Through her marriage to Reggie Kray, Roberta Kray has a unique and authentic insight into London's East End. Roberta met Reggie in early 1996 and they married the following year; they were together until Reggie's death in 2000. Roberta is the author of many previous bestsellers including *No Mercy*, *Dangerous Promises*, *Exposed* and *Survivor*.

ROBERTA
KRAY

BETRAYED

sphere

SPHERE

First published in Great Britain in 2020 by Sphere
This paperback edition published by Sphere in 2021

1 3 5 7 9 10 8 6 4 2

Copyright © Roberta Kray 2020

The moral right of the author has been asserted.

*All characters and events in this publication, other than those
clearly in the public domain, are fictitious and any resemblance
to real persons, living or dead, is purely coincidental.*

All rights reserved.
No part of this publication may be reproduced, stored in a
retrieval system, or transmitted, in any form or by any means, without
the prior permission in writing of the publisher, nor be otherwise circulated
in any form of binding or cover other than that in which it is published
and without a similar condition including this condition being
imposed on the subsequent purchaser.

A CIP catalogue record for this book
is available from the British Library.

ISBN 978-0-7515-7696-2

Typeset in Garamond by M Rules
Printed and bound in Great Britain by
Clays Ltd, Elcograf S.p.A.

Papers used by Sphere are from well-managed forests
and other responsible sources.

Sphere
An imprint of
Little, Brown Book Group
Carmelite House
50 Victoria Embankment
London EC4Y 0DZ

An Hachette UK Company
www.hachette.co.uk

www.littlebrown.co.uk

BETRAYED

Prologue

1965

The West End club was heaving, jam-packed with the usual Saturday-night crowd. The music was loud and the air thick with expectation. Lads circled the dance floor like wolves, leering at the girls, hoping to bag some prey before the end of the evening. The girls played it cool. His own gaze travelled through the strobing lights until it came to rest on a slim blonde swaying to the music. Laura Moss was wearing a white minidress and white knee-length boots. Her long fair hair, falling almost to the base of her spine, was swinging in time to her hips. She was dancing to the Supremes, 'Back in My Arms Again', and her face had a dreamy, contented expression.

He inclined his head, examining the contours of her body. His eyes blatantly raked her breasts, her hips, her long shapely legs before returning to her face again. A soft hiss escaped from his lips. It was a shame, he thought, but it had to be done. Having examined the problem from every angle, weighing up the pros and cons, he'd arrived at the only logical conclusion: she would have to be disposed of. She knew too much and couldn't be trusted to keep her mouth shut. In every war there was collateral damage – it was just the way of the world – and this was no different. He wouldn't sleep easy again until she ceased to be a threat.

Once he'd made up his mind it was like a weight had been lifted. He stood straighter and the tightness in his guts subsided. He lifted the glass to his mouth, swigged some whisky and smiled. The circles he moved in were dark and dangerous, savage places where life was worth nothing. Only the strongest could survive. To have a conscience, to think twice, to harbour even a twinge of remorse were weaknesses he could not afford. That was why he had no regret for the decision he'd made. It was him or her. End of story.

The only question left to answer now was how. It would be easy enough to put a bullet in her brain, but smarter to make her death look like an accident. That way there wouldn't be much of an investigation. An open and shut case; a few quick words from the coroner and job done.

He nodded, pleased to have sorted things out in his head. In truth, he wasn't going to kill her just because she knew too much. Laura Moss had taken him for a fool and that in itself was enough to sign her death warrant. Who did she think she was? A double dealer, a liar, a cheap little slut, that's what. His eyes grew dark with anger. He had a rule he always stuck to: no one messed with him and got away with it.

1

1975

Ten years later

The three girls sitting on the wall were at a dangerous age, no longer kids but still a few years off adulthood. They thought they knew it all as they swung their skinny legs against the warm brick, their elbows touching, their eyes drinking in the world around them. What they had was a six o'clock curfew. What they longed for was freedom, for their lives to properly begin, for all constraints to fall from them like chains.

There was nothing much to do except hang out. They had no money and no obvious means of getting any. Boredom coursed through their veins. On Sundays they were always at their most restless, knowing it was school the next day, knowing that the hours were ticking away and that tomorrow they'd be shut up in a classroom while a teacher tried to focus their scattergun minds on algebra or oxbow lakes or Dickens.

They were sitting in a line on the low wall near the entrance to the Mansfield estate. Chrissy Moss was in the middle with Zelda Graham to her left and Dawn Kearns to her right.

Chrissy's arms were tinged with pink where the sun had caught them yesterday. Zelda's were smooth, the colour of caramel, and Dawn's were pale, almost white, mottled with fresh and fading bruises. Chrissy didn't ask about the bruises any more; the blue, brown, plum-coloured marks were always there.

Behind them loomed the three tall towers which could be seen for miles. Chrissy gazed down at her pink flip-flops, at the chipped nail polish on her toes, and looked up again. Her Uncle Pete said Kellston was a shithole and the estate was a sewer, a place where all the local waste was dumped and forgotten about. That's when Nan got all huffy. *If that's how you feel, why don't you find somewhere else to park your arse?* But, of course, he didn't have anywhere else. He'd only just come out of jug. She wasn't exactly sure what he'd been in for – a robbery of some sort – but he'd been gone five years. It was cramped in the flat with him living there. She'd had to give up her bedroom and bunk in with Nan, who tossed and turned and seemed uneasy even when she did finally go to sleep, breathing wheezily into the darkness, muttering words that made no sense.

Nan was sad at how things had worked out for her kids. She didn't come right out and say it but she didn't need to. It was written all over her face. Pete, however hard he tried – and it wasn't very – couldn't keep on the straight and narrow. Laura had died in a terrible accident, falling under a train when she was twenty-three. Chrissy had only been four then and couldn't remember much about her mum. All that remained was the photo kept on the mantelpiece, a picture of a young laughing girl with fair hair flying in the wind.

Chrissy raised a hand to her forehead, shielding her eyes against the sun. They were watching everyone who came in and out of the estate. Just for something to do. Like security guards, only without the authority. Mainly they were watching the lads, grading them from one to ten. So far no one had got more than a four. It was a half-hearted sort of game, but it was better than nothing. They knew most of them, spotty oiks with mush for brains, boys who once upon a time had liked to pull their hair or call them names but now just stared at them through wary eyes.

The town hall clock struck two, echoing down from the high street. Music floated through an open window. *Come up and see me, make me smile ...* There was no breeze and the air felt thick and heavy. Frank Yates cycled by on his bike, half raising a hand as if about to acknowledge them but then speeding past. 'One,' Zelda said. No one disagreed. The Dunlap brothers mooched past with their hands in their pockets. 'Three,' Dawn said. 'Maybe. I don't know. Or a four?' Chrissy pulled a face. 'Three,' she said, 'and that's being generous.' She wasn't keen on the brothers: they smelled funny, musty, like they'd been left in a cellar for a long time. Carol Harper, a year above at school, waltzed by with her mother, putting her nose in the air and pretending not to see them. 'Snotty cow,' Dawn said.

People came and went. Nothing happened.

And then, out of the blue, *he* showed up. They didn't know his name but they'd seen him before. Chrissy instantly sat up straighter. They all paid attention as he approached the estate. Nineteen or twenty, tall, slender, wearing blue jeans and a black T-shirt. A bit of a swagger but not too much. Anyway, it was his face they were really staring at: sharp cheekbones stretched over olive skin, a generous mouth, eyes covered by a cool pair of shades. His dark brown hair, almost black, was straight and silky covering the nape of his neck. He stopped to light a cigarette a short distance from the entranceway.

'Ten,' Chrissy murmured.

'I dare you,' Dawn said. 'I dare you to talk to him.'

Chrissy shook her head, narrowed her grey eyes. 'You do it.'

'Go on.'

'No.'

'You have to. I dared you.'

The god was alongside them now, almost close enough to touch. Chrissy took a deep breath and leaned forward a little. A dare was a dare. 'Hey, how are you?'

He looked at her and grinned. 'Hey yourself.'

Chrissy felt the colour rise to her cheeks. She didn't know what to say next, was completely tongue-tied and just stared stupidly back at him.

It was Dawn who filled the awkward silence. 'You got a spare fag?'

He thought about this for a moment and then reached into his back pocket, pulled out a pack, opened it and offered it to her. 'Stunts your growth, you know.'

'Hasn't stunted yours,' Dawn said.

'I'm what they call the exception to the rule.'

Dawn pulled out a cigarette and popped it in her mouth. 'Ta. You got a light?'

He flicked open his lighter and held it out. Dawn lit the cigarette, took a drag and passed it to Chrissy, who hoped she wouldn't cough and embarrass herself. Although she nicked Uncle Pete's fags now and again, she hadn't quite got to grips with the art of inhaling.

'So what are you girls up to?'

Chrissy puffed out some smoke and quickly passed the fag to Zelda.

'We're just hanging,' Dawn said.

'Hanging, huh?'

'Yeah. What about you?'

'Oh, you know. Things to do, people to see.'

'What's your name, then?'

'Eddie,' he said. 'What's yours?'

'Dawn. And this is Zelda; this is Chrissy.'

Chrissy had a breathless sensation like her chest was being squeezed, the same giddy feeling she got when she saw David Essex on the TV. Eddie looked a bit like him except his hair was straighter. Finally, she forced herself to speak again. 'Do you live here?'

'No, I'm just visiting. A friend.'

'Your girlfriend?'

'Nah, not my girlfriend.' He glanced at each of them in turn and nodded. 'Well, it's been a pleasure, ladies. You have fun.'

'See you, then,' Dawn said. 'Thanks for the fag.'

Eddie walked on. Chrissy, Zelda and Dawn turned to watch him. He was a few yards along the central path when he suddenly stopped, turned around and came back. Chrissy felt her heart jump into her mouth. Maybe he was going to ask one of them out. Maybe it would be *her*. Even though he'd spent more time talking to Dawn, she wasn't without hope. *Please God, let it be me.*

But Eddie wasn't thinking about romance. He had something else on his mind. 'I don't suppose you girls could do me a favour?'

'Sure,' Chrissy said too quickly, eager to please.

Dawn was more cautious. 'What kind of favour?'

'Oh, it's nothing much. I've got a message for someone but I'm a bit pushed for time.' He glanced at his watch and frowned. 'You couldn't do it for me, could you? To be honest, I should be somewhere else right now. By the time I take the lift and . . . Would you mind?' He rummaged in his pocket, found some loose change and held up a coin. 'There's fifty pence in it for you.'

Dawn held out her hand. 'I'll do it.'

'We'll all do it,' Chrissy said, disappointed that he only wanted them to run an errand but not wanting to miss out on her share of the reward. They could buy pop *and* sweets with what he was offering. She didn't think to ask why he'd been standing around chatting if he was in so much of a hurry. 'What's the message?'

'It's for Anita, flat forty-eight, Haslow House. Just tell her Eddie sent you. Tell her . . . tell her the stock's come in and she can take her pick. Can you remember that?'

'The stock's in and she can take her pick,' Chrissy dutifully repeated.

'And the flat number?'

'Forty-eight.'

'Good. I can trust you, can't I?'

'Course you can,' Dawn said.

Eddie dropped the coin into Dawn's hand and grinned. 'Yeah, course I can. Ta, girls. I'll see you around.'

Chrissy slid off the wall and the other two followed. They stood for a while gawping at Eddie as he headed out of the estate and along Mansfield Road. He might have turned around and waved but he didn't. As soon as he was out of sight, they set off for Haslow House.

'What are we going to buy with it?' Dawn asked, twisting the coin between her fingers.

'Sherbet dips,' Zelda said, 'and Black Jacks and Flying Saucers and—'

'Love Hearts for Chrissy,' Dawn said, sniggering. 'She's got the hots for Eddie.'

'I don't.'

'Yes, you do.'

'No, I don't.'

8

'You gave him a ten.'

'So?' Chrissy had crazy pictures in her mind: she and Eddie strolling down the street, hand in hand; she and Eddie slow dancing in a nightclub; she and Eddie snogging in the moonlight. And okay, so maybe she was a bit younger than him, but she'd be fifteen in a few months' time, old enough to be taken seriously.

Dawn laughed. 'You *lurve* him, you *lurve* him,' she said in a singsong voice. 'Chrissy wants to marry Eddie.'

'I do not!'

'So why's your face gone all red?'

'Shut up!'

'Make me.'

Chrissy glared at her. Dawn could be annoying, maddening sometimes, the way she latched on to things and wouldn't let go. Like one of those yappy little dogs snapping at your ankles. 'I will!'

'Go on then.'

Zelda, forever the peacemaker, squeezed between the two of them and said, 'Let's just get this message sorted and then we can go to the shop.'

'She started it,' Chrissy said.

'No, I never.'

'Yes, you did.'

Zelda, sounding like a fed-up parent with two bickering kids, gave a long sigh. 'For God's sake, give it a rest.'

Chrissy linked her arm through Zelda's, a proprietorial gesture. Sometimes she wished it was just the two of them again, the way it had been before Dawn had moved onto the estate last year. Although she felt sorry for the girl, she didn't really like her. Dawn could be funny but she could be mean too; she knew where to find the weak spots and how to use them to

9

her own advantage. Did Zelda like Dawn more than her? Did Eddie? Her stomach turned over. She dropped what remained of the cigarette and ground it out with her heel. In all honesty she wished Dawn wasn't around any more.

2

Haslow House was almost identical to Carlton where the three of them lived. The same high-rise greying concrete, the same tiled foyer, the whole place tatty and strewn with litter. Only the graffiti was different. They went up in one of the juddering lifts, wrinkling their noses at the stink. There was still an atmosphere between Chrissy and Dawn, a simmering tension waiting to explode.

'I wonder what he meant by stock,' Zelda said.

'Dodgy gear,' Dawn said. 'Nicked stuff. Fags and booze and the like.'

'You don't know that,' Chrissy said.

Dawn rolled her eyes. 'What else could it be, stupid?

'Don't call me stupid. It could be anything.'

'Like what?'

Chrissy tried to think of something else but couldn't. 'Like anything,' she repeated.

Dawn gave a snort. 'Like puppies or kittens, you mean?'

'Piss off. I didn't say that.'

The lift ground to a halt and the doors creaked open. The three of them stepped out, checked the flat numbers and started walking towards flat forty-eight.

'It could be drugs,' Dawn said. 'Grass or coke. I bet Eddie's a dealer. He looks the type.'

'He's not a dealer.'

'How do you know?'

Chrissy didn't know but refused to believe it. Dawn was just trying to wind her up. Already she was building a picture of Eddie in her head, not exactly a knight in shining armour but someone basically good and decent. That was the sort of bloke she wanted, not the sort who would bring trouble to Nan's door. And not the sort who would smash her heart into a thousand pieces.

They stopped outside the flat and looked at each other. 'You do it,' Chrissy said to Dawn.

'Why me?'

'Why not?'

'*You* do it.'

Zelda sighed, reached out her hand and pressed the bell. They waited but no one came. Zelda rang again. This time there was movement from inside. They stared at the tiny circular eye in the door, shifting self-consciously from one foot to the other, aware of being studied. Eventually a bolt was slid back and the door was opened. A tall man, hard-looking, unshaven, gazed down at them. He was wearing a grubby vest and had tattoos down both arms.

'Yeah?'

'Is Anita in, please?' Zelda asked.

'We've got a message,' Chrissy said. 'From Eddie.'

'And why couldn't Eddie deliver it himself?'

The girls, not expecting to be cross-examined, glanced at each

12

other again. 'He ... erm ... I think he had something urgent to do,' Chrissy said.

The man was unimpressed. 'Lazy fucker. What's the bleedin' message then?'

'It's for Anita,' Zelda said.

'She ain't here.'

'How long will she be?'

'How the fuck would I know? You want to leave a message, leave it. If you don't, bugger off. Make your minds up. I ain't standing here all day.'

The three girls were in a quandary. Eddie had paid them to tell Anita, but he hadn't said what to do if she wasn't there. They dithered, shuffled, pulled faces. Someone had to make the decision, but no one seemed up for it. Zelda nudged Chrissy's elbow. 'Go on. You may as well.'

Chrissy didn't want to be the one to leave the message. What if Eddie found out and had the hump with her? But she also didn't want to stay here any longer than she had to. The bloke was getting antsy. She could see the darkness in his eyes, the growing irritation. *Never talk to strange men* was what her nan had always said when she was a kid. But she was grown up now – well, almost – and those warnings were only faint echoes. Quickly she blurted out, 'Eddie said the stock's in. You can take your pick.'

'Stock's in, huh?' He seemed to mellow a little, the hint of a smile playing on his lips. 'Well, that's something, I suppose.' His gaze roamed over them all and finally came to rest on Dawn. 'I know you, don't I?'

Dawn shook her head. 'Don't think so.'

'Yeah, you're Tina's sprog. Debbie, ain't it?'

'Dawn.'

'Yeah, Dawn. That's it. Sorry, love. How's yer mum these days? Haven't seen her for a while.'

'She's okay.'

'Glad to hear it.'

Mission accomplished, Zelda started to edge away – 'Bye then' – and Chrissy and Dawn followed suit.

They were halfway to the lift when the man called out. 'Hey, Dawn, come here a minute.'

Dawn hesitated, frowned, but then did as she was told.

Chrissy and Zelda watched as he bent to whisper something in her ear. Dawn nodded, said something in return. The man went inside the flat and closed the door. Dawn sauntered back along the corridor.

'What was all that about?' Chrissy asked.

'Nothing.'

'What did he say?'

'Nothing. I mean, nothing much. Just to ... erm, say hi to my mum.'

Chrissy didn't believe her. The bloke could have said that when they were all there – or just called it out. He hadn't needed to summon her back. 'What else?'

'Nothing. I told you.'

Chrissy stared at her. 'Why won't you tell us?'

'There's nothing to tell.'

'Who is that feller? What's his name?'

'Dunno.'

'He knows who you are.'

'He knows my mum, that's all.'

They got in the lift and went down in silence. Chrissy thought about Tina Kearns. Dawn's mum *was* well known on the estate, although not in a good way. She drank too much and had bad taste in boyfriends, men who were tight with their cash and quick with their fists. At least that's what Nan said, and Nan had the lowdown on all the neighbours.

They passed through the coolness of the foyer, through the doors and back into the warmth of the September air. Chrissy was still bothered by what they'd done. 'What if he doesn't tell Anita?'

'Why wouldn't he?' Zelda said.

'He might forget.'

Dawn laughed. 'Eddie should have done it himself, then, shouldn't he? It's not our fault.'

And that was true, Chrissy thought. They'd upheld their side of the deal so far as they'd been able. If the tattooed bloke had a bad memory, it wasn't down to them. Anyway, if the message was *that* important, Eddie would have found the time to deliver it personally.

As they headed towards the main gate, Dawn began to dawdle, dragging her feet.

'Come on,' Chrissy urged. 'He closes at half-two.'

Patel's was the only local shop that opened on a Sunday, but even Mr P. liked to have some of his afternoon off.

Dawn came to a standstill, stopping dead in the middle of the path. 'I'm going home,' she said. 'I don't feel so good.'

Chrissy stared at her. She didn't look sick. She didn't look any different to how she'd looked five minutes ago. 'What's wrong? What's the matter?'

'Cramps,' Dawn said, clutching her stomach in an overly dramatic fashion. 'I've got gut ache.'

Zelda put an arm around her, making sympathetic noises. Chrissy wondered what the time was. How long since they'd heard the two chimes from the town hall clock? First, they'd talked to Eddie and then walked over to Haslow to deliver the message. It must be fifteen, twenty minutes at least.

'We'll come with you,' Zelda said. 'We'll walk with you to the lifts.'

Chrissy turned her face away and raised her eyes to the

15

heavens. The trouble with Zelda was that she always saw the best in people. Anyone could tell Dawn was faking it.

'Nah, I'll be okay.' Dawn took the fifty pence coin out of her pocket and gave it to Zelda. 'You go to the shop. I'll see you tomorrow.'

Chrissy gave her a wave, trying to speed up the goodbyes. 'See you, then.' The thought had crossed her mind that Dawn might be trying to pull a fast one, to clear off with Eddie's money, and now she felt bad about it. But she still didn't reckon Dawn was sick. To make up for her unfounded suspicions, she said, 'We'll get you some sweets, keep them till tomorrow.'

'Ta,' Dawn said, glancing over her shoulder as she hurried back along the path.

Zelda gazed after her, head inclined, eyes full of concern.

'She'll be all right,' Chrissy said.

'She never goes home early.'

'She'll be all right,' Chrissy repeated, aware of the seconds ticking away. Although it was rare for Dawn to go home before they did – despite what she pretended she had no set time, her mum being unconcerned about when she left or when she came back – it was hardly something to worry about. 'Come on, it must be almost half past.'

Zelda didn't move. She waited until Dawn had gone into Carlton House and disappeared from view. Only then did she start walking with Chrissy towards the gates. From there they went along Mansfield Road and down to the high street. Were they going to make it? Chrissy increased her pace, flip-flops slapping against the pavement. Dawn had lost them a few vital minutes and she prepared herself for disappointment whilst still hoping she could be wrong. Another few yards – she broke into an ungainly jog – and then her worst fears were confirmed. The lights were off. The shop was closed.

Pressing their noses against the glass, they gazed mournfully through the window at the rows of sweets on display. It occurred to Chrissy, somewhat belatedly, that they should have come here before delivering the message. That way they could have safely secured their reward and kept their side of the bargain. As she pondered on this she was reminded of the tattooed man.

'I didn't like that feller at the flat. What do you reckon he said to Dawn?'

'She told you. He said to say hi to her mum.'

Chrissy didn't want to come right out and call Dawn a liar, even though that was what she thought. 'Just that?'

'What else?'

Chrissy shrugged. 'I don't know. It doesn't matter. What are we going to do now?'

'Go back, I suppose.'

Chrissy looked around, hoping she might spot Eddie, but there was no sign of him. The high street was Sunday quiet, almost deserted, with nothing in the way of distractions. She tried to think of something fun to do but drew a blank. They walked slowly back to the estate, saying little. For Chrissy, it wasn't a comfortable silence. Zelda seemed distant, distracted, as though she'd rather be somewhere else . . . or with someone else.

3

Eddie Barr was still in two minds as to whether he should jump ship. No sooner had he managed to wheedle his way into the firm last year than Joe Quinn had got his head caved in. A jury had decided that Quinn's two sons were guilty, but others weren't so sure. There were some who put Terry Street firmly in the frame, although Eddie reckoned Terry might have started that rumour himself. Anyway, whether he'd done it or not, Terry hadn't been slow in climbing into the dead man's shoes. But would it last? It was all very well seizing power, but hanging on to it was another matter altogether.

Already some of the more senior faces had left to form allegiances with other East End firms. Terry was too young to command the respect of the old guard. They weren't prepared to take orders from a bloke who hadn't even been born when they were helping Joe Quinn build his empire. Others had stayed, though – men like Vinnie Keane and John Haley. A turf war was looming – Kellston was up for grabs – and Eddie didn't want to end up on the wrong side.

Eddie sipped his pint while he considered his options. He was sitting in a dingy basement bar, a shebeen in King's Cross run by some dodgy Jamaicans. Reggae music pounded his ears. The only place to drink on a Sunday afternoon was in illegal joints like this one or in the comfort of your own home. He would have stuck with home if he hadn't had some business around the corner.

Eddie didn't like Jamaicans, didn't like coloured people full stop. He didn't like Chinks either, or Paddies or Yanks or spics come to that. Catholics, Jews and any mug who came from south of the river were also on his blacklist. On the whole, he wasn't crazy over anyone who didn't look or think like himself, and that included women. *Girls*, however, were a different kettle of fish. Girls were his living, his bread and butter. He knew how to charm and entice, how to make them trust.

Eddie thought about the trio sitting on the wall at the Mansfield, and grinned. He could have had any of them if he'd put his mind it, but especially the blonde. Chrissy, that was her name.

He'd seen the way she'd looked at him, her grey eyes wide as saucers, her heart full of yearning and soppy romantic notions. They were all obsessed with love at that age, with boyfriends and soulmates and happy-ever-afters. Yeah, he could have clicked his fingers and she'd have come running, but he knew better than to go down that road. Never shit on your own doorstep, right? It wasn't smart and always came back to bite you on the arse.

He glanced at his watch. The next trains in were from Manchester and Nottingham. He'd give it five minutes, time for the passengers to clear, before he went and examined the debris. The runaways were always easy to spot, aimless and bewildered, not sure what to do next now they'd finally reached their destination. He'd choose carefully, get chatting, buy the target a coffee and show her the kind of interest nobody else had ever bothered to do. Listening, that was the key – or at least pretending to. He'd heard all the stories a hundred times before.

When he was on the hunt, he had to keep his eyes open, check that the law weren't on the prowl, or any of those do-gooding social workers. He stayed away from the girls who were too young, although it wasn't always easy to tell. They lied about their age, their names, lied about most things. The biggest lie of all, of course, was the one they told themselves – that life would be perfect once they got away from home.

Eddie's two houses, the biggest on Albert Road, were doing well, but if another firm took over the manor all that could change. At the moment he had an arrangement with Terry, weekly payments so he didn't get any hassle, protection if he needed it. He resented paying but that was the way it was. If he wasn't forking out to Terry, it would be to someone else. Unless that someone decided they didn't want him on their patch any more.

The girls he picked up, the newcomers, didn't go straight to work. What he liked to think of as the introductory period was spent in one of his bedsits, where he'd begin to forge a relationship: feeding them, clothing them, taking them out and buying them gifts. There was partying. There was alcohol, weed and coke. It didn't take long for an attachment to be formed, for them to start to rely on him – and on the gear. Before they knew it, they were hooked and there was no going back.

It was Anita who ran the houses for him. Every establishment needed a madam and she was the best, keeping the customers in line, and the toms. She was the one who decided where to put the new girls once Eddie had prepared them. He didn't feel any guilt over what he did. It was every man for himself in this world, dog eat dog. He had a living to make and he had ambition. This was just the start. Kellston was all very well, but the real money was to be made in the West End. It was there, among the clubs and bars and escort agencies, that the future lay. He wanted punters with deep pockets, men who were prepared to pay top dollar for the privilege of screwing his girls.

He scratched his chin, drank a little beer, thought a bit more about Terry Street. Was the guy tough enough to survive what was coming? Was he smart enough, devious enough, vicious enough? His enemies were already closing in, testing, pushing the boundaries, looking for the weak spots. Others were circling round like vultures, waiting to pick the bones clean once he was toppled. If Eddie made a mistake and backed the wrong side, all his hard work would be for nothing.

He was torn. Better the devil you know, a voice whispered in his ear. Except he didn't really *know* Terry Street, wasn't exactly sure of his capabilities. And okay, Terry hadn't done badly so far, but it was still early days. Until he was challenged, there was no saying which way it would go. Even smart geezers ended up with bullets in their brains.

Eddie drained his glass, lit a fag and stood up. There was no need to make an immediate decision. He could think about it some more, weigh up his options, try and suss out which way the wind was blowing. In the meantime, he had work to do. He checked out the mirror as he walked towards the door, ran his fingers through his hair and admired his reflection.

4

Dawn didn't show up on Monday or Tuesday morning. On Wednesday Chrissy and Zelda waited at their usual meeting point by the gates to the estate until the last possible minute. Then, not wanting to be late, they set off for school.

'She must still be sick,' Zelda said. 'Do you think?'

Chrissy, who was secretly pleased to have Zelda to herself, nodded. 'Yeah, I guess.' She suspected Dawn was just bunking off, something she did these days with ever increasing frequency. 'She might be.'

'Should we go round and see her later?'

Chrissy grimaced. The last time they'd done that, Tina Kearns's feller had answered the door and given them a mouthful, told them to fuck off and not come back. Dawn said that Marlon worked nights and got the hump if he was woken up during the day. She had made them promise not to knock on the door again. 'What about that bloke? Is he still living there?'

'I dunno. I think so.'

Chrissy thought of the bruises on Dawn's arms. If they went to the flat and disturbed him, he might take it out on her. 'What if . . . you know, he gets mad again, has a go at Dawn after we've gone?'

'So what are we going to do?'

Chrissy reckoned Dawn would show up soon enough, probably tomorrow, but she wanted to please Zelda so she said, 'We could go round after dinner. He should be up by then, shouldn't he?'

Zelda nodded. 'Okay, let's do that.'

The school day passed slowly as it always did. Chrissy spent most of it gazing out of the window, daydreaming, or watching the second hand on the clock move lethargically round the face. She longed to escape from the classroom, away from equations and questions that she couldn't answer. The sun slanted across the playground, golden yellow, an invitation to go out and feel the warmth. The four walls closed in. The teachers' words slid over her, barely heard, unabsorbed. She envied Dawn her freedom. If she'd dared, Chrissy would have bunked off too, but she knew Nan would come down on her like a ton of bricks. Nothing got past Nan; she was the eyes and ears of the estate. It was like living with the police.

Back home Chrissy sat at the kitchen table, watching as the steak and kidney pie was doled out from the Fray Bentos tin. There were chips and boiled carrots, too. Uncle Pete was reading the sports pages in the evening paper, tutting over some article about his football team.

Nan put a plate down in front of him. 'It's the jobs you should be looking at, not that rubbish.'

'There are no jobs for the likes of me. No one wants to employ an ex-con.'

'You won't find out until you try.'

23

'I've been asking around.'

'Where? In the pub? Last time I checked, there weren't too many jobs going in the bottom of a pint.'

Uncle Pete threw her a look. 'Don't start that again, Mum.'

Chrissy was sick of hearing the conversation, which seemed to take place in one form or another every other day. She was half on his side – there was nothing worse than being constantly nagged – but half on Nan's, too. If Uncle Pete got a job, he might be able to find somewhere else to live and she'd get her bedroom back. She was still delighting in this thought when her own plate arrived, steam rising from the pie. 'Ta.' She picked up her knife and fork, ate some food and asked, 'Nan? Is that bloke still living with Tina Kearns? You know, the shouty one with the ponytail.'

'Marlon, you mean?'

'Yeah.'

'What do you want to know about him for?'

'Dawn hasn't been at school all week. We haven't seen her since Sunday. Me and Zelda are going to go round later and check if she's okay. Only last time we went, he got well narked about it.'

'Yeah, he's got a gob on him, that one. And Tina isn't any better. Out all hours, she is, gallivanting. I feel sorry for the poor kid. You want Pete to go with you?'

'Huh?' Uncle Pete said.

'It's not as though you're rushed off your feet. It'll only take five minutes. You can spare that for your niece, can't you?'

'It doesn't matter,' Chrissy said. 'We'll be fine on our own.'

But Nan had made up her mind. 'It won't do any harm to have him with you. That Marlon won't be so mouthy when he's faced with someone his own size.'

Chrissy glanced at Uncle Pete.

He looked back at her and winked. 'I don't know what she's talking about. I'm *way* taller than Marlon.'

Chrissy grinned. Uncle Pete *was* tall and he had muscles in his arms. Just the kind of person you needed in a scrap.

'Well then,' Nan said.

And the matter was settled. Although she wouldn't openly admit it, Chrissy was glad of the escort just in case Marlon did kick off – although it was probably all a waste of time. Chances were that Dawn was sitting on the sofa right this minute with a bag of chips in her hand and her eyes glued to the telly. Chrissy wouldn't have even bothered going to see her if Zelda hadn't suggested it.

There was butterscotch Instant Whip for afters. Once that was eaten there was the washing up to do; Chrissy washed and Nan dried while Uncle Pete made a brew and smoked a fag.

As soon as the tea was drunk, Nan glanced at the kitchen clock and said, 'You might as well get going then. And don't take all night about it.'

'Sorry about this,' Chrissy said as soon as they were out on the landing.

'Oh, you know what your nan's like, always looking for something to worry about.'

Chrissy was about to say that there wasn't any need to worry when she had second thoughts. He might decide to clear off to the pub instead.

They walked down two flights of stairs to Zelda's, and Chrissy rang the bell.

Zelda answered the door and called over her shoulder, 'Mum, I'm going to Dawn's. I won't be long.' She stepped into the corridor and glanced queryingly at Uncle Pete.

'Personal bodyguard,' he explained. 'In case Marlon doesn't mind his manners.'

'Oh,' Zelda said. 'Do you think he'll get mad at us, Mr Moss?'

Chrissy sniggered at Zelda's politeness – it was odd hearing someone call her uncle Mr Moss – but quickly straightened her face when Zelda glared at her.

'Marlon's always mad at someone,' Uncle Pete said. 'He was born that way. I reckon he came into the world griping and hasn't stopped since.'

They took the lift to the seventeenth floor and walked in silence to Dawn's flat. The bell didn't work and so Zelda knocked lightly on the door. Chrissy hoped that Dawn would answer, but when the door was opened it was the dreaded Marlon standing in front of them. She instinctively took a step back.

Zelda, however, stood her ground. 'Is Dawn in, please?'

'Nah,' he said. 'She ain't here.'

'Do you know where she is?'

As if she'd asked him to solve the square root of eighty-one, Marlon scowled. 'How the fuck would I know?'

Uncle Pete, who had been standing to one side, now moved into Marlon's view. 'Because she lives here, don't she?'

Marlon's attitude became marginally less confrontational. 'She ain't my kid, mate. I don't keep tabs on her.'

'So where's Tina?'

'Out.'

'Out where?'

Marlon shrugged. He wasn't a big man, nothing like as big as Uncle Pete, but sheer nastiness emanated from every pore. 'Dunno.'

'When did you last see her? Dawn, I mean.'

'Dunno, mate.'

'Well, *mate*, maybe you could have a think about it. Today, yesterday, the day before? It ain't rocket science. You must have some idea.'

26

'Kid comes and goes when she likes. I don't take no notice.'

'She was sick,' Zelda said. 'On Sunday she felt sick so she came home.'

Marlon gave another shrug. 'She'll be around someplace. With one of her pals, probably.'

'We are her pals,' Zelda said.

Chrissy tried to peer around him to the inside of the flat. The hallway carpet was filthy and covered in stains. A bad smell floated out, something rancid.

'You checked her room?' Uncle Pete asked.

'There ain't nobody here but me.'

'Well, just so we're sure. Come on, it won't take you a minute.'

Marlon curled his lip and glared at Uncle Pete. Then he muttered something under his breath, half turned around and yelled, 'Dawn! Dawn!' He waited and when there was no reply, turned back and said smugly, 'What did I tell you? She ain't here.'

Uncle Pete stared at him with a thin smile. 'You can check her room or I will.'

'You reckon?'

Chrissy felt her skin prickle. Was there going to be a bust-up? But surely even Marlon wouldn't be that stupid. She watched his mean little eyes narrow into slits like he was weighing up the odds if he was to try and stand his ground. But then, realising he was on a hiding to nothing, he did what he could to save face by standing aside, waving his hand and saying, 'Help yourself, mate. It's the second on the left.' Like the one thing he *wasn't* going to do was go and look himself.

Uncle Pete went inside. Chrissy and Zelda exchanged a glance but stayed where they were. There was no point in all of them trudging through the stinking flat. They waited on the landing as Marlon crossed his arms across his chest and followed the unwelcome visitor with his eyes. They heard a door open.

'Dawn? Are you here? It's Pete, Chrissy's uncle.'

There was a short delay – ten, twenty seconds – before the door clicked shut again. Another door opened.

'Hey!' Marlon called out. 'What do you think you're doing?'

But Uncle Pete ignored him. He clearly wasn't going to leave until he'd checked out the whole flat. Two minutes later he was back. He pushed past Marlon and joined them on the landing. 'She's not here.'

'What did I tell you?' Marlon growled. 'She'll be hanging round the estate someplace.'

'She'd better be or—'

'Or what?'

'Or the next visit you'll be getting is from the law.'

Marlon slammed the door in his face.

'So what now?' Chrissy asked.

Uncle Pete began walking towards the lifts. 'You and Zelda have a quick look round, check out wherever she usually goes. But don't take too long, okay? I don't want your nan giving me earache. I'll go down the Fox and see if Tina's there.'

They separated outside the lobby. Uncle Pete strode off towards the high street while Chrissy and Zelda started their search of the Mansfield. For the next twenty minutes they explored the wide concrete expanse of the estate, as well as the gloomy hidden parts, the long tunnels and passageways, the neglected corners and filthy spaces under the stairs.

Zelda walked quickly, her face tight with worry, her eyes darting left and right. 'Where can she be? Where would she go?'

'Anywhere.'

Neither of them knew for sure where Dawn went when she bunked off school. Perhaps she didn't even stay in the area.

28

Her absence didn't necessarily mean that anything was wrong. Zelda's anxiety, however, was contagious. Chrissy hadn't been that worried when they'd gone to Dawn's flat but now a feeling of uneasiness was creeping over her. She sucked in a breath and shivered.

They stopped anyone they knew and asked the same question over and over again. 'Have you seen Dawn Kearns today?'

The answer was always the same. 'Nah.'

'Yesterday?'

'Nah.'

The September evening was drawing in, the sky lowering, a chill starting to permeate the air. Zelda gazed back towards the main gates, squinting through the greyness.

'How long do you think your uncle will be?'

This wasn't a question Chrissy could answer with any accuracy. Knowing his fondness for a pint, Uncle Pete might stop for one or two or three. It would depend on whether he found Tina or not – and how urgent he thought the situation was. Was it urgent? They didn't know for sure how long Dawn had been missing, or even if she was missing at all.

'Not long,' Chrissy said. 'Unless Tina isn't in the Fox. Then he'll have to check the other pubs.'

They were standing halfway between Haslow and Carlton House, at a loss as to what to do next. Having searched all the obvious places, there was nowhere left to look on the estate. Well, not unless they started knocking on doors, and there were hundreds of those.

'She could be at the chippy,' Chrissy said. 'Or that Anita's flat. Do you think we should try there?'

'Why would she be at Anita's?'

'Perhaps she went back there on Sunday.'

'What for?'

'That bloke said something to her, didn't he? The one with the tattoos.'

'Only to say hi to her mum.'

'Maybe . . . maybe he said something else, too.' Chrissy gazed towards the banks of windows, some of which were now filled with light. She counted up the floors but wasn't sure which flat it was. 'Should we try? What do you reckon?'

Zelda shook her head. 'Will your uncle go?'

'I'll ask him when he gets back.' Chrissy understood her reluctance. She felt the same and was relieved she didn't have to follow through on the suggestion. The bloke had been like Marlon, surly and aggressive, at least until they'd passed on the message from Eddie. If they showed up looking for Dawn, he might think they were accusing him of something.

'Ta. I'd better go home now or Mum's going to worry,' said Zelda. 'It's getting dark. Will you let me know if he finds Tina?'

'Yeah, course.'

They began to walk towards Carlton House, all the time looking around as though Dawn might suddenly materialise from the gloom.

Chrissy asked, 'Do you think she could have run away? I'd run away if I had to live with Marlon.'

Zelda shook her head again. 'She wouldn't have done that, not without telling me.'

Chrissy bristled at the word 'me'. Not *us*, she noted, as though Dawn would only confide in Zelda. It was further proof, had she needed it, that the two girls had developed a closeness from which she was excluded. 'Well, maybe she doesn't tell you everything.'

Zelda shot her a look but didn't reply.

Chrissy instantly regretted the retort. Had it sounded bitchy? She didn't want Zelda to hate her. 'I just meant she might have left in a hurry, you know, not had time to . . . ' Her voice trailed off.

Zelda stayed silent as they walked quickly towards the entrance to Carlton House.

Chrissy tried to think of something better to say, something reassuring, perhaps, but nothing came to mind.

Zelda didn't speak again until they were in the foyer. 'I've still got her sweets.'

Chrissy reckoned Zelda was the only person in the world who wouldn't have succumbed to temptation and eaten them by now. Suddenly, Sunday seemed a long time ago, weeks rather than days. On Monday morning, on the way to school, they had spent Eddie's money at Patel's and divided the spoils into three. Chrissy had scoffed all her share at lunchtime, along with the salmon paste sandwiches Nan had made for her. She had spent the rest of the afternoon with a bad taste in her mouth, a gross combination of fish and chocolate and sherbet.

Zelda's voice was soft, tremulous. 'What if something's happened to her?'

'Like what?'

But Zelda wouldn't meet her gaze. Whatever she was thinking she couldn't speak out loud. She was too scared, perhaps, that it might be true.

5

Chrissy was surprised to discover Uncle Pete in the kitchen when she got home. He and Nan were sitting at the table and, as soon as she saw them, she knew the news wasn't good. Nerves fluttered in her stomach. Pete was puffing on a fag, grim-faced, and Nan was drumming out a beat on the tabletop with her fingertips.

'Finally,' Nan said. 'I was about to send out a search party.'

'I haven't been that long.'

'Long enough.'

'You didn't find her, then?' Uncle Pete asked.

'No one's seen her. What about her mum?'

'She's in the Fox. She reckons that Dawn's been staying at Zelda's for the past few days.'

Chrissy frowned. 'That's not true.'

'We know that, love,' Nan said. 'That's the worry. If *she* doesn't know where Dawn is, who the hell does? I'd say it's hard to believe, but I'd be lying. That woman's not fit to call herself a mother. What's the stupid tart thinking?'

Uncle Pete gave a snort. 'She ain't thinking, that's the trouble.

She's off her head, as usual. I tried to get her to come back but she wasn't having any of it. Just kept saying the kid was okay, she was fine, there was nothing to worry about. I couldn't get it through her thick skull that no one's seen her since Sunday.'

'You should have made her come back,' Nan said.

'And how was I supposed to do that? Grab her by the hair and drag her through the streets?'

'If that's what it took. She should be here looking for Dawn, not drinking herself silly down the Fox.'

'What are we going to do?' Chrissy asked.

Nan heaved herself to her feet and sighed. 'There's only one thing we can do. Put your coat on, love. We're going down Cowan Road.'

'You're going to report it?'

'Can't see what else to do. The sooner we tell them, the sooner they can get looking.'

Uncle Pete stubbed out his fag and stared at her. 'You sure about this?'

'You got a better suggestion?'

He hadn't, apparently, because all he did was lift and drop his shoulders. Uncle Pete steered clear of the law as much as he could, as did most of the tenants on the Mansfield estate. Nan wasn't a big fan, either, so Chrissy knew this was serious. Although Nan had no qualms about interfering in other people's business, she wouldn't go near the nick if she could possibly avoid it.

'What about Zelda?' Chrissy asked. 'I said I'd tell her if Uncle Pete found Tina.'

'You can tell her when you get back.' Nan grabbed her handbag – she was never without it – and bustled past. 'Come on,' she said. 'We'll not find that poor girl standing here.'

There was a queue at the desk in Cowan Road Police Station

33

but Nan wasn't prepared to join it. She marched straight to the front and, ignoring the tuts of the people behind her, placed her handbag firmly on the counter and declared, 'I need to see someone now. It's urgent.'

'Hey, missus,' a skinny woman protested. 'There's a queue here, in case you ain't noticed.'

Nan turned to glare at her. 'You got something more important than a kid gone missing?'

The woman pursed her lips but didn't pursue the objection.

Chrissy was proud of her nan, but a bit embarrassed by her, too. Now everyone was staring. She could feel her cheeks turning red as numerous pairs of eyes focused on them. The people in the queue were curious, eager to know more. The two of them were going to look mighty stupid, she thought, if it turned out to be a false alarm and Dawn wasn't missing at all. Maybe she was staying with another friend and Tina had just got confused. But what other friend? So far as Chrissy knew, she and Zelda were the only mates Dawn had.

The desk sergeant asked Nan a few questions, then told her to take a seat and said someone would be with her soon. They retreated to a row of hard plastic chairs set against the wall, where Nan placed her bag on her knee and clutched it with both hands as though someone might try and snatch it away from her.

'This lot wouldn't know urgent if it slapped them in the face,' Nan said, glancing up at the clock.

But it was only a few minutes before a door at the back opened and a bloke in a suit walked through. He was slim, thin-faced with pale brown hair swept back from his forehead. He stopped to have a quick word with the desk sergeant and then made his way over to where they were sitting.

'Mrs Moss,' he said. 'I'm DS Will Sutherland. Would you like to—'

'I know who you are,' Nan said sharply.

He gave a nod. 'It's been a while. I wasn't sure you'd remember me.'

'Not likely to forget, am I?'

Chrissy stared at him, wondering what the deal was between the two of them. Something to do with Uncle Pete, perhaps; he'd spent more time down this nick than he'd had hot dinners.

'Would you like to come through?'

Chrissy followed Nan and the cop along a corridor to a small sparsely furnished room with a window high up in the wall. A WPC, whose name she didn't quite catch, Jenny something, joined them shortly after they'd sat down at the table.

'You should be out looking for the girl,' Nan grumbled. 'Anything could have happened to the poor kid. You're not going to find her sitting here.'

DS Sutherland smiled patiently. 'I understand your concern but we've already despatched officers to the estate, and we'll be talking to Tina Kearns, too.'

'Good luck with that. She won't know what day it is, never mind where her daughter's gone. And that no-good Marlon's no better. It's a bleedin' disgrace. No one's seen Dawn since Sunday; she hasn't been to school or nothing. If it wasn't for our Chrissy here, no one would even know she was missing.'

'And Zelda,' Chrissy said. 'Zelda's worried, too.'

The DS looked down, referred briefly to his notes and then looked up again. 'So, the last time you saw Dawn was on Sunday? Do you want to tell me about it?'

Chrissy didn't want to, at least not all of it. The minute Nan heard about Eddie, about the message he'd asked them to deliver, she'd have a fit. Was there a way round revealing that? She could just not mention him, but then what if Zelda did? And Zelda would. She was bound to. Aware that a silence had fallen, one that she was supposed to be filling, she quickly said, 'We were just hanging out.'

'On the estate?'

Chrissy nodded. 'Yeah. Dawn went home about two-thirty, a bit before, said she wasn't feeling well. Gut ache, she said.'

'And earlier?'

'We were sitting on the wall by the gates.'

'Did you see anyone?'

Chrissy pretended to give it some thought. 'Frank Yates, the Dunlap brothers, Carol Harper.'

'Did you talk to them?'

'No.'

'And there was no one else?'

Chrissy squirmed in her seat, knowing that this was the moment of truth. An uncomfortable silence was filling up the room again. Eventually she took a deep breath and said, 'Well, there was Eddie.'

'Eddie?'

'I don't know his last name. I've seen him around, though. He's okay. He ... erm, he asked if we'd take a message to a woman called Anita in Haslow House.'

'What's this?' Nan asked sharply. 'You never said nothing about this before.'

'I forgot. Anyway, didn't think it mattered, did I? I mean, we all went there and we all came back so ...'

'What have I told you about talking to strangers?'

'He's not a stranger, not exactly.'

'Near as damn it. I thought I raised you to have some sense in your head. How many times have I said? You don't go—'

Thankfully DS Sutherland interrupted before she could really get going. 'Mrs Moss. If you could just let Chrissy tell us what happened.'

Nan glared at him but shut her mouth.

Chrissy told the story at speed, partly to get it over and done with and partly to stop her nan from chipping in again. Even as she was speaking, she was aware of how dodgy it all sounded. She kept her eyes on the policeman and saw him frown when she mentioned the tattooed man calling Dawn back. 'She said he just told her to say hi to her mum, but . . .'

'But?' the DS prompted.

'He could have said that at the door, couldn't he?'

'You think she was lying?'

Chrissy, who didn't want to say anything bad about Dawn now that she was missing, gave a shrug. 'I didn't mean that. It just seemed a bit weird.'

'But she didn't appear scared or anything? Worried?'

'No.'

Chrissy was asked to give descriptions, first of the tattooed man and then of Eddie. She gave as much detail as she could remember for the bloke at Haslow House but was deliberately vague when it came to Eddie. He couldn't have had anything to do with Dawn's disappearance – she was sure of it – and she didn't want to land him in trouble.

'You're certain that Eddie said "stock"?'

'Yeah.'

'What do you think he meant?'

Nan, who could never keep quiet for long, said, 'What does it matter what she thought? It's neither here nor there. Chrissy's told you everything she knows. Don't start trying to put words in her mouth. I know what you're like. You should be round at this Anita's finding out what's going on.'

'Thank you, Mrs Moss. We will be doing that.'

Chrissy could feel the friction between them, like two pieces of sandpaper rubbing together. She glanced at her nan – her lips were set in a thin straight line – and then back at Sutherland. What was it between those two? More than Nan's general dislike of the law. This was personal. But she didn't have time to dwell on it. He was asking more questions, like what Dawn was wearing on Sunday, what they'd talked about, what Eddie had said *exactly*.

It was the WPC, who up until now had been silent, who asked, 'Is it possible that Dawn has run away?'

'I don't know.'

'She never mentioned it? I mean, the idea that she might or that she wanted to?'

Chrissy thought about this, aware that the idea had crossed her own mind. The truth was that all three of them – herself, Dawn and Zelda – had talked about running away at one time or another, but not with any real intent. It was just something you said when you were narked at not being able to get your own way, usually after some family spat when you had the hump at not being able to do whatever it was you wanted to do. Although Dawn had good reason to take off, what with her mum and Marlon and the rest, Chrissy wasn't convinced that she had. 'Where would she go?'

'You can't think of anywhere?'

Chrissy shook her head.

It was another ten minutes before they were finally allowed to leave. In the foyer, Tina Kearns was raising hell, drunkenly swaying from side to side while she hurled abuse at the cops who'd brought her in. Everyone was watching. While Nan was distracted, storing up the juicy details to share with the neighbours, DS Sutherland said to Chrissy, 'We might need to talk to you again. Will that be all right?'

'I suppose so.'

'Try not to worry too much. And if you think of anything

else that could be helpful, just let your grandmother know. She can ring the station. Or drop by. Whatever's easiest.'

'Okay,' Chrissy said, even though she was pretty sure she'd told him everything she was willing to tell.

'You're a smart girl. Something else might come to mind.'

There was an edge to the way he said it, as though he suspected her of withholding information. Which, of course, she was, but nothing important. She'd kept quiet about Dawn faking the gut ache, for instance, but that wasn't what you'd call a *fact*, only her own opinion. And she hadn't mentioned that Dawn had asked Eddie for a fag or that Dawn, when she was in the mood, could be mean as a snake. She assumed what she hoped was an innocent expression. 'Erm, like what?'

Perhaps her acting skills weren't all they should be because Sutherland raised his eyebrows a fraction. 'Sometimes things come back to you. You'd be surprised.'

Chrissy was in the process of inching away, hoping that Nan had had her fill of the Tina Kearns show, when Sutherland said something unexpected.

'You look just like your mother.'

She stopped, startled, and stared at him. 'You knew my mum?'

'Back in the day.'

She would have asked more, only this was the moment, typically, that Nan chose to grab her elbow and start propelling her out of the door. Chrissy glanced over her shoulder but Sutherland was already walking off. *He'd known her mum.* For Chrissy, this was a piece of information worthy of note. She had stopped asking her nan questions a long time ago – she just got upset – and Uncle Pete never told her much, either. Now there was someone new, someone who might be able to shed light on what Laura Moss had really been like, someone who might tell her the things nobody else would.

6

Chrissy's excitement was short-lived. No sooner was she out of the door than she realised she might never get the chance to talk to DS Sutherland again. She could hardly pop into the station and start asking him about her mum, not unless ... well, not unless she came up with a good reason for being there in the first place. She had barely begun pondering on this when Nan launched into her.

'How many times have I told you, Chrissy? Don't talk to strangers and don't even think about taking money from them. I mean, what were you thinking? Going to that flat like that and ... I thought I'd raised you to have more bleedin' sense.'

'God, Nan, I'm not six years old.'

'You could have fooled me.'

'It was just a message. There were three of us. Nothing was going to happen, was it?'

Nan glared at her. 'Something *has* happened, young lady, or have you forgotten about Dawn?'

'You can't be sure that's got anything to do with it.'

'And you can't be sure it hasn't.'

Chrissy couldn't argue with this so she didn't bother trying. The tattooed bloke lurked ominously at the periphery of her thoughts. A bogeyman. She didn't want to bring him to the foreground, to dwell on what he might have done to Dawn. It was dark now as they walked back towards the estate and the air smelled different to how it did during the day. She sniffed, breathed it in. Nan continued with her lecture, but she wasn't really listening.

'Nan,' she asked as they passed through the gateway, 'how do you know that cop?'

'What?'

'The sergeant. DS Sutherland. He said he thought you might not remember him.'

There was a short delay before an answer came. 'Oh, he used to work at Cowan Road but then he moved away. It was years ago.'

'Why don't you like him?'

'He's the law, love. Why would I?'

Chrissy could see the sense in this, but she still thought there was more to it. 'Is that the only reason?'

'Can you think of a better one?'

There were a couple of panda cars parked outside Haslow House and these distracted Chrissy from her line of questioning. Both the vehicles were empty. Her gaze rose up the tower to the floor of Anita's flat and she wondered if the police were already inside. Her stomach churned at the thought of what they might find.

She moved a little closer to her nan until their arms were brushing. Being fourteen (almost fifteen), she didn't want to admit to feeling scared. They walked up the path to Carlton House, went through the doors and into the foyer. As they got into the lift, Chrissy asked, 'Can I go and see Zelda now?'

'You'll be seeing her in the morning.'

'Yes, but you said—'

'In the morning,' Nan said firmly. 'It's getting late.'

It wasn't actually that late but Chrissy knew better than to debate the point. She was already in Nan's bad books. The trouble was that Sutherland or some other cop would be round to talk to Zelda's mum, just to make sure that Tina Kearns's story didn't have any truth to it, and they were bound to talk to Zelda too. What would she say? Would she tell them about the row over Eddie? Well, it hadn't been a row exactly, more of a squabble, but the cops might wonder why Chrissy hadn't mentioned it.

She thought about this as they went up in the lift. Perhaps it didn't matter. After all, you couldn't remember everything that happened. If they pulled her up on it, she'd just say that she'd forgotten. She hadn't wanted to mention Dawn taunting her over fancying Eddie, not in front of Nan. It was embarrassing.

When they got inside the flat, they found Uncle Pete standing on the balcony. He was leaning over the railings, looking down on the estate. A thin line of smoke rose up into the night air from his cigarette.

'They brought that Tina Kearns in,' Nan said to him. 'Hollering like a fishwife she was. It'll be a good few hours before they get any sense out of that one.'

Uncle Pete looked over his shoulder and nodded. 'The law showed up about ten minutes ago.'

'Yeah, I saw the cars outside Haslow. Have they come out yet?'

'Not yet.'

Nan took off her coat and placed it over the back of the sofa. 'You'll never guess who else I saw down the nick.' She paused, glanced at Chrissy and said, 'Why don't you put the kettle on, love? I'm dying for a brew.'

Dying to get rid of me, more like, Chrissy thought. Nan was

about as subtle as a sledgehammer. She went into the kitchen but hovered just inside the door, hoping to hear what was said next. It had to be about the cop.

'We were interviewed by that sod Sutherland.'

'What? You're kidding. What the fuck is that bastard doing back?'

Normally, Nan would have pulled him up on his language, but not on this occasion. 'How would I know? But he's here all right. He ain't changed much neither.'

'His type never do.'

Chrissy pricked up her ears, hoping to learn more, but her nan must have gone out onto the balcony because now all she could hear was a murmur. She strained to catch the words but couldn't. She clicked her tongue, annoyed. Why did adults always keep things from you? It wasn't fair. Giving up on her eavesdropping, she crossed the kitchen, lit the gas, put the kettle on the hob and took three mugs off the drainer.

While she waited for the kettle to boil, Chrissy slopped milk into the mugs and added some sugar. She took a bourbon from the biscuit tin and nibbled on it. She gazed out of the window but it overlooked the back of the estate and everything was quiet there. No cop cars, no people, no nothing. A lot of the lamps were out – the local lads liked to throw stones at them – and the area was shrouded in darkness.

The tea was almost brewed when she heard the kerfuffle in the living room – voices, movement, sudden activity. She put her head round the door to see Nan quickly pulling on her coat.

'What is it? Where are you going?'

'Just nipping out for a minute, love.'

Before Chrissy could say anything more, Nan had scooted out of the flat. She went to join Uncle Pete on the balcony. 'What's going on?'

43

'There's an ambulance,' he said. 'It came just now.'

Chrissy hung over the railings, peering down at the scene below. The back of the ambulance was open and items were being passed out. More panda cars had appeared, too. She had an odd panicky sensation in her chest, like her heart had grown wings and they were flapping against her ribs. 'Does that mean they've found her? Have they found Dawn?'

'That's what your nan's gone to find out.'

A crowd had already started to gather outside Haslow, the residents emerging from all three towers as word spread around the estate that something was happening. A cop was trying to keep them in order, moving them away from the ambulance. The crowd shuffled back a little, heads bobbing as they attempted to see over the person in front of them, and then gradually edged forward again.

Chrissy's fingers gripped the cool metal. 'If the ambulance is here, doesn't that . . . you know, doesn't that mean that she needs help, that she's just been hurt, had an accident or whatever, rather than she's . . . ?' She couldn't bring herself to use the word dead, didn't dare speak it.

Uncle Pete didn't say anything.

She looked at him.

'Yeah,' he said, nodding. 'It might.'

But Chrissy knew he didn't believe it, any more than those down below believed it. They wouldn't all be standing there gawping if they didn't think something dreadful, something gruesome, was unravelling. She could see a good few of the neighbours, but not Zelda or her mum. The Dunlap brothers were standing to one side, shoulders slouched, hands in their pockets; they were pretending they weren't interested although, of course, they were.

It was only a couple of minutes before Nan appeared. She

pushed through the people and went straight over to one of the cops. He must have given her short shrift because she rapidly moved on to another. This officer shook his head, directing her back towards the crowd, but she wasn't having any of it. Chrissy could see her gesticulating, arms rising and falling as she tried to press home whatever point she was making.

Suddenly, a visible ripple ran through the spectators. Chrissy and her uncle leaned further forward but they were too high up to catch what was being said. Uncle Pete yelled down to a bloke who was a few floors down and also out on his balcony.

'Hey, Jacko, what's going on down there?'

'They've found a body, mate.'

Chrissy recoiled, a jolt passing through her heart. It was Dawn! It had to be. She felt cold and sick and dizzy. *A body*. She had reckoned she was prepared for the worst, but she wasn't. The news hit her as hard as a fist thumping into her guts, taking away her breath, leaving her limp and stupefied. All the bad thoughts she'd privately harboured – the resentment, the jealousy, the dislike – swirled around in her mind as if they had in some way contributed to Dawn's death.

'Go inside,' Uncle Pete said.

She didn't move. She couldn't.

'Chrissy!'

But still she continued to stand there, her feet fixed to the ground.

Eventually Uncle Pete took her arm and gently hauled her back into the living room. 'Come on,' he said. 'You don't want to see this.'

She slumped down onto the sofa and briefly covered her face with her hands. She wanted Nan. Why wasn't she here? Nan was the only person who could comfort her, who could make her feel safe. Tears sprang into her eyes. She was starting to shake as the full horror of it all gradually sank in.

Uncle Pete touched her lightly on the shoulder. His gaze darted towards the balcony and she could see that he longed to be out there, watching and witnessing, sharing in what was going on. But to his credit he stayed in the room with her, even if he couldn't stop pacing back and forth.

'They'll get the bastard who did this, Chrissy. He won't get away with it.'

Chrissy couldn't see how this was much of a consolation – it wouldn't bring Dawn back – but she knew he was only trying to help.

'Who could do that to a kid?' he muttered, shaking his head.

She didn't reply, even though she knew the answer. A monster in a white vest with tattoos down his arms. If only she'd made Dawn tell her what the bloke had said. He must have asked her to come back later, must have promised her something – something even more enticing than the shelves of sweets in Mr Patel's shop. But what?

Although it was probably less than ten minutes, it felt like hours before she heard the front door open and close. She leapt up as her nan came into the living room. She tried to speak but nothing came out. Her mouth opened and closed like a goldfish. Her throat felt rough as sandpaper.

'Jacko said they'd found a body,' Uncle Pete asked. 'It's her, then, is it?'

7

Nan's face was pale except for two bright spots of red on her cheeks. She was breathing heavily – she must have run along the corridor – and at first could only manage a thin tight smile as she looked first at Chrissy and then at Uncle Pete. Chrissy could feel her heart thumping in her chest. She wanted to put her hands over her ears, to deafen herself to the news she knew was coming.

'Well?' Uncle Pete prompted.

But then, amazingly, Nan shook her head. 'It's not Dawn.'

Chrissy's eyes widened in disbelief. 'What? It's not her? Not Dawn?' Relief crashed through her. It seemed impossible, incredible. She would have jumped up and down if her legs hadn't been so shaky. Instead she lurched forward, three unsteady steps until she was standing right in front of her grandmother. 'Are you sure, Nan?'

'It's a grown woman they've found. That Anita, from the sounds of it. They reckon she's been there a few days too. At least that's what people are saying.'

'So Dawn's still alive?'

Nan hesitated. 'Let's hope so, love.'

Chrissy's relief, her excitement, was instantly dampened. There was something cautionary in Nan's voice, something that wasn't quite right. 'What do you mean? If it's not her then ... I mean, she must be okay, mustn't she?'

'I'm sure she is.'

Except it seemed to Chrissy that Nan wasn't sure. Not in the slightest. 'But if she wasn't in the flat ...'

Nan nodded and gave her a reassuring pat on the arm. 'She's probably just gone off somewhere. I dare say she'll turn up in a day or two.'

Uncle Pete asked, 'Have they caught the bugger who did it?'

'What do you think? He'll be well gone by now. Miles away. Not going to hang around, is he? Not after he's done something like that.' Then she said to Chrissy, 'Put the kettle on, will you, sweetheart. I need a brew. I never got the chance to drink the last one you made.'

Chrissy wanted to ask more questions – how Anita had died, what the man had done to her – but they could wait. Nan, if she even knew the answers, would be more forthcoming with a strong cup of tea inside her. As Chrissy went to the kitchen, her thoughts were full of the tattooed devil who might or might not be miles away by now. What if he was still lurking someplace on the estate? She shivered. And what of Dawn? There was every chance she hadn't gone back to Anita's flat, every possibility she was still alive. But if that was true, why did she feel so bad? Why did she have this weight inside her, like a mighty great stone in her stomach?

She laid the palms of her hands against her guts, slowly breathed in and out, and tried not to panic. Dawn wasn't dead. She wasn't. *Please God*. If she prayed hard enough, maybe Dawn would come home.

8

The next morning Chrissy waited for Zelda by the entrance to the estate. It felt wrong for the sun to be out, for the sky to be so clear and blue and cloudless, as though the weather should be aware that bad things had happened and adjust itself accordingly. She frowned and gazed over at Haslow House, but there was no sign now of last night's activity or that the law had ever been there.

Despite intense interrogation, she hadn't been able to find out much more from Nan. Only that Anita had been stabbed, and Nan, she was sure, had only told her that because she knew she'd hear about it anyway. She didn't want to think about the man plunging in the knife, but the image wouldn't go away. It scared her, not only because murder *was* scary, but because she'd been so close to him herself. How easily he could have reached out and grabbed her, dragging her inside the flat and . . .

She stamped on the thought before it could become embedded in her mind. That the world was a perilous place was a given – her own mother had died at the age of twenty-three – but the dangers had never seemed quite so real before. To the tattooed man she would be a threat. He would know she could identify him, know that she could place him in the flat on Sunday.

Her eyes raked the estate as her pulse quickened. There was nothing to see other than a swarm of kids wearing the navy-blue uniforms of Kellston Secondary. She felt partly reassured. Safety in numbers, right? He wouldn't approach her in broad daylight, not with so many witnesses around. And anyway, Nan was probably right – the monster would be miles away by now.

She wished that Zelda would hurry up so she wasn't alone. On the way to school they'd be able to compare notes about what the cops had asked and what they'd said back. That way she wouldn't be caught out if Sutherland questioned her again. And they could talk about Dawn. Was Zelda still sure that she hadn't run away? Chrissy prayed she was wrong. Better Dawn had taken off than gone back to Anita's flat.

The Dunlap brothers, Charlie and George, came out of Carlton House and walked down the path towards her. They were always together, stuck like glue, and could almost have passed for twins – the same red hair and freckles, the same pale blue eyes – if Charlie hadn't been a couple of inches taller. He was the older by a year and was in her class. As they got closer, she looked the other way, not ignoring them, exactly, but just pretending she hadn't seen them.

But the brothers didn't walk on past. Instead they stopped right beside her.

'You waiting for Zelda?' Charlie asked.

'Yeah.'

'She ain't coming.'

'What?'

'She ain't coming,' Charlie repeated. 'Mrs Graham said to tell you.'

The Dunlaps lived on the same landing as the Grahams. Zelda's mum, who knew the girls met up every morning, must have waylaid the lads as they passed the front door. Chrissy tried to hide her disappointment, but her voice, even to her own ears, had a thin, whiney quality to it. 'Why? Why not?'

'Dunno.' Charlie paused, gave her an interested look, and added, 'Maybe it's 'cause of last night. Is it true that you talked to the law, that you were down the nick?'

'Who told you that?'

But he only answered the question with another. 'Is it true that Dawn Kearns is missing?'

'I suppose,' she said. 'No one's seen her since Sunday.' And then, eager to dispel any notions that she might be some kind of grass – talking to the police was generally disapproved of – she said, 'That's why I had to go down the nick. I didn't have a choice. Me and Zelda were the last ones to see her.'

'You think he's done away with her, too? The bloke from the flat, I mean.'

Even though the thought was constantly with her, Chrissy scowled at him. 'What sort of thing is that to say?'

Charlie just grinned, like it was all some sort of game. 'I heard they found something of hers in the flat.'

'Found what?'

'Her cardigan. That's what Frank Yates said. He said they found her cardigan there.'

Chrissy's breath caught in her throat. She gulped, not wanting to believe it, and ran her tongue over dry lips. 'What does Frank know about it?'

'I'm only telling you what he said.'

Chrissy knew Dawn hadn't been wearing a cardigan the last time she saw her, but that didn't mean she hadn't gone home and put one on. She stared at Charlie, wondering if he was winding her up – or if Frank had been winding *him* up. 'What colour cardi?'

'Dunno. You'll have to ask him that.'

'I will.'

The two brothers walked off, leaving in their wake that familiar musty smell. Chrissy wrinkled her nose, shifted her school bag from one shoulder to the other and stared after them. Now, more than ever, she wanted to talk to Zelda. She was tempted to go back to Carlton House and knock on the Grahams' door, but that would make her late for school and the last thing she wanted was detention.

Reluctantly, she went through the gate and started walking along Mansfield Road. She followed the brothers all the way down the high street, trailing behind, keeping her distance so she wasn't forced to talk to them again. If a cardigan had been found, wouldn't Nan have heard about it? But maybe she had and just didn't want to worry her.

It was clear as soon as she entered the school yard that everyone was talking about the murder. Most of the kids who came here lived on the estate and they'd all witnessed last night's drama. There was a slightly feverish atmosphere, half excitement, half shock. Groups huddled together, boys and girls, heads bowed as information was exchanged. She heard snippets as she passed. Casual violence was commonplace on the Mansfield, but a deliberate killing was something else.

She had a quick look round for Frank Yates but couldn't see him. As he nearly always cycled to school, she considered going to the bicycle sheds in case he showed up there. Should she? It was where the cooler, more rebellious, more intimidating kids hung out, smoking and snogging and taunting anyone who dared to step into their territory. She dithered, and by the time she'd made up her mind to do it the bell was ringing. With some sense of relief, she went inside instead. It felt odd to be without Zelda or Dawn. She was used to their company and didn't much like being on her own.

At morning assembly, after the hymn had been sung and the Lord's Prayer recited in a subdued mumble, the headmaster talked about the 'unfortunate incident' on the Mansfield estate without once saying the word murder. Chrissy was only half listening. She was peering along the rows trying to locate Frank. It was only when Mr Pierce mentioned Dawn's name that her ears pricked up.

'If anyone has seen Dawn Kearns over the last few days, from Sunday afternoon two-thirty onwards, or has any idea where she might be, please come and see me in my office.'

A few faces turned to look at Chrissy. She kept her eyes fixed straight ahead. Why were they staring at her? *She* didn't know where Dawn was. She wished she did. That sick feeling was swirling around in her guts again, a churning mixture of guilt and dread. With every minute that passed, the chances of Dawn still being alive seemed to grow smaller and smaller.

9

It was afternoon break before Chrissy got the opportunity to question Frank Yates. He was one of those oddballs, the sort who kept themselves to themselves. While most of the other lads were kicking a football around the yard, he was standing well apart, leaning against the wall with his nose in a book. He had a sullen, sulky kind of face, brown hair and brown eyes. Those eyes, full of suspicion, were gazing at her now.

'Charlie Dunlap says you told him that the law found Dawn's cardigan in the flat.'

'I didn't,' he said, his voice peevish.

'Oh.' Chrissy was annoyed and relieved in equal measure. 'So he just made it up?'

'I told him they found *a* cardigan. I didn't say it was definitely hers.'

Chrissy's relief was short-lived. Her heart missed a beat. 'How do you know what they found?'

'I saw the law put it in a bag. It looked like hers, that's all I told Charlie. Yellow with those pink bits on the cuffs.'

Chrissy frowned at the description. Dawn didn't have much of a wardrobe so what she wore she wore with regularity. Even so, she was surprised that Frank had recognised it. He didn't seem the type to take notice of any girl's clothes. 'Are you sure?'

'I was right there.'

'In the flat?'

'I didn't say they found it in the flat. It was down in the hall, under the stairs.'

'What?'

'Yeah, it was just lying there with all the rubbish.'

This put a different slant on things. Just because it was found in Haslow House, it didn't mean Dawn had been back there. She could have dropped the cardigan anywhere on the estate and someone else could have picked it – the type with no respect for other people's property – and chucked it in the stairwell. 'Did you tell them it was hers?'

Frank looked at her like she was stupid. 'Why would I do that? It might have been hers, it might not have been. It's not down to me. They can ask her mum, can't they?'

Chrissy nodded. 'I suppose,' she said, although she wondered if Tina was even aware of what clothes her daughter had.

'And I never told Charlie they found it in the flat.'

'Okay,' she said. 'I believe you. He's always making stuff up. Did you know the bloke who was living there, the one with the tattoos?'

'No.'

'You never saw him around?'

'I just said, didn't I?'

'You said you didn't know him. It's not the same thing.'

Frank raised his eyebrows as though she was just splitting hairs.

Chrissy looked away and stared across the crowded yard. She

still wasn't sure if the cardigan meant anything or not. It could have been missing for weeks. When was the last time she'd seen Dawn wearing it? She couldn't remember. Her thoughts flew back to Sunday. It suddenly occurred to her that Anita might already have been dead when the three of them had turned up with Eddie's message. Her hands clenched into two tight fists. No, that couldn't be true. Surely no one would answer the door if there was a dead body inside.

'Is that it?' Frank asked.

Chrissy looked back at him and nodded. 'I guess.'

Frank returned to his book.

Chrissy continued to stand there for a moment, still trying to figure everything out. Then she cleared her throat to get his attention again.

Frank looked up. 'What now?'

'Did you see her again? Dawn? On Sunday afternoon.'

'What do you mean *again*?'

'You know, after you cycled past us. By the gates to the Mansfield. It was about two o'clock. We were sitting on the wall.'

Frank shook his head. 'I wasn't out on Sunday.'

'You were.'

'I wasn't.'

'I saw you. You were, like, feet away.'

Frank's face turned beetroot red, the dark flush rising from his neck to his cheeks. 'You calling me a liar?'

Chrissy took a step back, surprised by the vehemence of his response. 'Okay, keep your hair on. I was just . . .'

Frank slammed his book shut. 'Just putting me somewhere that I wasn't. You've got it wrong, all right? Don't go saying any different. You've made a mistake. Whoever you saw, it wasn't me.' And with that he threw her an angry look and stomped off across the yard.

56

Chrissy watched him leave, bemused. She'd clocked him with her own eyes, plain as day – she would swear to it on her nan's life – and nothing he said could change that. So why the hell was he lying? The question continued to bug her as she headed back inside for the rest of the day's lessons.

10

By the time Chrissy left school at the end of the day, she was no closer to understanding Frank's denial. It didn't make any sense to her. But then boys were a mystery, full stop. Most of what they said and did was incomprehensible. If it had just been her word against his, he might have got away with it, but Zelda and Dawn had been there too. Not that Dawn could back her up, but Zelda certainly could. That was where she was going now, straight back to the Mansfield to see her.

Was it possible that Frank knew something about Dawn going missing? Well, she had told the law about seeing him on Sunday – he wouldn't be too pleased about that – so it was up to them to find out why he was lying. She couldn't see how he fitted in with her suspicions about the tattooed man, but maybe Dawn hadn't returned to the flat. The two events, the murder of Anita and Dawn's disappearance, might not be connected. She didn't much care for this theory but couldn't completely dismiss it.

Chrissy was walking down the high street, musing on all this, when she became aware of someone falling into step beside her. She glanced sideways and was startled to see Eddie grinning back at her.

'Hey,' he said. 'Good to see you again. It's Chrissy, isn't it?'

She nodded, feeling two strong and simultaneous emotions: joy at seeing him again and mortification that she was wearing her school uniform. 'Yeah, that's right.'

'I thought so. I never forget the name of a pretty girl.'

Chrissy smiled, aware that she was being flattered but pleased by it all the same. She could feel her heart thumping. It was hard to believe that he was right here, looking at her, speaking to her, like all her dreams come true. Then, as she recalled the events of last night, her smile quickly faded. 'God, I'm really sorry about your friend.'

Eddie frowned. 'What friend?'

'Anita,' she said. 'You've heard about what happened to her, haven't you?'

'Ah, *her*. Yeah, I heard, but she wasn't really a friend. I barely knew her as it goes. That message was just a favour for a mate.'

'Oh, okay.'

'Not that it isn't awful. I mean, murdered in her own flat, poor cow. Who'd do a thing like that? Have they arrested anyone yet? Do you know?'

Chrissy shook her head. 'I don't think so.'

'What did she say when you gave her the message?'

'Nothing.'

'Nothing?'

'She wasn't there.'

Eddie looked relieved. 'No harm done, then. That's good. You know what the pigs are like, always trying to make something out of nothing.'

Chrissy glanced away. What now? She thought about keeping

quiet, but he'd probably find out eventually. 'Erm . . . they know about the message. Sorry, but I kind of had to tell them.'

'Had to?'

Chrissy heard the sharpness in his tone and inwardly flinched. Now she'd annoyed him, the last thing she'd wanted to do. Quickly she tried to explain. 'Because of Dawn going missing. The man at Anita's flat said something to her, something we didn't hear – I mean, me and Zelda – and we thought . . . we thought that she might have gone back there later. Nan made me go down the nick with her. They asked who we'd seen that day, who we'd spoken to and so . . . ' Her voice trailed off into a whisper. 'Sorry.'

'What man? And who's Dawn?' Before she had time to reply, he continued, 'No, hang on, how about we grab a Coke and you can tell me all about it.'

Chrissy's eyes lit up. 'Okay.'

'The Wimpy,' he said. 'Will that do?'

'Okay.' Chrissy loved the Wimpy, especially as she rarely had the chance to go there. Money was tight in the Moss household and not be wasted. 'Yeah, let's do that.'

While they were crossing the road, she surreptitiously took off her tie and slipped it into her pocket. She was both excited and anxious. Simply walking beside him – she was trying not to stare – gave her butterflies in her stomach. She hoped some of the girls from school would be in the Wimpy; to see her with Eddie would make them all green with envy. At the same time, she prayed that none of the neighbours would spot her or she'd get a right bollocking from Nan when the gossip was passed on. Still, it was worth the risk.

In the event, the Wimpy only had a few customers and she didn't recognise any of them.

Eddie chose a table away from the window, beckoned the

waitress over and ordered a couple of Cokes. Chrissy saw the way the woman looked at him, the way she instantly became flirtatious, smiling too much and pushing out her chest.

'Anything else, love?' the waitress asked. 'Anything else I can help you with?'

Chrissy glared at her but she didn't seem to notice.

'I'll let you know,' Eddie said. 'If and when.'

The waitress grinned and walked away, wiggling her hips like they were something special.

Eddie turned his attention back to Chrissy. He pushed his sunglasses on to his head, leaned forward and said softly, 'So, you were telling me about Dawn.'

It was the first time Chrissy had really noticed his eyes. They were very blue with long dark lashes. 'She was with me on the wall, the small one with the short brown hair. You remember, don't you?'

'Only vaguely,' he said. 'I wasn't really looking at the other two.'

'Oh, come on.' Chrissy rolled her eyes, trying to act grown up, not the sort to fall for some sweet talker's blarney.

'I mean it. You were the only one I noticed. Don't you know how pretty you are? I bet you've got hundreds of lads running after you.'

Chrissy blushed, despite her desire to play it cool. She didn't put him straight. The truth was that no boy, not a single one, had ever shown an interest. When she looked in the mirror all she saw was a skinny, awkward girl with lank hair, a narrow face sprinkled with much-hated freckles, and a mouth that was too wide. 'Dawn was the one you gave the fifty pence to.'

A smile played around Eddie's lips as though he was more than aware of the effect he was having on her. 'And now she's gone missing?'

'Since Sunday. No one's seen her since then.'

The waitress came back with the Cokes and put them on the table. She flashed her teeth at Eddie, but he only nodded back. 'Ta.'

Once the woman had left, Chrissy gave him a quick summary of what had happened when they'd gone to Anita's flat. 'So that man with the tattoos, he could of . . . Do you know who he is? Do you know his name?'

Eddie shook his head. 'Not a clue.'

'Only he seemed to know who you were.'

As soon as she'd said it, she wished she hadn't. Eddie's face darkened, his eyes narrowing into slits. Then, almost instantly, he had wiped the expression and was smiling again. 'Can't think why that was. Like I said, I barely knew Anita. I only met her a couple of times.' He swigged some Coke and put his glass down. 'What did you tell the law about me?'

'Hardly anything,' Chrissy said hurriedly. 'Only . . . only that you asked us to deliver a message. And I wouldn't have told them that if I hadn't had to. They were going to talk to Zelda too so I thought I'd better be straight. I didn't want to get you in trouble or nothing.'

'I know that, hon. What did they say when you told them?'

'They asked me what I thought you meant by stock.'

'And what did you say?'

'Nothing. Nan said it was none of their business what I thought so I didn't need to answer.'

'Your nan sounds like a smart woman.'

'She doesn't trust the law.'

'And who can blame her? They don't care about the likes of you and me; they don't give a toss. If they can find a way to stitch you up, they will.'

Chrissy nodded as if she knew all about the misdoings of the police. 'They can't do that to you, though, can they? I mean, you never went near the flat. They can't blame you for what happened.'

Eddie gave a long, world-weary sigh. 'Wouldn't put it past the bastards. That's what you get for doing a favour for a mate. I should have told him to stuff his message, to take it himself. You try to help someone and end up in the middle of a murder case. And all for the sake of a bit of booze. That's all it was about, you know. Vodka, Scotch, gin. Anita used to buy a few bottles when he managed to get his hands on some cheap stuff.'

'But that's nothing to do with you.'

'Don't shoot the messenger, right? Except the law always do.'

'Can't you explain to them about your mate?'

Eddie's eyebrows shot up. 'I'm not a grass, hon. I couldn't show my face in Kellston again if anyone found out. I mean, the booze isn't strictly legit. Off the back of a lorry, if you get what I mean. No, I can't bring his name into it.'

Chrissy sipped her Coke, pleased that Eddie was confiding in her – he wouldn't be sharing this information unless he trusted her – but concerned about her part in his current situation. 'I didn't give the law a good description. There must be lots of Eddies in Kellston. They can't be sure it's you.'

'But what about your pal, Zelda? What did she say to them?'

'I don't know,' Chrissy admitted. 'She didn't come to school today.'

Eddie gave a wry smile. 'Oh well, I'll just have to keep my head down for a while. Maybe they'll nab the tattooed geezer and it'll all blow over.'

'Nan says he'll be miles away by now.' Then, realising that this didn't help Eddie much, she added, 'But he might not be. And even if he is . . . they could still catch him, couldn't they?'

'Let's hope so.'

'And maybe Dawn will turn up, too. Zelda reckons she wouldn't have run away, but I'm not so sure.'

'You must be worried about her.'

Chrissy nodded. 'It's been days now. The law found her cardigan, but not in the flat. It was under the stairs at Haslow. There's nothing to say she was ever in the flat but . . .'

'You reckon she might have been?'

'I don't want to think about it, not after what happened to Anita.'

Eddie lit a fag, inhaled and released the smoke in a long straight line. He inclined his head and gazed at her.

After a while, when he still hadn't spoken, she began to feel self-conscious. 'What?'

'Sorry, I shouldn't stare at you. I just can't help it. Tell me something about yourself.'

'What do you want to know?'

'Anything. Do you live with your nan?'

'And my Uncle Pete. In Carlton House.'

'What about your mum?'

'She died when I was four.'

Eddie frowned. 'That's a shame. It must have been tough on you. But you get on all right with your nan, do you?'

'Most of the time. She's okay.'

'Still, I don't suppose she'd be too happy about you being here with me.'

Chrissy, hoping to give the impression that she was mature enough to run her own life, lifted her chin and said firmly, 'She can't tell me what to do. Anyway, we're only having a Coke. There's nothing wrong with that, is there?'

'Nothing at all,' he agreed. 'But I am a bit older than you.'

'Not that much.'

'No, not that much, but I don't want to get you into trouble.

Perhaps it would be better if ... well, if we didn't tell anyone else about us meeting like this. Just for now. Until this Anita business is sorted out. You don't mind, do you?'

'I guess not.'

'I knew you'd understand. I bet you're good at keeping secrets.'

'I won't tell anyone, I swear.'

'Especially the law.'

'Especially the law,' she repeated.

'Good.' Eddie put out his cigarette and glanced at his watch. 'Okay, I'd better make myself scarce before the bastards track me down. Thanks again, Chrissy. Why don't you go first in case someone sees us leave together? You don't mind, do you? Better to be safe than sorry. You go on home and I'll sort out the bill.'

Chrissy, reluctant to bring the encounter to a close, especially when no further meeting had been proposed, sipped what remained of her drink. She gazed across the table at him, absorbing every inch of his handsome face. She wanted to grab hold of the moment, to keep it for ever, to never have it stop, but he was already reaching into his pocket for his wallet.

'Thanks for the Coke,' she said.

'You're welcome. Take care of yourself, hon.'

'You too.' Chrissy rose to her feet. 'Bye, then.'

'Bye. I'll see you soon.'

She wanted to ask when, but knew it wasn't cool. Instead she banked those words – I'll see you soon – in her memory. They meant something, didn't they? That this was only the beginning and not the end. As she opened the door, she glanced over her shoulder. Eddie was leaning on the counter, chatting to the waitress. She felt a sharp spurt of jealousy, like an arrow piercing her heart. Quickly she turned her face away in case he caught her looking.

11

Although it was getting on for half an hour since Chrissy had left school, she was in no rush. Nan wouldn't be back yet; every Thursday afternoon, from three to five – it was half closing at the butchers where she worked – she went to visit her old neighbour, Betty Cope, at Silverstone Nursing Home. The place wasn't far from the station, a big, forbidding building that had once been an asylum. They called it a home these days, but everyone knew that the people in it weren't right in the head.

She trailed up the high street, frequently glancing over her shoulder so she could catch sight of Eddie coming out of the Wimpy. He didn't. Well, maybe he'd gone to the loo or was making a phone call. She didn't want to think of him still talking to that waitress. No, he wouldn't be. Or if he was it was only to kill some time before he left.

She stopped when she came to Mansfield Road, peering back down the high street while she shielded her eyes from the low afternoon sun. She had a fluttery sensation in her chest, and her legs felt wonky, like her knees were in danger of giving way.

Still no sign of Eddie. She slowly counted to ten before giving up and turning the corner.

Chrissy was already aware that she wouldn't be able to keep quiet. She had to tell someone about what had just happened – she was too excited not to – and that someone would be Zelda. It didn't count as breaking a promise; the two of them told each other everything and she knew it wouldn't go any further. As she walked towards the estate, she tried to remember exactly what Eddie had said to her so she could repeat it word for word.

The Dunlap brothers were loitering by the gates and Chrissy thought about pulling them up on the information about Dawn's cardigan. Trouble was, she wasn't sure if they'd been lying or Frank had. She gave them a half smile as she passed, not wanting to be too friendly but not wanting to snub them either.

'Hey,' Charlie said. 'You heard about Marlon Pound?'

Chrissy stopped. 'Heard what?'

'They've hauled him down the nick.'

Chrissy couldn't see this as in any way newsworthy. After all, Marlon had been living with Tina and Dawn; the law were bound to want to talk to him. 'So what?'

'Just thought you'd want to know. They took him in this morning. Kicked up a right fuss, he did. Least that's what Mum says. Punched one of the cops in the face.'

'Has he been arrested?'

'Dunno,' Charlie said. 'Could have been.'

Chrissy stared at him. As usual, Charlie Dunlap only had half the story. 'Do they think he ... you know, has something to do with Dawn going missing?'

Charlie shrugged. 'That's what people are saying. It's been all day and he still ain't back. They wouldn't hold him, would they, if they didn't have a reason.'

'What about her mum? What about Tina?'

'They've let her go.'

Chrissy weighed up this new information, trying to balance it against her own theory of the tattooed man and Dawn returning to the flat. Perhaps she'd got it wrong. Perhaps Marlon was the one who'd done something bad. It wouldn't be the first time. She thought of the bruises on Dawn's arms and shuddered.

As if Charlie had read her thoughts, he said, 'That Marlon's a shit.'

'Yeah.'

This was followed by one of those awkward moments while the three of them stood around saying nothing. George stared at her, his expression blank. He was as silent as he always was; she'd only ever seen him talk to his brother.

'Okay,' Chrissy said. 'I'd better be off.'

She didn't look back as she walked on into the estate, but could feel their eyes on her. Quickening her pace, she hurried along the path towards the entrance to Carlton House. Once inside, she took the lift and went up to the ninth floor. The ascent was slow and juddery. As she watched the light over the doors creep from one number to the next, she slapped her hands impatiently against her thighs.

Eventually the lift reached its destination and she jumped out, dashed along the landing and knocked on Zelda's door. It was Mrs Graham who answered and she didn't seem pleased at the interruption. She folded her arms, looking stern.

'Oh, it's you.'

Chrissy, despite the chilly welcome, maintained her smile. 'Is Zelda in, please?'

'Sorry, but she's just about to have her dinner.'

'Is she all right?'

'She's upset,' Mrs Graham said stiffly. 'All this business with Dawn. It's shaken her up.'

'Yes, it's horrible. It's really . . . Look, I won't stay long. Could I just see her for five minutes?'

Mrs Graham shook her head. 'I don't think that's a good idea. There's been enough bother as it is. You go on home now.'

Then, before Chrissy could say anything else, the door was shut firmly in her face. She stood there, bewildered. What had that been about? Mrs Graham was usually so nice and friendly; this wasn't like her at all. And unless she was mistaken, there had been something accusatory in her tone – *There's been enough bother as it is* – as though Chrissy was about to add to it. Or had caused it in the first place. But how could that be? She hadn't done anything wrong. She hadn't even seen Zelda today.

Still confused, and disappointed at not being able to share her news about Eddie, Chrissy turned and walked to the stairs. While she climbed the two flights, she tried to figure out what Mrs Graham had been getting at. It was hardly Chrissy's fault that Dawn had gone missing or that Anita had been murdered, so what was with the attitude?

By the time she reached her own front door, Chrissy was none the wiser. The exchange still bugged her, though. She felt like she was being blamed for something she hadn't done. A wave of indignation rolled over her. Adults, she decided, could be just as baffling as boys.

She went inside and was surprised to find Nan home already. Her grandmother came out of the kitchen, scowling as she wiped her hands on her apron.

'Have you seen the time? Where have you been?'

Chrissy was about to claim she'd been at Zelda's – it wasn't a complete lie – but then had second thoughts. Nan was obviously in a mood and she didn't want to get caught out. 'The library,' she said. 'The school library. I had to get some books for homework.'

'And how long does that take?'

'It was busy.'

Nan, not surprisingly, didn't seem convinced. Chrissy was hardly renowned for her dedication when it came to such matters. 'Hanging round those school gates, more like. You think I was born yesterday? Go and get changed and then wash your hands. Dinner's almost ready.'

As Nan marched back into the kitchen, Chrissy looked at Uncle Pete, who was sitting on the sofa watching TV. 'What's with her?'

'Betty had one of her turns and the visit was cut short. So don't go giving her any grief. She's upset enough as it is.'

'She doesn't need to take it out on me.'

'You should get home on time, then.'

'Since when did you make the rules?'

'Since never. Don't be so stroppy. I'm just saying that she's had a bad day.'

'Haven't we all,' Chrissy snapped defensively, although this wasn't strictly true. Despite Zelda's absence and the weirdness of Frank Yates, her own day had been unexpectedly enhanced by Eddie's attentions. 'Dawn's still missing, remember?'

'Yeah, I know. Everyone's on edge so let's just keep things calm, huh?'

'Is it true about Marlon?'

'Is what true?'

'Charlie Dunlap said they took him down the nick this morning and they haven't let him go yet. Do you think that means—'

Nan put her head round the door and glared at her. 'Are you still here? What did I just tell you?'

'I'm going, I'm going,' Chrissy said. 'Keep your hair on.'

Chrissy went through to the bedroom, changed out of her school clothes and pulled on jeans and a long-sleeved T-shirt. It was sod's law that Betty had thrown a wobbler today. If it hadn't been for that, Nan would never have known what time she'd got back. Uncle Pete, even if he'd noticed, would never have grassed her up. Now, after dinner, instead of watching television she'd have to pretend to do the homework she didn't have.

Chrissy softly cursed Betty Cope. She didn't remember much about the woman – it was years since she'd last seen her – and the only memories she did have were vague and wispy: a slight, elderly woman who had lived along the landing when Chrissy was a child. Nan said Betty suffered from 'nerves', but that was just another way of saying she wasn't right in the head.

By the time Chrissy made it to the kitchen, dinner was already on the table: chicken Kiev with chips and beans. She sat down and picked up her knife and fork.

'Have you washed your hands?' Nan asked.

'Yes,' Chrissy lied, even though she'd forgotten all about it.

Nan gave her a sceptical look. 'Are you sure?'

'Course I'm sure.' Then, before Nan could demand proof of soap and water having touched her fingers, Chrissy quickly changed the subject. 'Have you heard about Dawn's cardigan? Frank Yates said they found it under the stairs at Haslow House.'

Uncle Pete, who was shovelling food into his mouth as though there was a famine on the way, said nothing.

Nan sighed and shook her head. 'It might not be hers. And even if it is ... well, it doesn't mean ...'

Chrissy plunged her knife into the Kiev and released the garlic butter. It made a satisfying squelchy noise. 'It must mean something. And why haven't the law let Marlon go yet? Charlie Dunlap reckons he's still down the nick.'

'Best place for him.'

Uncle Pete stopped eating long enough to say, 'They had me down there this morning, too.'

'What for?' Chrissy asked. 'What's it got to do with you?'

'We went to the Kearnses' flat last night, didn't we? They wanted to know if I noticed anything while I was inside. You know, anything odd.'

'But you didn't.'

Uncle Pete loaded up his fork again, lifted it to his mouth and said, 'That's what I kept telling 'em. If I'd seen something, I'd have said something. Stands to reason, don't it? Not that it puts him in the clear – he's had plenty of time to cover his tracks. And we all know what he's like. Blokes like him should be strung up.'

Nan, who was shifting her food around her plate without actually eating any of it, put her knife down. 'Don't you go getting any ideas. You've only just come out of jug. Leave it to the law to sort out.'

'He's a scumbag. He needs teaching a lesson.'

'And he'll get what's coming to him if . . . ' Nan glanced at Chrissy, pausing before she carried on. 'Just stay out of it, right? Think on, for once. I can do without visiting you in the Scrubs for the next fifteen years.'

It seemed to Chrissy that all the focus was on Marlon Pound. 'What about the tattooed man?'

'Don't go fretting about that,' Nan said. 'They'll find him soon enough.'

So far as Chrissy was concerned, soon enough couldn't come quickly enough – for her own sake and for Eddie's. It was all very well Nan saying not to worry, but she wasn't the one who'd stood right in front of the monster. And Eddie was caught in the middle of it, too; he would stay in the firing line for as long as the killer was on the loose. Even though it was completely obvious that he'd had nothing to do with the murder, the law might have a different point of view. Thinking about Eddie gave her goosebumps – she wanted to say his name out loud, to talk about him, but knew that she couldn't. Instead she said, 'Zelda wasn't at school today.'

'She was down the nick,' Uncle Pete said. 'I saw her there with her mum.'

Perhaps that was why Mrs Graham had been in a mood, Chrissy thought – no one liked going down the nick – although it didn't explain the bad vibes she'd got off her. 'Was it about the message, about the man at Anita's flat? Was that why Zelda was there?'

Uncle Pete shrugged. 'Probably. Why else?'

'Why didn't they talk to her last night?'

'Don't ask me, love. Maybe they did. Maybe they just wanted to run through it again.'

Chrissy frowned, wondering why *she* hadn't been asked to go back. 'Do you think they'll want to see me again?'

Nan heaved out another of her sighs. 'Why should they? You've told them everything you know, haven't you?'

'Yeah, course I have.'

'Well, then. That's the end of it.'

'It's not the end of it until they catch him. And until they find Dawn.' Chrissy looked at her uncle. 'Was it that Sutherland you saw down the nick?'

'Can we just drop this now?' Nan said sharply. 'Can we talk about something else?'

They ate the rest of their dinner in silence. There didn't seem to be anything else to talk about.

12

DS Will Sutherland glanced around the Fox and figured nothing much had changed in the years he'd been away. Well, it had been smartened up a bit since Joe Quinn's demise, given a fresh lick of paint, but that was about it. The pub was still frequented by the same clientele, an eclectic mix of the criminal, the law-abiding and the various shades of humanity that fell in between. Terry Street had bought the place for a song – or so DS Sutherland had heard – after Quinn's sons had been sent down.

He looked towards the bar where DCI Tony Gaul was waiting for their drinks. The chief inspector was a florid, overweight specimen with a face that could only be described as porcine. This was pretty apt, bearing in mind the man's occupation and the fact that he always had his nose in the trough. Once Gaul had been hand in glove with Quinn, the two of them carving up Kellston between them, and no doubt there was a similar arrangement in place with Terry Street.

Bent coppers. The Force was full of them. It had shocked

DS Sutherland when he'd first joined up, but not any longer. Back in the day he'd been innocent, sure of that thin blue line between right and wrong, convinced he was on the side of the angels. Now it was often hard to tell the difference between the good and the bad. Some cops were dirty because they saw it as the only way to win the war – the end justifying the means and all that – whilst others, including Gaul, were only interested in lining their own pockets.

Will hadn't wanted to come back to Kellston, but the choice hadn't been his. Sometimes you just had to do what you were told. The place was full of too many memories, reminders of a past he had tried to forget. He had made mistakes and they didn't sit easy with him. Coming face to face with Elsie Moss hadn't helped matters, either; he had seen the hate in her eyes and knew that she would never forgive him.

Laura would have been thirty-three now if she had lived. In his head, however, she would always be that wild, sensual, reckless girl, stunningly attractive and stupidly fearless. She'd got under his skin and even now, all these years later, just the thought of her caused his heart to miss a beat. Love was different when you were young: it grabbed you by the balls and made you physically ache. Nothing and no one would affect him quite so much again.

Will didn't know why he'd said what he had to Chrissy. She didn't really look much like her mother. Apart from the long fair hair, and maybe there was something about the mouth . . . No, he'd just said it because he'd wanted her to like him. It had been an impulse, a spur-of-the-moment thing and he regretted it now. His priority – so far as it was feasible – was to keep the Moss family at arm's length. He didn't need the past coming back to kick him in the teeth.

Gaul returned with the drinks, put the two pints of bitter on the table and sat down with his back to the wall so he could see the other customers. 'No sign of that fuckin' ponce, I take it?'

Will, aware that the ponce in question was Eddie Barr, said, 'No chance. He'll be keeping his head down.'

'I'll shove his bleedin' head down the khazi when I get hold of him.'

'That's what he's worried about.'

Gaul smirked. 'He'll soon crawl out from whatever stone he's hiding under. He's got a business to run, hasn't he? Can't lie low for ever.'

Will nodded his agreement, picked up his glass and said, 'Ta. Cheers!' even though he knew Gaul would have put the drinks 'on the slate', an unnecessary addition to a bill that would never be paid. 'He'll be shitting himself, case we've got him in the frame for Anita Jakes.'

'Who says we haven't?'

Will looked at him. 'Well, if what the girls say is true, Eddie didn't even go into Haslow House on Sunday. He left the message with them and—'

'That doesn't mean he didn't go back later. We don't know exactly when she died. Maybe he dropped by again in the evening, the two of them had a falling out – that sort can't look in the fuckin' mirror without picking a fight – and Anita ended up brown bread.'

'And the tattooed man?'

'We've only got those kids' word for it that he even exists. No one else on the estate has ever set eyes on the geezer.'

'So they say, but you know what that lot are like. Anyway, the girls said he recognised Dawn, that he knew her mum.'

'And Tina Kearns says she doesn't have a clue who he is.'

'I know who I'd rather believe. Why would the girls make up something like that?'

76

'Why would she lie if there's a chance he might have something to do with her daughter's disappearance? And our Eddie has a way with the fairer sex. Maybe he had a word, used that flimsy charm of his, persuaded them to cover his back. An imaginary devil with tattoos would fit the bill nicely. Someone to take the heat off him.'

Will frowned. 'I don't think so. Their stories are too similar – and their descriptions. I was talking to Zelda Graham this morning and—'

'Yeah, yeah,' Gaul said, flapping a hand dismissively. 'You're not getting my point, son. What I'm saying is that it's a *possible* scenario, the kind of scenario that should loosen Eddie's tongue when we finally catch up with him. If anyone knows who that whore killer is, it's him. He employed the tart, didn't he? Bet he kept a close eye on her too; his type doesn't trust anyone.'

It came as no surprise to Will that the DCI was prepared to threaten Eddie with a stitch-up if he didn't cooperate. That was the way the man worked. But it didn't help with the investigation. Eddie had gone to ground precisely because of Gaul's underhand methods; knowing what was waiting for him at Cowan Road meant he wouldn't come forward voluntarily.

Will, naturally, didn't voice his reservations. Getting on the wrong side of Gaul would be a big mistake. Instead he said, 'So what about Dawn Kearns? Is there a connection to Anita's murder or not?'

Gaul drank some of his pint and smacked his fleshy lips. 'There's no evidence pointing in that direction. I'm more inclined towards a domestic. That Marlon Pound's a piece of work. Got form, hasn't he. Likes to use his fists on women. Don't suppose he'd baulk at using them on a kid, either. Maybe he gave her a slap and she decided to take off. Couldn't blame her, could you? Crap mother, crap home, crap life. There's not much to hang about for.'

'Or maybe he did something worse to her.'

'And the body? How would he get it off the Mansfield without anyone noticing?'

'Risky,' Will said, 'but if he was desperate . . . early hours of the morning, perhaps. There wouldn't have been many people around then.'

'But the prick hasn't even got a car. The best he could do would be to dump her somewhere on the estate.'

Will played with the ashtray while he pondered on this. What if Dawn had still been alive when Pound had taken her off the Mansfield? Maybe they had simply walked off the estate. But no one was admitting to having seen them after two-thirty on Sunday, either alone or together. Hear no evil, see no evil, might be the mantra of most of the residents for most of the time, but it was different when it came to kids. The same rules didn't apply.

At first light another search had been made of the Mansfield, but nothing had been found other than the cardigan. There were no obvious bloodstains on it and the chance of forensics finding anything useful was slight; it had been lying in a heap of rubbish for God knows how long. Tina Kearns claimed it definitely belonged to her daughter – there was a button missing on the bottom left-hand side – but she couldn't say when she'd last seen Dawn wearing it.

At the moment Pound was still in a cell at Cowan Road. They had interviewed him twice and were now leaving him to sweat for a while. Tina's flat had been searched but nothing incriminating had been found other than a general lack of cleanliness. The place, squalid and stinking, should have carried a health warning. It was the kind of pit where even the rats had packed their bags and moved out.

'Maybe Pound's telling the truth,' Will said, playing devil's advocate.

Gaul, who resented any lowlife walking out of Cowan Road without one charge or another, made a grunting noise. 'We've still got him for assaulting a police officer.'

Pound's alibi as regards Dawn didn't add up to much. He claimed to have been asleep until about four o'clock on Sunday afternoon, and to have not seen her at all. It was hardly watertight but he was sticking to it. Tina had spent Sunday at a friend's, getting smashed on vodka, and hadn't got home until late at night. She was sticking to her story too – that Dawn had told her she was staying at Zelda's for a few days. They had let Tina go for now but doubtless she would be interviewed again.

'I need a slash,' Gaul said, rising to his feet.

While he was gone, Will turned his attention back to Anita Jakes. She had been forty-seven, a prostitute past her sell-by date and with enough nous to know it. She had put her experience to good use by teaming up with Eddie Barr and running his two houses on Albert Road. From talking to the toms who worked there, he'd got the impression that she hadn't been well liked. Too strict, too greedy, too cold hearted. No one had wanted to speak ill of the dead, but no one had managed to find anything good to say about her, either. They all claimed to know nothing about her private life and nothing about the tattooed man. Whether they were telling the truth was debatable. In their world, like on the Mansfield, it didn't pay to shoot your mouth off.

As Gaul came back from the Gents, Will noticed how the other customers instinctively stood aside to let him pass without him once having to utter 'Excuse me'. They all knew who he was. The chief inspector was neither liked nor respected by the local community, but he was feared.

Nobody was going to stand in his way. Nobody wanted to piss him off.

Gaul settled his bulk back into his seat, and said, 'Someone must know who our tattooed friend is, someone other than Eddie bloody Barr. If no one saw him around then either he was lying low or he'd only just arrived.'

'And he has to be familiar with the Mansfield. He knows Tina Kearns and he recognised Dawn, even if he did get her name wrong.' The lads at the station were still trawling through the records, trying to put a name to the mystery man. They were checking out all the likely suspects, anyone who might have been released from jail in recent weeks or was wanted on one charge or another. They were also trying to track down any relatives of Anita's, but to date they'd come up with diddly-squat: no husband, no kids, no siblings, not even a distant cousin. 'And the guy's distinctive, isn't he? All those tattoos on his arms. It's the kind of thing you remember.'

'Yeah, well, the residents of the Mansfield are renowned for their collective memory loss. And lots of villains have tattoos. I could reel off a baker's dozen right now. Trouble is, we don't even know how old the bastard is. He could be anything from thirty to sixty.'

Will nodded. It was true that Chrissy and Zelda hadn't been able to pin an age to the man. That was the trouble with fourteen-year-old girls: they thought everyone over twenty was geriatric. 'He was old,' Chrissy had said. 'Not *really* old, but . . . you know.' Will *hadn't* known, which was why he'd pressed her. 'Older than me or younger?' She'd pulled a face then, as though it was a trick question, stared at him for a moment and then shrugged. Zelda had been equally vague. 'He was . . . erm, about . . . I'm not really sure.'

They had established that the man was tall, broad shouldered and that his hair was short and brown, but that didn't narrow things down much. When it came to the tattoos, neither of them had been able to give an accurate description; there had only been an overall impression of swirls and pattern. The two girls had both agreed, however, that his accent was local. Where they differed was in their opinion as to whether Dawn might have gone back to Anita's flat. Zelda reckoned not, but Chrissy wasn't so sure. The man had spoken to Dawn out of earshot. What had he said to her? Maybe Dawn had told the truth about the exchange – a simple request to pass on his best to her mum – or maybe she hadn't.

It worried Will that Dawn could have been abducted – or worse. Although Gaul was of the opinion that the two cases were not connected – Dawn's fingerprints, taken from her hairbrush, had not been found at Anita's flat – a part of him was inclined to trust Chrissy's instincts. Perhaps, like her mother, she was good at reading people. And suddenly he was back to thinking about Laura Moss.

Will must have released an audible breath because Gaul turned to look at him, his eyebrows lifting slightly. 'What is it?'

'Nothing,' Will said. 'I was just thinking about someone.'

Gaul's face assumed a lecherous expression. 'Some tart, I bet. You never could keep it in your pants.'

Will thought this was rich coming from a bloke who'd screwed half the toms in Albert Road – and without paying a penny for the privilege – but he smiled and kept the tone light. 'I'm a married man, remember? It's always in my bloody pants.'

Gaul's mouth widened to show a row of tombstone teeth, stained brown by all the cigars he'd smoked. 'The old ball and chain, eh? You need to get out more.'

'Fat chance of that at the moment.'

They went back to discussing the murder of Anita Jakes,

but Will only had half his attention on it. Laura Moss danced around in his brain, making him wish, not for the first time, that he'd never come back to Kellston. There was something strange, ominous even, about her daughter being involved in his first major case since his return. It was just a coincidence, wasn't it? Nothing more, nothing less. These things happened. But like most cops, he was superstitious, always alert to omens and signs, to anything that might signal the approach of calamity. Try as he might, he couldn't quite shake off the feeling that disaster was heading his way.

13

Chrissy was relieved to find Zelda waiting by the estate gates on Friday morning. She hadn't fancied another day on her own, and was bursting to share her news about Eddie taking her to the Wimpy. She smiled and linked her arm through her friend's as they set off for school. 'What happened to you yesterday?'

'I had to go to Cowan Road with Mum and talk to the police. It took ages. They asked me all sorts and they wanted to know about Marlon, whether he ever . . . whether he was, you know, mean to Dawn or violent or whatever.'

'What did you tell them?'

'The truth,' Zelda said. 'She was always covered in bruises. The man's a pig.'

'Is that why he's still locked up? Because they think he's done something to her?'

Zelda's body stiffened and her voice rose in pitch. 'He *has* done something. He must have. I hope they never let him out.'

'Charlie Dunlap said he punched a cop.'

'You don't do that if you're innocent, do you?'

Chrissy nodded, even though she thought Marlon Pound was the type who'd punch a cop just for looking at him sideways. 'I suppose.'

'He belongs in jail, that one. He deserves everything he gets.'

Chrissy was silent for a while and then she said, 'I came round after school yesterday but your mum wouldn't let me in.'

'She's mad at you about the message stuff, about us going to the flat.'

'How come I'm getting all the blame?'

'You're not. She's mad at me, too. And she can't blame Dawn, can she? Not with her being . . . Anyway, she says Dawn doesn't know any better, but that we should.'

'What's that supposed to mean?'

'Just that no one ever taught Dawn right from wrong.'

Chrissy suspected that Mrs Graham blamed her more than Zelda and that she now had her labelled as a bad influence. 'We were only having a laugh,' she said defensively.

'I know.'

'And nothing happened, did it?'

'Something happened,' Zelda said. 'That woman got murdered. Mum says it could have been one of us.'

Chrissy had the feeling she was going to be in Mrs Graham's bad books for quite some time. She wished Dawn would come back from wherever she'd gone and then things could return to normal. Unable to hold it in any longer, she blurted out, 'I saw Eddie yesterday.'

Zelda stopped dead and stared at her. 'What?'

'Yeah, he took me to the Wimpy and bought me a Coke.'

'You have to tell the police.'

Chrissy laughed, but her laughter quickly faded when she saw that Zelda was serious. It wasn't quite the reaction she'd expected. 'Why should I tell the law?'

'Because they're looking for him. DS Sutherland said I had to tell him if I saw him again.'

'Well, you haven't seen him, have you? I did. And Eddie didn't have anything to do with Anita's murder. They're just trying to cause trouble for him.'

'Is that what he told you?'

'It's true. He didn't go anywhere near the flat.'

'So why did he buy you a Coke? What did he want?'

'Nothing. He was only being friendly.'

Zelda frowned. 'Did he want to know what was going on, about what the police had asked you?'

'No,' Chrissy lied. 'It wasn't like that at all.' Zelda was making it seem like Eddie had had some hidden agenda and it hadn't been like that. He *liked* her. He thought she was special. And although she wanted to tell Zelda about the things he'd said, to even brag about them a little, warning bells were going off in her head. 'He wanted to say sorry for getting us involved.'

'And that's all?'

'Yeah, that's all. You won't tell, will you? Do you swear? Nan will kill me if she finds out.'

Zelda didn't answer directly. 'DS Sutherland said that Eddie Barr's a bad lot, and we should stay away from him.'

It was the first time Chrissy had heard Eddie's surname and she rolled it over her tongue for a few seconds. 'Eddie's okay. He hasn't done anything wrong. He was only delivering the message for a mate.'

Zelda began walking again. 'The police are still looking for him, though.'

'Well, they can't be looking very hard. He was on the high street yesterday.'

'So why doesn't he—'

Before Zelda could cast any more aspersions on Eddie's

character, Chrissy quickly interrupted. 'Oh, I didn't tell you about Frank Yates, did I?'

'What about him?'

'We were talking yesterday and he said he wasn't out on Sunday and he didn't see us by the gates.'

'So?'

'So why would he say that? He rode right past us. We were playing that game and . . . You saw him. We all did. I don't get why he'd deny it. Do you think he knows something about Dawn?'

'No, of course not.'

'Why is he lying then? I mean, what does he think – that he's invisible?'

'It won't be anything to do with Dawn. He's just scared of the police. He got in trouble a few months back and now he reckons they're out to get him.'

Chrissy couldn't imagine what kind of trouble Frank could have got into, unless it was for reading too much. 'What did he do?'

'Nothing. That's the thing. They claimed he'd been with a bunch of lads who nicked a car, but he hadn't. Anyway, ever since then he's had a thing about the police, thinks they're going to try and stitch him up. That's probably why he said he wasn't there on Sunday, just in case they try and pin something else on him.'

Chrissy could have said, 'Just like Eddie,' but she didn't. 'How come you know all this and I don't?'

'My mum knows his mum. Mrs Yates said they had him down the station for hours, trying to get him to admit to theft. They even gave him a caution. Now he's scared they'll pack him off to borstal the first chance they get.'

'Why didn't you tell me?'

86

'It's only Frank,' Zelda said, as though no one could possibly be interested in anything he did. 'It's Dawn we should be worried about.'

Chrissy heard a hint of accusation in her tone. 'I *am* worried,' she insisted. 'It's all I've been thinking about. Why do you reckon Tina Kearns said that Dawn was staying at your place?'

'Because she was covering her back, I suppose. She never knew where Dawn was. She never cared either.'

'*Did* she ever stay round yours?'

Zelda hesitated. 'Sometimes. Not that often. Only when Tina was off on one of her benders. She didn't like being alone in the flat with Marlon.'

This was something else Chrissy hadn't known about. Not the Marlon bit – no one would want to be alone with him – but the fact that the two girls had spent time together without her. She felt wounded by it. There had been a time when she and Zelda had often had sleepovers, but all that had changed when Uncle Pete had moved in. Without a bedroom of her own it had become impossible. And Nan wouldn't let her stay at Zelda's if Zelda couldn't be invited back. She wondered when it had started but didn't ask for fear of sounding jealous or petty. Instead she said, 'Do you want to come round this evening after school? You could stay for dinner. Nan won't mind.'

'I can't. Mum won't let me. I'm grounded because of the whole message thing.'

'How long for?'

'Until I've learnt my lesson.'

'So you can't come out tomorrow, either?'

'No chance. Not this weekend or next weekend. If Mum has her way, she'll keep me locked up until I'm twenty-five.'

'She'll get over it.'

'Not in a hurry, she won't. She's talking about moving. She

says the Mansfield isn't a safe place to live. She doesn't even want to stay in London.'

'You can't move,' Chrissy said, startled. 'She doesn't mean it, does she?'

'She's does. She's deadly serious. If she could she'd pack our bags and we'd be out of here tomorrow. She reckons Dad can drive a bus anywhere so there's no reason to stay.'

Chrissy couldn't imagine a future without Zelda. Despite Dawn, despite everything that had happened, they were still best friends and had been since primary school. 'But where would you go?'

'Mum's got family in Dover – my Auntie Sheila. It's by the sea. It's nice there.'

'But it's miles away,' Chrissy groaned. 'We'd never see each other.'

'You could visit. It's not that far on the train. Or you could get a coach.'

But Chrissy knew she'd never be able to afford the fare. Or rather Nan would never be able to. 'Tell her you don't want to go. You can change her mind. I know you can.'

Zelda didn't seem inclined to take up the fight. 'Nothing but bad things happen here. It's a horrible place. That Anita woman was murdered, Dawn's gone missing and . . . You know what it's like. Look what happened to your mum.'

Chrissy was bemused at her mother being brought into it. 'That was years ago, and it was an accident.'

'Was it?'

Chrissy slipped her arm out of Zelda's, took a step away and stared at her. The question had been phrased more as a challenge than a query. 'What do you mean?'

Zelda's face reddened and she shook her head. 'Nothing.'

'You wouldn't have said it if it was nothing.'

'I'm not supposed to talk about it.'

'It's a bit late for that. Come on, you can't start and not finish. Tell me!'

'It was only that ...'

'Only what?'

Zelda glanced down at the ground and then back up again. 'Some people say it wasn't an accident.'

Chrissy stiffened, a chill running through her. She felt the hairs on the back of her neck stand on end. 'What people? Who are you talking about?'

'Just, you know, people on the estate. People who were around back then. They told my mum and ... she said it was none of our business and I shouldn't say anything to you.'

'Told your mum what, exactly?' Chrissy's mouth was dry and she quickly ran her tongue along her lips. 'Told her what?'

Zelda's face twisted and her eyes grew wide. 'That maybe it wasn't an accident, that maybe someone pushed her.'

'That's not true! It's not! Nan told me it was an accident. She wouldn't have said that if ...' Chrissy swallowed hard, trying to keep her composure, but it was already a lost cause. 'Who pushed her?'

'I don't know.'

'Yes, you do.'

'All I know is that she got in with some West End crowd. There was a bloke she was seeing, but I can't remember his name. Lennie or Lou or ... no, hang on, I think it was Luther, but I never heard his surname.'

'Why would this Luther want to hurt her?'

'He was a gangster, I think.'

A *gangster*? Chrissy's head was starting to spin. 'So why wasn't he arrested? Why didn't he go to jail?'

Zelda lifted and dropped her shoulders. 'It's only gossip;

there's no saying any of it is true. You know what people are like round here.'

But it was too late for Zelda to backtrack. Chrissy didn't want to believe it, *couldn't* believe it, but now that it was in her mind, she was unable to get it out. 'It's rubbish,' she said weakly. 'I'd know if my mum had been murdered.'

'Course you would. Forget about it. I shouldn't have ... Come on, we'd better get to school or we'll be late.'

Chrissy wanted to turn right around and go home, but there wasn't any point. Nan would be at work by now and she could hardly stomp into the butcher's demanding answers in front of all the customers. There was Uncle Pete, of course, but he was probably still in bed and, even if he was up, she doubted if she'd get a straight answer from him.

Chrissy wished Zelda hadn't told her. Why had she? She understood that it had been something to do with guilt because Zelda *wanted* to move away. The sturdy roots of their friendship, once so deep, had shrivelled and died. Without Dawn, there was no one to stay for – and Dawn, Zelda seemed to have decided, was never coming back.

The two girls didn't link arms again. They walked together and yet separately, barely talking. An awkwardness had fallen between them. A rift had opened up, dark and gaping, and neither of them knew how to close it.

14

Chrissy's concentration, never that good even under normal circumstances, was shot to pot for the rest of the day. She couldn't settle to any of her lessons and got told off on numerous occasions for staring out of the window. Distracted by what Zelda had told her, she was unable to focus on anything other than what might or might not have happened to her mum. Was it a fact or just idle gossip? But even gossip came from somewhere; it didn't just materialise out of thin air. There was usually a nugget of truth even if it did get twisted and distorted in the retelling.

She grabbed her bag and hurried out of school as soon as the afternoon bell went, not even bothering to wait for Zelda. As she raced down the high street, Chrissy wondered why she hadn't been more curious about the manner of her mum's death. She'd accepted Nan's version of events without probing any further. But then again, why shouldn't she have? Nan's reluctance to talk had seemed entirely natural, bearing in mind the loss of her daughter at such a young age. But what if there *was* more to it?

It made her feel weird, unsteady, to think of her mother dying like that. One moment she must have been standing on a platform at Kellston station, and the next ... What platform had it been? What time? Where had she been going and who with? Chrissy didn't know the answers to any of these questions and they spun around her head, faster and faster, until she couldn't think straight any more.

When she finally reached the Mansfield, she was hot and bothered and thoroughly confused. It would be sensible, she knew, to try and get her thoughts in order before doing anything else. But she was too impatient. She went up in the lift, strode along the landing, poked her key into the lock, pushed open the door and dashed into the kitchen. Nan, who was busy peeling spuds, must have seen the expression on her face because she put the knife down and frowned.

'What's happened?'

Chrissy didn't even pause for breath. 'Zelda said Mum didn't die in an accident. She said she was pushed under that train. Is it true, Nan? Is it right that Mum was murdered?'

Her grandmother, clearly taken aback, took a moment to recover herself before saying, 'And since when did Zelda Graham become the world expert on our family history?'

'Someone told Mrs Graham, that's all. So is it true or not?'

'Of course it's not true.'

Chrissy watched her closely. 'Why are people saying it, then?'

'Got nothing better to gossip about, that's why. People say all sorts of stupid things, especially stupid people. If you believe everything you're told on this estate, you'll have a head full of nonsense by the time you're twenty-one.'

'But how can you be sure it was an accident?'

'Why would anyone want to kill her? She never hurt a fly, that girl, not in her entire life. As good as gold she was. And if you don't believe me, perhaps you'll believe the coroner. Accidental death, that's what he said at the end of the inquest. You think he'd say that if it was a lie?'

Chrissy wasn't entirely sure what an inquest was, or a coroner come to that, but it all sounded official so she responded with a shrug.

Nan picked up the knife again and continued peeling the spuds as if she'd made her point and the exchange was over. But Chrissy hadn't finished yet.

'I still don't see why people think she was pushed. Zelda says she was seeing a gangster, some bloke called Luther something.'

'"Zelda says, Zelda says." That girl doesn't have a clue what she's talking about. There was nothing like that going on. Your mum wasn't seeing Luther Byrne; she just worked for him.'

'What sort of work?'

'A bar in the West End, in Mayfair.'

'Why was she working for a gangster?'

'He wasn't a gangster, love. He was just a businessman.'

'So was she dating someone else?'

'No one serious. She wasn't going steady.'

Chrissy wondered how much Nan had actually known about her daughter's private life. There were plenty of things that *she* got up to that Nan knew nothing about. Perhaps it had been the same with Mum. 'What about my dad?' she asked. 'Did she ever see him again?'

Nan gave a snort. 'That fly-by-night,' she said. 'Once he found out she was up the duff, he was off like a dog with its tail on fire. The sod never showed his face again. Not that I'm sorry; she was better off without him. Good riddance is what I say.'

Chrissy had never had any interest in her father, mainly because he had never had any interest in her. What kind of man scarpered at the first sign of trouble? Not the sort that she'd ever want to have around. Brian Lockheed had been his name, although it wasn't on the birth certificate. He'd been a mechanic, working at a garage in Dalston. That was as much as she knew – or wanted to know.

'You tell that Zelda to mind her own,' Nan said. 'She shouldn't be poking her nose into other people's business.'

Although things were strained between Chrissy and Zelda, an old loyalty automatically kicked in. 'It's not her fault, not really. She's scared 'cause of Dawn going missing. And Mrs Graham wants to move away, to leave Kellston for good; she says too much bad stuff happens here.'

'Thinks she's too good for the Mansfield, does she? A cut above. Well, she's no better than the rest of us.'

Chrissy hadn't meant that, but rather than try to explain – it would probably only make matters worse – she returned instead to the subject of her mother. 'So where was Mum going on the night she died?'

'She was on her way to work.'

'Was it late?'

'Not especially. About half-seven.'

'It was dark, though?'

'Of course it was dark. It was November.'

'Was she on her own?'

'Yes, she was on her own. Now have you got any more questions or can I get on with the dinner? I need to get these spuds on or we'll be eating at midnight.'

Chrissy had lots more to ask but she could see that Nan's patience was wearing thin. She wasn't sure why she chose her final question. It just popped into her head out of nowhere. 'How did Mum know that cop? You know, the one we talked to down at Cowan Road? Sutherland.'

'Who says she knew him?'

Instinct told Chrissy to keep her mouth shut about what he'd said to her while Nan had been distracted by Tina Kearns. 'No one. I just thought he might have investigated Mum's death.'

The frown between Nan's eyes deepened for a second before swiftly clearing again. 'That moron couldn't investigate his way out of a paper bag. Now, go and get that uniform off. I don't want you getting your dinner all over it. I won't have time to wash it out tonight.'

Nan seemed to have forgotten that it was Friday and there was no school tomorrow. Or that Chrissy was fourteen and more than capable of getting a fork to her mouth without dropping food all over herself. Well, most of the time.

'And don't you go bothering your uncle with all this nonsense,' Nan said. 'He'll only get upset and then God knows what he'll do.'

Chrissy went to the bedroom and mulled over everything as she changed into jeans and a T-shirt. Did she believe what Nan had told her? The problem with adults was that they only ever told you half the truth. She still couldn't see how her mum could have just fallen in front of a train. Unless she'd been drunk. Unlikely if she was on her way to work. Had there been other passengers around, witnesses to the event? And what about the train driver? The police must have looked into all of this, but she had no way of knowing what they'd found out. Nothing suspicious, she presumed, if the death had been classed as an accident. But what about Luther Byrne? Boyfriend or employer? Maybe both. She carefully stored his name away, certain that she would need it one day.

15

Eddie Barr was in a funk, sick of trying to dodge the law and sick of the small room in the B&B where he was currently holed up. Big blowsy roses, a faded shade of pink, adorned the walls, a noisy pattern that made his head ache. The whole place stank of old cooked cabbage and sweat, and something else he couldn't quite put his finger on. Perhaps it was simply disappointment. No one dreamed of ending up in a dump like this. He couldn't wait to get away – the room was driving him stir crazy – but he wasn't going to take the risk until it was dark.

One small window overlooked the street below and this was where he'd been standing for the last half hour. He smoked another cigarette while he waited for night to fall. He usually did good business on a Friday; it was payday, after all. The punters would fill up on booze and then make their way to Albert Road. With Anita gone, however, there was no one to keep the tarts in line. Turn your back for a minute and they'd screw you over. He could almost feel his profits leaking away.

It hadn't been safe to go to the houses – the filth were probably keeping watch – and so he'd put in a phone call instead, told Colleen that she was in charge and made a few veiled threats about what he'd do if he found the takings were down. She was the best of a bad lot, but he didn't trust her. The sooner he could find someone to replace Anita, the better, but there was sod all chance of that while he was stuck here.

He thought of his flat, smart and stylish with its leather sofa and king-size bed. No hope of going back there until this business was sorted out. His face twisted as he glanced around the room. He didn't belong in a pit like this. It was beneath him. He was Eddie Barr, man about town, smart and successful with money in his pocket. Where he *should* be was in the West End, rubbing shoulders with the rich and famous.

A snarl distorted his lips. All this was Anita's bloody fault. If it hadn't been for her bad judgement he wouldn't be hiding out in this godforsaken hole. The minute he'd clapped eyes on Vic he'd known he was trouble: six foot two of pumped-up muscle, eyes like empty pools and all the charm of a psychopath. Who she shacked up with was her own business – there was no accounting for taste – but anyone with an inch of nous could have seen that it wasn't going to end well.

Eddie waited as the light shifted into silvery grey and then into dusk. He had two choices: either he could sit tight and wait for Vic to be found – which could be weeks, months even – or he could try and square things with the law. Really there wasn't a choice at all. He couldn't afford to play the fugitive while his business went down the pan. If it wasn't for that fuckin' Gaul he'd have no problem walking into Cowan Road, but the chief inspector was a malicious bastard, the worst kind of filth, the sort who'd find a way to stitch him up without a shred of evidence.

No, there was only one solution: he'd have to talk to Terry

Street and get him to sort it out. After all, isn't that what he paid him for every week? Or, rather, paid Vinnie Keane, as he was the one who turned up every Monday with his hand held out. Protection money – and now he needed protecting. If he could get Terry to have a quiet word with Gaul, this could be nicely smoothed over and everything would get back to normal. The plan, in his mind, seemed perfectly feasible. He could only hope that Terry thought so too.

When he judged that it was dark enough, he put on his jacket and headed out, glad to be escaping from his squalid surroundings. He walked quickly with his head down and his shoulders hunched. Within minutes he had crossed the border between Shoreditch and Kellston and began weaving through the back streets until he came to Yelland Road.

Terry lived on the top floor of a smart modern block of flats, set back from the road with space for parking in front and a communal garden out back. His car, a black Mercedes, was there, which hopefully meant that he was, too. Eddie raised his eyes to the top of the building and saw that the lights were on. He lowered his gaze, had a quick look round, reassured himself that he was alone and then walked up the path to the front door.

There was an intercom system with a bank of buzzers. None of them had names on, only the number of the flat. Very discreet. He pressed the right button and waited. It was answered almost immediately.

'Yeah?'

'It's Eddie.'

'Eddie who?'

This put Eddie in an even blacker mood. How many Eddies did the fucker know? 'Eddie Barr,' he said through gritted teeth. 'I need to talk to you.'

There was a long pause, as though Terry was thinking about it, then he said, 'Hang on. I'll be right down.'

Now Eddie was even more pissed off. Why couldn't he just buzz open the door and let him in? Perhaps he had company, the type he didn't want anyone knowing about. Shit, he hoped it wasn't Gaul. Quickly he glanced over his shoulder at the parked cars, searching for any motor that might belong to a cop. Nothing stood out.

He turned back and peered into the lit foyer, which had a tiled floor and what appeared to be a palm tree right in the middle of it. Like it was fuckin' Spain or somewhere. The seconds ticked by and turned into minutes. Eddie jigged impatiently from foot to foot. What was he playing at? As if he didn't have better things to do than stand around waiting on Terry bloody Street.

Eventually he saw the lift slide open. Terry walked across the foyer, without any hint of urgency, and opened the front door. He didn't apologise for keeping him waiting. 'Eddie,' he said. 'What can I do for you?'

'I need a word. Is there somewhere we can talk?'

'Sure.'

'Not here,' Eddie said. 'Not on the doorstep.'

'What about the Fox?'

'Are you kidding me? Half the bleedin' nick drink in there.'

'Ah, yeah,' Terry said. 'I heard about your spot of bother. Gaul's none too pleased, by all accounts. He's been looking for you.'

'I know he has. Why do you think I'm keeping out of his way? No, it needs to be some place private.'

Terry stepped out and closed the door firmly behind him. 'Round the back then.' He smirked. 'There shouldn't be too many pigs lurking in the undergrowth.'

Eddie tried to hide his irritation at not being invited in, like he was some no-mark loser. Fuckin' rude, that's what it was, but he couldn't afford to let his feelings show. He needed Terry's help and he needed it urgently. 'Fine,' he said.

Terry led the way round the side of the building to an oblong of lawn with trees and shrubs. Light from the rear windows of the flats cut through the darkness. There were two wooden benches, one on either side, and Terry chose the left-hand one. He sat down and stretched out his legs.

'I like it here. It's peaceful, don't you think?'

Eddie was feeling anything but peaceful. He gave a thin smile as he joined Terry on the bench. 'I've got a problem.'

'This about Anita Jakes?'

'It's about that bastard Gaul trying to stitch me up. He knows I didn't even go to her flat on Sunday – Vic's the one who did her in, that shit she was shacked up with – but he's still got me in the frame.'

'Who told you that?'

'I heard a whisper,' Eddie said. 'He needs an ID on Vic Hooper, some background, and at the moment I'm the only one who can give it to him. If I don't, he'll make sure I pay, charge me with perverting the course of justice or whatever.'

'So why don't you tell him? What's the big deal? You don't owe that bloke nothin'. He wasted Anita, for God's sake.'

'I'm not a bloody grass.' What Eddie really meant was that he didn't want Vic to find out that he'd grassed him up. Cowan Road was as leaky as a dripping tap. If Vic heard he'd been talking, Eddie would be sharing mortuary space with Anita. Any normal person who'd committed a murder would do a runner, be miles away by now, but that psycho wasn't normal. He could be holed up anywhere, including Kellston.

Terry looked at his watch as though he had places to be, people to see. 'So what do you want me to do about it?'

'Have a word with Gaul,' Eddie said. 'He'll listen to you. Ask him . . . *tell* him to leave me alone.'

'And why would I want to do that?'

'As a favour,' Eddie said. 'And it makes good sense. How am I supposed to operate while I'm being hassled? And if I'm not making money, you're not going to get paid.'

Terry shot him a glance. 'You found someone to replace Anita yet?'

'I'm working on it.'

'Tricky business, finding someone you can trust.'

'Tell me about it.'

'So what's the deal with this Vic?'

Eddie took it as a good sign that Terry was asking. He wouldn't be doing that if he wasn't going to help. 'Vic Hooper,' he said. 'Least that's what Anita said he was called. Showed up a few months back. He's local but he's not been around a while. Did a stretch in the Scrubs, six or seven years, I think. There's plenty know him on the estate but they're too shit scared to tell the law his name. He's the sort who bears grudges.'

'Hooper,' Terry said, before shaking his head. 'Nah, it doesn't ring any bells.'

'Big fucker. Almost as big as Vinnie, but twice as nasty.'

'Don't let Vinnie hear you say that. He prides himself on being the nastiest fucker in town.'

Eddie wondered if there was some kind of underlying threat in the words, a timely reminder of the force Terry could bring down to bear if anyone tried to cross him. He stared but it was hard to read his face in the gloom. Terry was only a year or so older than him – twenty-five or twenty-six – but he'd already acquired the demeanour of a gangland boss. 'So what do you think? You reckon you could talk to Gaul?'

Terry placed his palms on his thighs, leaned forward a

little and gazed into the darkness. 'You know what I'd do if I was you?'

Eddie waited. 'Yeah?'

A smile played on Terry's lips. 'I'd get the fuck out of Kellston.'

'What?'

'Gaul's got it in for you. Anyone can see that. If it's not this, it'll be something else. He doesn't like you, hates your guts, and he's never going to leave you alone. You're better off out of it. Go someplace else and start again.'

Eddie jumped to his feet and glared down at Terry Street. Rage was flowing through him, making his blood boil. 'Go someplace else? What's your fuckin' game? You want me out of the way. Is that it? So you can move in and take over my houses, take over my girls? Three years I've spent building up my business and now you think I'm going to throw it all away. Well, fuckin' Gaul's not going to drive me out and nor are you!'

Terry gazed calmly up at him, unmoved by the outburst. 'I'm just telling you like it is. No one's trying to steal your girls. Take them with you. What difference does it make where they work from? I'm trying to give you some good advice here, Eddie. You should listen. Sometimes you have to cut your losses before you lose everything.'

'I'm not losing nothin',' Eddie hissed.

'Have it your own way. Maybe Gaul will get run over by a bus and you won't have to worry any more. Or maybe he won't.'

Eddie didn't know what to do. He wanted to lash out with his fists but had enough sense left to be aware it was a fight he wouldn't win. He fell back instead on hollow words. 'No one pushes me around and gets away with it.' Then, before Terry could respond, he turned on his heel and walked back across the lawn. He thought he heard a low mocking laugh as he retreated.

16

It was almost ten o'clock on Saturday morning when Chrissy was woken by raised voices coming from the living room. She rubbed her eyes and groaned, sure that she hadn't been asleep for more than ten minutes. Nan had tossed and turned all night, eventually getting up to make a cup of tea at some time in the early hours. It had been a while before she'd come back again, slipping into bed with a sigh.

'You all right, Nan?'

'Just a touch of indigestion, love. Nothing to worry about. You go to sleep.'

But Chrissy *had* been worried. Nan had been acting oddly all evening, distracted, like she had something on her mind. All those questions Chrissy had asked, perhaps – and what had been said about people claiming her mum's death wasn't an accident. She almost wished she hadn't brought it up.

The exchange was still going on, not an argument, exactly, but more of a heated discussion. She got out of bed, put on her dressing gown and went through to the living room. Nan and

Uncle Pete were in full flow and didn't even notice her come through the door.

'It's a bleedin' liberty,' Uncle Pete was saying. 'Someone should do something. This estate is a big enough shithole without the likes of him on it. I should have turned that flat over when I had the chance, had a proper look round.'

'You did look round and what did you find? Nothing.'

'If I had five minutes with that bastard . . .'

'You don't know that he's done anything. If the law let him go then—'

'All that means is that the morons can't prove anything. Doesn't mean he's innocent.'

'Doesn't mean he's guilty, either. I've told you before: stay out of it, Pete. You want to end up back inside again?'

'And what if it's Chrissy next? How are you going to feel then?'

'What do you mean, me next?' Chrissy asked.

Their heads jerked round in unison, surprise showing on their faces. There was a short silence before Uncle Pete said, 'That Marlon Pound's been released. He's back on the estate.'

'Have they found Dawn?'

'No,' Nan said. 'Not yet.'

'What about the tattooed man?'

'I don't think so, love. But I'm sure they will in a day or two.'

Uncle Pete stood up and pulled on his denim jacket over his red T-shirt.

'Where are you going?' Nan asked.

'For a walk.'

'Don't you go near that Marlon. It's only going to end in trouble. Pete? Are you listening to me?'

But Uncle Pete wasn't. He was already in the hall and a few seconds later the front door opened and then slammed shut.

Nan stood up and smoothed down the front of her apron.

She stared for a moment at the space Uncle Pete had occupied, frowning at the emptiness. Then she said, 'You go and get dressed, Chrissy. I'll make you some breakfast.'

Chrissy ate her cornflakes in the kitchen, studying Nan while she pretended not to. It occurred to her that Nan was starting to look old, not *really* old, not like Betty Cope, but kind of crumpled round the edges. She had been a good-looking woman when she was young – there was a photograph in the bedroom of her wedding day – but now her fair hair was streaked with grey and there were lines on her face. Grandad had died before Chrissy was born, a stroke when he was only forty-two. It seemed that the Moss women didn't have much luck with their men. She thought of Eddie and wondered when she'd see him again.

'So what are you going to do today?' Nan asked.

'Dunno.'

'Well, you be careful, all right? You and Zelda stick together and don't get into any trouble.'

Chrissy didn't tell her that she wasn't welcome at the Graham home or that Zelda wasn't allowed out for the foreseeable. She didn't want Nan getting the hump about Mrs Graham's superior ways – or any ideas about grounding Chrissy, too. 'Okay.'

'And make sure you're back for lunch.'

'I will.'

As she left the flat Chrissy had no idea of what she was going to do for the next few hours. Usually she would hang out with Zelda and Dawn, but there was no hope of that today. She was stuck on her own. The lift doors opened and she stepped out, walked across the foyer and through the main door.

It was warm outside and the air was very still. She tried not to think too much about what had happened to Dawn. She pushed it to the back of her mind with all the other stuff she'd been

105

accumulating, a jumble of half-answered questions, of lurking fears and quiet regrets. But she couldn't get beyond the fact that she'd longed for Dawn to be gone – and now she was. *Be careful what you wish for*, Nan sometimes said, and now Chrissy understood what she meant.

She glanced up towards the windows of Zelda's flat, hoping to see her there, but they were empty. What was she doing? Playing records in her room, perhaps: Marvin Gaye, Stevie Wonder, Smokey Robinson. Zelda loved Motown; when the music was playing, she would close her eyes and smile.

Chrissy looked round for Uncle Pete but couldn't see him. He was angry because the law had let Marlon Pound go. Zelda would be mad, too. They both thought he was guilty, but Chrissy wasn't so sure. Well, guilty of being a nasty piece of work, but that didn't make him stand out on this estate. She was still more inclined to believe her own theory: that Dawn had gone back to Anita's flat where something dreadful had happened.

Out of habit Chrissy strolled to the low wall by the gates but decided not to sit down. With no one to talk to there didn't seem any point. She didn't want to be perched there all alone like some Billy No-Mates. Instead, she carried on walking, out of the estate, along Mansfield Road and onto the high street. She had a vague hope of bumping into Eddie and wandered down to the Wimpy. Peering through the window, she could see that it was busy inside but he wasn't there.

Disappointed, she walked on for a while until she reached Station Road, where she turned around and started to walk slowly back. The streets were packed with Saturday-morning shoppers, women with prams and bags and harassed faces. She saw a few girls from school but no one she knew well enough to stop and talk to. The day seemed to stretch ahead, and not in a good way. She felt lonely and adrift. There was no fun in roaming around if you didn't have friends to share things with.

She went into Woolies to kill some time, meandering up and down the aisles until she reached the record section, where she browsed through the albums, trying to decide what she'd buy if she had money to spend. David Bowie? Roxy Music? She moved on to the pick 'n' mix, tempted to slip a few pink shrimps into her pocket. Was anyone looking? Her gaze flicked to the left and right but she lost her nerve and couldn't do it. Dawn had been an expert in nicking sweets, so fast you wouldn't even know she'd taken anything.

Chrissy's next port of call was the green, an oblong of scruffy grass about the size of a football pitch that ran between the high street and Barley Road. There wasn't much to it other than a few trees and the occasional shrub. A sign saying no ball games was displayed by the entrance. There were some people walking their mutts, and a couple of oldies taking a break on one of the wooden benches.

She ambled around the perimeter, chewing things over. An idea came to her: she should go to Zelda's and apologise for the incident with Eddie. She could tell Mrs Graham that she was truly sorry, that she'd made a mistake, done something stupid blah blah, and that none of it had been Zelda's fault. Maybe even cry a little. Perhaps then she'd be forgiven and allowed to spend time with Zelda outside of school again. Perhaps she would even be invited in.

There was only one snag to this plan: Zelda might not *want* to spend time with her. Things hadn't gone well yesterday. It seemed to her that their friendship was on the brink, that it could easily topple over the edge if steps weren't taken to put it right. She had to try and build bridges before Zelda let her mother talk her into moving away. Perhaps it was too late already. The thought of this made her feel cold inside.

Although she feared rejection, Chrissy resolved to give the plan a go. She cut across the green and was heading up the high street when the door to Patel's opened and DS Sutherland came out with a packet of fags in his hand. He didn't see her and carried on walking as he stripped the pack of its cellophane, took out a cigarette and lit it. She followed at a distance, while she tried to make up her mind whether to speak to him or not.

He crossed the road, dodging between the cars, and she did the same. He stopped to stare into Connolly's, his gaze roaming over the café customers. Was he looking for Eddie? She hung back, pretending to study the TVs in the window of the Radio Rentals shop. When he moved on, she moved on, too. This was more fun than she'd expected. She watched him surreptitiously, careful not to stare, and questioned the investigative abilities of a cop who didn't even realise he was being tailed.

They carried on up the high street. If she was going to approach him it would have to be soon. She didn't want to end up chatting on the forecourt of Cowan Road where the world and his dog could see her. It was always iffy talking to the law, even if you did have a legitimate reason. She glanced round to make sure no one she knew was in the vicinity, then increased her pace, drew alongside him and said, 'Hi.'

Sutherland started a little, as if he'd been lost in thought. 'Oh, hello there. It's Chrissy, yeah?'

She nodded. 'Yeah. I was just wondering if you had any news about Dawn?'

'Sorry, not yet.'

'But you've let Marlon Pound go.'

Sutherland's eyebrows shifted up a notch. 'News travels fast on the Mansfield. Who told you that?'

'Someone saw him,' she said, careful not to mention Uncle

Pete's name. 'One of the neighbours. Does that mean he didn't have anything to do with Dawn going missing?'

Sutherland puffed on his fag and glanced at her. 'Investigations, as they say, are still ongoing.'

'What about the tattooed man?'

'Likewise,' he said.

'Do you think Dawn's all right? Do you think she's just run away?'

'Do *you* think she could have run away?'

'I don't know,' Chrissy said. He'd asked her this before when she'd been down Cowan Road with Nan, and she'd given the same answer then. Sutherland was being tight-lipped, but that didn't come as any big surprise. The law never told you more than they had to. 'What about her cardigan? What was it doing under the stairs?'

'You ask a lot of questions,' he said.

'It's the only way to find out anything.'

A smile twitched at the corners of Sutherland's lips. 'You could be right. Truth is, we don't have too many answers at the moment. I'm sorry, I wish we did but . . .' He shrugged his shoulders. 'I don't suppose you've seen Eddie again?'

'No,' Chrissy lied. Then, because she couldn't resist, she added, 'Has he done something?'

'I've no idea. He seems to be avoiding us.'

'Oh.'

'Eddie Barr's not a nice guy. I'd stay well away from him if I were you.'

'I hardly know him. I only spoke to him that once.'

Sutherland gave her a sideways glance. 'But you liked him, huh?'

Chrissy winced, suspecting that Zelda had told him the whole story about the game and the dare and the rest. 'Not

109

really. I was just bored, you know. It was something to do. That's the only reason I talked to him.'

'You should be careful. He's the sort to take advantage.'

'Okay.' Chrissy knew better than to try and defend Eddie. The smart thing to do was to keep her mouth shut and change the subject. 'There's something else I wanted to ask you.'

'Ask away.'

'How did you know my mum?'

The question took him by surprise. He came to a halt for a moment, took a long drag on his cigarette, blew out the smoke and stared at her. 'Your mum?'

'Yeah, you said I looked like her.'

Sutherland stopped staring and began walking again. 'To be honest, I didn't know her that well. We weren't friends or anything. She lived on the Mansfield and that was part of my patch back when I first worked in Kellston. I just used to see her around.'

Chrissy didn't believe him. Partly this was because he was acting shiftily, but also because she was smart enough to realise that you didn't recall what someone looked like from all that time ago – at least ten years – unless they'd made a big impression. 'But you remembered her?'

'Well, she was down the station a fair few times, bailing out that brother of hers. How is your uncle these days? Staying out of trouble, I hope.'

'Yeah.'

'Glad to hear it.'

'You didn't work on the case, then? You know, when she died?'

'No, that wasn't me.'

'Do you remember who it was?'

'Sorry, it was a long time ago.'

'Do *you* think it was an accident?'

110

They had reached the corner of Cowan Road and Sutherland seemed eager to get back to the station, upping his pace and taking long strides so Chrissy almost had to jog to keep up with him. 'That's what the coroner said.'

'But what do you say?'

'Why should I say any different?'

Chrissy felt like she was being stonewalled. His face had a tight, strained look, as if the conversation wasn't one that he wanted to have. 'I just heard something, that's all. I heard that it wasn't. An accident, I mean.'

'And who told you that?'

'Someone.'

'Maybe that someone was trying to cause trouble. You shouldn't believe everything people tell you.'

'They said she could have been pushed.'

Sutherland shook his head. 'I can't see why anyone would have wanted to hurt her. Your mum was a good person.'

'I thought you didn't know her very well.'

'From what I *heard*,' he said. 'Look, people spout all sorts of rubbish. It doesn't mean it's true. Accidents happen, Chrissy. It's sad, very sad, but that's just life.'

Chrissy wasn't convinced, still suspecting he had known her mum better than he was letting on. She wanted to ask why Nan and Uncle Pete disliked him so much, but couldn't think of a subtle way of doing it. Instead she said, 'Have you ever heard of a man called Luther Byrne?'

'Christ, that's a name from the past.'

'Was my mum going out with him?'

'I've no idea. I shouldn't think so, not if she had any sense.'

'What do you mean?'

'Let's just say he was never on the side of the angels.'

'Was he a gangster?'

'I'm not sure if I'd call him that exactly, but ...'

Chrissy, still walking too fast for comfort and getting slightly out of breath, waited for him to finish. He didn't. 'But?' she prompted.

Sutherland didn't answer immediately. His face had taken on a more concentrated expression, as though he was deliberating over what to say next. 'He wasn't the sort of man you'd want to cross. He had ... how can I put it? ... something of a reputation.'

'A bad one?'

'Yes.'

'Is he still around?'

By now they were outside Cowan Road. Sutherland stopped again, dropped the butt of his fag and ground it into the pavement with his heel. 'I've no idea. I don't think so. Can I give you a bit of advice?' Before she had time to reply he continued. 'There are some individuals in this world who it's best to stay away from, Eddie Barr and Luther Byrne being two of them. Now, I can see you're a bright girl, that you've got brains, so I know you'll do the smart thing and make the right choices. I can rely on you, yeah? It's for the best, I promise.'

If there was one thing Chrissy couldn't stand it was being patronised, but she nodded and smiled, thanked him and said goodbye. As she walked off, she wondered why it was that when some people demanded you act a certain way you immediately wanted to do the opposite.

17

As soon as Chrissy entered the Mansfield, she knew something was wrong. The estate had been busy when she'd left but now the space around Carlton was eerily quiet – too still, like the calm before a storm. This wasn't a normal Saturday morning. Where were the lads kicking a ball around, the women gossiping to their neighbours, the men coming and going? Nothing was as it should have been.

It was only as she got further along the path, when she looked up at the tower, that she became aware of faces at windows and of small groups gathered on balconies. Like an audience waiting for a show to begin – but not a good kind of show. Her stomach shifted. Something bad was on the way, something grim. She could feel it in her bones.

Frank Yates cycled past, pedalling furiously.

'Hey, Frank!' she yelled after him.

At first, she thought he was ignoring her or that he hadn't heard, but eventually he slowed, steered the bike through a U-turn and came back to her. 'There's going to be trouble,' he said, before she even had the chance to ask him anything. 'I'd get inside if were you.'

'What trouble? What's going on?'

He looked scared. 'They're going to sort out Marlon Pound.'

'What? Who is?'

'Because of Dawn. They reckon he's done her in. And the law ain't doing nothin' so . . . ' Frank's gaze rose towards the top of the tower and quickly slid down again. 'It's going to be soon.'

Her gaze traced the same path as his and came to rest on a group of men making their way up the external staircase. They were already close to the seventeenth floor.

'Jesus,' she murmured. In the middle of them was Uncle Pete. At least, she thought it was him. He was too far away for her to see him clearly but she could just make out the fair hair and the flash of red from his T-shirt. She shuddered, knowing exactly what the men were going to do. This was justice Mansfield style, with no questions asked, no trial, no judge or jury. 'What if they've got it wrong?'

Frank's face was pale but his eyes were bright. 'Girls don't just disappear.'

'Some do. They run away or . . . ' Chrissy couldn't think of an 'or' so she just shrugged.

'I'm going. You should too. You don't want to be here when the law show up.'

Chrissy's gaze rose towards the top of the tower again. She stood with her head tilted back, her neck craned. The men were still moving, advancing towards the Kearnses' flat. They were almost there. She wanted to do something to stop them, but there was nothing she could do. Her throat felt tight and she couldn't breathe properly. It was like she'd forgotten *how* to breathe.

'I'm going,' Frank said again, and this time he did, pushing down on the pedals of the bike, wheeling around and cycling away. She watched him pass under the arch and disappear. Now she needed to leave too, to start running, to get inside, to tell Nan what was going on. But her legs wouldn't shift. Her body was a dead weight, dense as lead. She was rooted to the spot.

It was shortly after that the yelling started – a woman's voice, Tina's. It had to be. She couldn't make out the words; it was just a noise of protest, high-pitched, plaintive. The men, who must have pushed their way inside the flat, were now out on the balcony. There was some kind of a scuffle going on. Male voices floated down to her, angry and insistent. She put her hand at right angles to her forehead to shield her eyes against the sun, to try and get a better view.

Was that Marlon up against the railings? She sensed rather than saw the attack, her imagination filling in the missing pieces: a beating, a battering, the rush of fists against flesh. Panic coursed through her. The fingers of her left hand curled, her nails piercing the skin of her palms. She wanted it to stop – but what she wanted didn't matter.

It happened so quickly that she didn't have time to react. One second the space above her was empty, the next it was filled by a dark object, like a weird, oversized bird, plummeting out of the sky. Her jaw dropped open. Time stood still. A hundred thoughts flashed through her head but she could process only one of them.

It was *him*. It was Marlon.

She had to get away. She couldn't. He was hurtling down, coming nearer and nearer until … Her eyes automatically closed at the moment of impact, as his body made contact with the unforgiving concrete only yards away from her. There was a dull, dreadful thump and then a terrible silence. She wouldn't look. She would never open her eyes again. She was there on the concourse and yet she wasn't. She felt removed, distant, severed from the here and now.

And then the screaming started from high above, harsh piercing cries that cut through the air.

And then the wailing of a police siren, the sound growing closer.

And then the adrenalin kicked in.

Chrissy's legs finally discovered their muscles and she sprinted towards the tower. She must have covered half the path, running blind, before her eyes flicked open. *Don't look back*. Her heart was beating wildly and there was a strange buzzing in her ears. She had almost reached the doors, extending her arms to push her way in, when something compelled her to stop. She couldn't help herself. Twisting round, she glanced over her shoulder at the broken remains of Marlon Pound, at the spread-eagled limbs and the pulpy mass of his skull. She looked only for a second but it was enough to burn the image on to her retinas for ever.

18

Chrissy staggered across the foyer to the lifts. One of them was out of order and the other three were in use. She cried out in frustration, banging her fist against the button. Her hands were clammy and shaking. She waited and waited. It felt like for ever before one of the lifts finally made it to the ground floor.

She stumbled in – it was empty – and as the doors were closing the reflex happened in her throat. Her stomach heaved and she threw up on the floor. For a while she stayed hunched over, trying not to breathe in, trying not to think about what had just happened.

Marlon Pound was dead. Marlon Pound was splattered on concrete.

The lift slowly ascended. The motion of it made her want to be sick again. She gagged but nothing came out other than a long string of saliva that hung from the corner of her mouth until she wiped it away with the back of her hand. One moment you were alive and the next you were dead. One split second and everything could change.

The lift came to a halt and the doors opened. She lurched out in a daze. Tears were running down her cheeks but she wasn't even aware of them. The landing was deserted and she walked along it like a somnambulist, one foot in front of the other, her mind suddenly blank. It was only when she reached home, when she turned the key in the lock and went inside, that she was jerked back to reality.

There was an acrid smell of burning in the flat. She went through to the kitchen where Nan was leaning over an old metal bucket, fanning the flames of a fire that was devouring something red. Uncle Pete's T-shirt was in the process of being destroyed. Had there been blood on it? There must have been. He'd already changed into a fresh white shirt and was standing by the window, smoking furiously while Nan disposed of the evidence.

'I didn't know they were going to throw the bastard off, did I? That fuckin' Jacko! Just give him a slap, that's what we agreed, see if we could get him to talk.'

'He's not going to do much talking now,' Nan said.

'What about Tina? Shit, she's going to tell the law, isn't she? She's going to name names.'

Chrissy, standing in the doorway, had the curious feeling that she might be invisible, that she wasn't here at all, or that this might just be some sort of complicated nightmare. Perhaps nothing bad had happened. Perhaps she would wake up any moment and the dream would crumble away. But then Nan looked up and saw her, her eyes widening in alarm.

'Chrissy! What are you doing home?'

Chrissy opened her mouth and then found she couldn't speak. Like there was a great big wodge of cotton wool wrapped around her vocal cords. She pushed a strand of hair back from her face and felt the dampness of vomit on it. Disgusting. She could smell it too, now, even above the stink of the fire.

Nan left the bucket and walked over to her. 'Chrissy?'

The kitchen shifted slightly, moving out of focus, becoming blurred around the edges. The sides of the table, of the cooker, of the window, grew shadows. There was an odd echoey feeling in her head, as though all her thoughts were being bounced around an empty chamber. She tried to concentrate on Nan's face but that wasn't right, either; it seemed to slip and slide, refusing to take on its familiar form. Greyness was descending, like a veil being drawn across her mind . . . and then her legs betrayed her.

When she came round, Chrissy was lying on the sofa in the living room. The smell of the fire had been replaced by a sharp lemony air freshener. At first, she felt woozy and confused but then it all came rushing back to her. She groaned, not wanting to remember.

'Here, have some of this,' Nan said, shoving a glass of water under her nose. 'Just take little sips.'

Chrissy did as she was told.

Nan nodded. 'You'll be all right, love. You just fainted, that's all.'

Uncle Pete was hovering behind Nan, still smoking. The same cigarette or a different one? She only wondered because it would give her some idea of how long she'd been out. This was a better thing to think about than a man falling from the sky.

'Get those ashes sorted,' Nan said to him. 'Wash them down the sink. And then rinse out the bucket.'

Uncle Pete disappeared into the kitchen.

Chrissy passed the glass back to her grandmother. She swung her legs over the side of the sofa, waited to see if she felt okay and then slowly pulled herself into a sitting position. Even after drinking the water her mouth felt dry. She ran her tongue over her lips. 'I saw him, Nan. I saw Marlon Pound fall.'

119

Nan sat down and put an arm round her. 'Oh, love, that's a terrible thing to see. Try not to think about it.'

Chrissy leaned against her. She could hear the water running in the kitchen and the clatter of the bucket as it was put back under the sink. She wanted to turn back time, to start the day again, to create a reality where none of this had happened.

'He wouldn't have known nothin' about it, sweetheart. He'd have been dead before . . . well, you know.'

Chrissy hoped this was true.

'Was Zelda with you?' Nan asked.

'No, she couldn't come out. She was doing something. Will I have to talk to the law?'

Uncle Pete came back into the living room. 'You don't want to get involved.'

'She *is* involved,' Nan said. 'She was right there, wasn't she? Why didn't you think before you went storming round? Now look what you've done.'

'I've already told you. It was never meant to happen that way. We only wanted to give him a scare, shake him up a bit, try and find out what he'd done to that poor kid.'

'Oh, and how did that go, exactly?'

Uncle Pete didn't reply. He crossed the room, shoved his hands in his pockets and stared out of the window.

Nan was angry but she'd never betray one of her own. 'I'll say you were here all morning, that you never went out.'

Uncle Pete turned and Chrissy could see the fear in his eyes. 'And what about Tina? What's she going to say?'

'That woman's never sober. It'll be our word against hers.'

19

It was ten minutes since they'd scraped Pound's remains off the ground and taken them away. Not a pleasant sight. DS Will Sutherland, aware of eyes watching, of a multitude of faces pressed against glass, felt like an actor on a stage. Hundreds of possible witnesses stared down from Carlton House but the chances of any of them talking were slight. Even cold-blooded murder wouldn't be enough to loosen the tongues of Mansfield residents.

'Fuckin' vigilantes,' Gaul said. 'We got any names off Tina Kearns yet?'

'The doctor's still with her. She's hysterical, apparently. Not surprising after her boyfriend got thrown off the seventeenth floor.'

'Yeah, well, they might have got the wrong man.'

Will nodded. It was only three hours since Pound had been charged with assaulting a police officer, bailed and released. There had been nothing, other than opportunity, to suggest that he'd been involved in the disappearance of Dawn Kearns.

If he'd had any sense he'd have stayed away from the estate, but good sense had never been part of Marlon Pound's make-up. 'Maybe we'll get something from the door-to-door.'

'And maybe pigs will fly,' Gaul said drily. 'What about the delivery bloke? Get anything useful from him?'

'Jim Bolton. He only got here after it happened. He didn't see Pound fall. He reckoned he saw a girl, though: teenager, long fair hair, pink T-shirt. She was running towards the doors of Carlton.' Will hesitated before sharing his next piece of information. The last thing he wanted was to see Elsie Moss again, but it couldn't be avoided. 'I think it might have been Chrissy Moss. I met her in the high street this morning and she asked if there was any news. I'm pretty sure she was wearing a pink T-shirt.'

'Let's go and have a word, then. You know which flat it is?'

'Yeah, ninth floor.'

They walked together to Carlton House and went through to the foyer. One of the lifts was out of order and another had a pool of vomit on its floor. The smell made Will want to gag. Of the remaining lifts they chose the lesser of two evils, got in and travelled up the tower in silence. As they strode along the empty corridor – all the residents had gone to ground – their footsteps sounded abnormally loud, like a small advancing army. Will stopped outside the Mosses' flat and rang the bell.

Elsie Moss opened the door and looked them up and down. 'Oh, it's you. I was wondering when you'd show your faces.'

'Can we come in?' Will asked. He gestured towards the chief inspector. 'This is DCI Gaul.'

'I know who he is. I suppose you're here about my Chrissy.'

'It was her, then? She saw what happened to Marlon Pound?'

'She saw him fall, if that's what you mean. Now don't you go upsetting her. She's been through enough as it is.'

'We understand,' Will said. 'We'll be as quick as we can.'

Elsie nodded and stood aside. 'You do that.'

They went through to the living room where they found Chrissy Moss curled up on the sofa. Despite the warmth of the day she was wrapped in a blanket and looked white as a ghost. She raised her head as they came in, her eyes wide and stricken.

'There's a couple of police officers here to see you, love,' Elsie said. 'You just tell them what you saw and then they can get on their way.'

There were two armchairs and Will sat down on the one closest to Chrissy. He smiled at her. 'Hi. How are you doing?'

She gave him half a smile back.

'Your son not around, Mrs Moss?' Gaul asked as he settled his bulk into the other chair.

'What's this got to do with him?'

Gaul gave her one of his unsettling looks. 'Is he here or not? It's a simple enough question.'

Elsie sat down on the sofa beside her granddaughter. 'He's in the khazi. You want me to drag him out or can you wait five minutes?'

Will looked around the room, while his nose absorbed a sharp, artificial citrus smell. His eyes briefly came to rest on the mantelpiece, where a photograph of Laura had pride of place. It gave him a jolt seeing her again and he quickly averted his gaze. Returning his attention to Chrissy, he said, 'I'm so sorry you had to see what you did. It must have been dreadful. Could you talk us through what happened? Whatever you remember could be useful.'

Chrissy opened her mouth and then closed it again as though she didn't know where to start.

'You walked back with me,' Will prompted. 'From the high street?' He saw her glance at her grandmother and immediately knew that she hadn't mentioned the meeting. Or that she'd been probing for information about her mother's death. 'You asked me about Dawn, yeah? If we'd got any news on her.'

Chrissy nodded, clearly relieved that he hadn't said any more. 'Yeah, about Dawn.' She pushed her chin into the blanket and took a deep breath. 'And then I came straight back here. To the Mansfield, I mean. I was walking along the path and—'

'Did you see anyone?' Gaul interrupted. 'Speak to anyone?'

Chrissy hesitated, thought about Frank, frowned but then shook her head. 'No. I was on my own. There was no one else around. I just . . . I just looked up for some reason and there he was . . . falling. And there was a scream, high, a woman's scream. I don't know if it was after or if it was while he was . . .' She rubbed her face with the blanket. 'I can't remember.'

'That's okay,' Will said reassuringly. 'Take your time. When you looked up did you see anyone at all, some people on one of the upper balconies, perhaps?'

'No, all I saw was *him*. And I started running 'cause I just wanted to get away and then I looked back and he was lying on the ground and . . .' Her lower lip quivered and she swallowed hard. 'He was all . . . broken and there was blood coming from his head and . . .'

'Does she really have to go through all this?' Elsie asked. 'You can see the poor girl's in shock.'

'And a man's dead,' Gaul said. 'We have to find out who killed him.'

'You won't do that sitting here,' Elsie snapped. 'She's told you everything she saw. If anything more comes back to her, I'll be sure to let you know.'

'Maybe she should see a doctor,' Will said.

Elsie gave a snort. 'What, so he can shoot her full of drugs? How's that going to help? No, I'm perfectly capable of taking care of my own granddaughter, thank you very much.' She glowered at the two policemen. 'All she needs is a bit of peace and quiet.'

There was the sound of a toilet flushing, of footsteps on the hall carpet and then the door to the living room opened and Pete Moss walked in. 'Oh,' he said, as though he hadn't realised they were there. 'I heard what happened. You here to see Chrissy?'

'And you,' Gaul said. 'You mind telling us where you were this morning between eleven and half past?'

'Me? What's that got to do with anything?'

'Just answer the question.'

'I was here,' Pete said, glancing at Elsie. 'Wasn't I, Mum?'

'Didn't get out of his pit until gone eleven,' Elsie said. 'I virtually had to drag him out. "You should be looking for a job," I told him, "not sleeping the whole day away." I mean, there's three mouths to feed in this household and money doesn't grow on trees. I can't be expected to keep everyone.'

'In bed, then,' Gaul said. 'Well, that's convenient.' He looked across at Chrissy. 'So you didn't see your uncle at all this morning?'

Chrissy shook her head. 'Not until I got home.'

'You sure?'

'Of course she's sure,' Elsie said. 'Are you calling her a liar?'

'No one's calling her that,' Will said, trying to keep things calm. Gaul always thought he could intimidate people – and usually he was right – but Elsie Moss was more than a match for him. She'd defend her own with her last breath.

Gaul stood up and went over to Pete Moss. 'Show me your hands.'

'Huh?'

'Your hands,' Gaul repeated. 'Palms down. Show me your knuckles.'

Pete Moss's hands were in his pockets. 'And if I don't?'

'Then we'll take a trip down the station and carry on this conversation there.'

'Just show him, for God's sake,' Elsie said. 'You've got nothing to hide.'

With a show of reluctance, Pete took his hands out of his pockets and held them out. 'You see? Nothing, right? I never touched the guy, never went near him. Why would I want to throw Pound off a balcony? It's crazy. I mean, the kid's still missing. If he did have something to do with it, he can hardly talk now.'

While all this was going on, Will was watching Chrissy. Did she know more than she was letting on? It was hard to tell. Her face had taken on a closed expression. She suddenly looked younger than she was, more of a child than a teenager. She would recover from this – in time – but there'd be other ghosts to haunt her. The truth about her mother was still out there, buried but not so deeply that it couldn't be unearthed. His gaze flicked over to the photograph of Laura Moss. Secrets rarely stayed hidden for ever. A careless remark, an ill-considered action, and everything could fall apart.

20

As if she'd been holding her breath, Chrissy let out a long sigh as the two police officers left. She had been aware of DS Sutherland's eyes on her, watching, noting her reactions. Did he suspect her of lying? It had been a bad moment when the fat cop had asked Uncle Pete to show his hands. He'd been looking for bruises, for scrapes, for anything that would prove an assault on Marlon Pound. But there'd been nothing, which meant, surely, that Uncle Pete was innocent. Well, not completely innocent – he had been there – but less guilty than some of the others.

Nan came back into the living room, looking fraught. She glared at Uncle Pete. 'I don't know what you're grinning about. It's not over yet.'

'They can't prove anything.'

'And what about Tina Kearns?'

'She can't have put the finger on me, can she? They must have talked to her by now.'

'Maybe, maybe not. It's early days. All I'm saying is don't count your chickens.'

'I'm not counting anything. It was just good to see that bastard's face when he couldn't put me in the frame.'

Chrissy thought she'd have made a run for it if she'd been in Uncle Pete's shoes, got as far away from here as possible. Instead he'd chosen to brazen it out, to take his chances or whatever. He must have been in one of the lifts while she was waiting in the foyer. And, of course, it wasn't sensible to run – that just made you look guilty – but on the other hand it was better than spending the next fifteen years banged up.

There was a dull thump in the centre of Chrissy's temples. She hadn't told the truth, either. She hadn't even mentioned talking to Frank Yates. He was the one who'd warned her, who'd told her what was coming. It had been a split-second decision to keep this information to herself. Frank was scared of the law so she didn't want them turning up on his doorstep. He might panic, blurt something out, even start naming names. Did he know Uncle Pete was involved? It wasn't a chance she'd been prepared to take.

'How are you doing, love?' Nan asked.

Chrissy forced a smile. 'I'm okay.'

'Good. I'll put the kettle on, then.'

Hot sweet tea was Nan's answer to all of life's problems, big or small. There was nothing that couldn't be cured by a brew. Chrissy, still cocooned in the blanket, watched as Uncle Pete went over to the door that led out to the balcony. He reached out his hand as if to depress the handle but then withdrew it again. She could sense the battle that was going on his head: he wanted to find out what was going on, who else the law was visiting, but didn't want to take the chance of being seen.

From the kitchen came the sound of water rattling into the kettle, the chink of mugs, the dull click of the fridge opening and closing as Nan took out the milk. Normal noises, ordinary ones, and yet they seemed out of place. She frowned, trying to make sense of it but failing. Fear crept back inside her. Perhaps she'd be safe if she stayed right here on the sofa and never went out again. Her thoughts flew to Marlon Pound. A shiver crawled up her spine. Zelda had been right about bad things happening on this estate. Two people had died within the space of a week, a tattooed murderer was on the loose and Dawn had disappeared into thin air. And what about her mother? She had noticed Sutherland glance at the photograph, quickly looking away as though he didn't want to be caught staring.

Had Chrissy been less rattled she might never have asked the question. 'Uncle Pete? How did DS Sutherland know Mum?'

He was too jumpy, too distracted, to exercise caution. Turning from the door, he spoke before thinking, forgetting perhaps how little she knew. 'That shit screwed her over good and proper. If it hadn't been for him, she'd still be here. She'd never have—' He stopped abruptly, realising what he was doing, and glanced towards the kitchen as if worried that Nan might have overheard.

'Never have what?'

'Nothing. It doesn't matter.'

She could have pressed him but she didn't, remembering – although it was too late now – Nan's instruction not to mention what people were saying about Mum's 'accident'. Except she hadn't said anything about that, had she? Not directly. All she had asked about was Sutherland. Uncle Pete's answer, however, had been enough to back up what she already suspected – that the sergeant had known her mother a damn sight better than he was prepared to let on.

129

21

Will Sutherland was only half listening as Gaul had a quiet rant about people taking the law into their own hands. At intervals, he made an appropriate grunt of agreement, just to show he was paying attention. Laura Moss was on his mind again.

'We'll round up the usual suspects,' Gaul said. 'One of them might squeal.'

Will tried to focus, to concentrate on what his boss was saying. He wasn't entirely sure who the 'usual suspects' were any more. Although some faces remained the same – only a little older than they had been – there had been changes since he'd last been here. New families, new villains, had moved on to the estate and he was still acquainting himself with the worst of them. The Mansfield was a breeding ground for criminality: robbers, burglars, rapists, muggers, dealers, pimps and toms were all crammed into its high concrete towers. Those residents of a more law-abiding bent quickly learned to turn a blind eye to anything they saw and a deaf ear to anything they heard.

'Gutteridge, Layton, Dunlap, Thomas, Fielding,' Gaul continued. 'And anyone else who hangs out in that crowd.'

'Is that Jack Layton?' Will asked. 'Jacko?'

'That's the one.'

Will knew that Layton had once been friendly with Pete Moss and probably still was. They'd done some jobs together, including a post office robbery back in the sixties. Yeah, Jacko was just the type to appoint himself judge and jury when it came to the likes of Marlon Pound. The man didn't object to waving a gun at innocent clerks and bystanders, but was happy to take the moral high ground when it suited him. 'What's your take on Moss? You reckon he was in on it too?'

'More chance that he was than he wasn't.'

Will didn't want Pete Moss to be involved. He could feel those strings from the past tugging at him again. The more contact he had with the family, the more chance there was of some unpleasant truths coming out. 'You reckon he'd throw Pound off a balcony with his niece standing underneath? Seems kind of callous.'

'Not if he didn't know she was there.'

They took the lift up to the seventeenth floor and made their way to the Kearnses' flat. It was a crime scene now, crawling with Forensics. As he stood by the open door – the second time he'd been here this morning – Will's nose twitched with disgust at the smell. The place wasn't fit for a squat, never mind a home to raise a child in. He could see straight through to the living room, where there were empty vodka bottles littering the floor, overflowing ashtrays on the coffee table and used plates and mugs lying wherever they'd been put down. A layer of dust covered all available surfaces. Grime had run riot, embedding itself into every nook and cranny.

Forensics were still dusting the flat and the balcony, working laboriously to try and lift every print. Gaul lowered his voice as he talked to one of the officers so he wouldn't be overheard by any eavesdropping neighbours. Will knew that the chances of finding useful prints were slight and that even if they did the owner could easily claim that they'd been here on a different occasion. It would make a reasonable defence in court. Tina was the sociable sort, always up for company. People came and went all the time.

There were bloodstains on the floor of the balcony, probably from Marlon's busted nose. The attack would have been fast and frenzied. And then, when the job was done, the assailants would have legged it, split up and scattered to the four corners of the estate – and probably further. It would be a help if one of them had dropped something, or ripped something, in the rush to escape, but as yet nothing incriminating had come to light.

When it had been established that no definite leads had been discovered, Will and Gaul went to the flat next door where Will gave a couple of short rings on the bell.

It was answered by a PC called Jenny Walbroke, an efficient officer in her early twenties.

'She's out cold, guv,' Walbroke said, standing aside to let them in. 'Asleep in the spare room. The doc doesn't think she'll be fit to talk before tomorrow.'

There was an elderly lady sitting on the sofa in the living room, small and thin with her grey hair crimped into a tight perm. She put the newspaper she was reading to one side and stared at them through suspicious eyes.

'This is Mrs Travis,' Walbroke said. 'Margaret Travis.' Then she introduced Will and Gaul.

'I don't see why I can't answer my own front door,' Margaret complained. 'It's like being under arrest.'

Gaul nodded and said, 'You don't need to stay, Mrs Travis.

If there's somewhere else you can go until tomorrow? PC Walbroke will make sure Tina isn't disturbed.'

'I'm going nowhere,' Margaret said firmly. 'This is my home. Anyway, you think I'm leaving her alone with you lot? No chance! She needs her rest and I'm going to make sure she gets it.'

Will could see that, despite a superficial fragility, Margaret Travis was made of steel. He wondered what else she was going to make sure of: that Tina didn't blab, perhaps, when she finally came round. Was she really looking out for her neighbour or did her allegiances lie elsewhere? He hadn't made up his mind up yet.

'Did you see what happened?' Gaul asked.

'I've already said, haven't I? I've already told her,' Margaret said peevishly, glancing towards Jenny Walbroke. 'I heard a commotion, that's all, yelling and the like. By the time I got outside, they'd all scarpered.'

'Got any ideas who might have done it?'

'That's your job, not mine.'

'Thanks for your help,' Gaul said sarcastically. 'If it's inconvenient for you, we can always move Tina to the hospital.'

'She's not going anywhere. Hasn't she been through enough today? No, she's staying put. She's staying right here where I can keep an eye on her.'

'There's a chance Marlon's attackers may come back,' Gaul said, clearly trying to alarm her. 'They won't want Tina telling us what she saw.'

'Tina's not saying nothing; she's out like a light. And isn't that why madam's here?' Margaret said, glancing at Walbroke again. 'Though God knows what use a scrap of a girl like her would be if those brutes did show up.'

Walbroke arched her eyebrows but said nothing.

Will, who favoured a less confrontational approach than his boss, sat down beside Margaret and smiled. 'Do you live alone, Mrs Travis?'

'Widowed,' Margaret said. 'My Norman's been gone ten years now.'

'I'm sorry to hear it.'

Margaret threw him the kind of look that implied she didn't give two hoots for his condolences, but her tone became marginally more affable. 'Had a heart attack, didn't he? I've two daughters but they don't live local. I don't want to be bothering them with all this.'

'How long have you known Tina?'

'Since she moved here last year, her and Dawn.' Margaret's face tightened as she mentioned Dawn. 'Poor girl. I don't suppose you've found her yet?'

Will shook his head. 'I'm afraid not.'

'Tina isn't what you'd call the best of mothers but she's not a bad person. She's been through hard times. Thinks she can find comfort in the bottom of a bottle – and maybe she does for a while – but as soon as she's sober again . . .'

'What sort of hard times?'

Margaret rolled her eyes as if the answer was obvious. 'The usual sort. Violence, booze, *men*.'

'Would you include Marlon Pound on that list?' Gaul asked.

'I don't like to speak ill of the dead.'

Will glanced around the room. This flat couldn't be more of a contrast to the place they'd just visited. The windows were gleaming, the carpet hoovered, every surface dusted and polished to within an inch of its life. The smell of Mr Sheen hung in the air. Margaret Travis was obviously a fastidious woman – or perhaps just a bored one. And bored people tended to pay attention to what their neighbours were up to.

'Did Marlon and Dawn get on, do you know?'

'You'd have to ask Tina that.'

'But you must have got an impression.'

Margaret pursed her lips. 'Shouldn't you be out there looking for the people who killed him? You won't find them sitting here talking to me.'

Gaul stood in the centre of the room, glaring at the wall as if he'd like to smash through it, drag Tina Kearns from her bed, shake her into consciousness and get the names he so badly wanted. 'You must have some idea who did this, Mrs Travis. Did Tina not say *anything* to you?'

'She was hysterical, Chief Inspector, in shock – and who wouldn't be after witnessing something like that?'

Will knew that Tina had refused to go to hospital, refused point blank to go anywhere except to Mrs Travis's. Other than forcibly removing her from the building, they'd had no choice in the end but to submit to her wishes. Now it was just a waiting game. Hopefully, she'd cooperate once the medication had worn off and she was back in the land of the living, but there was no way of knowing.

Gaul, making little attempt to disguise his frustration, pushed his hands into his pockets and said, 'We'll see you later, Mrs Travis. If anything comes back to you in the meantime, please tell PC Walbroke.'

Will got to his feet, politely said goodbye and followed his boss to the front door. Gaul beckoned Walbroke outside and kept his voice low.

'Keep an eye on that one,' he said, inclining his head towards the living room. 'Don't leave her alone with Tina, not for a minute.'

'I won't, guv.'

'Call us as soon as Tina wakes up. Whatever the time is.'

'Yes, guv.'

Gaul gave a low growl. 'And see if you can get anything else out of the old biddy. I reckon she knows more than she's letting on.'

'I'll try my best.'

'Use that charm of yours, huh?' Gaul said, looking her up and down and winking at her. 'Pretend she's your new best friend.'

Walbroke smiled thinly and withdrew inside.

In the lift, Gaul muttered to himself while the steel box made its slow descent. Then he turned to Will and said, 'Run a check on old Ma Travis when you get back to the station. There may be more to her than meets the eye.'

'You think she's got ulterior motives?'

'Ulterior motives,' Gaul repeated in a high-pitched singsong voice. 'Jesus, since when did you learn to speak like some fuckin' poncy lawyer?'

Since he'd married Belinda, Will thought, but he didn't share the information. Instead he laughed, got out his cigarettes and offered one to Gaul. 'You don't trust her.'

'I don't trust anyone on this bleedin' estate.'

Outside in the air that was fresh as it ever got in Kellston, they stood smoking on the main path. Although Pound's body had been removed, some evidence of the crime still remained: a staining on the concrete, a spattering of blood and bone and tissue. Will turned his face away.

'I had a call this morning,' Gaul said. 'One of my snouts. He wants to meet up this afternoon. Reckons he can put a name to our tattooed man.'

'Is he reliable?'

'As reliable as any of them are.'

'Does he live on the Mansfield?'

But Gaul wouldn't be drawn. He was, like all cops, fiercely protective of his informers. They were a valuable asset, a precious commodity, people who were prepared to grass for money or favours or revenge. 'I'll let you know how it goes.'

22

Will felt out of sorts for the rest of the day. Part of this was down to the long stream of lowlifes he had to interview, all denying they'd had anything to do with the attack on Marlon Pound, all armed with shit alibis from their wives or girlfriends, all grinning back at him from across the table as if they knew he had nothing and all *they* had to do was hold their nerve. He'd have liked to find a way to wipe those smug expressions right off their faces.

But this wasn't the only reason he felt fractious. Tonight he had dinner with his in-laws to endure, and the thought of it – three, maybe four hours of unmitigated tedium – cast a dark shadow over his already irritable frame of mind. Belinda's father, a barrister, was a pompous braggart, her mother the sort of woman who did good works and sat on endless committees. Neither of them liked Will and the feeling was mutual.

The Chart family were, as Will's mother would have put it, 'a cut above', and never tired of demonstrating the fact. They bored him now but once he had been charmed by them.

Belinda – attractive, classy, sophisticated – had seemed unobtainable, beyond his grasp, which had made him want her all the more. Desire had blinded him. Lust had grabbed him by the balls. He hadn't realised until it was too late that she was an empty shell, vacuous, all style over substance, and now he felt trapped. This wasn't good news, not when you'd only be married for four years.

Belinda had recently been talking about having a baby. Will had been thinking about a separation. He didn't hate his wife but he didn't love her, either. The thought of all those years stretching ahead filled him with dread. Coming back to Kellston had triggered something in him, a kind of panic at what the future held. And Laura Moss was back inside his head, a constant reminder of what might have been.

You've made your bed, now lie in it. Another of his mother's favourite phrases. Except, of course, you didn't have to damn well lie in it. There were always choices. He just wasn't sure if he had the guts to make them. Perhaps he was having some kind of mid-life crisis – he'd be forty in a year's time – and it would pass. He didn't want to make any rash decisions, but rash decisions were all he could think about.

Will played with the papers on his desk, hoping that the phone would ring. Some news about Tina Kearns or Dawn or their tattooed killer or any other matter requiring the kind of attention that meant he wouldn't be able to make dinner tonight. Of course, he could always lie about it, put a call through to Belinda and say he had to work late, but he had done that last time and it would only mean another row.

He opened the file on Dawn Kearns and began rereading the reports and statements. There must have been something that they'd missed. The cardigan bugged him. With so few clothes to choose from, would she really have been so careless as to lose it? And if she hadn't, who had thrown it in the stairwell? Someone trying to cover their tracks, someone who'd panicked, someone who'd had to get rid of it in a hurry. There was still the possibility that she'd simply run away, but Zelda Graham didn't believe that and he didn't think he did either.

The door-to-door had yielded nothing useful, and it hadn't helped that Tina had been unable to provide a recent photo. They'd talked to most people who'd passed the three girls on Sunday, but none of them had new information. Carol Harper claimed not to have noticed them. Frank Yates had claimed he wasn't there at all. Which meant either Chrissy Moss had been mistaken or Zelda Graham had. Was it important? He didn't think so, but scribbled down a note to follow it up.

Will went through Marlon Pound's statement line by line. Gaul had put pressure on him – everything but the thumbscrews – but the man hadn't broken. And if he had killed Dawn, then where was the body? She'd been missing for a week. He swore softly under his breath, angry and frustrated. Tina Kearns had been convinced of Pound's innocence but that didn't mean much. Her head was a mess, her brain addled by alcohol.

Thinking of Tina shifted his attention on to Margaret Travis. Nothing had come up on the search; she was clean as a whistle. Norman Travis, however, was a different matter. He'd done time for burglary, a series of short stretches, although his last conviction had been eight years before he'd died. He wasn't sure how useful any of this was, other than as an indicator that Margaret might have friends in low places. It wasn't fair, he knew, to visit the sins of the husband on the wife, but when it came to investigating murder it paid to know all the facts.

Will raised his head and looked around the room. It was busy, filled with cops coming and going, cops on phones, cops chatting, cops slurping coffee to fend off the tiredness. It felt odd to be back here after so long. Despite his previous stint, he was still the new boy at Cowan Road, still finding his feet, still in a position of having to prove himself to his fellow officers.

God, he hated Kellston. West End Central was where he'd been stationed for the past eight years and he missed his old colleagues and the buzz of working in Mayfair and Soho. The transfer had come out of the blue and he wondered if Gaul had specifically requested him – someone he could trust, someone to cover his back. Will's predecessor, a sergeant called Hobson, had allegedly been making noises about corruption at the station – bribes, planted evidence, conspiracy – and had quickly been shifted to some remote location where his loose mouth could only be heard by a few disinterested locals and a field full of sheep.

Will owed Gaul, and Gaul knew it. The DCI had saved his arse over the Laura Moss affair, covered for him, twisted the truth and buried the relevant paperwork. All this made Will nervous, on edge, aware that the favour could be called in at any time. He had made a mistake and wouldn't be allowed to forget it.

He lit a fag, sat back and contemplated his situation: shit transfer, shit marriage, shit life. Well, he only had two options; either he walked away or he stuck it out and made the best of it. This applied to his job and his marriage. He wondered where it had all gone wrong, but didn't need to think about it for long. The second he'd set eyes on Laura Moss his world had changed for ever.

23

Terry Street could have passed on the information over the phone, but he preferred to conduct this sort of business in person. That way there could be no misunderstandings. The terms could be laid down and everyone was clear as to where they stood. Anyway, it amused him to put Gaul out, to make him drive to this greasy spoon in Kilburn. Everything of value should require a little effort.

While he waited, Terry quelled the rumbling in his stomach with a chicken sandwich. Then he drank his tea, lit a smoke and considered his position. Since stepping into Joe Quinn's shoes he'd faced multiple challenges, most of which, even if he did say so himself, he had overcome with ease. Of course, some of the old guard had jumped ship but that was only to be expected; old men, like dinosaurs, didn't like change. He was better off without them. Slowly he was building up his own firm, making new contacts, consolidating what was his and taking care not to step on the wrong toes.

His arrangement with Gaul – you scratch my back and I'll

scratch yours – had got off to a rocky start. For years the DCI had been hand in glove with Quinn and he hadn't taken kindly to this state of affairs being abruptly terminated. But Terry had worked on him, cajoled, subtly flattered, charmed and eventually talked him round. Now the two of them, if not exactly best mates, had come to an understanding that was mutually beneficial.

Speak of the devil. The door to the caff opened and Gaul walked in. The DCI was a big man, wider and heavier than he should have been, and with a grey, unhealthy pallor.

Gaul glanced around, spotted Terry, came over to the table and sniffed disdainfully. 'Nice joint,' he said, as though he was more used to dining at the Ritz.

'Sorry I had to drag you out here. I've got a bit of business and won't be back in Kellston till late.' Terry always assumed the same tone with Gaul, respectful without being ingratiating. Nobody liked an arse licker. 'Thought you might want to know about this sooner rather than later.'

Gaul pulled out a chair, heaved his bulk into it and put his elbows on the table. 'Well?'

'You want a brew?'

'Let's just get on with it, shall we?'

Terry shook his head at the approaching waitress, and threw her a smile. Then he turned his attention back to Gaul. 'Anita Jakes. I've heard a whisper.'

'What kind of whisper?'

'A name. Vic Hooper. Mean anything to you?'

Gaul curled his lip, irritation sliding into his eyes. 'You're wasting my time. Hooper's banged up.'

'*Was* banged up. My contact says he's been out a few months now.' Terry looked towards the phone on the wall. 'Go and check if you like. Give the station a call.'

Gaul didn't move. 'Hooper wasn't covered in tattoos.'

'Maybe he's been busy since he came out. Or maybe he had them done inside; something to fill those long empty hours. Anyway, my contact swears Hooper was shacked up with Anita so . . .'

'And this contact of yours, he's reliable, is he?'

'No, he's not reliable at all, but in this case I believe him. He's got good reason for wanting Hooper caught.'

The light dawned in Gaul's eyes. 'We talking Eddie Barr here?'

'He came to see me. Seems to think you're trying to stitch him up for some reason. He wanted me to have a word with you, pass on Hooper's name, and see if he couldn't straighten things out.'

'And you agreed.'

'No.'

'But here you are.'

'On my own terms, not his. I don't like the scrote, never have.'

'And yet you still do business with him.'

'Business is business. But I'm not here to do any favours for Eddie. I just reckoned the name might be useful to you.' Terry didn't come right out and state the obvious – now you owe me one – but it was understood. 'I told him it might be time to move on.'

'I'm sure he appreciated the advice.'

Terry grinned. 'I wish I could say that was true. Sadly, he's the type who doesn't take kindly to any kind of advice, no matter how well intended. I mean, the bloke's running a knocking shop, for Christ's sake – last time I checked that wasn't even legal.'

Gaul and his colleagues at Cowan Road had always turned a blind eye to the activities on Albert Road, partly because it contained the problem of prostitution to the one area, but mainly because of the backhanders they received. 'If we close him down,' the DCI said slyly, 'someone else will just take over.'

'Yeah, that's probably true. Well, after a decent interval. But perhaps the new owner will be less greedy than Eddie, more prepared to give a decent amount back to the ... community.'

Gaul gazed at him across the table, his eyes full of greed. 'There's always that possibility. I'll give it some thought.'

Terry stubbed out his fag in the ashtray, pleased that a deal was on its way to be being brokered, but careful not to show it. He didn't mind paying to get rid of Eddie; it would be worth every penny. Truth was, he didn't want the bloke on his patch any more. Although he did plenty of business with men he didn't like – present company included – there was something about that lowlife which made his flesh creep.

With the more pressing proceedings out of the way, Terry moved on. 'I hear you had some bother at the Mansfield this morning.'

'So what's new?' Gaul said gruffly. 'If I had my way, I'd burn the bleedin' place down.'

'Put yourself out of a job if you did that. Bet the residents of those three towers account for half the crime in Kellston.'

'More than fuckin' half.'

'I hear they threw some geezer off a balcony.'

Gaul's eyes grew sly again. 'Don't suppose you've heard any whispers about *that*.'

'Nothing,' Terry lied. 'I've been out of Kellston all day.' What he'd actually heard was that a girl was missing and the victim had been in the frame. Some kind of kiddy fiddler. Terry didn't have much in the way of morals, but he drew the line at that. The bastard had got what he deserved.

Gaul gazed at him for a while, perhaps trying to figure out

if he was telling the truth or not. Then he heaved himself to his feet. 'You got any idea where I can find Eddie Barr?'

'Under a stone, I imagine.'

'Very helpful.'

'He's not been in the Fox for a while. You could try the Hope. He drinks there sometimes.'

Gaul gave an abrupt nod and walked out of the caff.

Not even a thank you, Terry said to himself, for the useful piece of information about Hooper. Not that he'd been expecting one. Gaul didn't do manners. He sat back, pleased with how things had gone. It always left a bad taste in his mouth doing business with the law, but nothing a stiff Scotch couldn't get rid of.

24

On Sunday morning, Chrissy woke to a feeling of trepidation. She'd had bad dreams, had been expecting them, but these weren't to do with a man falling out of the sky. Instead she had seen Dawn standing at the open door to Anita's flat, laughing and beckoning her in. 'Come on, come on, your mum's inside.' And Chrissy had recklessly rushed forward, hope replacing reason, only to hear the door slam behind her, for Dawn to disappear, for the tattooed man to place his hand on her shoulder, his fingers digging so hard into the blade that she thought he would crush it. 'Hello love, I've been waiting for you.'

She had jerked awake then, breathing heavily, her heart racing. Her gaze had searched the darkness. Every shape in the room, usually so familiar, had taken on a threatening quality: he was the wardrobe, the chest of drawers, the shadow by the window. For a long time, she had lain there, imagining horrors. Trembling, she had moved closer to Nan in order to feel the reassuring warmth of her body.

Eventually, when tiredness had overcome fear, she had fallen asleep again. But there had been no rest. Now she was outside Carlton House, walking away from the tower. There was no one else around but she could feel eyes watching from windows. As she approached the gate, she saw someone waiting there. She knew it was Eddie but he looked different, as though he was wearing a mask. That was when the black flies had come, big as bluebottles, swarming round her, getting in her hair and eyes and mouth. She had tried to flap them away, but the more she'd fought, the more they'd multiplied, until all she could see was darkness and all she could hear was the buzzing in her ears.

The two dreams echoed in Chrissy's head as she got up and got dressed. She glanced at the alarm clock – it was a quarter to nine – before pulling back the curtains. It was grey outside, and wet, the rain coming down in long, straight lines so that it barely touched the window pane. She stood for a while, trying to shake the nightmares from her mind, but the harder she tried the clearer they became.

On her way to the bathroom, she passed the open door to Uncle Pete's bedroom. The blankets had been thrown back from the bed as though he'd risen in a hurry. She listened for his voice but couldn't hear it. The flat was unusually quiet. Even the radio was off.

In the kitchen, Nan was slouched at the table, staring into space. Her face was pale and anxious. Although the rest of her body was still, her hands were involved in a restless dance, the fingers twisting together, separating, joining together again. Chrissy's first thought, an awful thought, was that the law had come while she was asleep.

'Where's Uncle Pete?'

Nan looked up, startled, and one of her hands rose to her chest. 'Jesus, Chrissy, you gave me a fright. How long have you been standing there?'

'Has something happened?'

'No, of course not.'

'So where is he?'

Nan sat up straight, tried to smile, but she couldn't erase the worry from her face. 'He's gone to see that Jacko. I told him he shouldn't, best to stay away at a time like this, but does he ever listen? No, your uncle was born with two deaf ears. The law's still crawling all over the place, watching all the comings and goings, I should imagine, but he thinks he knows best.'

'He'll be careful,' Chrissy said. 'They can't watch everywhere.'

'And God knows what Tina Kearns is going to say when she's back in the land of the living.'

'Haven't they talked to her yet?'

Nan shook her head. 'The doctor pumped her full of something to calm her down. But it won't be long now.' She glanced at the clock on the wall. 'Margaret Travis took her in. They've had one cop inside and another out all night, just so there's no funny business.'

Chrissy was never surprised by what her grandmother knew; she was like a magnet for information. Uncle Pete said the neighbours couldn't take a piss without Nan hearing about it. 'Maybe Tina won't remember. I mean, not all of the ones who were there. It happened so quick . . .'

'Well, we can hope.'

Chrissy put a match to the grill. 'You want some toast, Nan?'

'No, ta, love. I had a slice earlier.'

While she waited for the bread to brown, Chrissy leaned back against the sink and folded her arms across her chest. She wanted to tell Nan about her dreams – perhaps if she shared them, they'd dissolve and disappear – but sensed that now wasn't the right time. Her grandmother had other things on her mind, serious things. What if Uncle Pete was sent back to jail?

Murder. You got a long stretch for that. He'd be old when he came out. Fifty, maybe. It didn't bear thinking about.

Nan sighed into the room. 'I told him Jacko was trouble, stirring things up like that, getting everyone all hot under the collar. It was always going to end bad.'

Chrissy thought back, trying to remember how many men had been on the stairs. About ten, she reckoned, or maybe more. What were the odds of Tina being able to pick out Uncle Pete from a group that size? Except he'd been down the Fox last Wednesday, trying to reason with her, trying to make her understand that her daughter was missing. That wasn't good; it might mean he'd stand out for her.

'How are you, love?' Nan asked, as if suddenly recalling what Chrissy had witnessed yesterday.

'Yeah, I'm okay. I'm fine.'

'It'll pass, given time. Try not to dwell on it.'

Chrissy seemed to be accumulating a list of stuff not to dwell on: Marlon Pound, bad dreams, the chances of Uncle Pete going back inside. She pulled out the grill tray and flipped the bread over with the tips of her fingers. 'He's got an alibi. Uncle Pete. You told the law he was here.'

'They won't believe that, love, not in a million years. I'm his mum, ain't I? I'd swear he was the Queen of England if it helped him get off.'

'Maybe Tina won't blab.'

'We'll just have to wait and see.'

Chrissy stared out of the window at the low grey sky. She wondered what Eddie was doing, where he was. She didn't believe what Sutherland had said; he'd lied about her mum so she was sure he'd lied about Eddie, too. You couldn't trust the law, not as far as you could throw them. Eddie wasn't a bad person. He was just unlucky. She wished she could see him again, talk to him; he'd understand how she was feeling.

'Is that toast burning?'

Chrissy quickly turned off the grill, plucked out her slightly charred toast and sat down at the table. She scraped off the burnt bits around the edges and smeared the rest with butter and jam. Nan stood up and started moving round the kitchen, wiping a cloth across surfaces that were already clean, picking up mugs and putting them down, watching the clock as she tried to kill time.

Normally Chrissy would have skedaddled as soon as breakfast was over, but she didn't want to go out today. Outside was dangerous. Outside was a place where bad things happened. She didn't want to see the spot where Marlon's body had hit the ground or hear that thump in her head again. And anyway, it was still raining, coming down in sheets, like the sky had been holding it all in for weeks.

Nan went through to the living room to find something else to do. Chrissy washed up her plate and put it on the drainer. What now? Sundays were always tainted – at least during term time – by the knowledge of school the next day. Twenty-four hours to make the most of her freedom before she was locked up again. Last Sunday the sun had been out and she'd been sitting on the wall without a care in the world. How could so much change in such a short period of time? She wished she could wipe it all out and start again. She wished Uncle Pete would come back.

25

Where Will Sutherland wanted to be was tucked up in bed with a glass of water and a fistful of aspirin, but instead he was parked outside Carlton House, waiting for Gaul to honour him with his presence. Nine o'clock on the dot, the DCI had said, and it was already quarter past. Bloody typical! He could have had an extra fifteen minutes shut-eye. After examining his face in the rear-view mirror – not the best he'd ever looked – he cupped a hand to his mouth, breathed into it and sniffed the result: minty toothpaste, underlain with just a hint of Courvoisier. Hopefully, he'd get away with it.

He hadn't meant to drink so much last night, hadn't meant to drink at all, in fact, but half an hour of the in-laws had been enough to weaken his resolution. John Chart was such a pompous ass that it simply wasn't possible to be sober in his presence. Memories of the evening kept floating back to him and none of them were good. The highlight had come over dinner as the conversation shifted, fatefully, onto politics and the treacherous subject of Northern Ireland. Now, if he'd had any sense, he'd have kept his big mouth shut, but the wine had made him reckless. What exactly had he said? Something along the lines of: 'You reap what you sow.' From which Chart had inferred that he was some kind of IRA sympathiser and it had all been downhill from there.

Will gazed through the windscreen at the pouring rain. Officers had kept an all-night vigil on the estate, front and back, in case one of their suspects tried to do a runner. To his knowledge, none of them had, although it wouldn't be that difficult to slip away without being noticed. The Mansfield was like a rabbit warren, full of tunnels and passageways, twists and turns. Numerous escape routes for those who had a mind to it. To run, of course, would be like an admission of guilt, but sometimes there was one who lost his nerve.

His thoughts drifted back to last night. Belinda had driven them home, throwing him angry sideways glances. 'What the hell is *wrong* with you?'

As though a question like that could be answered in a twenty-minute journey, or by a man who had drunk so much he could barely string a sentence together. And so he hadn't bothered trying. Now she'd have the hump with him for a few days or a week or for however long she wanted to cling on to the resentment. She wasn't just mad because of last night – that was simply the icing on the cake – but because she'd married a jerk and it didn't reflect well on her judgement.

Gaul's beige Volvo finally appeared at the gates. Will leaned forward, opened the glove compartment, found a packet of mints and popped one in his mouth. He waited for Gaul to pull alongside before getting out of his own car and getting into the DCI's. It smelled of sweat and cigar smoke and an artificial lemony scent that came from a piece of cardboard dangling from the rear-view mirror. The latter reminded him of the smell in Elsie Moss's flat.

Gaul didn't apologise for being late – he never apologised for anything – but instead glanced at Will and said, 'I hope you're feeling better than you fuckin' look.'

Will could have made up an excuse, some story about an upset stomach or a family crisis that had kept him up all night but, in the end, he didn't have the energy to lie. It was all too much effort. 'We're ready. Everything's in place.'

'Any sign of trouble?'

'All quiet.'

'Good. Let's get her out of here before anything changes.'

Will nodded. The plan, arranged yesterday, was straightforward enough. A lift would be requisitioned so that Tina could be brought out of the building as quickly as possible. The landing and the foyer would be guarded by uniformed officers. A car would be waiting by the front doors to take her straight to Cowan Road. If it all ran smoothly, they should be in and out in a matter of minutes.

Will got out of the Volvo and, despite the rain, stopped for a moment to gaze up at Carlton House, his eyes scanning the balconies, the windows, the stone staircase that ran up the side of the tower. He didn't need any problems. It was always smart to be on your guard on the Mansfield, but today the place was likely to be even more tense than usual. If it all kicked off, they'd have to be prepared.

Gaul strode on ahead, his raincoat flapping round his legs. A few quick strides and Will had caught up with him. They went into the foyer, spoke to the officers there, made sure everyone knew what they were doing and then got into the lift.

'Vic Hooper,' Gaul said, as soon as the doors had closed. 'Mean anything to you?'

Will had been thinking about Tina Kearns and the sudden change of subject caught him off guard. 'Should it?'

'We're going back a fair bit, fifteen years maybe, but he used to run some girls on the Albert Road – including Anita Jakes. Big bastard, over six foot. Got a temper on him. Real shithead. I thought he was still inside but turns out he's been back on the Mansfield for the past few months.'

'Yeah, yeah, I remember him now. You think he's our man?'

Gaul gave a nod. 'He's got a sister in Whitechapel. I put in a call and got the local plod to go round and check it out. Stupid sods didn't keep the back covered. He was over the wall and away before they'd even got through the front door. She didn't deny he'd been staying there though. Said Vic wasn't the type of person you ever said no to.'

'She's got a point.'

'Still, at least we know who we're looking for now.'

26

Will and Gaul got out of the lift and walked together along the landing to Margaret Travis's flat. A uniformed cop was standing outside and he straightened up as he saw them approaching.

'Any trouble?' Gaul asked.

'No, guv.'

'Visitors?'

'No, no one's been near.'

Will knocked on the door and it was answered by PC Jenny Walbroke. She'd done a long shift and she looked tired. Not shit tired, the way he looked, with bags under his eyes and skin the colour of fag ash, but just a little worn around the edges. There were other officers, he thought, who'd have used the opportunity to curl up on the sofa and kip for most of the night, but he could tell that this hadn't been the case with her.

'She slept straight through,' PC Walbroke said softly. 'I checked on her several times. She just got up ten minutes ago.'

'How is she?' Will asked.

'Jittery.'

Gaul looked over her shoulder. 'You get any information out of Ma Travis?'

'No, guv. I tried but she's sticking to her story that she didn't see anything and Tina didn't tell her anything.'

'Very convenient,' Gaul said. 'Okay, let's get Tina out of here.'

They went through to the living room where Tina was perched on the edge of the sofa with both hands tightly clasped around a mug. She was in her mid-thirties, a thin, scrawny blonde who looked older than her years. Her bare legs, streaked with narrow blue veins, seemed impossibly pale against the dark grey of the sofa. She must have noticed Will staring because she took one hand off the mug, glared at him and then tugged at the hem of her skirt.

'Morning, Tina,' Gaul said. 'How are you doing?'

'How do you think?'

'Let's get going, then.'

'What?'

'We're taking you down Cowan Road. We can have a chat there about what happened.'

Tina pursed her lips. 'I'm not going nowhere.'

Margaret Travis, who'd been lurking at the kitchen door, came into the living room. 'Give her a chance. She's only just woken up.'

'Best to get it over and done with,' Gaul said firmly.

'We can talk here,' Tina said. 'We don't have to go nowhere.'

But Gaul wasn't having any of it. 'Come on, love. We need to do this properly. You want to catch the bastards who murdered Marlon, don't you?'

Tina thought about this for a moment, glanced at each of them in turn and then focused her attention on the floor. 'It all happened so quick. I didn't see much, not really. I answered the door and they barged in and ...' She shuddered, put the mug down and crossed her arms over her chest. 'There was a lot of shouting and stuff. It's all kind of blurry.'

'But you recognised some of them,' Gaul said. 'You must have done.'

Tina didn't reply.

PC Jenny Walbroke sat down beside her on the sofa. 'I know it's scary, Tina, but you can't let them get away with it. We'll take care of you, keep you safe. You won't have to worry about anything.'

'I can keep meself safe,' Tina snapped back.

Will knew that once Tina named names she could never come back to the estate. And she knew it too. She would have to be placed in a safe house until the trial was over and then found somewhere else to live. His headache was getting worse, chiselling into his skull. He just wanted this to be over, to return to the station and grab some black coffee. 'You can't stay here,' he insisted. 'It's impossible. You do realise that, don't you? Even if you refuse to help us, those thugs aren't going to leave you alone. They won't trust you to keep your mouth shut. We're looking at a murder charge here, a long stretch inside, and they're not going to take the chance that you might change your mind.'

'Yeah,' Gaul said, quickly taking up the baton. 'You're a marked woman, Tina. If you don't cooperate, if you don't play it smart, you'll end up like Marlon. Is that what you want?'

'There's no need to try and scare the poor girl to death,' Mrs Travis objected. 'If she can't help, she can't.'

Gaul shot her an angry look. 'You're not doing her any favours.'

Mrs Travis glowered back at him.

PC Walbroke stuck with the softly-softly approach. 'We'll take care of you, I promise. You really can't stay. You do see that, don't you? We can't protect you here, not twenty-four hours a day.'

Tina chewed on her nails. 'And what's supposed to happen when my Dawn comes back and I'm not around?'

'You don't have to worry about that,' PC Walbroke said. 'If she . . . *when* she comes back, if you're not here she'll go and find her friends, won't she? We'll make sure they know to bring her down the station.'

'And what if that lot get hold of her first?' Tina said, nervously glancing towards the window as if Marlon's killers might already be scaling the walls to the seventeenth floor.

'They won't hurt a kid,' Will said with more confidence than he felt.

'You don't know that.'

'You're not much use to her dead, Tina,' Gaul said with his customary bluntness. It was clear that his patience was running out. 'You've got two choices: either you stay here and take your chances – and believe me, they're slim – or you come with us now and we'll take care of you. What about Marlon? Don't you want justice for him? Or are you happy to let those bastards get away with it?'

'Easy for you to say,' Tina whined. 'You won't be the one having to stand up in court.'

'Better that than the alternative.'

Tina continued to gnaw at her fingernails. Will could almost see the cogs slowly turning in her brain. 'I need a drink,' she said. 'A proper one.'

'Let's get that statement sorted and then we'll see what we can do.'

It was perhaps the hope of some alcohol that finally made up Tina's mind. She rose carefully to her feet and looked towards Mrs Travis. 'Will you keep an eye out for Dawn, tell her what's happened?'

'Course I will, love.'

The landing was checked and then double-checked before they left the flat. Uniforms guarded the corridor. The lift was waiting and the four of them got in. No one spoke. Slowly the lift descended towards the ground floor. Will hoped that the bloody thing wouldn't break down. He held his breath until they reached terra firma and the doors opened again.

More uniforms were waiting in the foyer. Will was starting to sweat, partly down to the tenseness of the situation and partly down to his hangover. They couldn't afford for anything to go wrong now. It had been decided that PC Walbroke would accompany Tina to the station, someone familiar who could keep her calm. Will and Gaul would follow on behind.

The rain had eased a little, but storm clouds still hung overhead. Will passed through the main doors first, his eyes scanning the area, as alert as he could be to any imminent threats. The car was only yards away. They had almost reached it when a bellowing male voice echoed down from somewhere up above them.

'Keep yer mouth shut, Tina, or you're a fuckin' dead woman!'

Tina stopped dead in her tracks, her mouth opening, her eyes becoming wild with fright.

Will looked up at the balconies, his gaze jumping from one to the next, but the man had already disappeared.

'I'll have those bloody shitheads,' Gaul snarled.

Will quickly bundled Tina into the waiting car before she could have second thoughts.

27

Margaret Travis was gratified to suddenly find herself the centre of attention. As soon as the police had left, the women descended on her like a murder of crows. She hadn't had so much company since Norman's funeral. Pots of tea were made and biscuits distributed. Some of the neighbours had come purely for the gossip, others – and she knew who they were – to find out how the land lay.

Naturally, she was going to make them work for the information they wanted. If she gave away the goods too soon, everyone would disappear and she'd be on her own again. She was, however, quick to establish that she, personally, had seen nothing and told the police nothing. She'd lived on the estate long enough to know that grasses never prospered.

'That woman copper was on at me all night, trying to put words in my mouth, but I told her straight: "I'm an old woman, dear, slow on my feet. By the time I got out to the balcony it was all over and done with." Anyway, my eyesight's not what it was. I couldn't have identified anyone even if I *had* seen them.'

All eyes were on her, all ears pricked up.

Margaret, relishing being centre stage, beamed brightly back. The questions came and she took her time answering them. There was much tutting and shaking of heads. What was the world coming to when something like this could happen? Did she think that Marlon Pound *had* done something to Dawn? What state was Tina in now? Did she know who the men were? Was Tina coming back?

Elsie Moss was sitting at one end of the sofa, Jacko's wife Pam at the other. Elsie wasn't saying much – which made a change – but she was listening intently. Pam, on the other hand, couldn't shut up. The two women were clearly worried and had good reason to be. Margaret had some sympathy for them – she knew what it was like to have your loved one behind bars – but there was nothing she could say to make them feel better. What the men had done couldn't be undone. They would have to pay the price.

'So Tina's going to give a statement?' Pam asked. 'Is that what's happening?'

'They didn't give her much choice, love. Said she wouldn't be safe staying on the estate, not with what she'd seen.'

Margaret had seen plenty, too, more than she was letting on. She'd heard the men tramping down the corridor and then all the fuss outside Tina's door. From her living room she could see out onto next door's balcony. There had been a lot of noise, a scrum of bodies, but she'd recognised some faces. A mob, that's what they'd been, a lynch mob. She couldn't be doing with that kind of justice.

Elsie Moss got up and said she had to be going. 'I don't want to leave Chrissy on her own for too long. She's still all shaken up, poor kid.'

Margaret saw her to the door, pressed her arm, said she

hoped Chrissy would be all right. Elsie looked like she had the weight of the world on her shoulders. As the woman walked off, Margaret stood and watched her for a moment. Some people were just dogged by misfortune. She remembered Laura and what had happened to her. A nice girl, but she'd got mixed up in some funny business. Everyone knew that her death hadn't been an accident. It had all been brushed under the carpet because there were those who preferred it that way.

Life wasn't fair and that was the truth of it. If anyone had asked, she could have told them about that cop always sniffing around Laura and the fact that she'd seen them together more than once. She'd told her Norman but he'd said, 'Best stay out of it, love. It's none of our business.' And so she had stayed out of it . . . well, for the main. She'd only told a few people, sworn them to secrecy, and it wasn't her fault if they'd told others.

Margaret shut the door and went back to the living room. She looked around her guests and smiled. 'Now, who's for another cuppa?'

28

Once Tina Kearns had started talking there was no stopping her. Having made the decision to name names, she wanted to make damn sure that the charges would stick. The only way she was going to sleep easy at night was if Marlon's killers were behind bars. Jacko Layton was the first out of the hat – no surprise there – quickly followed by Pat Dunlap and John Fielding. Then it was 'Pete summat, you know, the bloke who came down to the Fox last week, the one who said my Dawn was missing.'

Will winced into his coffee when Pete Moss's name came up. He'd been secretly hoping that Pete really had been in bed when the mob had descended, but no such luck. Why couldn't that idiot ever steer clear of trouble? Laura had spent so much time, so much effort, trying to keep him out of the slammer but he never learned his lesson. And now here he was heading straight back inside again. Her big brother had always been her Achilles heel. She'd have done anything for him – and had. Will had taken advantage of that, but so what? He wasn't going to feel bad about it. All's fair in love and war.

Once Tina had been through what happened several times and exhausted all the names she knew, they moved on to the book of mugshots. While she leafed through the pages, her brow furrowed with concentration. She rubbed her eyes. She worried on her lower lip and sighed. Gaul shifted impatiently in his chair. He wanted to round up the suspects again as soon as possible. Everyone would know where Tina was by now and what she was doing. There was every chance that some of them would make a run for it.

It was another fifteen minutes before Tina identified two others: Jimmy Watling and Larry Bates. This brought the total up to six. What she couldn't tell them was exactly how many men there had been – she thought nine or ten – or which ones had been responsible for throwing Marlon off the balcony. She was sure, however, that it was Jacko who had punched him.

'He was wearing knuckledusters,' she said. 'I remember. Marlon was on the ground. There was blood all over him. Jacko and a couple of others picked him up and dragged him out onto the balcony. They pushed me out of the way and then . . . '

Up until this point she had been curiously calm – perhaps the sedative was still swimming through her bloodstream – but suddenly the horror caught up with her. Will watched as her face crumpled and the tears began to flow.

'He didn't do nothin',' she said, wiping her nose with the back of her hand. 'He never hurt my Dawn.'

Will didn't know if this was true or not. All he was sure of was that the men had gone to the flat with the intention of causing harm. They had taken the law into their own hands and now Marlon Pound was dead.

'Okay,' Gaul said, turning to Will. 'Let's bring them in.'

'Are we done?' Tina asked.

'For now.'

'So can I have that drink? I need a drink.' Tina's gaze was full of pleading. 'You said I could.'

'Just one more thing,' Gaul said. 'What can you tell me about Vic Hooper?'

Tina hesitated for way too long. 'Who?'

'You know, our tattooed friend, the one you claimed to have no knowledge of. The shit who murdered Anita Jakes. Don't fuck me around, love. I can sit here all day and wait if I have to.' As if to prove his point, Gaul leaned back and folded his arms.

Tina stared at him through watery eyes. For a moment it seemed like she was going to stick with her denial, but pragmatism quickly got the better of her. No cooperation, no booze. Her shoulders slumped. 'I didn't know that was his name. Hooper, I mean. I only met him a few times.'

'So why deny it?'

'Why do you think?' Tina whined. 'He killed Anita, didn't he? I didn't want nothin' to do with it.'

'How did you meet?'

'Anita showed up at the flat with him a few months back, said he was an old mate of hers and . . .'

'And what?'

'That he was, you know, looking for a bit of company.'

It didn't surprise Will that Tina had been turning tricks in her spare time, and he wondered if Marlon had known what she was doing while he was out at work.

'I thought he was okay at first, but I was wrong. He's got a screw loose, I'm telling you.' She wiped her nose again and made a snivelling noise. 'Likes it rough, if you know what I mean. I saw him a few times but it wasn't worth the aggro. After that, I tried to avoid him.'

'Did Dawn know him?'

'No.'

'She never met him when he came round?'

'No, she was always in bed by then.'

'But he knew *her*, at least he knew who she was. How was that?'

Tina shrugged. 'Dunno. Perhaps he saw us together. Perhaps Anita told him. But look, Dawn wouldn't have gone back to Anita's flat, I know she wouldn't. She's a smart kid. She'll come home soon, I'm sure she will.'

'Let's hope you're right. Have you got any idea where Hooper might be right now?'

'No. Why would I?'

Gaul stood up. 'Have a think about it. Places he might have mentioned, mates, that kind of thing.'

'He never said nothin'.'

'It would have helped if you'd told us about him before.'

Tina rubbed her face and mumbled into her hands.

'What was that?'

But she just shook her head. 'It doesn't matter.'

Will left the room with Gaul and they headed towards the incident room. It was going to be a busy afternoon. The suspects in Marlon Pound's killing would all have to be picked up, interviewed again and charged. 'She's hardly what you'd call a reliable witness.'

'Well, she's the only one we've got . . . for now.'

Will understood what he meant. Under pressure, any of the suspects could cave in and turn Queen's evidence. Murder tended to focus the mind. Loyalty, keeping schtum, never being a grass was all very well until you were staring down the barrel of a life sentence. With a deal on the table there was a chance the men would turn against each other like rats in a sack.

Will's headache had receded to a soft regular thump at the back of his brain. It was still there, though, a constant reminder of the sins of last night. Although he had no choice but to return to the Mansfield, he was going to make damn sure that he wasn't the one to arrest Pete Moss. There was only so much drama anyone could take over twenty-four hours.

29

Chrissy wandered from the living room to the kitchen and back to the living room. She hoped Nan would come back soon. Or Uncle Pete. Someone to distract her from the bad thoughts that kept crowding in, someone to tell her that everything would be okay. Last night's dreams kept creeping into her head. She squeezed shut her eyes and opened them again. She could almost taste the black flies in her mouth.

Pressing her face against the window, she gazed down on the estate. The rain had washed over the ground, creating puddles in the potholes and rivers in the gutters. Wet litter lay in sodden mounds. There were still four panda cars parked out front and a number of uniforms milling around. A police van had just pulled up too. She watched but no one got out.

A young couple went by, their arms linked together, their shoulders touching. A man strolled towards the gate, his dog straining on its lead. Mrs Yates, Frank's mum, appeared along the path that led from Haslow House. She was walking briskly, black bag in hand, probably going to visit a patient. Mrs Yates was a district nurse, tending to all the sick people in the neighbourhood. She was the one who'd told Mrs Graham about Frank being in trouble with the law. Chrissy wondered if she'd spoken about her mother's 'accident' too.

She could ask Frank but didn't really want to. He might tell someone else who'd tell someone else and then Nan would eventually get to hear about it. Anyway, he wasn't exactly friendly. He wouldn't even have stopped to warn her about the trouble yesterday if she hadn't yelled after him.

Chrissy heard the front door open and moved away from the window. Nan bustled into the living room, looking anxious.

'Is your uncle back yet?'

Chrissy barely had time to answer before the front door opened and closed again. Uncle Pete came in, puffing on a fag. His hair was wet, slicked back, as though he'd been standing out in the rain.

'Tina's going to talk,' Nan said. 'She's down the station giving a statement.'

Uncle Pete shook his head. 'Jacko says she won't.'

'Jacko doesn't know his arse from his elbow. Wishful thinking, that's all that is. You should get out of here, Pete, while you still can.'

'And go where?'

'I don't know, anywhere. What about your mate in Croydon? Tina's going to tell them everything. That Gaul's going to make sure of it.'

'I couldn't go even if I wanted to. It's too late. The whole place is crawling with filth now; they're watching all the exits. Anyway, I wasn't there, was I? I was right here in bed.'

Nan gave him a doleful look. 'They won't believe that if Tina says different.'

'Jacko says—'

'I don't care what he says and you shouldn't either. Tina's not coming back, not ever. She's too scared. That Gaul's put it into her head that if she does then the same thing that happened to Marlon will happen to her. So she's got nothing to lose, has she? She'll tell it how it was. And she'll put the whole bloody lot of you behind bars.'

Uncle Pete slumped down on the sofa, but immediately jumped up again. He went over to the balcony, pulled open the doors and stepped outside.

'There's still time to get out of here,' Nan said, following him. 'They can't be everywhere. You could go over the wall at the back.'

Chrissy watched as Uncle Pete leaned over the railings, his shoulders tight. He made a quick survey of the ground beneath and then stood up straight again. She could tell from the way he was smoking, fast drags, in and out, that he was racked with indecision. 'If they catch me, I'll look guilty.'

'So don't let them catch you.'

'But if they do . . .'

'I've got some money,' Nan said, reaching into her handbag and taking out her purse. 'It's not much but it'll pay for your train fare with a bit left over.' She glanced back at the clock on the mantelpiece. 'Come on, Pete. You've got to decide. You've got to make your mind up.'

Chrissy's stomach was twisting. She could hear the urgency in Nan's voice, sense the fear. She didn't know what to say and so she kept quiet. What was the right thing for him to do, the smart thing? If Tina identified him – and she was bound to – then he was going to go to jail. Wasn't he better off on the run than behind bars?

Uncle Pete came back into the living room and stubbed out his fag in the ashtray on the coffee table. He began to pace from one side of the room to the other. Then he stopped and gazed around as if the answer might lie in the walls or the sofa or the photograph of his sister. Nan shoved the money at him, trying to force it into his hand.

'Take it.'

Right at that moment the knock came on the door. Four loud raps. A copper's knock. Everyone froze. It was too late.

30

Divide and rule was the order of the day. That and finding the weakest link. The afternoon was slipping away as Will and Gaul continued to interview the suspects in Marlon Pound's murder. Jacko Layton, John Fielding, Pat Dunlap and Jimmy Watling had all, unsurprisingly, gone down the 'No comment' road. They were seasoned lags, experienced, the sort who knew it was better to keep their mouths shut until the full extent of the evidence against them was clear.

Pete Moss was sticking with his story of having been in bed. He sat grim-faced and determined. 'I wasn't there.'

DCI Gaul drummed his fingers on the table. 'Tina Kearns reckons different.'

'Well, she's wrong. She's just confused. Or she wants to land me in it.'

'And why would she want to do that?'

'She's got the hump with me, ain't she? 'Cause I showed her up down the Fox last week, told her she should be looking for her kid instead of pouring vodka down her neck.'

'Your niece is a friend of the missing girl, isn't she?' Will chipped in.

Pete glared at him. 'So?'

'So maybe you're more bothered than most about finding out what happened to Dawn Kearns.'

'Everyone's bothered. I'm no different to anyone else.'

'But maybe *you* were bothered enough to try and find out if Marlon Pound had something to do with it. I mean, she goes home on Sunday and there's nobody there but him ... and next thing she's disappeared. Easy to put two and two together. Maybe you got together with a few mates and went round for a chat. Maybe you reckoned he'd be a bit more forthcoming when he was dangled off the balcony by his ankles.'

Pete leaned forward, his eyes flashing. 'Don't even try and pin this on me. I had nothin' to do with it. You ask my mum. I was in bed. I was nowhere near the place.'

'Shame your mates don't remember it that way,' Gaul said.

Pete gave a hollow laugh. 'Yeah, right. You think I'm falling for that pile of bollocks? I wasn't there, okay? End of story.'

It all went on in much the same vein for the next fifteen minutes. Will was glad when the interview finally came to an end. There was too much bad blood between him and Pete Moss, too much history.

By the time Larry Bates was brought up from the cells it was getting on for four o'clock. He was the youngest of the suspects and they'd deliberately left him to sweat while they went through the motions with the others. Larry was twenty-one, a petty thief with sawdust for brains. He was a follower rather than a leader, the sort who was easily led and who looked up to the likes of Jacko Layton.

It was obvious that Larry was the one they could turn. He was inexperienced, naive, the weak link that they needed. They would put the pressure on until he broke. With luck, it wouldn't take too long. Not that Will was in any hurry to get home – Belinda would still be seething – but he wanted to make the breakthrough before the end of the day.

The good cop/bad cop routine, even though it was a cliché, still worked with the callow ones. Will pretended to look at his notes before looking up and shaking his head. 'So, Larry, you've got yourself in a right old mess, haven't you? You want to tell us about yesterday?'

'I don't know nothin',' Larry said, predictably. 'You've got it wrong. I weren't there.'

'Tina Kearns says you were.'

'I don't know no Tina Kearns.'

Gaul put his big fleshy hands on the table and hissed out a breath. 'Don't waste our time, son. You know you were there, *we* know you were there, so let's just cut to the chase. Tell us exactly what happened, the whole story, and maybe you won't have to spend the next twenty years in jail.'

Larry smirked. 'If you can't prove nothin', you can't put me away.'

'Who do you think a jury's going to believe? You or Tina?'

'I weren't there.'

'Where were you?'

'At home. Didn't go out all morning. Had a skinful, didn't I, on Friday night. Felt like shit. You ask my mum, she'll tell you.'

'That's the thing about mums,' Gaul said, 'they're always loyal. Shame the same can't be said about mates.'

Larry stared at him.

'Yeah, when push comes to shove it's their own skins they're looking to save and no one else's. Still if you don't mind taking the rap, that's up to you.'

Larry's cockiness was starting to wane. He fidgeted in his

chair, glanced at his solicitor and then back at Gaul. 'I ain't taking the rap for nothin'.'

'What, so you're saying that you weren't the one to chuck Pound off the balcony? That's not what we've been hearing. We've been told it was you. We've been told that you got ... how shall I put it? ... a little carried away. They only wanted to scare him but you took it a step too far.'

'That's crap.'

Gaul, having put the knife in, continued to twist it. 'Personally, I don't much care who did it. I think you're all to blame. Do you know what we call it? Joint enterprise. It means the whole bloody lot of you were in it together and you'll all go down.' He looked at Will. 'Let's just charge him and get it over with. I've had enough for one day.'

Larry's eyes grew wide. 'What? You can't do that. I didn't—'

'Hold on,' Will said to Gaul, working to an age-old script. 'Give the lad a chance. Maybe he needs a minute. I mean, if he just went along for the ride, had no idea what they were going to do, then that's going to count for something in court. It could mean the difference between twenty years and five, maybe even less if he decides to cooperate.'

'But that's not what he's saying, is it?'

Will returned his attention to Larry. 'You want to take a break, carry on in fifteen minutes? Do you want to do that? It's up to you.'

Larry frowned while he thought about it.

Silence filled the room.

Gaul glanced at his watch, feigning impatience. 'Take your time. It's not as though we have homes to go to.'

'Give him a chance,' Will said, the voice of reason. 'He wasn't to know his mates were going to try and stitch him up.'

'Then he should choose better mates.'

Will sighed and nodded as though this was a truth he couldn't dispute. 'Thing is, Larry, they're taking you for a fool. A scapegoat, that's what they're looking for, someone to shift the blame on to. Are you just going to lie down and let them walk all over you?'

Larry's mouth fixed in a tight straight line. 'They wouldn't do that,' he said through gritted teeth. 'You're lying.'

'Really? Are you sure? Only there aren't any second chances here. Their truth or yours? It's down to you.'

'You haven't ever been inside, have you, lad?' Gaul said.

'What's that got to do with anything?'

'Fresh meat. They're going to eat you alive. You'll be some old lag's bitch before you've even had breakfast.'

The solicitor protested but it was already too late. The seed had been planted in Larry's mind and it was only going to grow.

Will picked up his notes and rose to his feet. 'Fifteen minutes, then. Think about what we've said.'

Out in the corridor Will and Gaul looked at each other and grinned. They both knew that when they came back Larry was going to sing like a canary.

31

Eddie Barr was well pleased when he heard about the latest trouble on the Mansfield. With most of the local force occupied with yet another murder, he reckoned they wouldn't have the manpower, or the inclination, to search for him too. Still, he drove twice around the block just to make sure they weren't watching his flat. He'd borrowed the motor, a clapped-out Cortina, off a mate, and wouldn't be sorry to hand it back. His beloved red Spitfire was still parked on the forecourt of Victoria Mansions but he hadn't dared go near it since Anita's body had been found.

Fortunately, things had moved on since then. A mob had stormed round to some geezer's place yesterday and thrown him off the seventeenth-floor balcony. Something to do with that missing girl Chrissy had told him about. Well, who said miracles didn't happen? Life was full of surprises. Now he had the opportunity to go home, have a long, hot bath and relax for a while.

'God bless the fuckers,' he murmured.

When he was sure it was safe, Eddie parked up and had a good look round. He had checked out of the B&B – good riddance to it – and intended to stay here for the night. Maybe longer. It was worth the risk. So long as he was careful not to put on the lights in the front room when it got dark, he reckoned no one would be any the wiser.

He got out of the car, retrieved his bag from the boot and walked over to the front door. It was annoying, all this subterfuge, all this skulking in the shadows. If Terry Street hadn't been such a double-crossing bastard everything could have been sorted by now. His lip curled as he recalled the conversation they'd had. Some people had no respect. They thought they could push you around and get away with it.

Quickly he tapped in the code, waited for the click, shoved open the door and slipped into the foyer. Victoria Mansions wasn't as flash as Terry's block but it was smart enough. He could live without the lift and the palm tree. Anyway, this was only his first step on the property ladder. He had big plans for the future. By the time he was thirty he intended to own a bloody big house with electric gates and a swimming pool. No one, least of all the likes of Terry, was going to stand in his way.

Eddie jogged up the stairs to the second floor, glad to be home. Tomorrow he'd visit Albert Road, check on the girls and pick up the takings. He wondered if the law had been hassling them. Although he paid Terry to keep DCI Gaul sweet, Anita's death had thrown a spanner in the works. They were greedy bastards, both of them. He paid through the nose and they still weren't happy.

After glancing along the corridor – all quiet – he let himself into the flat, dropped the bag in the hall and went through to the living room. What he needed now was a stiff drink and a comfortable chair. He had barely taken a few steps before he realised something was wrong: an instinct, a prickling, a sense of things not being how they should be. Then his eyes fell on the bottle of Glenfiddich, half empty, standing on the coffee table with a glass beside it.

Eddie sensed the movement rather than heard it. He whirled around and his heart leapt into his mouth. *Shit.* Vic Hooper was standing in the doorway, all six foot whatever of him, and he didn't look happy. His eyes were unnaturally bright, his mouth twisted. Bulging arms dangled by his sides like resting weapons.

'Hello, Eddie. I was wondering when you'd get home.'

'How the fuck did *you* get in?'

Hooper grinned, although not with any friendliness. 'That's not much of a welcome, mate. You should get a better lock on the door – those Yales aren't what you'd call secure.'

As making a run for it wasn't on the cards – there was nowhere to run to – Eddie stayed very still and tried to play it cool. 'What are you doing here?'

'Take a guess.'

Eddie didn't want to. He didn't like the look on Hooper's face, didn't like the tone of his voice. The bloke was probably drunk – pissed on his whisky – but he was off his head on some junk too. His pupils were pinpricks, his skin sheened with sweat.

'You grassed me up, Eddie. I don't like grasses.'

'What? What the fuck are you talking about? I didn't grass you up, man. I haven't been anywhere near the law. Where do you think I've been? In the bleedin' B&B from hell, that's where, just so I *didn't* have to talk to the fuckers.' Eddie spoke quickly, trying to get it all out before Hooper shut him up for good. 'You're way off the mark. That copper, Gaul, he's been trying to grab me all week, but I gave him the slip. I'm no grass. I never said a word, I swear it.'

'Nice try, but someone gave the filth my name. Now, who

180

could that have been? Sure as fuck wasn't Anita – she's mighty quiet these days. I was keeping my head down, you see, bit of bother with some boys south of the river. Only you and her knew who I was. Even that tart Tina only knew me as Vic.'

Eddie could feel the panic rising up in him. He had to think fast. A knife, a thin stiletto, was strapped to his ankle but he knew that Hooper would be on him before he had a chance to grab it. No sudden movements. Nothing that would make him lash out. And then it came to him – a bloody brainwave – and he almost cried out in relief.

'It wasn't me. It was one of those girls, you know, the ones who came up with the message for Anita. Gaul showed her some mugshots and she picked you out. That's what I heard. That's what happened, man. It was nothin' to do with me.'

Hooper's eyes bored into him, dark pools of evil. He stared and stared. 'But you were the one who sent her with the message, Eddie. If you hadn't done that . . .'

Eddie was thinking about the knife again, wondering if it was worth the risk. 'Yeah, yeah, that was a mistake. I shouldn't have done that. But you can get rid of her, no one can prove anything. She's the one you want and I can find her for you. Her name's Chrissy.'

'Chrissy what?'

'I dunno, but she lives on the Mansfield.'

'Where on the Mansfield?'

'I don't know exactly.'

'Not much use to me then, are you, Eddie?'

Eddie, desperately pursuing his goal of self-preservation, moved swiftly on. 'I can find her. You can't go near that estate or Gaul will have you. The law's all over it. Some bloke was wasted yesterday. I can get hold of her, though. Tomorrow. We can meet somewhere. You decide. I'll bring her to you.' He stopped, ran his tongue over dry lips and thought about that other girl who'd disappeared. Dawn, that was her name. Maybe Hooper hadn't just killed Anita, but her too. 'What do you reckon?'

'What's wrong with right now?'

'Like I said, the estate's crawling with filth. If they pick me up, that's it. And anyway, it's getting on.' Eddie glanced at his watch. 'She's not going to be out and about. She'll be at home having her tea or something.'

'In the morning then.'

'No, the afternoon's better. That way I can get her on her own. You don't want her mates tipping off the teachers if she doesn't turn up at school.' Even while he was talking, trying to buy time, Eddie was thinking about what he was *actually* going to do. He didn't intend to be an accessory to murder, especially of a young girl. No, once he'd got rid of Hooper, he was going to get back in his car and scarper. 'I'll bring her to you tomorrow. Just say where and I'll be there.'

Hooper took a step forward and Eddie instinctively stepped back. The big man grinned, showing a short row of upper teeth with black gaps at the sides. 'What's wrong, mate? You seem kind of edgy.'

Eddie shook his head, trying to feign a composure that he didn't feel. His hands had gone clammy and his pulse was racing. 'What do you say? You can sort it out with the girl face to face.'

'Tomorrow, huh?'

'Yeah, just say where. It's not a problem.'

'Here,' Hooper said. 'You can bring her here.'

Eddie's heart sank. 'Are you kidding? It's not safe. The law keep checking to see if I'm home yet. I only dropped by to get some clean clothes and then I'm off back to the B&B. If they find me here ... if they find *you*, we'll both be for it.'

'Now you see I've been here all day, Eddie, and not a sniff of the law. Funny that. Makes me wonder if you're being straight with me. For all I know you could be talking bollocks. You could be planning on doing a runner the minute you get out of here. Maybe even put in a call to the law. You wouldn't do anything like that, would you, mate? Not to an old pal. You wouldn't say you're going to do one thing and then do another?'

'No way, man,' Eddie said. 'I'm only looking out for you.'

Hooper's mouth stretched into that devil's grin. 'That's good to hear. But you know what I think? I reckon we'll be just fine here. It's a good a place as any to spend the night. You and me can have a nice chat, have a drink together, have a catch-up.'

Eddie couldn't think of anything he'd rather do less, but he nodded and said, 'Sure. If that's what you want.'

Hooper sat down on the sofa, picked up the bottle and poured himself a whisky. He looked up at Eddie. 'You just going to stand there?'

Eddie sat down in the armchair.

'You want a drink?' Hooper asked.

'Yeah. Ta.'

'Better get yourself a glass then.'

Eddie stood up again and crossed the room. His nerves were jangling. There were bottles of vodka and gin on the sideboard and he considered picking them up, one in each hand, and smashing them over Hooper's head. Would the bastard even notice? It was better, he supposed, to humour him for now. At least until he thought of a better plan. Perhaps, when Hooper was drunk enough, the psycho would fall asleep and he could sneak out of the flat. Or stab him through the heart. Except then he'd have to get rid of the body.

Eddie grabbed a glass, walked back and put it on the coffee

table. Hooper sloshed some whisky into it and slid it across the table.

'Cheers.'

'Cheers,' Eddie repeated, downing half the whisky in one.

'You want to give me the knife, Eddie?'

'Huh?'

Hooper gestured towards Eddie's ankle. 'Just in case you get any ideas.'

Eddie hesitated, reluctant to relinquish the only weapon he had. But then he looked at Hooper's face, dark and menacing, and quickly bent, pulled the knife free and passed it over.

'There,' Hooper said, placing the knife beside him on the sofa. 'Now I don't have to worry about you doing anything you shouldn't.' He took a pouch out of his pocket, opened it and started rolling a cigarette. 'So, tell me about the bitch who grassed me up.'

32

Breakfast on Monday was a dismal affair. Chrissy played with her cornflakes, squashing them against the bottom of the bowl with the spoon. Her appetite was gone. Nan peered down into her mug of tea as though an answer could be found there as to why things always went so wrong. Uncle Pete, along with the others, had been charged with the murder of Marlon Pound. They were up in court this morning, where they'd make their pleas before being remanded to jail.

'Are you going to go, Nan?'

'It'll only take five minutes, love. Not much point in traipsing across London for that.'

'I could come with you.'

'You've got school and I've got work.'

Chrissy didn't want to go to school. She didn't want to have to listen to the other kids talking about Marlon or have to answer their questions about what it was like to see a man falling from the seventeenth floor. 'Do I have to?'

'Yes, you have to.'

'They'll all be going on about what happened.'

'Best get it over and done with, then. They'll find something else to gossip about soon enough. Are you going to eat those cornflakes or just play with them?'

'I'm not hungry. Where will they put Uncle Pete?'

'God knows. A local nick, hopefully, but they'll want to split them up. Make sure there's no conspiring before the trial.' Nan lifted the mug to her lips and took a sip of tea. 'He should have stayed well clear of that Marlon – and Jacko, come to that. The boy doesn't have the sense he was born with.'

'How long will it be before the trial?'

'Months,' Nan said. 'Not till after Christmas.'

'We can visit, though, can't we?'

'Course we can, so long as he's not too far away.'

Chrissy sighed. 'It's not fair, is it? I mean, Uncle Pete wasn't the one who did it. Why should he be charged with murder? He didn't know what they were going to do.'

'Well, he should have thought on, shouldn't he? Nothing good ever happens when that Jacko's involved.'

'So why doesn't he tell the law it wasn't him, that he was there but he didn't have anything to do with it?'

'Because then he's going to have to say who *did* do it, and that means giving evidence against his so-called mates. No, I know what Pete's like; the silly bugger would rather do a long stretch than be labelled as a grass.'

'They should admit to it then, the ones who did push him off,' Chrissy said indignantly. 'They shouldn't let Uncle Pete take the blame.'

'That lot won't admit to nothin'. They'll deny it till the cows come home.'

'Didn't Tina see?'

'There were too many of them, love. They were all crowded

round and ... it was over by the time she realised what they'd done. I don't reckon she knows if it were one of them or two or ... No, she can't say for sure.' Nan put down her mug and glanced at the clock. 'Lord, is it that time already? You'd better look lively or you'll be late.'

Chrissy reluctantly got to her feet. She leaned over and kissed her nan on the top of her head. 'I'll see you later.'

Nan nodded in an absent-minded fashion as if her thoughts were already somewhere else.

As she walked down the steps, Chrissy recalled the moment yesterday when the law had come to arrest Uncle Pete – not Sutherland or Gaul but two different cops – and although he'd made a few objections his heart hadn't really been in it. He'd known by then that Tina must have identified him. He'd known too that he'd lost his chance to scarper.

'Don't worry, Mum,' he'd said as they took him away in cuffs. 'They've got the wrong man. I'll sort it out. It'll all be fine.'

Except it wouldn't be fine. Uncle Pete could deny he'd been at the flat till he was blue in the face, but Tina Kearns had seen him there. She was going to stand up in court and point her finger straight at him. Not today, though. Today was just the first stage, when he'd claim he was innocent. He wouldn't get bail. He wouldn't be coming home. He might not be coming home for a very long time.

33

Will Sutherland came out of the magistrates' court with a smile on his face. Job done. Larry Bates, having decided to come clean, had given them three more names yesterday, bringing the total up to nine. The trio had been rounded up last night. Eight of the accused had just been charged with murder and all had pleaded not guilty. Only Larry had been absent from court. He'd been persuaded to turn Queen's evidence and would be kept in a safe place until the trial. With his testimony and Tina's, they should be sure of getting convictions.

Larry's story pretty much tallied with hers, citing Jacko Layton as the ringleader. Fielding and Dunlap had figured large, too. It was those three, he said, who had pushed Pound against the railings, lifted him up and threatened to drop him over the edge if he didn't fess up to what he'd done to the girl. Naturally, Larry had played down his own part in the miserable affair, claiming that he hadn't even wanted to go to the flat. 'But you don't say no to Jacko. You can't.' Will suspected he hadn't been quite as reluctant as he'd made out.

He lit a fag, crossed the road and went into a café he knew. Here he ordered a coffee and sat down by the window to watch the world go by. It was likely, he thought, that a few more of the accused would come forward before the trial, trying to make a deal now they knew that Larry Bates had turned. They wouldn't want to take the rap for something that they hadn't done. Although they were all guilty to some extent, some were more guilty than others.

Pete Moss had thrown him a few dirty looks during the hearing, as though the whole thing was personal, as though Will was responsible for his predicament rather than it being a consequence of his own actions. He'd always been the same. Even ten years ago, Laura had been fighting a losing battle. She'd tried her best to keep him out of jail and lost her own life in the process.

At least Elsie hadn't been in court, for which he was grateful. She had her own beliefs, her own understanding of what had happened in the past and nothing he could say would ever change that. Not that he even wanted to try. For women like Elsie, the law was the enemy and that would never alter.

He gazed out through the window, watching the girls go by and trying not to leer. At what age did you pass from a red-blooded male to a dirty old man? Laura had always turned heads wherever she went. He wondered how some girls learnt to walk how they did, heads held high, as though they owned the world and everything in it.

It wasn't fair to compare Belinda to Laura, but he still did. He couldn't help himself. Laura Moss had thrilled him like no other woman ever had. That wild, dangerous streak in her had set his pulse racing. She'd been clever too – not in a bookish sort of way, but in her ability to always get what she wanted. She could wind men round her little finger while she looked at them with the eyes of an innocent. But that had been half the appeal, hadn't it, the game the two of them had played: never being entirely sure of each other, always trying to be one step ahead?

Will knew he should get back to the station but he lingered for a while longer. Sometimes he liked to be alone, anonymous, to feel his inconsequentiality within the vastness of the city. In a strange way, it made him feel better, as though nothing he did really mattered. For many people this would be a depressing thought but he found it the very opposite, like a burden being lifted from his shoulders. You did your best. You carried on. In the end you were no more important than a speck of dust floating in the air.

34

Eddie Barr had experienced the night from hell, forced to endure seemingly endless hours of Hooper's rants and ramblings. The bloke was deranged, demented, a complete raving lunatic. Any hopes that Hooper might doze off at some point had come to nothing; fuelled up on cocaine and booze, on pills and coffee, he'd been as wide awake as a sentry, and as watchful.

Eddie had been on the lookout for opportunities, chances to get away, chances to grab the knife, but there had been none. Now his nerves were stretched to breaking point and exhaustion was setting in. What the hell was he going to do? Hooper was after retribution and wouldn't stop until he got it. His list of grievances was as long as his arm, an irrational tangle of insults and injuries. He had killed Anita, apparently, because 'the bitch wouldn't shut the fuck up', and clearly didn't have any regrets about it.

It was still in Eddie's mind that Hooper could have killed the missing kid, too. The man was capable of it, capable of anything. And now he had Chrissy in his sights. Originally,

Eddie had suggested going alone to pick her up in the car, his actual intention being to head for the hills the minute he got out of the flat, but then Hooper had insisted on coming with him.

'The thing is, old pal, you might just forget to come back.'

'I wouldn't do that, man, I swear. I mean, where am I going to go? I live here. This is my home.'

Hooper might have been high as a kite, but he still knew a line when it was fed to him. 'Don't give me any of your bullshit, Eddie. It pisses me off. It makes me want to push your face through that fuckin' wall. We're going together, okay? You and me. End of story.'

'Okay, okay. If that's what you want.'

Eddie had let it drop. Now, as morning slipped into afternoon, he was aware of time running out. He kept telling himself, trying to convince himself, that for as long as he was useful, Hooper wouldn't kill him. But there was nothing rational about the man. His mood was constantly changing: genial one minute, dark as thunder the next.

But Hooper needed him. That was the bottom line. Although he'd seen Chrissy before it had only been briefly and there was every chance – especially if he'd been off his head – that he wouldn't recognise her again. There would be loads of girls around when school finished for the day. He'd need Eddie to pick out the one who'd betrayed him. And Eddie was prepared to do it, but only if could find a way to distance himself from what would happen next.

Slowly, carefully, he set about trying to persuade Hooper that it was a bad idea to bring Chrissy back to the flat. There was the law to think about, and the neighbours, not to mention the fact that the girl probably wouldn't get in the car in the first place.

'I hardly know her,' Eddie said. 'And she's going to clock you straight away. She might freak out, start screaming or something. No, it's just not going to work.'

'You got a better fuckin' idea?'

'Yeah, I've got a better one. Listen to this.'

35

Chrissy had spent the day in a state of restlessness, too pre-occupied to concentrate, and it was a relief when the school bell finally went. All she'd been thinking about was Uncle Pete and what was going to happen to him. She had tried to stay away from everyone except Zelda, but she had heard the whispers and known that her classmates were talking about her. Well, not just her but anyone who was connected in some way to Marlon Pound's murder.

She grabbed her coat and set off for home on her own – Zelda was staying late for music practice – but had barely cleared the gates when the Dunlap brothers joined her.

'Have you heard?' Charlie said.

'Heard what?'

'About this morning. I went home at lunch. Dad's been sent to Wandsworth, but he never did nothin'. The bloody filth are stitching him up.'

'Do you know where Uncle Pete's gone?'

Charlie shook his head. 'Mum didn't say. She heard

194

something, though: some slag's going to give evidence against them. One of the ones who was there on Saturday. Can you believe that? What a fucker.'

'Who is it?'

'Dunno.'

'You reckon it's true?'

'Yeah, course it is. He's turned Queen's ain't he? Going to save his own skin by making up shit about everyone else.'

Chrissy's heart sank. She glanced at George – his face was all pale and crumpled like he was going to cry – and quickly looked away. It made her want to cry, too. Suddenly she didn't want to hear any more. Deep down she'd still been hoping for a miracle, that somehow the charges would be dropped, but she knew that wasn't going to happen now. 'God, I've forgotten my history book. I'll have to go back.' Then, in case they had any ideas about waiting for her she quickly added, 'I'll see you tomorrow.'

Chrissy walked back against the tide of kids, weaving along the pavement until she got to the school gates. Here she stopped and looked over her shoulder to make sure the Dunlaps had moved on. She couldn't see them but she still loitered for a while, just in case. She wanted to go home and dreaded it at the same time. Nan would be upset and there wouldn't be anything she could say to make her feel better.

When she was sure the coast was clear, she set off again. While she walked, she wondered which jail Uncle Pete had been taken to, hoping it was a London one, or at least one not too far away. It would be hard for them to visit if he was shipped out of the city. And what about the grass Charlie had been talking about? That wasn't good. Uncle Pete couldn't go on denying that he wasn't there when there were two people prepared to testify against him.

Chrissy was approaching the main drag of the high street

when she heard footsteps behind her and then a voice calling out her name.

'Hey, Chrissy!'

Even before she turned, she knew who it was. *Eddie.* She whirled around, her heart pumping. Well, God hadn't provided the exact miracle she'd wanted, but if she'd had a list this would have been up near the top.

'Hi,' she said, while she tried not to look as pleased as she felt. He was wearing shades, a baseball cap and a smile bright enough to light up the darkest of days.

'You okay?' he asked. 'I've been worried about you.' He touched her lightly on the wrist. 'I heard there was more trouble on the estate.'

It was the touch that set her off, the feel of his hand against her skin. Tears instantly sprang into her eyes. 'I'm all right. How are you?'

'You don't look all right.'

'No, I am,' she insisted. 'It's just . . . you know.'

'Is it true some bloke got chucked off a balcony?'

Chrissy nodded. 'I saw it. I saw him fall. It was Marlon Pound, the man who lived with Dawn's mum. There was a whole bunch of them who went round and . . .'

'Jesus, what did they do that for?'

'They reckoned he knew what had happened to her.'

'And did he?'

Chrissy gave a shrug, not trusting herself to speak. Just thinking about it all made her feel shaky.

'Jesus,' he said again. 'Must have been awful seeing that. You okay? No, course you're not. It's terrible. I wish I could do something. Look, I'd buy you a Coke but I've still got the law on my back. I'm worried they might spot me so I'd better not hang about.' He glanced around, looked back at her. 'I don't like leaving you when you're upset, though. Do you fancy a walk? Somewhere quieter?' He nodded across the road. 'What about the cemetery? We can have a proper chat. I don't suppose the law will be sneaking around in there.'

Chrissy didn't think twice. She didn't care where they went so long as they were together. In truth, she'd have walked on hot coals, strolled across a battlefield, so long as he was there beside her. As they crossed the road, she shot him a series of fast little glances, trying to fix his features in her mind – his cheekbones, the way his lips curled up, his dark hair lying at the nape of his neck – so she could bring them out like snapshots and look at them later.

'I'm glad I ran into you again,' he said.

'Me too.'

They passed through the gates into the tranquillity of the cemetery. There were a few people on the main path and so Eddie veered off to the left. 'It's nicer down here,' he said. 'It's more peaceful. It's where all the older graves are.'

The path was narrow but there was just enough room for them to walk side by side. Their arms brushed occasionally, fleeting touches that made Chrissy catch her breath. The grass was much longer here, up to their shins and woven through with wildflowers and weeds. Even though they weren't that far from the street, the traffic was only a faint distant drone. It was like being in another world, a world that only she and Eddie inhabited.

'Can I tell you a secret?' he said.

'Of course you can.'

'It wasn't just an accident, me running into you today. I was hoping to see you again.'

'Were you?'

'I've been thinking about you a lot.'

Chrissy felt nervous and excited at the same time. Was he going to kiss her? She wanted him to but was afraid she'd do something wrong. She'd never kissed a boy before and the thought of it gave her butterflies in her stomach.

Eddie glanced over his shoulder as if checking that they really were alone. He seemed suddenly tense, uneasy. Perhaps he was as nervous as she was.

'Are you all right?' she asked him.

'Yeah, yeah, I just . . . Sorry, I'm kind of paranoid about the law at the moment.' He laughed. 'I keep expecting DCI Gaul to jump out from behind a bush.'

'Oh, I've met him. I didn't like him.'

'What's to like? He's got it in for me but I don't know why. I never did nothin' to him. You'd think the fat slob had better things to do than harass innocent people.'

'I know. It's not fair, is it?'

'It's hard to find anyone to trust these days.'

Chrissy hoped he trusted her. Did he? She felt too shy to ask. They were passing a tall grey stone angel on a plinth and she raised her eyes to gaze at it. The hands were joined in prayer, the face lifted towards heaven. It was like a sign, she thought, an indication that she was being blessed.

They reached the end of the path where it branched into two, one side leading down to a row of mausoleums, like miniature houses built for the dead, the other winding back towards the main part of the cemetery. Eddie stopped abruptly.

'What's the matter?' she asked.

'I . . . er, I need a slash. Sorry. I won't be a minute.'

Chrissy watched him walk down the slope, drinking him in, but then quickly averted her eyes in case he looked back and saw her gazing at him. She studied the graves, old faded headstones covered with ivy and surrounded by grass and nettles. Names from the past. They had died young in those days. It made her sad to read the ages – seven, thirteen, eighteen. She hoped Eddie wouldn't be too long. When he came back, they would kiss, come to an understanding. He would ask to see her again and she would say yes, and that would be the beginning, the start of something special.

So absorbed was she by this dream that she didn't hear the sound of approaching footsteps. Or maybe there was nothing to hear – the ground was damp after the rain – and nothing to alert her other than a feeling, a sixth sense that someone else was present. She half turned, almost expecting to see Eddie, even though she knew he'd be coming from the opposite direction. The hand clamped over her mouth before this thought had been properly processed, and seconds later she was dragged backwards and hurled to the ground.

The breath flew from her lungs on impact, shock waves running through her body. Before she could cry out, he was on top of her, punching and cursing, calling her a bitch, a slag, a grass. His fist drove into her jaw. She heard the crack of breaking teeth. She felt a stinging pain on her shoulder, her arm. She knew who he was now – the man with the tattoos, the man of her nightmares. There was only fear and panic. She struggled, tried to bite at his fingers, but he was too powerful.

'Move and you're dead! You're fuckin' dead!' he spat into her face.

She was on her back, trapped by the weight of him. She saw the flash of silver and felt the sharpness of the blade against her throat. Engulfed by terror, the fight went out of her. A blankness descended. She'd had it. She was beaten, defeated. There was only one hope and that was Eddie. He'd be back soon. He'd save her. Where was Eddie?

The man reached down, roughly pushing up her skirt,

groping between her legs, pulling at her pants. She heard the thin metallic sound of a zip being released. Beyond his shoulders she could see the branches of a tree, almond-shaped leaves, a stripe of grey sky. There was nothing she could do to stop what was happening. He was forcing her legs open, pushing himself into her, tearing her apart. Harsh guttural sounds escaped from his mouth. His breath was a stench in her face. And all the time the blade was at her throat. She was going to die, here, in this place, surrounded by the dead.

It felt like for ever. Eternal hell. She closed her eyes. His hate bored down on her, into her. Her body, racked with pain, silently screamed. She was being crushed, torn apart, obliterated. She prayed to God. She thought of Nan and Uncle Pete and Zelda. Where was Eddie? Why hadn't Eddie come? It was too late now. The brute was killing her. His filthy grunts were all she could hear. Everything hurt. Everything was agony. Why wouldn't it stop?

And then, abruptly, it did. There was a strange cracking crunching sound before the tattooed man swayed on top of her and then slowly toppled sideways. She felt the weight of him removed, heard a dull thump and then a dragging noise. She lay very still, limp and useless, unable to comprehend what was going on. There was someone else here. Eddie? It had to be. He'd come at last. She tried to open her eyes but couldn't see properly. Not darkness exactly, but a grey swimming mass.

Then a voice. A man's but not Eddie's. 'Don't try to move. I'm going to get help. I won't be long.'

And then the pounding of running steps on grass. She opened her mouth to beg, to plead, 'Don't go! Don't leave me!' but nothing came out. She was dumb, unable to speak. Her throat hurt. Perhaps she was dead already. She turned her head slightly, blinked hard, but her eyes still couldn't focus. There was something, she thought, lying a little way apart from her – a solid mass, a lump. It wasn't moving. It wasn't doing anything. It took her a moment to realise that it must be *him*.

Panic surged through her again. He would wake up, stand up, finish what he'd started. She tried to get to her feet but her body refused to cooperate. Her head rose a few inches and then dropped back against the ground again. She felt sick, confused, dizzy. Above her, a bird flapped its wings and flew up into the sky. That was the last thing she remembered until the sound of voices brought her round again.

36

As soon as he had passed out of sight of Chrissy, Eddie had broken into a sprint, hurtling past the row of mausoleums, cutting across the cemetery, forging a path through the long grass and brambles until he came to an old gate that led out of the churchyard. Here, in order not to attract attention, he had slowed to a brisk walk and made his way to the high street.

What now? He didn't have the keys to the Cortina – they were still in Hooper's possession – but he did have the key to the Spitfire. All he had to do was get back to the flat, retrieve the car and take off. A black cab was passing and he raised his arm to hail it, scrambled into the back and said, 'Victoria Mansions, Foster Road.'

He was sweating, stressing, his heart hammering in his chest. *Stay calm. Don't lose your nerve.* He kept his mouth shut and the cap pulled down over his eyes. He thought about what was happening at the cemetery. He hadn't had a choice, had he? It was her or him. Hooper wanted blood, retribution, and wasn't going to stop until he got it. Eddie had stuck to his side of the bargain, luring the girl to a quiet place where Hooper would be waiting; now the rest was up to him.

But what if something went wrong, if she managed to escape and grassed him up to the law? No, that wasn't possible. Hooper wouldn't let her live. He couldn't afford to. The bastard was unhinged, psycho. Eddie had managed to convince him that Chrissy was the cause of all his problems and if he removed her there would be no one to connect him to the murder of Anita.

The journey was a short one, but it felt interminable. Too many arguments were tumbling through his head, too many internal wrangles. Maybe he shouldn't run. Wouldn't that make him look guilty? Maybe he should just stay put. But what if someone had spotted him going into the cemetery with the girl? Well, he could just say they'd had a row and he'd stormed off. He'd had no idea what was going happen next, had he? And anyway, chances were that no one had noticed, or if they had they wouldn't be able to identify him. He'd get rid of the cap and the shades, maybe all the clothes he was wearing. But what if Hooper came back to the flat, decided to lie low there, decided that was the safest place to be? He'd be back to square bloody one.

The driver pulled up outside the flats and Eddie leaned over to pay him. He got out of the cab, looking all around, almost expecting to see a cop car waiting. No, it was too soon. It could be days before the girl was found, maybe months if Hooper hid the body. Hardly anyone went to that part of the cemetery these days. It was neglected and overgrown, a jungle in places. A corpse could lie there for a long while until the stink alerted someone.

Gaul was the only cop who'd be looking for him right now and that was over something else. And maybe, hopefully, the fat bastard had better things to do. With all the recent trouble at the Mansfield, he would be too busy to make house calls. Resentment seethed in Eddie's breast: first Gaul and now Hooper. What had he done to deserve any of this? It was so fucking unfair. He'd worked damn hard for everything he'd got and now it was all falling apart.

He glanced towards the Spitfire, trying to make up his mind about what to do next. Hooper could be back any minute. Or he might not be coming back at all. He had the Cortina; the smartest thing, surely, would be to scarper. But Hooper wasn't smart or rational or predictable. There was no saying which way he'd jump.

Eddie began walking towards the car. He'd get out of here, put some distance between him and Kellston until the dust settled and he could see what was what. Yeah, that was the best choice. Except – he stopped and looked around again – maybe he was being too hasty. There was cash in the flat, over five hundred quid, money he might need over the coming weeks. Clothes, too. What difference would a few minutes make?

He dithered, pulled in both directions, unable to decide. Shit. The longer he stood there, the less time he had. Eventually, he came down on the side of the flat. While he collected his things, he would keep an eye out for the Cortina. If Hooper showed up, he could just head for the top landing and wait there until the coast was clear.

With what he hoped was a failproof plan, Eddie strode over to the front door, opened it and sprinted up the stairs. He unlocked the flat and walked inside. Immediately he hurried over to the window to look down on the forecourt. No sign of the Cortina. Good. Quickly, he went to the bedroom, emptied the bag he had brought back yesterday, stuffed it with fresh clothes and the money and prepared to leave.

Another thought occurred as he was heading for the door. What would happen when Hooper was caught? And he would be, he was bound to be eventually. And if he was still driving the Cortina, it wouldn't take long for it to be traced back to its owner. He should ring his mate later, tell him to report the car stolen. Eddie was starting to sweat again. Would Hooper grass him up when he was nabbed, tell the law it had all been his idea? If that was the case, he might never be able to come back to Kellston. He'd be on the run for the rest of his life. Maybe he should take more with him.

He went back to the bedroom and began emptying the wardrobe and the drawers, throwing the contents on the bed and quickly sorting through them. He took everything out of the bag and transferred it to a bigger suitcase. Why hadn't he thought all this through last night? Because he'd been trapped in the flat with a lunatic, that was why. No one could think straight when a man like Hooper was sitting on their sofa with a knife lying beside him.

Eddie dragged the suitcase into the living room, went over to the window and looked out again. Still no Cortina. He glanced at his watch. It was getting on for ten minutes since he'd arrived. Wouldn't Hooper have been back by now if he was coming? Just then the phone began to ring. He jumped. Hooper? Or maybe Gaul – or one of his lackies – checking to see if he was home yet. He let it ring out, holding his breath. Time to go. Time to get the hell out of the place.

He locked up, alert to the sound of any footsteps, to any sound at all. Everything was quiet. Then he began to walk down the stairs, taking them as fast as he could with the heavy suitcase tugging on his arm. He'd head for the south coast, he thought, get a breath of sea air. Bournemouth, perhaps, or Torquay. A change of scene couldn't do any harm. And maybe he'd make a few new friends while he was there, pretty girls looking for a good time.

Eddie was starting to believe his luck might be changing as he lumbered down the last flight and hurried around the corner into the foyer. That was when the man stepped out straight in front of him. For a moment he thought it was Hooper and his blood turned to ice. Then, realising his mistake, he breathed out a sigh of relief and frowned.

'What the fuck are you doing here?'

It was the last thing Eddie ever said.

37

DS Will Sutherland watched as they put Chrissy Moss onto the stretcher and carried her towards the waiting ambulance. The girl, who was barely conscious, was in a bad way, severely beaten, punched, cut and probably raped. His face twisted, his hands clenching into two tight fists. He saw awful things every day, had become immune to most of it, but this was different. The sheer brutality of it appalled him. It was made worse, of course, by the fact he knew her, that she was Laura's daughter.

'Go with her,' he said to PC Jenny Walbroke. 'Stay at the hospital. See what she can remember.'

'Yes, guv.'

He shook his head. What kind of monster could do that to a kid? Well, he didn't have far to look for an answer. The body of Vic Hooper was lying only yards away. At least he was pretty sure it was him from all the tattoos. A knife was still clasped in his hand. Dr Larsen, the pathologist, was kneeling by the corpse, examining the spot where the skull had been caved in. The scene of crime officers were busy searching for the weapon.

Gaul came up the narrow path, nodded at Will and went over to talk to Larsen. A minute later he was back.

'Blow to the head with a blunt object.'

'I'd never have guessed,' Will said.

'What the fuck was she even doing here?'

'Who knows? Meeting someone, I imagine. Or maybe she just fancied a walk and had the misfortune to run into our friendly neighbourhood psychopath.'

'Who appears to have hit some misfortune of his own. Larsen doesn't reckon the girl could have done it. She wouldn't have had the strength.'

'So, a third party. A bloke. Someone who heard what was going on and came to the rescue.'

'Could have been a woman.'

Will shook his head. 'I don't think a woman would have left her in the state she was in. Or if she had it would only have been to run and get help. And it was a man who rang nine nine nine, asking for the police and an ambulance. I'm presuming it was the same person.'

'Which begs the question of where he's gone.' Gaul's gaze flitted over the old graves, as if he hoped one of the occupants might be kind enough to furnish him with an answer. 'Why disappear?'

'Could have just taken fright, I suppose, when he realised Hooper was dead. Got in a panic. Didn't fancy the possibility of a murder charge.'

'Do we know where the call came from?'

'A phone box at Kellston station. I've sent someone over to talk to the staff there, see if anyone saw him.'

Gaul pushed his hands into the pockets of his raincoat. 'The girl might be able to tell us more. Has her grandmother been informed?'

'Any minute now. I've arranged for her to be taken to the hospital.'

'You've been busy. That family hasn't had much luck recently.'

'I'm not sure how much luck has to do with it.' Will was running through recent events in his head, searching for connections. 'Anita Jakes, Marlon Pound. Chrissy had links to both those murders.'

'Not random, then. You think Hooper could have been following her?'

'I don't know. I had a quick word with the manager here and he didn't notice her pass the office, either on her own or with someone else. But he was busy, a meeting with a funeral director, and there are people coming and going all the time.'

'Other entrances, too. There's nothing to say she came in that way.'

There was a shout from behind and both men turned. An officer was pointing towards the ground. They walked over to join him and stared down at a block of sandstone about the size of a hand. The edge was smeared with blood and tissue and whatever else had been smashed out of Hooper's brains.

'Not much chance of any prints, I suppose?' Gaul asked.

'You suppose right, but we'll take it back to the lab and have a look.'

Will lifted his eyes and surveyed the area again. This was a lonely part of the cemetery, quiet and neglected. It was possible, he thought, that Chrissy Moss hadn't come here voluntarily. She could have been snatched off the main path, the knife put to her throat to silence her before the terrifying march to the place of her assault. Against that monster, she wouldn't have stood a chance.

The pathologist had finished and procedures were being put in place to move Hooper's body.

'What goes around, comes around, huh?' Gaul remarked.

'So they say.'

'Still, it saves us the bother of a trial. Someone did us a favour getting rid of that pile of scum.'

'There's always a bright side,' Will said drily.

A young uniformed PC was walking quickly towards them. He had a nervous expression, as though aware that the news he was about to deliver wouldn't be welcome. He stopped in front of Gaul and cleared his throat before speaking. 'Er, excuse me, guv, but I've been told to let you know that there's been an incident at Victoria Mansions.'

Gaul glared at him. 'And? Am I the only fuckin' cop at Cowan Road? Jesus. In case you haven't noticed,' he continued, flapping a hand towards Hooper's body, 'I'm kind of busy at the moment.'

'It's just . . .'

'Just what?' Gaul roared.

The young cop flinched, his cheeks flushing red. 'A man's been shot, guv, killed. Sergeant Beatty thought you'd want to know. The victim's name is Eddie Barr.'

38

Chrissy wasn't sure how long she'd been in the hospital. Five days, six? Maybe longer. She couldn't remember much at all about when she'd first been brought in. They had given her injections that took the pain away but made everything hazy, like she was drifting through mist. Now, as the world began to come back into focus, she could feel the throb in her mouth and the dull ache of her bruises. Every time she moved her body hurt.

The details of what had happened were slowly returning, drop by drop, as if her memory was drip-feeding her only as much as her mind could manage. She could be staring at the ceiling or be partway through a bowl of soup when something else would suddenly come back to her. If the choice had been hers, she would have turned off the tap and erased the attack from her head altogether.

And then there was Eddie. They hadn't told her at first, not until she'd started asking about him. It was the policewoman – Jenny, that was her name – who had broken the news as kindly

211

as she could. But no amount of kindness could blunt the sharp horror of the truth. *Eddie was dead.* At first Chrissy had been certain that the tattooed man must have killed him. That was the only thing that made sense. But he hadn't died at the cemetery; he'd been at the block of flats where he lived. How could that be? And Jenny had said that they didn't know, not yet, that they were still trying to piece it all together.

Chrissy was trying, too. She thought about Eddie a lot. He'd cared about her. He'd said so. He'd said she was pretty. But then she remembered him glancing over his shoulder as they walked along the path, uneasy, on edge, as though he suspected they were not alone. But that didn't mean ... except, it might.

She was in a small square side room with white walls and a sink in the corner. Sometimes she got scared at night when Nan and the policewoman weren't here. Even though she knew that Hooper was dead, she still imagined the door slowly opening and a tattooed arm appearing round the side of it. She would wake in a cold sweat and reach for the night light, trying to chase away the shadows and the fear.

Someone had saved her but nobody knew who. It seemed to Chrissy that no one knew very much, that everything was shrouded in mystery. She would try and recall the voice of the man – the man who'd smashed Hooper over the head – but it was only the words she remembered. She didn't reckon there'd been anything unusual about the accent: just local, London. She hadn't seen his face. Young, middle-aged, old? Tall, short? Jenny had gently probed, but Chrissy still wasn't able to help. He had saved her, that was all that mattered, and for this amazing act she'd always be grateful.

Nan tried her best to say the right things, to support and console her. 'You're not a victim, Chrissy Moss. You're a survivor. You'll get through this. I know you will.'

But Chrissy felt empty inside, hollowed out. She had only survived by chance, by the intervention of a stranger. Death had been ready to snatch her. At the moment she couldn't see a way through, couldn't see any light at the end of the tunnel. Perhaps that would change. Perhaps, when she was stronger, she would find the courage she was going to need to carry on.

39

1985

Ten years later

Chrissy put the loaded tray down on the counter, took out her order book and walked back across the café. It was Saturday, a quarter to three, and Connolly's was still packed. She'd been on her feet since seven and her legs were starting to ache. In another fifteen minutes her shift would be over, and it couldn't come soon enough.

Charlie Dunlap looked up as she approached, leaned back and folded his arms. "Bout time,' he said. 'You could die of bloody thirst in this place.'

'We're busy, in case you hadn't noticed.'

'Four brews,' he said. 'And if you could get 'em here before tomorrow, we'd be grateful.'

'Anything else?'

Charlie's gaze blatantly raked her body. 'Well, if you're offering, love. Be rude to say no, wouldn't it?'

Chrissy knew he was just showing off in front of his mates, hoping to get a rise out of her, but she didn't oblige. 'Four teas, then.'

As she was walking away, she heard him say, 'Jesus, I wouldn't touch that with a bargepole.'

Chrissy was passing a table with a half-drunk cup of coffee left on it. Six months ago, she'd have picked up that cup, strolled back and, regardless of the consequences, poured its contents over Charlie Dunlap's stupid head. Now, showing admirable restraint, she just kept on walking. She wasn't going to lower herself to his standards – and couldn't afford to lose this job.

When Chrissy looked back over the past ten years, much of it was a blur. She had taken refuge in oblivion, in drink and drugs and meaningless encounters, unable to deal with what had happened to her. She had played truant from school and left when she was sixteen without a single qualification. She'd had and been fired from countless jobs in shops and restaurants and cinemas and factories, often turning up late or not at all. The years had drifted away and, by the time she'd realised she was on the road to nowhere, half the eighties were already over. The royal wedding of Charles and Diana, the Falklands War, the assassination of John Lennon and God knows what else had come and gone, barely touching on her consciousness.

Chrissy collected the teas from the counter, put them on a tray and walked back along the aisle, taking care to avoid the shopping bags and random, outstretched legs. By now the four men were chatting up a couple of girls on a nearby table. Charlie was doing most of the talking. He had a high opinion of himself and liked to pretend he was some kind of gangster, although he was actually nothing more than a two-bit villain and wasn't even good at that. He had all the planning skills of a five-year-old and was in and out of jail like a yo-yo.

But the girls were lapping it up, giggling and flicking back their hair. They were young and impressionable and she had been the same once. She thought of Eddie Barr and her skin prickled. Perhaps something showed on her face, a spasm of disgust, because as she put the mugs on the table, Charlie stopped talking, looked at her and frowned.

'What's wrong with you?'

'Nothing.'

'Try telling your face that.' He grinned at the girls, always loving an audience. 'You just can't get the staff these days.'

'And here was me thinking exactly the same about the customers.'

'Ah, darlin',' he said, putting a hand to his chest. 'Don't go getting all jealous 'cause I'm chatting to some pretty girls. You know you love me really.'

The girls giggled again.

So much for female solidarity, Chrissy thought. Feminism hadn't made too many inroads into Kellston yet. She glanced at Charlie's brother George, who appeared to be fixated on her breasts. He was staring at them like he'd never seen a pair before.

'Something on your mind?'

George didn't reply.

'He's just admiring the view,' Charlie said. 'You should be flattered.'

'Well, hey, newsflash – I'm not.' There was something about George that always made her uneasy. She could deal with Charlie and all his Jack the Lad nonsense, but she never knew what was going on in his brother's head. There was a creepiness about him, a touch of the sinister. She'd heard he'd been lifted by the law over some young girl he'd tried to pick up, although Nan said he'd been released without charge. That didn't mean he was innocent, though.

Before her imagination could run riot, Chrissy threw George a disapproving glare and beat a hasty retreat. She was aware of his eyes following her as she went to take another customer's order. So what? She wasn't going to let it get to her, wasn't going to let *him* get to her. Sometimes when things, people, got under her skin, the old temptations rose up in her again. A part of her still yearned for the oblivion she'd nurtured for so long. It called to her like a siren, enticing her back.

Don't go there. Don't think about that.

Now that she was clean – and it had been a struggle – she intended to stay that way. Keeping busy was her main priority. The less time she had to think, the better. This evening she'd be working again at a cocktail bar in the West End. The basic wage wasn't much but the tips were good. It meant she could finally contribute to the household instead of relying on Nan for everything.

At three o'clock Chrissy went to the back room, grabbed her coat and bag, said her goodbyes and left the café. Charlie called out something as the door was closing but she didn't catch it. Probably for the best. She doubted it was anything complimentary. 'Bloody Dunlaps,' she muttered as she walked towards the Mansfield.

She had more than one reason to dislike the family. Uncle Pete was still doing time because Pat Dunlap, Jacko Layton and John Fielding had refused to admit that they'd been the ones to chuck Marlon Pound off the balcony. In court Larry Bates had proved to be an unreliable witness, frequently changing his story and contradicting himself. With the judge unable to decide who had done what, he'd sent all of them down, bar Larry, for fifteen long years.

Uncle Pete had to serve two-thirds of that sentence and his time was almost up. In a few months he'd be a free man again. Chrissy regretted not having visited as often as she should have over the past decade – she had been too drunk or too hungover or had just completely forgotten about it – and not just for his sake. Poor Nan had been forced to make the long journey to Parkhurst on her own, a miserable trip that included a ferry ride across the Solent.

Chrissy regretted a lot of things. She had viewed herself as weak and worthless, a victim, and had set out on the road to self-destruction. When she looked back on it all, she realised she'd just been finishing Hooper's job for him. He hadn't managed to kill her that day but he had murdered her spirit. She had let him take away ten years of her life. And not just him, of course; Eddie had played his part, too. She knew now that he must have conspired with Hooper, must have served her up as the sacrificial lamb.

Of course, she hadn't just woken up and seen the light. It had taken more than that to drag her out of the black hole of despair. She had come home one afternoon to find Nan in the kitchen, all red-eyed and tearful. It had sent a shock wave through her. Nan *never* cried. She was the strong one, the resilient one, the stalwart of the family. For her to break down meant that something seriously bad was going on.

'What's wrong? What's happened? Is it Uncle Pete?'

Nan had shaken her head.

Then, realising it was a Thursday, Chrissy's thoughts had turned to someone else. 'Is it Betty?' Nan's friend must be getting on now, in her eighties, if not older. 'Is she . . . ?'

But Nan had shaken her head again, pulled out a hankie from her sleeve and vigorously blown her nose. 'It's nothing. Don't take any notice. I'm fine, love, absolutely fine.'

Suddenly Chrissy had found herself seeing her nan like a stranger might: an exhausted woman, her face lined and weary, her life so full of troubles that the burden was too much. She realised what she had put her through and felt the awful anguish of being responsible for someone else's misery. It was all very well playing Russian roulette with your own existence, but when that was hurting someone else you had to stop, stand back and take a good, hard look at yourself.

And that was what Chrissy had done. Families were supposed to stick together, to watch out for one another, and it couldn't be a one-way street. The tears had welled up in her eyes and she had sat down beside Nan and taken her hand. 'It's my fault. I've been so bloody stupid. I'm sorry, I'm really sorry.'

'You've got nothing to be sorry for.'

Which was Nan all over, never blaming those closest to her, just trying to carry on as best she could. Even when it was killing her. All the times Chrissy had gone AWOL for days on end, off on some bender, oblivious to the desperation it caused, to the sleepless nights and constant worry. It must have been a nightmare. Chrissy had sworn she would change and, after a few minor setbacks, she had.

She felt the breeze on her face as she strolled towards the estate. It was a pleasant autumnal afternoon with some thin sunshine and just the hint of a nip in the air. There was no point in looking back. She had to keep focused, keep her gaze straight ahead. The future was what mattered, not the past. What she needed, she thought, was something to keep her away from temptation, a project or a cause to occupy her mind. Perhaps she could become a hunt saboteur or an animal rights activist or join the CND. Then another idea occurred to her. A name popped into her head from long ago: Luther Byrne. Yes, why not? Finding out what had really happened to her mother might bring her some closure. It didn't exactly fall into the category of not looking back, but it would give her purpose, and that was what she needed at the moment.

40

Cordelia's was situated in the heart of Soho. It was a popular cocktail bar, the type of place where half the customers – actors, pop stars, footballers – came to be seen, and the other half to people-watch. This wouldn't have made it any different to dozens of other West End bars if Terry Street hadn't added a frisson of danger to the mix. There was a rumour – a rumour he had cultivated himself – that the cream of London's underworld also drank here. It was surprising how many people, men and women, were fascinated by the idea of rubbing shoulders with the criminal classes. They might not have been so keen, Chrissy thought, if they'd grown up on the Mansfield.

With her shift about to start, she sat down, took her high heels out of her capacious handbag, slipped them on and winced. Despite soaking her feet for half an hour when she'd got back from Connolly's, her arches were still aching. Having to stand at the bus stop for twenty minutes hadn't helped matters, either. Still, hopefully it would be worth it when she counted out the tips at the end of the evening.

Chrissy stood up again and studied her reflection in the long mirror. Six months of clean living had made a substantial improvement to her appearance. Her skin was clear now and her long fair hair was glossy. There was no physical trace of the mess she had been, no outward indicator of the abuse she'd inflicted on her body. All that remained was the memory.

She smoothed out the front of her dress and checked her tights for ladders. Every waitress wore an identical little black dress, with just enough cleavage on show to titillate the men without offending the women. Flirting was a big part of the job and she didn't always find it easy. Having to look happy while some lecherous old geezer appraised her vital statistics was always a trial. And then there were the gropers. What *they* needed was a damn good slap, but this, unfortunately, was frowned upon. Giving them what they deserved was not in keeping with good customer service. She glanced up at the clock, pushed back her shoulders and prepared to do battle.

Cordelia's was busy and for the next three hours Chrissy didn't stop, ferrying trays of overpriced cocktails from the bar to the customers, collecting glasses, wiping down tables, emptying ashtrays, laughing at unfunny jokes and smiling until her face ached. She sashayed down the aisles, swinging her hips to avoid any amorous advances. Now, after three months, she was able to spot the individuals who were likely to have wandering hands and to make sure she was suitably alert.

At around ten o'clock she noticed DCI Gaul sitting with a group of men at one of the tables across the other side of the bar. Business or pleasure? Maybe, for him, there was never a dividing line. Soho was outside his official jurisdiction, but a minor detail like that wouldn't bother him. He was drinking an amaretto sour, smoking a fat cigar and looking pleased with himself. It wasn't the first time she'd seen him in here and he never paid for his drinks: Terry always picked up the tab.

Chrissy was glad she wasn't Gaul's waitress. It was hard to be polite to people you despised. Everyone knew he was bent but nothing was ever done about it. He was as bad as the men he locked up. She still held him at least partly responsible for Uncle Pete's long sentence. The police had known who'd actually killed Marlon – Larry Bates had grassed up the three men – but they'd still gone ahead with murder charges for the whole lot of them.

She didn't like it either that Gaul had been at the cemetery after Hooper had attacked her. He must have seen her lying there, half naked, beaten and raped. It made her feel revolted, humiliated, to think of his eyes on her. She was glad she hadn't had anything to do with him afterwards. With Hooper and Eddie Barr both dead, there hadn't been much investigating to be done, at least not for her case. And when it came to Eddie, she suspected no one really cared who'd put a bullet in him.

Chrissy tried to push the past out of her mind. It just churned up her guts and brought back too many feelings of helplessness. That wasn't the person she was any more. She could no longer allow herself to be defined by what had happened. Taking a deep breath, she painted a smile on her face and advanced on her next customers.

Twenty minutes later, when she was on her way to the back room to take a break, she ran into Terry Street. On impulse, she stopped and asked him if he'd ever heard of a man called Luther Byrne. 'He used to own a bar in Mayfair but it was ages ago. I mean, over twenty years.'

'Sorry, love, a bit before my time. Doesn't ring any bells.'

'Oh well, it doesn't matter.'

'Any reason why you're looking for him?'

'He was a friend of my mum's. I was hoping ... I just thought ... but he might not even be in London now. People move on, don't they? It's okay.'

'I could ask around, if you like.'

Chrissy hesitated. If Luther Byrne had been connected to her mum's death, she didn't want him to hear that she was on the hunt for him. DS Sutherland had said he was the kind of man she should stay away from. He'd warned her about Eddie, too, but she'd refused to listen. This time she was going to be more careful. 'No, you're all right. Thanks, though.'

Terry looked at her curiously. 'Why not?'

'I ... er ... I don't want to put you to any bother.'

'It's no bother,' he said.

And now Chrissy didn't know what to say. 'Erm ...'

'I can be discreet, if that's what you're worried about.'

Chrissy wasn't sure what constituted discreet in Terry's eyes. 'It's probably a waste of time.'

'Leave it with me,' he said, giving a nod. Then he strode off into the bar.

Chrissy went on to the back room, made herself a strong black coffee and sat down. Had she done the right thing in asking Terry? She mulled it over for a while but didn't come to any firm conclusions. Well, it was too late now. And sometimes you just had to be brave and go for it. Of course, if Luther had been connected to her mum's death, she could be storing up all sorts of trouble for herself. He wouldn't take kindly to her stirring up the past. Nan still seemed to believe it had been an accident, but maybe that was easier to deal with than the thought that her daughter could have been murdered.

When Chrissy went back to work, she saw Terry sitting at the table with Gaul. They looked very pally, laughing and joking together, and her earlier misgivings crept back. She didn't trust Gaul and didn't want him knowing any more of her business than he already did. It was all very well Terry *saying* he'd be discreet, but would he be? She was just a waitress in his bar, whereas Gaul was ... Well, she wasn't exactly sure of the nature of their relationship, but Terry didn't pick up the tab for just anyone.

Chrissy tried to get her mind back on the job. The latter part of the evening was always harder than the start. Too many drinks lowered inhibitions and heightened emotions. Harmless banter quickly flipped into something nastier, manners turned to aggression. It didn't take much for matters to escalate. And it wasn't just the men who were guilty of bad behaviour; there were some women who could pick a fight with a tablecloth.

Fortunately, Vinnie Keane was on hand to deal with the worst offenders. At over six foot five he towered over most people, a great bear of a man who rarely had to lift so much as a finger to persuade a punter that now was the time to go home. It took a brave person – or a foolish one – to argue with him.

Chrissy was always glad of his presence. Usually, like tonight, he was seated at the bar, keeping a surreptitious eye on the room. All it took was a quick wave or a quiet word in his ear if it looked like someone was about to kick off. Minutes later the offending party would be out of the door with the minimum of fuss. She had never heard him raise his voice or see him cause any kind of commotion.

Happily, the rest of Chrissy's shift passed without event. As the final customers left, she heaved a sigh of relief. She was bushed. It had been a long day and all she wanted was her bed. As she eased off her high heels, Terry put his head round the door.

'Chrissy? Could I have a quick word?'

'Sure.' She slipped on her flats and went out to meet him, away from the prying eyes and ears of the other girls.

'Luther Byrne,' he said.

'Oh, have you found out something?'

'You mind me asking why your mum wants to find him?'

'She doesn't,' Chrissy said. 'Sorry, I should have explained. *I'm* the one who's looking. Mum died a long time ago.' She wasn't sure how much to say. She didn't want to lie, but didn't want to tell the whole truth, either. 'I've heard he was a good friend of hers and just … I suppose I'd like to find out more about her. It's difficult talking to my nan; she still gets upset about it all.'

Terry nodded as though he understood. 'I'm not sure how helpful any of this is going to be. He did have a bar in Mayfair – it was called Rascals – but he sold it years ago. Someone reckons he had a gallery, selling paintings and the like, in the West End, but whether it's still there or not …'

'Do you know whereabouts?'

'Sorry, but you could always try the phone book.'

Chrissy hadn't thought of that. A private number might be ex-directory, but a business would be listed. 'I don't suppose you know what it was called?'

Terry shook his head. 'This Luther, was he ever in trouble with the law?'

'Is that what Gaul said?'

'Ah, so you know the chief inspector.'

'I live in Kellston. *Everyone* knows that man.' Then, concerned that the two of them might be mates and that what she'd said sounded disrespectful, she quickly tried to qualify the remark, 'Although I'm sure he's … I mean, I don't know him well, so …'

Amused by her attempts to backtrack, Terry grinned. 'You

don't have to be polite on my account. I can't stand the bastard. If I never saw him again it would be too soon.'

Chrissy was relieved not to have put her foot in it. 'So what did he say about Luther?'

'Not much, other than what I've told you, but I reckon there's no love lost between the two of them. He got kind of twitchy when the name came up, wanted to know why I was asking. I didn't tell him, of course, which pissed him off even more. Yeah, I reckon there's bad blood between him and Luther.'

'I'm starting to like Luther Byrne.'

'Yeah, well, I'd watch your step. Being on the wrong side of Gaul won't do you any favours.'

'I'm not looking for any trouble. Whatever went on between the two of them has nothing to do with me. I just want to find out about my mum.'

'I get that,' he said, 'but sometimes trouble can come looking for you.'

Out of the blue Chrissy thought of the cemetery in Kellston and a thin shiver ran through her.

'Are you all right?'

'Yes, fine.'

'I didn't mean to worry you about Gaul.'

'You didn't. You haven't. Honestly. I'm just a bit chilly.' She rubbed her bare arms, even though it was warm in the corridor.

Terry took a pack of cigarettes from his pocket, opened it and offered her one.

'No, ta. I've given up.'

He lit up, inhaled and blew out a gentle stream of smoke while he continued to gaze at her. 'Look, are you in a hurry or do you fancy going for a drink?'

Chrissy was surprised, even flattered by the invitation, and for a moment she was tempted. But it wasn't a good idea. For one, he was married – it was hardly fair on his wife – and for two she didn't need any messy complications in her life. However, she didn't want to cause offence so she tried to turn him down tactfully. 'Thanks, that's really nice of you but Nan's not been too well lately so I think I'd better get back. I don't like to leave her on her own for too long.'

Terry knew he was getting the brush-off but fortunately didn't get the hump about it. He was confident enough to take it on the chin: win some, lose some. 'Another time, perhaps.'

Chrissy smiled without committing herself. 'Good night, then. And thanks for the info on Luther.'

Fifteen minutes later, while she was waiting for the night bus – she wasn't going to waste her wages on a taxi – she wondered if she'd made the right decision. Perhaps she should have taken him up on the offer. Why not? He was attractive, smart, charming. It would have meant a bit of fun and excitement. But now wasn't a good time to get involved with anyone, never mind her married boss. And then there was the little matter of what he did for a living. Terry wasn't just the owner of some West End cocktail bar – he ran most of the East End and had done for years.

No, she'd made the right choice, the grown-up choice. She'd diced with danger for too long. Nothing good would come from a dalliance with Terry Street. She'd either end up out of a job or with a broken heart or, knowing her luck, both. 'Congratulations, Chrissy Moss,' she murmured. 'You've finally done something sensible.'

She was peering down the street, shifting from one foot to the other and willing the bus to come into view, when a dark-coloured car drew up beside her. The driver leaned across and pushed open the passenger door.

'You want a lift?'

Instinctively, she took a step back. Some chancer, she thought, on the pick-up. But then, as she bent down to look, Vinnie Keane's face came into view. Feeling slightly embarrassed about her hasty retreat, she quickly stepped forward again.

'Which way are you going?' she asked.

'Kellston, of course. Aren't you going home?'

Chrissy had a moment of hesitation – how well did she really know Vinnie? – but then instantly put aside her reservations. He'd never done anything to make her feel uncomfortable and she'd never heard the other girls say anything bad about him. She climbed into the car and fastened her seat belt.

'Ta,' she said. 'I didn't know you lived in Kellston.'

'Barley Road, the far side of the green.'

'Oh, nice.'

'Well, it's hardly Hyde Park but there are worse places.'

'Thanks for stopping. I was starting to think that bus was never going to come.'

'No problem. I wasn't just going to drive on by, was I? Not when we're going in the same direction.'

'How did you know? I mean, that I live in Kellston too?'

'I've seen you around.'

Chrissy sneaked a sideways glance at him. She wasn't even sure how old Vinnie was. Older than Terry, she reckoned. In his forties or thereabouts. But still in good condition. And although he didn't have Terry's striking good looks there was something interesting about his face. Lived-in was the phrase that came to mind. 'So how come I've never seen you?'

'I guess I'm just one of those blokes that nobody notices.'

'Because you're so small and insignificant?'

'Now you're just hurting my feelings.'

Chrissy liked a man with a sense of humour – the dryer the better. She saw him yawn and said, 'Tired?'

'Knackered. It's been a long night.'

'You're kidding me, right? You've got it easy. All you have to do is sit there. I'm on my feet for six hours.'

'Mental fatigue,' he said. 'It's very draining waiting for something to happen.'

'You should try a shift in my shoes.'

'I've never looked good in a little black dress.'

Chrissy raised her eyebrows. 'It's the high heels you need to worry about.'

'Thanks for the tip. And talking of which, I don't get many of those coming my way. No one cares about the poor schmuck sitting at the bar. At least you get some reward for all your hard work.'

Chrissy, relaxed now, smiled and gazed out through the windscreen. There was something altered about London in the early hours of the morning. It was never empty but it took on a different face, becoming a place inhabited by a normally hidden population of night workers, insomniacs and drifters. There were those with nowhere to go and those making their way home after clubs had closed or parties finished. A few skulking cats kept watch on their territory, eyes luminous in the darkness. She liked this other side of the city; once the daytime bustle was over, a kind of peace descended.

Vinnie was easy to talk to and the journey passed quickly. With so little traffic it didn't take long to get to Kellston. The streets were virtually empty, the lights off in most of the houses. Everyone was tucked up in bed and asleep.

'Where to?' he asked.

'The Mansfield. Carlton House. It's the first block you come to when you go through the gates.'

'Yeah, I know it.'

Two minutes later, Vinnie was pulling up beside the tower.

Chrissy took off her seatbelt, turned to him and said, 'Ta for the lift. I appreciate it.'

'Thanks for the company.'

She smiled, got out of the car, leaned down and said, 'Thanks again. See you next week.' As she walked up the path and went into the foyer, she was aware that the car hadn't moved off yet. She got into the lift, turned around and pressed the button. It was only then, as the lift doors were closing, that Vinnie finally left.

Chrissy liked that he'd waited until she was safely inside before going. It seemed a courteous, gentlemanly way to act. She was all for equality but it was nice to feel that someone was looking out for you. As the lift ascended, she wondered if he'd expected her to invite him in for a coffee or something, the something being a lot more than a hot drink. But he hadn't hinted at it or made any kind of move on her. In truth, she didn't have a clue about Vinnie's personal life, whether he had a wife or a girlfriend, and it was hardly the sort of question you could come straight out and ask without it seeming like you might have an interest yourself. And she didn't. Absolutely not. She was single, in control and staying that way. No complications, right? Although, having said that, Vinnie did have his good points . . .

41

There should have been better things Will Sutherland could be doing on a Sunday morning than sitting in his car in a Whitechapel back street, but it was a sad reflection on his life that there wasn't. No one to eat a late breakfast with, to pore over the newspapers with, to go back to bed and have lazy sex with. So he was working on the premise that doing something was better than doing nothing, even if that something was waiting for an unreliable snout called Ned Langley.

To his left was a row of boarded-up shops, to his right a derelict factory with crumbling blackened walls. The view was less than inspiring. The whole street had an abandoned, hopeless feel to it, as though everyone had just given up, moved out and left the place to decay. The pavements were cracked, the gutters swimming in litter. A grand advertisement for the state of the economy and the ruin of a community. The sky was low and grey, full of rain.

He checked his watch. Langley was ten minutes late but that wasn't unusual. The man did sod all and still didn't turn up when he said he would. Will decided to give him another five and that was it. There was a limit to his patience. Waiting around gave him time to think, which was precisely what he didn't want to do.

A couple of weeks earlier, he'd seen Belinda going into a cinema with her current husband and their two kids. He had watched from a distance, feeling oddly removed, like he was viewing his life as it might have been. Was he sorry for screwing up his marriage? He still felt ambivalent about it: half regretful, half relieved. The break-up, of course, had been entirely down to him. A brief affair – if it could even be called that – with Jenny Walbroke. He had thrown a grenade into his marriage, exploding every last remnant of trust.

Will wondered what Jenny was doing now. Last he'd heard, and that was a while ago, she was a DS in Manchester. Probably a DI by now. She was the ambitious sort, and good at her job. What she wasn't so good at was spotting seriously bad relationship material. He'd let her down, unsurprisingly, screwing things up like he always did. He rolled his eyes and sighed. But it was water under the bridge, past history; there was no point in dwelling on it.

Eventually, just as he was about to call it a day, Will glanced in the rear-view mirror and saw Ned Langley approaching. The man couldn't have looked shiftier if he'd tried: he was walking fast, shoulders hunched, his head going from side to side as he nervously examined every doorway, every blank window, for potential witnesses. Informing was a risky business – the consequences, if caught, would be dire – but it could be lucrative too if the information was sound. Langley didn't just do it for the money, though; he was one of those blokes with a chip on his shoulder, the sort who felt ill-used by the world and needed the satisfaction of some underhand redress.

When Langley reached the car, he had one final look round before getting in.

'Morning, Mr Sutherland.'

'Barely,' Will replied, gazing pointedly at his watch. 'Didn't we say eleven-thirty?'

'Yeah, sorry about that. A bit of business I needed to attend to.'

Will glared at him. Langley was in his late fifties, tall and thin with a narrow, unshaven face and wary eyes. His clothes were shabby and he smelled like he hadn't had a wash in a week. Will cracked the window open an inch to let in some slightly fresher air. 'We're all busy,' he said. 'You think I haven't got more important things to do than hang around here all day?'

'You know what them buses are like, Mr Sutherland. I had to wait bleedin' ages.'

'So what have you got for me?'

Langley shifted in his seat, looked over his shoulder and then back at Will. He spoke quickly and quietly as though afraid that someone might overhear. 'Warehouse job on the Raleigh Industrial. One of them units. Next Thursday morning, early hours. It's that Pritchard mob.'

'Which unit?'

'One full of electricals is all I know. TVs, videos, irons and the like. Stuff that's easy to shift down the pub. Shouldn't be too hard to figure out.'

'They got an inside man?'

'Nah, they reckon the guard's a lazy fucker – spends most of his shift pissed or asleep. Easy to take by surprise.'

'Any weapons?'

'Not shooters, if that's what you mean. Just the usual. Couple of bats in case the guard plays up.'

'Okay. Well, give me a bell if you hear anything else before Thursday.'

'I'll do that, guvnor.'

Will waited for Langley to leave but he didn't. 'You know the deal, Ned. If the job comes off, you'll get paid. Otherwise . . .'

'Nah, it ain't that.'

'What is it, then? You got something else for me?'

'It's just a whisper, somethin' I heard.'

'I can get rumours down the pub.'

Langley hesitated as if in two minds whether to share the information. He ran a hand over his stubbly chin. 'It's about that George Dunlap.'

'What about him?'

Another pause before he continued. 'That girl who went missing. Years back. You know, Dawn somethin'?'

'Dawn Kearns?'

'Yeah, that's the one. There's people saying he might have had somethin' to do with it.'

'Dunlap was just a kid back then.'

Langley threw him a sceptical glance. 'Not that young. Thirteen or so. He weren't a toddler or nothin'. Anyway, you reckon kids aren't capable of doing bad stuff?'

Will hadn't thought about Dawn Kearns in a long time. The search for her had continued for a while but eventually petered out. His own opinion, not that anyone was interested, was that Vic Hooper had killed her and disposed of the body. It would explain why the bastard had gone after Chrissy Moss, believing perhaps that she knew more than she did.

'And you lot picked him up, right? Recent like,' Langley continued. 'Trying to talk that girl into getting in his car. Scared the poor kid half to death. What grown man does that to a twelve-year-old? It ain't natural, is it? And who's to say it ain't the first time?'

It was true that Dunlap had been pulled in for questioning

a fortnight earlier over offering a lift to a girl called Chantelle Scott. She had taken fright and run away. Later, her mother had taken her to Cowan Road to report the incident. George Dunlap's response was that it had been raining and he recognised Chantelle from the estate. 'It was pissing down and she was getting soaked. I was just trying to do her a favour. I thought she knew me but ... Shit, I didn't mean to scare the kid.'

Dunlap had been given a warning, and advised to keep his favours to himself in future. At the time it had been hard to tell whether the incident had been a genuine misunderstanding or something more sinister. George, like his brother, had form for ABH, petty theft and burglary, but nothing of a sexual nature. However, just because it had never been flagged up, didn't mean it hadn't happened.

Langley got out of the car, bent down and muttered, 'No smoke without fire. That's all I'm saying.'

'The mantra of the lynch mob.'

'Huh?'

'Never mind,' Will said. 'Take it easy. I'll see you around.'

Langley shut the door and hurried off down the street, looking as furtive as when he'd arrived, his head still swivelling from side to side.

Will started up the engine while he turned things over in his mind. It was true that the Dunlaps had passed by the three girls on the day of Dawn's disappearance, but then so had lots of people. Because the focus had been on Marlon Pound and Hooper, nobody had looked that closely at the brothers or the other kids. What if that had been a big mistake?

As he wound his way through the Whitechapel streets, he weighed up the odds of George Dunlap having being involved. The bloke wasn't what you'd call law-abiding, but that didn't make him guilty. The whisper Langley had heard could easily

235

have come from someone trying to cause trouble, someone with a grudge, someone who'd heard about the Chantelle business and decided to link it to the Dawn Kearns case. Maybe Langley had even made it up himself, unable to resist the temptation to drop a little poison in Will's ear.

The more he thought about it, the more inclined he was to dismiss the connection. It wasn't the actual killing that he found impossible to believe – these things happened – but how two young teenage boys could dispose of a body so efficiently that it still hadn't been found to this day. Unless ... well, unless they'd had some help. Their father, Pat Dunlap, for example, who was currently serving out a sentence for the cold-blooded murder of Marlon Pound. If he was capable of that, then what else was he capable of?

Will drummed his fingers on the steering wheel while he contemplated this. Not impossible, he decided. Perhaps he'd call in at Cowan Road, pull the file on the Kearns case and take another look. He yawned, shook his head. 'The trouble with you, Sutherland,' he murmured, 'is that you have too much time on your hands.'

42

When Chrissy got back from Patel's, she found Nan sitting in the kitchen sorting through a pile of paperwork. She dropped the *News of the World* on the table, switched on the kettle and said, 'What are you doing?'

'Looking at these forms for housing. Your uncle's going to need somewhere to live when he comes out.'

'He can always stay here for a while.'

'You know what he's like: if he moves back in, he'll never move out again. No, he needs his own flat. There's not space here for the three of us. You shouldn't have to give up your room, and I don't want him kipping on the sofa making the place look untidy.'

'You want a hand? Those forms can be complicated. I'll just make a brew and then we can look at them together.'

'You're all right, love. Frank said he'd pop round later and help me fill them out.'

'Frank?'

'Frank Yates.'

'Since when did you two get so pally? I thought you didn't like him. You called him a leftie do-gooder.'

'I never said that.' Nan thought about it. 'Well, I might have done, but perhaps I was a bit hasty. I mean, he's young, isn't he, to be a councillor? But we had a chat at the residents' meeting and I mentioned your Uncle Pete's situation and he said there's plenty of flats empty on the estate.'

'Well, it's not like people are queuing up to live here.'

'Exactly. So why can't my Pete have a flat? Anyway, Frank said he'd help all he could, that there's ways and means when it comes to these applications. You have to know what to write.'

While Chrissy made the tea, she wondered why Frank had ever come back to the Mansfield. He'd gone off to one of those fancy universities and got himself a good degree in economics or whatever. If he had any sense, he'd be working in the City now, raking it in like all those wheeler-dealer wide boys, instead of attempting to solve all the probably unsolvable problems of Kellston. Still, she supposed she had to give him credit for trying.

'He reckons there's a good chance, then?'

'Wouldn't bother otherwise, would he?' Nan said. 'And it'll be good for your Uncle Pete to have a place of his own. It can be hard when you first come out, hard to adjust. If he wants some company, he'll know where we are.'

'You're worried about him.'

'Course not,' Nan said brusquely. 'He'll be fine once he's settled.'

But Chrissy knew she was worried, and not just about Uncle Pete settling back into normal civvy life. There'd be other things to deal with, too. Most of the men who'd been convicted with him would also be returning to the Mansfield. There'd be scores to settle, perhaps, over who'd said what in court, and who'd taken the blame for things they hadn't done. She put the two mugs of tea on the table, pulled out a chair and sat down. 'Yeah, he'll be fine.'

'Frank reckons we might get a grant for carpets and a bit of furniture. And there's always the charity shops for the rest. We'll soon make it nice and comfortable.'

'I can help out,' Chrissy said. 'I can buy some stuff.'

'You've not got money to burn.'

'I wouldn't be burning it, would I? I'm earning now; I've got my wage from the caff, and some decent tips from Cordelia's. We can go shopping together when the flat comes through.'

Nan looked like she was going to raise more objections but then, after mentally reviewing her finances, perhaps, just smiled and reached out to pat her hand. 'Ta, love. You're a good girl.'

Not that good, Chrissy thought, thinking of all the heartache she'd caused. She still had a lot of making up to do and this was just the start. 'Anyway, it's good of Frank to give up his time, especially on a Sunday. Nice of him.'

'It is,' Nan agreed. 'He's a decent sort. There's not many who give a damn about the people on this estate. He's got a good heart. And pleasant, too, always a kind word for everyone.' She gave Chrissy a quick, almost sly look. 'Yes, he'd be quite a catch for the right girl. You could do a lot worse.'

Chrissy spluttered out a mouthful of tea. 'What? Where did that come from?'

'He likes you.'

'No, he doesn't. I haven't spoken to him in years. I'm barely on nodding terms with the bloke.'

'Well, he's definitely got a soft spot for you. Whenever I mention your name, he gets all tense and flushed, doesn't know where to put himself.'

'You're imagining it.'

'What's wrong with him?'

'I'm not saying there's anything wrong but ...' Chrissy still thought of Frank as that awkward, touchy, brooding boy she'd known at school. Somehow, she couldn't see him as a grown man.

'But what?'

'Stop trying to matchmake. You're completely wrong.' Chrissy had a sudden vivid memory of Frank standing in the school yard ten years ago, his face burning with anger. *You calling me a liar?* 'God, the only reason he gets all tense is because he *doesn't* like me.'

'Have it your own way,' Nan said smugly.

Chrissy wondered where Nan got her ideas from. It was probably just wishful thinking. Her grandmother was of a generation which still considered – despite overwhelming evidence to the contrary – that being married was the ideal state for any woman. 'I wouldn't go buying a new hat just yet.'

Nan gave a rueful shake of the head. 'You're getting on, you know. If you're not careful, you'll end up on the shelf.'

'I'm twenty-four, Nan. And maybe I don't mind being on the shelf.'

'You'll find someone, love, and then you'll think different.'

Chrissy raised her eyebrows but said nothing. The truth was that she hadn't ever had a proper boyfriend, not anyone steady. She'd had flings, brief liaisons, one-night stands – all when she was numbed by drugs or booze – but never got close to any real kind of intimacy. To achieve that she would have to put her trust in a man, and that was something she could never do.

'Pass the paper over, will you?' Nan said, putting aside the housing forms. 'I need some good gossip.'

Chrissy gave her the newspaper, watched her turn the pages for a minute, then finished her tea and went to the loo. On the way back she passed the little cupboard in the hall with the phone on it. Inside the cupboard was the phone directory and a copy of Yellow Pages. She popped her head round the living room door – from here she had a clear view of the kitchen – and checked that Nan was still absorbed in the *News of the World*. Then she quietly retreated back into the hall.

Quickly she retrieved the phone directory and made straight for the end of the Bs. There were pages of them. Eventually she found Byrne – there were a fair few of these, too – and ran her finger down the list until she came to L. Next, next, next . . . and suddenly there it was: Byrne, Luther, with an address in Highgate. 48 Coleridge Avenue. Chrissy stared, almost startled by the ease with which she'd found it. It had to be him, didn't it? She couldn't imagine there being more than one Luther Byrne in London. Well, unless it was his father or his son.

There was a knock on the door and Chrissy jumped. As she shoved the directory back into the cupboard, she called out, 'I'll get it, Nan.'

She opened the door to find Frank Yates standing there. He was dressed casually in jeans and a shirt, and had one of those zip-up leather document holders under his arm.

'Hi,' she said.

'Hello, Chrissy. Is your grandmother in?'

'Sure. Come in. She's in the kitchen.' As she led him through the living room, she said, 'Thanks for doing this. It's good of you.'

'No problem. How is Pete these days?'

'All right, I guess. Looking forward to getting out.'

'It's been a long time.'

Chrissy glanced over her shoulder. 'It has.' She took the opportunity to search for any signs of awkwardness, but he seemed completely at ease and not the slightest bit flustered.

There, she'd been right all along. Nan was way off the mark. Frank had as much interest in her as she had in him.

'Nan, it's Frank.'

Nan was already on her feet, fussing around, putting the kettle back on and organising mugs. 'You'll have a brew, won't you, Frank?'

'Thanks, Mrs Moss. I'd love one.'

'Oh, call me Elsie. We don't stand on ceremony here. You sit yourself down. I'll only be two ticks.'

'I'll leave you to it then,' Chrissy said.

'Why don't you stay?' Nan asked. 'Have a cuppa with me and Frank.'

But Chrissy wasn't falling for that one. She didn't trust Nan not to make some clumsy attempt to try and fix her up with him. How embarrassing would that be? 'I've just had one. Sorry, I've got things to do.'

'What things?'

'I'll see you later.'

Chrissy was out the front door before any further interrogation could take place. She had nothing against Frank, and he was good-looking enough, if you liked that kind of thing: intense brown eyes, floppy brown hair, an almost sulky kind of mouth. But he was one of those driven types, she thought, always having to be doing something. Exhausting. It was Nan, she suspected, who had the soft spot, although not in a romantic way; maybe she just wished that her own son was more like him.

Chrissy took the lift down to the ground floor, walked to the main gate and then strolled down Mansfield Road and along the high street to the green. It was one of those grey drizzly days, where the sky can't quite decide whether it wants to rain properly or not. She breathed in the London air, relieved to be out of the flat. She had needed to escape from Nan's attempts to

242

play Cupid, but also wanted to be alone to think about Luther and what she was going to do next.

Now she had his phone number – or probably did – she could easily ring him up. But what if he just fobbed her off, or didn't want to talk? What if he hung up on her? What if his wife answered – he could easily have a wife – and asked her what it was all about? What was she supposed to do then? If she refused to say, it could seem suspicious, but she didn't want to have to explain to someone else before she'd even spoken to him.

Chrissy began to walk in a diagonal line across the green, ignoring the paths. The grass was soft and springy under her feet. It would be better if she could speak to Luther face to face, but she could hardly just turn up at his house. That would be intrusive, even a bit weird. And she could hit the same problem with the wife. No, she needed a better plan. Perhaps, if he still had the gallery, she could go and speak to him there. This seemed a more sensible idea and she resolved to check out the Yellow Pages when she got back.

Because she was in no hurry to get home – she wanted to be sure Frank Yates had gone first – she carried on walking until she was almost at Barley Road. Here she stopped and stared at the terrace of three-storey houses, idly wondering which flat was Vinnie's. Her gaze travelled from left to right, examining the curtains at the windows and trying to decide which ones were most likely to be his. Then she got to thinking how mortifying it would be if Vinnie looked out and saw her standing there like some crazy stalker. Quickly she turned around and strode back the way she'd come.

When she came to the wooden bench near the high street, she pulled out a tissue from her pocket and wiped the rain off the seat before sitting down. It was both exciting and nerve-racking knowing that she could be about to make contact with

Luther Byrne. What would he be like? What would he be able to tell her? Perhaps, finally, she would discover the truth about her mother's death. A note of caution sounded in her head: the truth could be hard to deal with, painful and upsetting. And what if Luther was more enemy than friend? She had to consider that, too. If that was the case, he wouldn't be happy about her showing up out of the blue. But she refused to listen to her own objections. Yes, there could be trouble but she'd cross that bridge when she came to it.

43

It was Wednesday before Chrissy got her next day off. Once Nan had left for work, she got up, had some breakfast and reviewed her plan of action. It had taken a while but she'd eventually found what she was looking for in the Yellow Pages. The Byrne Gallery was located in Bond Street, one of the fanciest parts of the West End, and that's where she was going this morning. Well, if she didn't lose her nerve beforehand. It was such a big step, momentous, and she didn't want to make a mess of it.

She dressed carefully, choosing a smart navy suit and a cream blouse. Then came hair and make-up: hair neatly swept up in a bun, make-up subtle. First impressions could count for a lot and she wanted to be taken seriously. That fear still niggled in the back of her mind – what if Luther *was* some kind of gangster? – but she couldn't afford to dwell on it. And anyway, she'd be safe enough in the gallery. It was a public place and there'd be other people around.

Chrissy was still telling herself this as she sat on the bus heading for Oxford Circus. She was also trying to work out how to introduce herself when she got to the gallery. If she was unprepared, the words were likely to come out in a jumble, a garbled version of what she really wanted to say. She tried out various sentences and eventually settled on, 'Hello, my name's Chrissy Moss. I believe you knew my mother, Laura.' And then he would say something back and, hopefully, things would flow from there.

The bus trundled on, the streets becoming busier as the West End approached. She fidgeted, crossed her legs and uncrossed them. Butterflies invaded her stomach. She tried to visualise Luther in her head but had nothing to go on other than her imagination. Nan wouldn't be happy if she knew what she was doing, but she couldn't let that influence her. Still, it was something else to add to that long list of things to feel guilty about.

By the time she got off the bus, her heart was starting to race. Instantly, she was absorbed into the crowd like a drop of water into a rushing river. She walked at speed along Oxford Street, carried by the current, sliding one way and then another to avoid collisions. There were people all around her, voices, the roar of traffic. Smells invaded her nose: sweat and perfume, fag smoke, exhaust fumes.

She swung left into New Bond Street, where the crowd thinned out and there was more space to move. Now, feeling a sudden reluctance to reach her destination, she slowed down and began to examine the window displays. The shops here were exclusive, pricey, full of beautiful clothes, jewellery and antiques. How could anyone afford such luxuries? It was another world, a place for the rich and privileged.

Eventually she arrived at where she was supposed to be. The Byrne Gallery was double-fronted, its wide windows framing a selection of gilt-framed paintings. She didn't know anything about art but presumed they must be good if they were being sold in Bond Street. Whilst pretending to examine them, she shifted her gaze to the interior where a blond-haired, smartly dressed man was sitting behind a desk with a phone pinned to his ear. Too young to be Luther, she thought. This man was only in his late twenties.

Furtively, she checked out the rest of the gallery but there was no one else in sight. That didn't mean Luther wasn't there, though. There must be back rooms and offices, places where pictures were stored and deals were made. Even a kitchen where you could make a cup of tea. All she had to do was go in and ask for Luther Byrne. It was easy, simple – so why were her feet rooted to the spot?

She stood staring intently at one of the paintings – a smudgy seascape in shades of grey and blue – while she tried to persuade her legs to move. The door was only a few steps away. *Just do it.* She could hear the quickness of her own breath, feel the weight of expectation in her chest. *Come on.* Then, before her nerve failed her completely, she forced her body into action, sidled along the pavement, pushed open the door and went inside.

The man, who was just putting down the phone, looked up at her and smiled. 'Good morning.'

'Hello,' she said. 'Is Mr Byrne here, please? Mr *Luther* Byrne.'

'Sorry, he's not in today. Can I help you at all?'

Disappointment coursed through her. Although this was partly mitigated by the knowledge of having found the right place, her face still fell. 'Erm, no, thank you. I don't think so.'

'Were you interested in something in particular?'

Chrissy shook her head. 'Could you tell me when he'll be in again?'

'Tomorrow, I should imagine.'

'Oh, right.' That was no good for Chrissy. She'd be at work tomorrow, and by the time she finished and caught a bus to the West End, the gallery would be closed. It would be another week before she'd be able to try again. She sighed and was about to leave when the man said something unexpected.

'It's not about the job, is it? Did the agency send you here? I told them Mr Byrne was interviewing at home.'

Chrissy only had seconds to respond and did so before she'd even thought about it. 'In Highgate?' she said, as if she knew what he was talking about.

'Yes, at the house.'

'Ah, I see. I'm at the wrong place.'

'I don't understand why they sent you here. I told them quite clearly where to send all the applicants.'

'It was probably my mistake,' Chrissy said. 'It was all a bit last minute. I may have got confused. Will he be interviewing all day?'

'It depends on whether he finds someone suitable or not.'

'Of course.' An idea was forming in Chrissy's head. Perhaps, rather than rushing in and immediately telling Luther Byrne who she was, she should take some time to get to know him first. What if those rumours about his gangster past were true? It would be better, surely, if her approach was a more cautious one. With no clue as to what the job was – something domestic, she presumed, if he was interviewing at home – she tried some fishing. 'Do you think I'd be suitable?'

He studied her for a moment, a smile playing around his lips. 'Well, let me see. Are you cool under pressure, thick-skinned, infinitely patient?'

'Ice cold,' she said. 'With the patience of a saint.'

'Then you're in with a chance.'

'Good,' she said, although this didn't bring her any closer to figuring out what the job actually was.

'Are you sure you want it?'

248

'Why not?'

The man leaned back and folded his arms across his chest. He was bored, she suspected – the gallery was empty – and wasn't displeased to have someone to pass the time with. 'Between you and me, Mrs Byrne isn't the easiest woman in the world.'

'His wife?'

'No, his mother, his widowed mother. And this is the third time he's had to advertise in as many months. They don't stay, you see. They say they will but . . . ' He stopped and raised his hand to his mouth. 'I shouldn't really be telling you all this.'

'It's all right. I won't say a word, I promise.'

But he wouldn't be drawn any further. 'My lips are sealed. Mr Byrne wouldn't be happy if he knew I'd been scaring off the applicants.'

'Okay,' she said. 'I'd better get to Highgate, then.'

'Good luck.'

'Thanks.'

Chrissy gave him a wave as she left the gallery. She walked back towards Oxford Circus, full of purpose. An opportunity had been thrown into her lap, so she might as well take it. *When one door closes, another one opens.* That was another of Nan's infinite sayings. And maybe on this occasion it was absolutely true.

44

As the Underground train hurtled through the tunnel, Chrissy pondered on the wisdom of what she was doing. It was tricky turning up for an interview when you didn't even know what the job was. Housekeeper, cook, cleaner? When you were rich you could afford to employ other people to run around after you. What if it was a nurse he was looking for, a carer for his mother? It would be hard to explain why she was applying for something she had absolutely no qualifications for. But no, it didn't matter; she would just say there must have been some kind of misunderstanding with the agency.

Anyway, she would get the measure of Luther Byrne during the interview, and then, when she was deemed unsuitable for the post, she would casually say as she was leaving, 'You're not the Luther Byrne who used to own Rascals, are you?' And he would say 'Yes', and she would say, 'What a coincidence! My mother used to work there.' Then it would seem like chance that they'd met, rather than her having actively sought him out.

Chrissy changed trains at Camden and caught the High

Barnet branch of the Northern line. The stops went by: Kentish Town, Tufnell Park, Archway, until they reached Highgate. She got off and took the escalator up to the ticket hall, where she asked for directions to Coleridge Avenue.

From the Tube she had a fifteen-minute walk to the Byrne residence. She had never been to Highgate before and its greenness surprised her. It didn't feel like London at all, at least not the London she knew. This place was clean and leafy and the air smelled different. It occurred to her as she strolled through the quiet streets that her mother may have taken the same route and seen more or less the same things.

When she reached the house, she stopped to take a good look at it. It was an imposing, red brick building, three storeys high, with the kind of windows that are divided into little squares of glass. There was colour in the top panes of the windows, bright, gem-like gleams of red and blue and yellow. A vine snaked across the left side of the house, and a pair of cream pillars flanked the front porch.

Before her nerves could take hold again, she pushed open the gate, walked up the drive, took a breath and pressed the bell. After thirty seconds or so the door was answered by a plump, middle-aged woman wearing a black dress and a white apron. The housekeeper, she presumed.

'Hello. I'm here to see Mr Byrne about the job.'

The woman's eyebrows shifted up as if what she saw didn't quite tally with what she was hearing. 'The job?' she repeated. 'Are you sure, only . . . Never mind, I suppose you'd better come in.'

None of this was very reassuring to Chrissy. Not that she wanted the job, but she appeared to have been found wanting even before she'd crossed the threshold. She went inside, entering a hall that was bigger than her living room at home. It was cool here, but gloomy. The walls were panelled in wood, and the only natural light came from a single narrow window.

'Wait here,' the woman said, before disappearing along a corridor that led off to the right.

Chrissy did as she was told. She looked around. She examined the parquet floor, the ceiling, the grandfather clock that claimed it was ten to eleven but which seemed to be ticking with infinite slowness. There was a pedestal with a glass dome on top of it. The dome contained a stuffed fox, its fake eyes gleaming, its expression quizzical, as though it was puzzled as to how it had ended up in this alien place. She wrinkled her nose, feeling sorry for the creature.

Several minutes passed. Should she sit down? If Mr Byrne was interviewing someone else, she might have to wait a while. There were two chairs near the door and both of them looked old, antique, like they were worth a few bob. She gave one a gentle prod but was afraid to sit on it in case it collapsed beneath her.

The hands on the clock shifted to eleven and she began to wonder if she'd been forgotten. She cleared her throat, the rasp sounding unnaturally loud in the echoey hall. She looked left and right along the length of the corridors, where numerous rooms were located, all with their doors closed. Where was everyone? Doubts were starting to creep into her head again, fierce worries that this was all a big mistake.

Then suddenly there was movement, the sound of a door opening, of heavy footsteps coming towards her. Quickly she retreated. She straightened her shoulders, linked her hands behind her back and tried to look professional. Her first impressions of Luther Byrne were good. The man who came around the corner was in his late fifties, grey-haired, about five foot nine, with a pleasant face, a neat beard and deep-set, intelligent eyes. But these favourable impressions didn't last for long.

He stopped dead, stared at her, scowled and said, 'For God's sake. No, no, you're not suitable at all.'

'I don't understand,' Chrissy replied, startled by the outburst.

'Didn't the agency tell you? Over fifty, I said. The woman has to be over fifty.'

Because Chrissy couldn't think of anything else to say she answered simply, 'Why?'

Before Luther could respond, another voice, cut-glass and female, came from behind him. 'Why indeed? It's an excellent question.'

Chrissy peered round Luther to see an elderly woman leaning on a stick. Although old – she must have been eighty if she was a day – her face was still full of life. She had strong features, a firm mouth, and was impeccably dressed in a pale mauve twin-set that was probably cashmere.

'For heaven's sake, Mother, what have you got in common with some chit of a girl?'

'And what have I got in common with all the dull, dreary women that you usually employ? If you're hoping to bore me to death, you're going the right way about it. Now, seeing as she's taken the trouble to come here, I think the least we can do is to give her a chance.'

Luther gave a snort. 'Fine, have it your own way.' He looked at Chrissy and said, 'In the drawing room, then. I take it you have a name?'

'Christine,' she said. Then, concerned that the surname Moss might ring a few bells in his head, she plucked a different one out of the air. 'Christine Cope.' Betty, she was sure, wouldn't mind her having it on temporary loan.

'I don't recall any Cope on the list the agency sent.'

'It was rather last minute,' Chrissy said.

'Last minute? How did that come about, exactly? I still don't understand why they even sent you. I specifically told them—'

'Oh, please, Luther,' Mrs Byrne interrupted. 'Can we save the interrogation until we're all sitting down?'

As they walked towards the drawing room, Chrissy felt the simmering tension between mother and son. An ongoing clash of wills. She glanced at each of them in turn. Luther's eyes were full of irritation, his mother's full of triumph.

45

The drawing room was light and spacious, but furnished in a style that belonged to another age. Chrissy quickly looked around. Everything was elegant, beautiful, as perfect as the day it had been bought – and that must have been a hundred years ago. It was like a room caught in time, like something from one of those stately homes she had seen in magazines while she was waiting at the dentist. There were tall bookcases and paintings on the walls. Beyond the windows was a well-tended garden filled with trees and shrubs. A late-blooming rose, pink and blowsy, lifted its face towards the sky.

Everyone sat down. Chrissy could feel her heart beating in her chest, and wondered how long it would be before her lack of suitability was discovered. She had only got this far because Mrs Byrne had wanted to spite her son. The old lady was intriguing but formidable; she had an imperious quality, as though she was used to giving orders and having them obeyed.

Luther Byrne crossed one elegant leg over another, gazed at Chrissy and asked in a dry voice, 'So, Miss Cope, what makes you think you would make a good companion for my mother?'

Chrissy tried not to look like a rabbit caught in headlights. A companion? She hadn't been expecting that and wasn't entirely sure what it entailed. Just hanging out with her? Talking to her, taking her places? Now she understood why Luther had been so incredulous. But a desire to prove him wrong rose up in her. 'I suppose it does seem odd to you, with the age difference and everything, but I was raised by my grandmother and enjoy the company of older women. Nan always says that it does her good having someone young to chat to.'

'Yes,' Luther said. 'That's all very well, but do you know anything about art, about literature?'

'Not really,' Chrissy said.

'Politics? Current affairs?'

'Erm . . .'

Luther gave a thin smile. 'I take it you *can* read?'

'Of course,' Chrissy said, her hackles rising.

'My mother's eyesight is very bad. She needs someone who can read to her in a competent fashion.'

'I can do that.'

Mrs Byrne remained silent, her head cocked slightly to one side, her gaze fixed on Chrissy. Her face was impassive and it was impossible to tell what she was thinking.

Luther's expression was one of bored disdain. 'Tell us a bit about yourself, Miss Cope.'

'As I said, I was raised by my grandmother. My mother died when I was young. I'm twenty-four and I live in the East End, near Shoreditch. I'm hard-working, loyal and honest. I'm working in a café at the moment, but I'm looking for something a little more . . . interesting.'

'And what did you do before the café?'

Chrissy thought back to all those jobs she'd managed to lose and thought it best to keep quiet about them. Instead, on the spur of the moment, she came up with what she hoped would be a plausible explanation for the gap in her employment history. 'Unfortunately, Nan's not been too well for the last few years. I've been taking care of her until recently.'

Finally, Mrs Byrne spoke again. 'Is she dead?'

The bluntness of the query caught Chrissy off guard. She felt guilty enough foisting a mystery illness on Nan without killing her off too. 'Oh, no, but she's . . . she's had to go into a nursing home. I still visit, though, of course.'

Mrs Byrne leaned forward and peered at Chrissy through pale eyes. 'What does she look like, Luther?'

Luther stared at Chrissy for a moment. 'Young,' he said. 'Slim, fair hair.'

'What colour are her eyes?'

Chrissy, who found it objectionable being talked about as though she wasn't there, said, 'Grey. Her eyes are grey. She's five foot four, eight stone, and she's wearing a navy suit and white blouse. She isn't beautiful but she's passably attractive when she makes the effort.'

There was a visible twitch at the corners of Mrs Byrne's lips, although it was hard to tell if this was the result of amusement or displeasure. Chrissy didn't much care. She didn't like being patronised by these people, even if they were rich as Croesus. Already she had learned enough to know that Luther was not the approachable sort – there wouldn't be any cosy chat about her mum – and that Mrs Byrne was either extremely rude or very eccentric. It was better, she decided, to make her excuses and leave.

Chrissy rose to her feet. 'Look, I can see you don't think I'm right for the position. That's fine. I don't want to waste any more of your time.'

Luther stood up too, looking relieved. 'I'll get Mrs Parry to show you out.'

But Mrs Byrne had other ideas. 'You know, I think we'll give her a try. Make the arrangements, Luther. She can start on Monday.'

'Mother!'

'Why not? She can't be any worse than the others. Dolts or harridans, the lot of them. A change is as good as a rest. Isn't that what they say?'

Luther scowled, a red flush suffusing his cheeks. He looked like he was going to make a further objection, but instead he simply raised and dropped his hands in a gesture of exasperation. 'Suit yourself. On your head be it.'

Mrs Byrne nodded as if another small victory had been notched up. 'It'll be pleasant to have someone young around the house. Liven the place up a bit.'

Chrissy, shocked by this unexpected development, didn't know what to do next. Surely, she should be stating, right now, that she didn't want the job? Except that little voice was whispering in her ear again. If she took it, she would be able to find out more about Luther Byrne. And she wouldn't have to stay for long. A few weeks, a few discreet questions and she might have all the answers she wanted.

Still undecided, Chrissy asked, 'What hours would I be expected to work?'

'Ten till four,' Luther said stiffly. 'Monday to Friday. The salary is a hundred and fifty a week.'

Chrissy's eyes widened. That was more than she earned at Connolly's and the hours were shorter. With Uncle Pete coming out soon, the extra money would be a godsend.

'Is that agreeable?' he asked.

'Yes,' Chrissy said. 'Yes, that's fine.'

258

'Very well. I'll contact the agency and let them know we've hired you.'

And now Chrissy had a problem. 'I ... erm ... didn't exactly come though the agency. Not directly.'

'So where *exactly* did you come from?'

Chrissy had to think on her feet. 'Well, someone I know applied for the job and the agency were going to send her, but then she found something else. Anyway, she thought I might be interested so she passed on the details to me and ... erm ... here I am.'

Luther gazed at her through disapproving eyes. 'I take it you have references.'

'References?'

'Yes.'

'I'm sure they'll give me one at the café,' Chrissy said, even though she wasn't sure at all. And then it occurred to her that she'd given a false name to Luther and so any reference that she might persuade Mr Connolly to give her wouldn't be of any use. 'Although I've only been there six months so ...'

Mrs Byrne came to her rescue again. 'Those references aren't worth bothering with. No one ever produces a bad one, do they? All full of the same nonsense about how wonderful the person is, how clever, how reliable, how trustworthy. They're not worth the paper they're written on.'

'Now you're just being ridiculous,' Luther said.

'You'll have to excuse my son, Miss Cope. He tends to become irascible when he doesn't get his own way.'

If by irascible she meant downright rude then Chrissy wasn't going to argue with her. 'Perhaps you'd like more time to think about it ...'

'Monday,' Mrs Byrne said firmly. 'Please don't be late.'

46

Chrissy decided to take the Tube to King's Cross and catch a bus home from there. It was more straightforward than going to Liverpool Street and getting the overground train to Kellston. While she was making these mundane decisions, her brain was still trying to process how she'd managed to acquire a well-paid job in the Byrne household. Of course, she knew it had been more down to mother/son hostility than to any good impression she had made.

While she waited on the platform, she wondered how her mum could ever have been involved with a man as arrogant as Luther Byrne. It didn't make any sense. She recalled those words he'd spoken, 'On your head be it,' as if only bad things could come from Chrissy being hired. He clearly didn't trust her, probably imagining she'd run off with the family silver at the first opportunity. And what about all that gangster stuff? Luther wasn't like any gangster *she'd* ever come across. Perhaps Nan had been right and it was just idle gossip.

There was a stirring of air in the tunnel, followed by a gentle roar as the train approached. The Tube was quieter at this time of day and she was able to get a seat without any trouble. As she sat down, she attempted to figure out if it had been smart or stupid of her to accept the job. Smart insofar as it was more money for less work, and she could pursue her investigation into Luther Byrne, but stupid if her deception was ever found out. Still, what was the worst that could happen? He could only fire her, and that would hardly be a novelty. Except, of course, that might not be the worst . . .

Chrissy shivered despite the warmth of the carriage. For all she knew, Luther could be a very dangerous man. Just because he lived like a toff didn't mean he wasn't capable of bad things. And he certainly wouldn't win any prizes for civility. He was the sort who thought he was better than everyone else – superior, maybe even above the law. The sort, perhaps, who could get away with murder.

She stared at the tunnel walls rushing past, a curvy blur of soot-coloured brick. Well, she didn't have to turn up on Monday, didn't ever have to see the Byrnes again. She could still walk away from all this. They didn't have her right name, didn't even know where she lived. She could disappear without a trace. But then all her questions would remain unanswered. Sometimes opportunities only came along once: you either grabbed them or let them slip through your fingers.

Chrissy was still considering her options when she got off the train at King's Cross. The escalators were busy with long lines of passengers going up and down. She kept to the right-hand side, giving her legs a rest as she travelled up towards the station concourse. With nothing else to look at, other than the back of the person in front, she gazed across at the other escalator.

Her eyes were running absently over the descending passengers – man in tracksuit, woman carrying baby, elderly gentleman – when a girl's face suddenly clicked with her. It took a moment for the features to register in her brain, for the synapses to snap, for the connection to be made. And then a shock wave ran through her. It couldn't be. It was. *It was Dawn!* She looked over her shoulder as the distance between them increased. Then she yelled out her name.

'Dawn! Dawn!'

The girl twisted her head and looked up, locking eyes with Chrissy for a second before quickly turning away again. No sign of recognition. No smile. No wave. No acknowledgment at all. But Chrissy was sure. Ten years might have passed, but the face was still recognisable.

Now she was almost at the top and Dawn was almost at the bottom. Chrissy didn't think twice. She dashed up the last few feet, swung left and hurried down the descending escalator, almost stumbling as she rushed to catch up. Her pulse was racing, adrenaline coursing through her veins. *Dawn wasn't dead.* But when she reached solid ground, she had no idea which direction to go in next. Which line? Which tunnel? There were too many options. She bobbed up and down, trying to spot her in the crowd. She couldn't.

Chrissy chose the nearest platform. As she arrived a train was just pulling in. She pushed through the other passengers, jostling elbows, apologising as she went, trying to see everyone who was getting on. No Dawn. She covered the length of the train, peering through the windows, but the one face she wanted to find was absent. Frustration flowed through her. The doors closed and the train pulled out.

She retraced her steps, wondering which way to try next. Randomly she chose the opposite direction, walking fast, searching the platform but with the same result. It was too late. Dawn was gone. To carry on looking was pointless. She could hear the rumble of trains arriving, trains leaving, the distant sound of a guitar. Every few seconds a new flood of people washed through the tunnels. She stood to one side, bewildered.

Was it possible that she'd been wrong? Had her mind been playing tricks?

Slowly she made her way back to the escalator, replaying the sighting in her head, trying to capture that moment when she'd first noticed the girl. And she had turned, hadn't she, when Chrissy had called out her name? It *had* been her. She was certain of it.

47

Will Sutherland stared out of the window of Connolly's. A dull Thursday morning in Kellston, he thought, and by that he meant dull in every sense of the word. The sky was grey and overcast, his mood one of dreary boredom. He needed something to lift him out of the doldrums. Having passed on his snout's information to the Robbery Squad, it was now down to them. Hopefully the gang would be caught red-handed and he'd get some credit for having provided the intelligence.

His own investigation – or rather re-investigation – into Dawn Kearns's disappearance had hit a brick wall. He had gone back through the case file and discovered, unsurprisingly, that Pat Dunlap had never been interviewed, and the two boys had only been spoken to briefly. He couldn't help thinking that an opportunity had been missed. And now it was too late. All he had to go on was a hunch and that was hardly enough to start demanding detailed answers as to what the three of them had been doing ten years ago.

He drank some coffee, hoping the caffeine might perk him

up. Although there didn't appear to be much happening in Kellston, other than the usual, an eye was being kept on the Mansfield in case the residents got any ideas about following in the footsteps of Broadwater Farm. It wasn't that long since the tragic death of a mother on the Tottenham estate had sparked off a violent confrontation between the residents and the police. There seemed to be unrest in most of London's poorer districts, smoking embers waiting to burst into flames. And people like Frank Yates didn't help, stirring up the locals with all his talk of inequality and social injustice. Yeah, the place was a sinkhole but it wouldn't be improved any by a full-scale riot.

Gaul, of course, wouldn't give a damn if it all kicked off. He'd welcome the opportunity to settle old scores and crack a few skulls. His idea of law and order was *Do as I say, not as I do*. Still, he'd be retiring in under a year, and Will was counting off the weeks. Once he was gone it would be like a weight being lifted. Will would no longer be beholden to him, no longer obliged to cover his back.

It was quiet in the café, that mid-morning lull between breakfast ending and the start of serving lunch. Only a couple of tables were occupied. Will glanced across to where Chrissy Moss was leaning against the counter chatting to May Connolly. He was pleased that things had improved for her, that she was holding down a job and staying out of trouble. There had been a time – and it wasn't that long ago – when he'd been sure that her life was only heading in one direction, and that was the gutter. He'd have put money on her ending up in Albert Road, touting for trade with the other toms, trying to get enough cash together for the next fix or the next drink.

Twice she had been brought in for drunk and disorderly, and twice he had intervened to let her off with a verbal caution. He couldn't forget what she'd been through. He couldn't forget that she was Laura's daughter. It had been hard watching her walk down that path of self-destruction, but hopefully she had turned a corner.

As if she sensed her eyes on him, Chrissy glanced over. He smiled and raised his cup to indicate that he'd like another. She smiled back and nodded. A minute later she brought the fresh cup of coffee and put it down in front of him.

'How are you?' he asked.

'Good, thanks. You?'

'Not so bad. You're looking well.'

Chrissy grinned. 'Looking sober, you mean.'

'Did I say that?'

'You didn't have to. But that's okay. We all make mistakes, right? It just took me a while to figure mine out.'

'Some people never do that.'

'Some people never screw up in the first place.'

'Only the boring ones.'

Chrissy picked up his empty cup. 'There's a lot to be said for being boring.'

Seeing as she wasn't exactly rushed off her feet, Will decided to continue the conversation and, because it had been on his mind, to try and get her take on the events of ten years ago. 'You know, I've been looking at the Dawn Kearns case again and I can't help thinking we missed something. It's been bugging me. What do *you* think happened?'

Her reaction took him by surprise. She visibly started, her face turning pale. 'What?'

'Sorry, I didn't mean to upset you.'

'You haven't. It's just . . .'

'Just what?'

Chrissy left a long pause. She swallowed hard, glanced away and then back at him. 'It's nothing. You took me by surprise, that's all.'

Will could have kicked himself. For her that time wouldn't just be about Dawn's disappearance, but also Hooper's brutal attack – a traumatic experience she was probably still trying to put behind her. 'Sorry,' he said again. 'I shouldn't have mentioned it.'

'No, it's all right. Honestly. It's odd, though. I've been thinking about her, too. All this time and she's never been found. Are you reopening the case? Have you got new information?'

'It's never really been closed. And no, nothing new, I'm afraid.'

Chrissy looked pensive for a second and then said, 'Why do you think you missed something?'

'It's just a hunch. I could be wrong, but . . . it's that not being able to see the wood for the trees thing. Do you know what I mean? There was so much going on – Anita Jakes, Marlon Pound – and it all got kind of tangled together.'

'Do you think she could still be alive?'

Will didn't want to be too blunt – the girls had been friends, after all – but he didn't want to raise any false hope either. He tried to think of a diplomatic answer, but came to the conclusion that there wasn't one. 'It's . . . unlikely.'

'I suppose so.' Chrissy had a quick look round the caff to make sure nobody required anything, satisfied herself that her assistance wasn't needed and focused on Will again. She lowered her voice, even though nobody else was close enough to hear. 'Could I ask you about someone else? Luther Byrne. You told me once that I should stay away from him, that he had a "reputation", and I've been wondering what you meant by that.'

Will was surprised by the question, caught off guard. 'Why do you want to know about Luther Byrne?'

'He's the only person who seems to have been close to my mum – well, apart from Nan and Uncle Pete, and they don't like talking about her. It upsets them, I suppose. I understand that.

And I heard Luther was a friend of hers ... or that she worked for him, at least. At a bar called Rascals in Mayfair.'

'That closed down years ago.'

'Yes, someone told me that. But I thought, if I could find him, he could tell me more about Mum. I feel like I barely know her. It's strange; she's this huge part of my life and yet she isn't. Does that make any sense?'

Will got how she wanted to connect to that part of her that had been lost, to flesh out the shadows, to make the ghost come to life, and for a moment he was tempted to help her on that journey. There was a lot he could tell her about Laura, so much, but it wouldn't be a good idea. 'Of course it makes sense, it's natural. But I don't think Luther will be much use to you. I don't even think they were close. She just worked for him for a while.'

'I've been told it was more than that.'

'Have you? Well, I can't say for sure one way or the other, but Luther wasn't a pleasant character. He was on our radar for a while, up to all sorts: illegal gambling, fraud, extortion. And there were rumours about ...' Will paused. 'I probably shouldn't be telling you all this.'

'It was years ago. What difference does it make now?'

Will, wanting to discourage her from trying to find Luther Byrne, decided not to hold back. 'There was drugs and prostitution too. And rumours of underage girls. The bloke was into all kinds of dodgy stuff.'

'He sounds delightful. So, I should stay away from him, right?'

'That would be my advice, for what it's worth. I've got no idea where he is now. He probably isn't even in London any more.'

'No, perhaps not. Okay, thanks. I'd better get on.'

'You take care of yourself.'

'Ta,' she said. 'I'll do my best.'

Will watched her for a moment, thinking about the past,

about Dawn, about Laura. History coiled around him, all the things he couldn't change and all the things he wanted to. There was a tightness in his chest. Don't get maudlin, he told himself. There's nothing worse than a sentimental cop. He picked up his coffee and stared out of the window.

48

At five o'clock, as Chrissy walked back to the Mansfield, she wondered why she hadn't told Will Sutherland about seeing Dawn yesterday. She almost had – it had been on the tip of her tongue – but then she'd changed her mind. Once it was said it could never be unsaid. She needed some time to think about it.

Although Sutherland had been good to her, she didn't quite trust him. He was a cop, after all, and cops always had their own agenda. Strange, though, how the subject of Dawn had come up today. A coincidence? Perhaps he did have new information. Perhaps he knew that she was still alive.

Having slept on it, Chrissy was still convinced that she'd seen her. It was possible, however, that Dawn didn't want to be found. She certainly hadn't hung about yesterday. She had looked straight at Chrissy and then she'd scarpered. But a lot could happen in ten years. She could be married, have a family, be living under a different name entirely. Maybe the last thing she needed was the law knocking on her door and raking up the past.

But there were questions that needed answering. If it hadn't been for Dawn's disappearance, a whole chain of events would never have been set in motion: Marlon Pound wouldn't have been murdered, and Uncle Pete and the others wouldn't have spent the last ten years banged up. An explanation was needed if nothing else. Why the hell had she gone missing and where had she been?

Chrissy was still turning these questions over in her head as she walked on to the estate. She was almost at Carlton House when she saw Frank Yates coming out of the door. He smiled when he saw her, said hello, but would have walked on past if she hadn't stopped him.

'Hi Frank. Could I have a quick word? I just wanted to ask you—'

'No news yet, I'm afraid,' he interrupted. 'It's likely to take a few weeks, maybe even longer. The paperwork only went in on Monday and the housing department isn't renowned for its speed ... or its efficiency. I'm hopeful, though. I'm sure we'll manage to get Pete something.'

'No, it's not about that.'

'Oh.'

Chrissy hesitated. She needed some advice, some *good* advice, and Frank seemed to be the go-to person these days. Plus, he didn't much care for the police, which was a bonus. But she still couldn't quite bring herself to say the words. 'You're going to think I'm mad.'

'Let's presume that I won't.'

'Believe me, you will.' She took a deep breath and said, 'It's about Dawn. I saw her yesterday.'

Frank frowned, shook his head. 'What? You couldn't have.'

'I did. I saw her at King's Cross.'

'But she's ...'

'Dead? I don't think so.'

'You spoke to her?'

'No, I didn't exactly ... She was on the other escalator, but when I called out her name she turned and looked at me. It was her. I'm telling you.'

'So you only saw her from a distance?'

Chrissy heard the scepticism in his voice and bristled. 'Not a distance. It was just a few feet. I went after her, but she'd gone. I couldn't find her.'

Frank chewed on his lower lip for a moment. 'Was she the only person who turned around? Only sometimes, you know, when you hear someone shouting, you turn automatically, even if it isn't your own name.'

'I knew you wouldn't believe me.'

'I'm not saying that.'

'So what are you saying?'

'It's been ten years.'

'I saw her, Frank,' Chrissy insisted, her voice rising. 'I saw her clear as day.'

'Okay, okay,' he said, raising his hands, palm outwards. 'Have you told the law?'

'No.'

'Why not?'

Chrissy shrugged. 'I don't know. What can they do?'

'Look for her, I suppose.'

'They can't search the whole of London. And she'd have come forward, wouldn't she, if she wanted to be found? It's odd, though, because that Sutherland was in the caff this morning and he asked me about her. Well, what he actually said was that he thought they might have missed something back then.'

'Missed what?'

'I don't know. He was being cagey about that, just claiming that he had a hunch.'

'Perhaps he's looking to stir things up on the estate, start some rumours.'

'Why would he do that?'

'Why do the law do anything?' Frank frowned, thinking over what she'd said. 'Have you told Zelda about seeing Dawn?'

Now it was Chrissy's turn to frown. 'Zelda? God, I haven't heard from her in years.'

'Oh, only I thought she . . . '

'Have you seen her? Is she back in London?'

Frank looked embarrassed, his mouth turning down at the corners. 'Sorry. She said she was going to get in touch with you, so I presumed . . . It was a while ago, a few months. She's working for a firm of solicitors in Spitalfields. I bumped into her at a council do and we had a quick chat and she asked after you and . . . I'm sure she *will* be in touch. She's probably just been busy.'

Chrissy hadn't thought about Zelda in a long time. The Grahams had left the Mansfield shortly after Hooper's attack, deciding that it wasn't safe to stay in a place where girls went missing or got attacked in broad daylight. She and Zelda had exchanged letters for a while – it was before Nan had got the phone installed – but eventually they'd fizzled out. Distance had proved too great an impediment to a friendship that had already been on the rocks.

'Like you say, she's probably been busy.'

Frank nodded, looking keen to get away. 'I should go. I've got a meeting in fifteen minutes.'

'Okay.'

'Bye, then. Give my best to your nan.'

Chrissy nodded. As he walked off, she stood and thought some more about Zelda. The fact her old friend hadn't been in touch didn't surprise her that much, but it did make her sad.

People changed, grew apart, went their separate ways and that was just life. She remembered a Sunday from long ago – three girls sitting on a wall, elbows touching, none of them knowing that everything was about to change for ever.

49

Nan was in the kitchen when Chrissy got home, removing a pair of pork chops from a sheet of greaseproof paper while she listened to the news on the radio. Chrissy asked the same question she always asked on Thursdays.

'How was Betty today?'

'Oh, not so bad.' This was Nan's standard answer, although occasionally it was 'Not so good.' Betty had a form of dementia and didn't always remember her.

'She must be getting on now.'

'We're all getting on,' Nan said. 'How was your day? Was it busy at the caff?'

'It's always busy.' Chrissy took off her coat and hung it over the back of a chair. 'Here, pass those spuds over and I'll peel them.'

'Ta, love.'

While Chrissy set to work peeling the potatoes, she glanced at her grandmother and said, 'I saw Frank as I was coming in.'

Nan looked pleased. 'Did you have a chat?'

'There's nothing on Uncle Pete's flat yet, but he'll let us know if he hears anything. He did have some other news, though: apparently Zelda's back in London. He bumped into her at some council do.'

'How long has she been back?'

'I'm not sure. Frank said a few months.'

'She's not exactly rushed round, then.' Nan pottered at the kitchen counter, getting together dinner plates and cutlery. 'You two should go for a drink together.'

'I don't even know where she's living. She works somewhere in Spitalfields, I think.'

'No, I meant with Frank.'

Chrissy stopped peeling and stared at her. 'Why on earth would I want to go for a drink with Frank?'

'Why not? You should give him a chance. He's hard-working, sensible, kind, and he's not bad-looking. What more do you want?'

'He's not my type.'

'He might grow on you.'

'Give it up, Nan. It's never going to happen.' And then, in order to distract her, Chrissy revealed another piece of news. She had made the decision today, although whether it was a wise one only time would tell. 'Guess what? I've got a new job. '

Nan almost dropped the plates she was holding. 'What? Where? I thought you liked it at the caff.'

'I do. I mean, I did. It's okay, but it's not the best job in the world, is it? I'm on my feet all day and the pay's not exactly great. Anyway, I was up West yesterday and I called in at this agency and—'

'You didn't say anything about that.'

'I know. I wanted to think about it. I wasn't sure if I wanted the job or not, but I've decided to take it. The hours are better and so's the pay.'

'What is it then?'

'It's . . . erm . . . it's working for an elderly woman in Highgate. Mrs Parry, she's called.' Chrissy hated lying but she couldn't mention the Byrne name, not without Nan's antennae going into overdrive. 'She's blind – well, almost – and needs some help.'

'You're not a nurse.'

'It's not nursing, Nan. I'm not going to be a carer.'

'What will you be doing, then?'

Chrissy wasn't entirely sure of the answer to that. The finer details of her future employment had got lost somehow in the unnerving nature of the interview. 'Just helping round the house, going shopping and such. Keeping her company, mainly, until her son gets home from work.'

'That sounds like an odd sort of job.'

'I suppose she gets lonely on her own. Anyway, I start on Monday. I've told them at Connolly's.'

'It'll be further to travel.'

'It's not too bad.' It crossed Chrissy's mind to tell her about Dawn, but she decided not to. Nan might think she was back on the booze again, seeing ghosts on escalators. Was Frank likely to mention it? She hoped not.

'What's she like, this Mrs Parry?'

'Oh, nice enough. I think we'll get on all right.'

Chrissy had decided to take the job early this morning, before she'd talked to Sutherland. What he'd told her about Luther Byrne made her question the wisdom of her choice, but there was no going back now. Her need to find out about what had really happened to her mum was stronger than her fear of Luther. It had to be done. She had to know. So, on Monday morning, come rain or shine, she'd be painting on a smile and stepping straight into the lion's den.

50

DCI Gaul sat back in his chair, put his feet up on the desk and reached for his glass of whisky. As he raised it to his lips, he said, 'The Dunlap boys? Where the fuck did that come from?'

'I don't know. We never really looked at them, did we? I mean, not properly. We just thought they were kids and dismissed them. What if we got it wrong? It's just been bugging me, that's all, what really happened to Dawn Kearns.'

'Why? What's changed? You've always had Hooper in the frame.'

'It was a theory.'

'And now you've got a new one. Haven't you got enough work to do without dredging up old cases?'

'I like to be thorough. And one of my snouts mentioned something, too, reckons the Dunlaps knew more about it than they ever let on.'

'You can't trust snouts. You know what they're like, fuckin' stirrers, the lot of them.'

'Perhaps. But it's something to think about.'

Gaul rolled his eyes. 'Well, here's something else to occupy your mind. I saw Terry Street on Saturday and he told me there are questions being asked about Luther Byrne.'

Will was cautious in his reply. 'Who was asking?'

'He wouldn't say.'

'What sort of questions?'

'Where he is, what he's doing, that kind of thing.'

'Is that a concern?'

Gaul glared at him. 'Of course it's a fuckin' concern. What's wrong with you?'

Will had to make a fast decision. He didn't want to land Chrissy in it, but if Gaul found out that she was the one asking, and he hadn't mentioned it, then there'd be hell to pay. 'I don't think it's anything to worry about. I reckon it was Chrissy Moss. She works for Terry sometimes, doesn't she, at that bar of his?'

Gaul looked blank for a second, but then the name came back to him. 'You're talking about *Laura* Moss's daughter, right? The one who was attacked?'

'Yeah.

'So how the fuck is that nothing to worry about?'

'Because it isn't. Someone told her years ago that her mum worked for Luther and so she thinks he can tell her about Laura – you know, personal stuff, what she was like and all that. She was asking me about him this morning in the caff and—'

'This morning? How come I'm only hearing about this now?'

'I haven't seen you all day and I didn't think it was *that* important. She isn't going to pursue it. I told her what a bastard he is. She's just curious, but I put her straight. She's a smart girl. She won't do anything stupid.'

'Are we talking about the same girl who went for a walk in Kellston cemetery with Eddie bloody Barr?'

'That was years ago. She was just a kid.'

Gaul sneered. 'You'd better be right. It won't be good for you if she starts poking around in the past.'

But Will knew he was only bothered about covering his own back. With retirement looming Gaul didn't want any incriminating truths rising to the surface; he had a pension to think about. 'She doesn't know where to find him, and she isn't going to look. Why would she after what I told her?'

'I wouldn't be so sure.' Gaul sipped his whisky and peered at Will over the rim of the glass. 'That Bobby English was there when Terry was asking – you know, the moron who runs the White Swan in Holborn – and he mentioned the gallery so I couldn't deny it. I dare say Terry passed the information on.'

'She didn't say anything to me about that.'

'No, well maybe she's not been quite as open and honest as you think. And maybe she's got other reasons for wanting to track down Luther.'

'Like what?'

'What do you reckon?'

Will picked up his own glass and stared down into it for a moment. If Chrissy did find Luther and got him to talk, it could open up a whole can of worms. 'Like I said, it's nothing to worry about.' But this time there wasn't quite so much conviction in his voice.

51

On Friday Chrissy did the early shift at Connolly's and was finished by two o'clock. She walked down to the Spar and picked up bread and milk and loo paper. While she shopped, her head was somewhere else, distracted by thoughts of Zelda. Perhaps she should be the one to make the first move, to get back in touch. It could be that Zelda felt awkward after all these years, unsure as to whether an attempt to renew the friendship would be welcome. Or perhaps her old friend just didn't want to see her.

Chrissy feared rejection, but she also feared throwing away the opportunity to rekindle something that had once been important. She had no close friends now, no one she could really trust. Well, there was Nan, of course, but that was different. What if pride was holding Zelda back, too? They might never meet again. She resolved to ask Frank where Zelda worked next time she saw him. He might even have her phone number.

On her way back to the Mansfield, Chrissy was passing the café again when the door opened and Charlie Dunlap walked out. 'Hello, darlin',' he said. 'How are you today?'

'Fine, thank you.'

Charlie fell into step beside her, and Chrissy's heart sank. The last thing she wanted was to be stuck with him all the way home. She turned her head slightly to look across the road, searching for a shop that she urgently needed to visit. Patel's wasn't far away. Once they drew level with it, she'd make her excuses and leave.

'Lucky us bumping into each other like this. I wanted to have a word.'

This sounded ominous. 'Oh?'

'I reckon you can guess what it's about.'

'No,' Chrissy said.

Suddenly Charlie moved in front of her so she had to stop walking. He leaned in, putting his face too close to hers, and she caught a whiff of that odd musty smell he'd always carried with him as a kid. 'You and Sutherland.'

'What?'

'I saw the two of you yesterday having a cosy chat in the caff. What was all that about?'

Chrissy instinctively wanted to draw back, but refused to give him the satisfaction. She stood her ground and stared right back. 'It was, if I remember rightly, about him ordering a cup of coffee.'

'It doesn't take that long to order a bleedin' coffee.'

Chrissy wasn't exactly sure what she was being accused of, other than consorting with the enemy, but Charlie's voice had a nasty edge to it. 'It's called making small talk. You know, "Warm for the time of year, isn't it? Quiet in here today." That sort of thing. What do you expect me to do, ignore him?'

'Someone's been spreading rumours about George.'

'And you think it's me? Jesus, I've got better things to do than talk about your brother.'

'Oh yeah?'

282

'Oh yeah,' she echoed. 'Now, do you mind getting out of my way?'

Chrissy stepped to one side, but he did the same.

'We ain't finished,' he said.

'I think you'll find we are.'

A familiar voice came from behind Chrissy. 'You heard what the lady said. Get out of the way.'

Chrissy turned to see Vinnie Keane, and his looming presence couldn't have been more welcome.

Charlie immediately stepped back, but wasn't about to lose face completely. 'We're in the middle of a conversation, mate.'

Vinnie looked at Chrissy, one eyebrow raised. 'Got anything more you want to say to our friend here?'

'No.'

'Well, there you go,' Vinnie said. 'Time to make yourself scarce, son. It's never good to outstay your welcome.'

Charlie Dunlap's gaze flicked between Chrissy and Vinnie, but it didn't take him long to make a decision. Even fools didn't argue with six foot five of muscle. He only considered it for a few seconds – his eyes resting on Vinnie's bulk – before throwing her a dirty look and scuttling off down the high street.

'What a jerk,' Vinnie said. 'One of the Dunlaps, right?'

'Charlie,' she said.

'If you don't mind me asking, what was that all about?'

Chrissy took a moment to get herself together. Charlie hadn't scared her so much as taken her by surprise. It was unpleasant being accused of something you hadn't done. 'He saw me talking to DS Sutherland yesterday, in the caff, and now he's got this idea in his head that I've been talking about George. I mean, why would I? It's ridiculous. As if I haven't got better things to do than talk about George stupid Dunlap.'

'The paranoia of the guilty,' Vinnie said.

Chrissy looked at him.

'Charlie, I mean. George has probably been up to something, and he thinks you might know what it is.'

'Why would I know?'

Vinnie grinned. 'No reason. That's why it's called paranoia.'

'Great. So now I'm in the frame for being a grass.'

'I wouldn't lose too much sleep over it.'

'Easy for you to say.'

'They're idiots, both of them.' Vinnie looked towards Connolly's. 'Hey, are you in a rush or do you fancy a coffee?'

'Not in there. I've only just finished a shift. I've had enough of the place for one day.'

'What about the Wimpy, then?'

Chrissy wrinkled her nose.

'You done a shift there too?' Vinnie said.

Chrissy smiled, feigning a self-possession she didn't feel. She hadn't set foot in the Wimpy since going there ten years ago with Eddie Barr, but that was a story she didn't want to share. 'No, it's just . . . Okay, why not? Let's do that.'

'You sure?'

Chrissy nodded. There was only so long you could avoid a place; it was time to put the past behind her. 'Yeah, I'm sure.'

'You want me to carry that?' Vinnie asked, gesturing towards the carrier bag she was holding.

'Thanks, but it's not heavy. I'm fine.'

They turned and set off down the high street, walking side by side. Chrissy noticed how people's eyes were drawn towards Vinnie, fast furtive glances, before they quickly looked away again. 'You got the day off?' she asked.

'Late night. I've only just got up. That's why I need the caffeine.' He left a short pause and then said, 'I hope you didn't mind me stepping in back there?'

284

'Why should I?'

'Some women take offence at that kind of thing. You know, as if I was presuming you couldn't sort it out on your own. You've got to be careful these days: you open a door, offer to carry someone's shopping, try to give up your seat on the bus, and suddenly you're a sexist pig. Believe me, it's a minefield.'

'Well, now I come to think of it . . .'

Vinnie grinned. 'Okay, I'll buy you a coffee to make it up to you.'

'You think I can't buy my own coffee?'

'Right then, you can buy *me* a coffee.'

They continued in this mode, the banter going back and forth, until they reached the Wimpy. Chrissy tried to push all thoughts of Eddie aside as they went in through the door. Inside, it looked much the same as the last time she'd been here – same colour walls, same layout, same hissing coffee machine. Only the girl at the counter was different.

Chrissy bought the drinks and deliberately chose a table as far away as possible from the one she'd sat at with Eddie. The Wimpy was less than half full and all of the other customers were teenagers. She squeezed into the booth opposite Vinnie, willing herself to stay composed. She couldn't let the past dictate the present and yet a shiver still ran through her.

'You okay?' Vinnie asked.

'Why wouldn't I be?'

'Don't let that scrote Dunlap get to you. He's just a little shit.'

Chrissy didn't put him straight about what was really on her mind. 'I know. It's just annoying when someone has a go at you for something that you haven't done.'

'So what *were* you talking to Sutherland about?'

'Jesus, not you as well. It was just chitchat, everyday stuff, nothing important and certainly nothing about George Dunlap.'

Vinnie drank his coffee and stared at her.

Chrissy stared back. 'What?'

'Did I say anything?'

'It's what you're thinking that worries me. I'm not a grass. I wouldn't ever tell the law anything.'

'I know. I wasn't . . . I'm just a nosy bastard. I can't help it.'

'You should go to the doctor. I'm sure you can get something for that.'

'Thanks. I'll consider it. Anyway, how have you been? Busy week?'

'Eventful.' Chrissy wondered how much to share with him, and decided to stick to the bare essentials. 'I got a new job.'

Vinnie's face fell before he quickly smiled and nodded. 'Oh, well done. Congratulations. What is it? Does that mean you won't be working at Cordelia's any more?'

Chrissy felt a small rush of pleasure that he'd betrayed some disappointment at the news. 'No, I'm going to stay on for a while. I only do Saturdays so it won't make any difference.' She went on to give him the same version of her new job as she'd given her nan. Although she instinctively trusted Vinnie, her instincts had betrayed her in the past. She wasn't going to take any chances.

'Well, good luck with it all.'

'Thanks. So how about you? How's your week been?'

'Same as usual.'

'Do you like working for Terry?'

'I've worked for worse. You know where you stand with him. There's no side. What you see is what you get. He's not a bullshitter.'

'That's always an advantage.'

'Yeah, Terry's all right. What do you think of him?'

'Sure, he seems okay.'

'Just okay?'

Sensing that he was on a fishing expedition, Chrissy narrowed her eyes. 'What's wrong with okay?'

'No, nothing, it's just that I noticed the two of you chatting on Saturday night and I wondered if . . .'

'What? If there was something going on?'

Vinnie shrugged. 'Just being nosy again.'

'No, there isn't anything going on. He's not my type.'

'How come?'

'He's married.'

'Ah, I see. That doesn't bother most girls.'

'I'm not most girls.'

'Yeah, I'm beginning to realise that.'

Chrissy, not entirely sure if this was meant as a compliment, briefly met his gaze and then looked away. Her eyes roamed the room. Suddenly Eddie was back in her head with all his pretty lies and deceit, telling her how special she was, how he couldn't stop thinking about her. She shifted in her seat, sipped some coffee, put the cup down and picked it up again.

'Sorry,' he said. 'I've made you feel uncomfortable. I shouldn't have asked about Terry. It's none of my business.'

'No, it's not that. It's this place.' She had a quick look round again, lowered her voice and said, 'It's full of kids, isn't it? Makes me feel old.'

Vinnie laughed. 'Yeah, 'cause you're so ancient. How old are you? Twenty-two, three?'

'You know what I mean. And I'm almost twenty-five.'

'Exactly. If anyone should be feeling their age round here, it's me.'

'You're not *that* old,' she said.

'Ta, that makes me feel a whole lot better.'

'You're welcome.'

Vinnie leaned forward, linking his hands on the table. 'So what do you twenty-somethings like to do in your spare time?'

'Sleep,' Chrissy said.

'You're a sad generation.'

'We're a tired generation.'

'You ever manage to eat in between all this sleeping?'

'It's been known.'

Vinnie's mouth slowly widened into a smile. 'Perhaps we could do that together sometime.'

'Are you asking me out to dinner?'

'Would you say yes if I did?'

Chrissy hesitated, remembering all her good intentions. Now wasn't a good time to be getting involved with anyone. Now was the time to stay focused, to keep her emotions in check, not allow herself to be distracted.

Vinnie's smile faded a little. 'Don't give me an answer now. Have a think about it and let me know.'

52

Chrissy parted from Vinnie at the green, and headed back to the Mansfield. She swung the carrier bag by her side as she walked, feeling pleased by how things had turned out, but not entirely sure if she should be pleased. She hadn't given him a definitive answer – that could wait until tomorrow night – but was inclined to accept the dinner invitation. Why not? Yes, well, she didn't really want to go there: the list might be a long one. But what really mattered, she thought, was that there was a connection between them, that they clicked in a way that felt right.

As she passed through the gates to the estate, Chrissy became aware of a disturbance in front of Carlton House. A small crowd had gathered to watch a drunk woman, stumbling around and hurling abuse. The Dunlaps, of course, were right in the middle of it all, loudly mocking her. They pushed their faces into hers, drew back, advanced again. They sneered and swore, jeered and goaded. There was nothing those two boys liked more than an opportunity to torment someone weaker than themselves.

She was watching this spectacle, wondering if she should

intervene – drunks weren't always grateful – when she suddenly realised who the woman was. It couldn't be. She drew closer and took a longer look. It was. A decade had passed, but Chrissy still recognised her. Tina Kearns was back on the Mansfield, off her head and shouting about Dawn.

'One of you bastards knows what happened to her! Tell me! Tell me, you shitbags!'

Chrissy's first thought was to get inside and call the police. They needed to come and pick Tina up before everything turned nastier than it already was. But was there time? The Dunlaps, along with others on the estate, had every reason to want revenge. Tina Kearns had given evidence in court, and that evidence had sent down fathers and brothers, sons and friends. That she was a victim herself wouldn't matter to them.

Chrissy didn't want to take the chance of leaving the woman alone. She pushed through the crowd, approaching with caution. 'Hello, Tina. Do you remember me?'

It was clear from the expression on Tina's face that she didn't have a clue who she was. A pair of pink-rimmed eyes stared vacantly back at her. But she'd stopped yelling at least, which was progress of some sort.

'It's Chrissy,' she said. 'Dawn's friend.'

Tina took a swig from the vodka bottle. 'Chrissy?'

There was still no recognition there. 'You remember. Me and Zelda? We were friends with Dawn.'

It was Zelda's name that triggered the memory. 'Yeah, yeah, Zelda.' Tina looked around, peering at the crowd. 'Is she here, love? I have to talk to her.'

'No, she doesn't live here any more.'

Charlie and George were closing in again, their hard faces full of malice.

Chrissy gently took hold of Tina's elbow before the brothers could pounce and started walking her towards the gates. 'Why don't we get away from here, go somewhere quieter?' Even as she was saying it, she couldn't think where. Connolly's, perhaps. She could buy Tina a coffee and try to get her sobered up a bit.

But Tina wasn't playing ball. As if her brain had suddenly caught up with what her legs were doing, she stopped dead in her tracks and wouldn't budge. 'I'm not going nowhere, not until I find out about my Dawn.'

Chrissy knew better than to argue with a drunk. 'That's okay. That's fine. We'll stay here, then. But let's get inside, huh? We can talk there, away from all these people.'

'Are we going to see Zelda?'

Chrissy was about to repeat what she'd said before, but then decided that now was no time for the truth. If she wanted Tina to shift, she'd have to tell her whatever she wanted to hear. 'Sure, let's do that.'

Tina raised the bottle to her mouth, drank another inch of vodka, turned to the crowd again and yelled, 'What the fuck are you lot staring at!'

A ripple of laughter ran through the onlookers. The residents of the Mansfield took their entertainment where they could find it, and a drunken woman shouting the odds was as good as anything else. The Dunlaps weren't laughing, though.

Charlie spat on the ground. 'You've a fuckin' nerve coming back here, Tina Kearns. Fuckin' grass!'

'Fuckin' grass!' George echoed.

Chrissy knew they had to get away, and fast. But where to? Nan wouldn't be too pleased if she took Tina to the flat. In the end, the only safe place she could think of was Frank's. He wouldn't thank her for it, but she was pretty sure he wouldn't turn them away. Quickly she linked her arm through Tina's and began pulling her towards Haslow House.

For a horrible moment, Chrissy thought the brothers were going to follow, but as she glanced back over her shoulder saw that they'd become involved in an altercation with a bloke in the crowd. Taking advantage of the distraction, she hurried Tina along. Trying to instil a sense of urgency into someone who was three sheets to the wind was no mean feat, but eventually they reached the tower. She bundled Tina into the lift and swiftly pressed the button to close the doors.

'This place always was a dump,' Tina said.

Chrissy hoped Tina wasn't going to puke. The lift smelled bad enough already. 'Can't argue with you there.'

'Which one were you again?'

'Chrissy.'

'Oh, yeah. Chrissy. You know what happened to my Dawn, Chrissy?'

'No. I wish I did.'

'Someone fuckin' knows. Someone in this godforsaken dump knows what happened. Ten years it's been now. Did you know that?' Tina didn't wait for an answer. 'The pigs don't give a damn and nor does anyone else. It ain't right. It ain't bloody right.'

Chrissy could see the pain in her face and wanted to tell her that Dawn was still alive, that she'd seen her, but wasn't sure if she should. One fleeting glimpse at King's Cross – was that enough to raise a mother's hopes? She was still debating this when the lift ground to a halt and the doors opened.

They walked along the corridor, Tina stumbling in her heels. Chrissy found the right flat, rang the bell and prayed that Frank was in. Her prayers were answered when he opened the door.

'Hi,' Chrissy said. 'Can we come in for a minute?'

Before Frank could reply, Tina had pushed past him and staggered inside. 'Where's the bog, hon? I really need a piss.'

'Off the hallway there, first on the left.'

Tina staggered off, the bottle still hanging from her hand.

Frank turned to look at Chrissy. 'Is that who I think it is?'

Chrissy went inside too and closed the door behind her. 'Look, I'm really sorry about this. I didn't know where else to go. Tina's wrecked, and the Dunlaps are probably forming a lynch mob even as we speak. Can you ring Cowan Road and get someone to come and pick her up? She's not safe on the estate.'

'What's she even doing here? I thought she was—'

'Can you just make the call?' Chrissy said. 'Please?'

Frank hurried through to the living room and picked up the phone. While he was talking to the cops Chrissy went into the kitchen and put the kettle on. The kitchen was clean but untidy, the counter strewn with files and papers. Frank's mum had died a few years back and he was living alone now. All her pots and pans were neatly stacked on the shelves, gathering dust. A single plate was drying on the drainer, along with a knife and fork.

'What did they say?' Chrissy asked as Frank joined her again.

'They're going to send someone over.'

'Good. Thanks for sorting that. And I'm sorry, I really am, but you know what those Dunlaps are like. I didn't know what else to do.'

'It's okay.'

'Do you mind if I make some coffee?'

'I'll do it.' Frank took three mugs out of a cupboard and cleared a space on the counter. 'She's taking a risk coming back here, even after all this time. Do you know where she's living now?'

'Not a clue. I presume the police found her somewhere new after the trial.'

The loo flushed and thirty seconds later Tina came back and tottered through to the kitchen. She put the vodka bottle on the counter, smoothed down her red miniskirt and stared at Frank. 'You're a good-looking boy,' she said. 'What's your name?'

'Frank.'

'Well, Frank, it's very nice to meet you.'

'And you.'

'I've always liked the name Frank. It's solid, isn't it? A proper man's name.'

Frank didn't seem to know how to respond so he just smiled vaguely while he edged away from her, grabbed the jar of Nescafé and started spooning coffee into the mugs.

'I used to live in a flat like this,' Tina said. 'Me and my Dawn. Did you know Dawn, Frank?'

'Yes, we went to the same school.'

'Did you, hon?' Tina sighed.

Frank poured boiling water into the mugs, gave the coffee a stir and pushed one of the mugs towards Tina. 'Here.'

Tina stared at the coffee like it was poison.

It was the first time Chrissy had had the chance to take a proper look at her. The years hadn't been kind – or maybe the booze hadn't. She'd lost a few teeth and her cheeks were hollowed out. Her body was thin, skin and bone, and her bleached blonde hair hung in long lanky strands around her face. She seemed to have forgotten about Zelda, which was fortunate.

Tina took a swig from the bottle of vodka, slammed it down on the counter and said, 'No one round here gives a fuck about my Dawn.'

'Yes, they do,' Chrissy said. 'We all miss her, don't we, Frank?'

'Yeah, course.'

Tina glared at them both. 'Not that lot out there. They don't give a toss.'

For the next ten minutes Tina's mood ran the gamut from anger to self-pity. She raged at the world and then wept at her loss. She cursed, ranted, accused, calmed down, cried and then started the whole circle again. She scribbled down her phone number on the top edge of a newspaper, ripped the strip of paper off and gave it to Chrissy. 'Here. You call me if you ever hear anything about my Dawn. Do you swear?'

Chrissy put the scrap of paper in her pocket. 'Yes, I swear. Of course I will.'

Tina drank more vodka.

Frank and Chrissy watched the clock while they tried to say the right things. It felt like for ever before the doorbell finally rang.

Frank rushed to the door and came back with DS Sutherland and a couple of uniforms.

Tina stared at them for a moment and then turned accusing eyes on Chrissy. 'You rang the fuckin' law, you bitch!'

'No, I didn't,' Chrissy said, trying to avoid a row. 'It must have been someone on the estate. How could I? You've been with us the whole time.'

Tina swayed from side to side while her muddled brain attempted to figure out if this was true or not.

'What are you doing on the Mansfield, Tina?' DS Sutherland asked calmly. 'You shouldn't be here. It isn't safe. You know that.'

'I just want some answers about my Dawn. I'm not going to find them in fuckin' Kent, am I?'

'Come on,' Sutherland said. 'Let's get you back to the station. We can talk about it there.'

Tina got as far as the hall before she started kicking up a stink. While the three police officers tried to keep her under control, Chrissy and Frank stayed out of the way in the kitchen.

'Sorry,' Chrissy said. 'You must be cursing me.'

'Only under my breath.'

'Yeah, well, I don't blame you. I feel bad for her, though.

I know she was never the best mother in the world, but you wouldn't wish what happened on anyone.'

'She was a terrible mother,' Frank said.

'Even terrible mothers have feelings.'

Frank sipped his coffee. 'Why didn't you tell her? About seeing Dawn, I mean.'

Chrissy went over to the sink, emptied out what was left in her mug and gazed out of the window at the London horizon. 'I don't know. I thought about it, but then . . . I can't be a hundred per cent sure, can I? And if I did tell her, then what's she going to do – hang around King's Cross for the rest of her life on the off-chance Dawn might show up again? That seems worse than saying nothing. I could tell the law, I suppose, but I doubt they'd do much about it.'

'Maybe, if she is out there, she doesn't want to be found.'

'Yeah, I thought about that, too.' Chrissy turned on the tap, rinsed out the mug and placed it on the drainer. 'It's hard, though, when you don't have any answers. It's better to know one way or the other, isn't it?'

'I suppose.'

Voices were still coming from the hall: intermittent shouts from Tina, murmurings from the cops. Getting her out of the flat was proving to be an ordeal.

'Frank? Could I ask you something?'

'Sure. What is it?'

'Did your mum ever say anything to you about my mum?'

'Like what?'

'Like her death not being an accident. That she was murdered?'

Frank spluttered into his coffee. 'Jesus, where's this come from? No, she never said anything like that.'

'It's just she knew a lot of people, didn't she? Being a nurse. She must have heard stuff when she was out and about.'

'She wasn't a gossip.'

'No, I didn't mean that. Sorry. I wasn't . . . I just wondered if she'd mentioned it.'

'No, not a word.'

'What about a man called Luther Byrne?'

'No. Why on earth do you think your mum was murdered?'

Chrissy wasn't sure why she was talking to Frank about this. It was just hard keeping it all to herself. 'It's what Zelda's mum said, apparently. Years ago. Something she'd heard. And I know this estate is full of rumour and gossip, but . . .'

'But?'

'I think it might be true. Nobody wants to talk about it, not Nan or Uncle Pete, not the law, no one. It's hard to explain. Something just feels wrong. No, it's more than that. Do you reckon I could get the police reports on the accident?'

'I don't see why not. Might take a while, though.'

'I think I know who did it. I just have to get the evidence.'

Frank, who probably believed she had a screw loose, nevertheless continued to humour her. 'You should go to the police if you think you know something.'

'No way. They're the last people I'm going to—' Chrissy turned from the sink to see DS Sutherland standing in the doorway. 'Oh, hello.'

'Just to let you know we're off now. We'll arrange to have her taken home, and hopefully she'll stay there, but give us a bell if she turns up again.'

'We will,' Frank said.

Sutherland nodded and left.

Once he was out of earshot, Chrissy said, 'Do you think he heard what I said?'

'Does it matter?'

Chrissy wasn't sure but she thought it might.

53

Three hours later Will Sutherland was still mulling over what he'd overheard. It had come as no big surprise – Chrissy had mentioned Luther Byrne to him in the caff – but now she was getting Frank Yates involved, and talking about the reports on Laura's accident. For Chrissy's own sake, he wished she'd leave well alone. Nothing good ever came from digging up the past.

Will gazed across the table at Tina Kearns, who was busy scoffing a plate of indifferent canteen food. She still wasn't sober but she was less drunk than when they'd picked her up. It would be another hour or so before the transport would arrive at the station to take her back to Kent. Whether she'd stay there or not was another matter altogether. She'd been fortunate today, but if she showed up on the estate again she might not be so lucky. He was trying to press this point home but wasn't sure how much she was actually taking in.

'You know Jacko and the rest are going to be out before too long? You need to keep your distance from the Mansfield. Tina, are you listening to me?'

Tina stopped eating for a moment and looked at him. 'Huh?'

'Jacko and the others. They'll be out before Christmas. You really think they'll be happy about seeing you on the Mansfield?'

'I ain't done nothing wrong,' she said.

'You're right, you haven't. But they're not going to see it that way. You gave evidence against them; so far as they're concerned, you're responsible for having them banged up. That's why we moved you out of London, to keep you safe, to keep you away from them.'

'Those scumbags deserved all they got.'

'No one's arguing with you there.'

'I need to find out what happened to Dawn.'

'Of course you do. I know. I get it. And we haven't closed the case; we won't ever close it until we find her.'

'Yeah, well, you ain't got too far with that in the last ten years.'

Will drank some tea, unable to refute the statement. 'So how come you ended up at Frank Yates's flat today?'

'The blonde girl took me there. That one who said she was a friend of Dawn's.'

'Chrissy Moss.'

'Chrissy, yeah.'

'Why there?'

'I dunno, do I?' Tina scooped up another mouthful of cottage pie and said, with her mouth full, 'I think . . . I dunno . . . I think it had something to do with seeing Zelda.'

'Zelda left years ago. She moved away with her parents.'

Tina frowned. 'Did she?'

'She and Dawn were close, weren't they?'

'They were mates.'

'And Frank? Was he a mate, too?'

Tina poked around in the mince as if suddenly realising that what she was eating wasn't exactly haute cuisine. 'I don't remember him.'

Will wasn't keen on Frank Yates; he was one of those lefties, always banging on about social injustice and bad housing and police brutality. Although Yates was on his list of people to talk to again about Dawn Kearns, he didn't know if it was worth the grief. There was every chance the councillor would accuse him of harassment.

'And the Dunlap brothers,' Will continued. 'Charlie was in Dawn's class at school. She ever mention them?'

But now Tina, despite her limited sobriety, was starting to wonder where he was going with the questions. 'What are you asking me about them for? You think they had something to do with it?'

'No,' Will said quickly, before she could get any ideas in her head. 'No, nothing like that. It's just that they all used to hang out on the estate. Kids often see things they don't realise they've seen, or hear stuff that doesn't make much sense at the time. I'm simply trying to look at any avenues that might not have been explored.'

'Yeah, right,' Tina said, as though he was just bullshitting her. 'I thought you lot had that freak Hooper in the frame.'

Will had thought this once, but the evidence had only ever been circumstantial. Now his suspicions were running along different lines. 'There was nothing to prove Dawn ever went back to Anita Jakes's flat.'

'She wouldn't have,' Tina said with the same insistence she'd used a decade ago. 'You only had to look at him to know he was crazy.'

Will nodded, finished his coffee and decided to leave it at that. He couldn't offer her any fresh hope, and the chances of her being able to give him new information were zero. 'Just promise me you won't come back to the Mansfield.'

'I ain't promising nothin'.'

'It's not helping, Tina.'

Tina pushed aside her plate and lit a fag. 'Then find out who took her, Mr Sutherland. If you don't, I fuckin' will.'

Gaul's office was warm and stuffy, and the rain lashing against the windows gave it an almost claustrophobic quality. It smelled of sweat and stale tobacco. 'What's she trying to do, start a bleeding riot?'

'She's trying to stir up something, that's for sure,' Will said.

'Where is she now?'

'I've left her in the canteen with Jackson. He can babysit her until the car arrives, make sure she doesn't do a runner.' Will leaned against the wall with his hands in his pockets. 'Do you think it's worth bringing in the Dunlaps?'

'And asking them what?'

'Just to go over what they were doing the Sunday Dawn disappeared.'

'It was ten years ago. Do you remember what *you* were doing that day?'

'We could bring all of them in, all the ones who were kids back then, see if anyone gets jumpy.'

'We could,' Gaul said. 'If we didn't have anything better to do.'

Will pushed off the wall, walked over to the window and stared out at the rain. 'There's something else. While I was at Yates's flat, I heard Chrissy Moss tell him that she's going to try and get hold of the accident reports on her mother. She thinks Laura was murdered, and she thinks she knows who did it.'

Gaul shook his head. 'Jesus, you'd have thought that girl would have had enough trouble in her life without going looking for more.'

'What if she finds Luther Byrne?'

'What if she does? He's not going to tell her anything.'

'You sure of that?'

Gaul gazed up at the ceiling for a while. 'Perhaps you should have a word with her.'

'I've tried that.'

'Then try harder. I don't need this crap. Sort it out, Will, or I'll do it for you.'

54

Chrissy felt some apprehension as she got ready for her first day of work in Highgate. She changed her clothes twice, even though Mrs Byrne wouldn't be able to see her, at least not with any clarity. But it felt important to look the part. She eventually settled on a pale blue dress, simple in style and modest in length.

Before leaving the flat, she sat down on the bed, and under the title new job wrote out the Byrne address on a piece of paper, folded it in two and slipped it into the bedside drawer.

She knew she was probably being melodramatic, but if something bad did happen to her, if she didn't come home one day, then at least the law would know where to start looking. That the information was there to be found made her feel a little safer. She stood up, put on her raincoat and went through to the living room.

'Okay, Nan, I'm off. Wish me luck!'

'Good luck, love. Have a good day.'

'You too.'

Ten minutes later, Chrissy was on the bus heading for King's

Cross. She was early – it was still only eight-thirty – but she wanted to make sure she got there on time. Arriving late on her first day wouldn't make a good impression. While she looked out of the window, watching the world go by, she hoped she wouldn't make a fool of herself. Her actual duties were still somewhat obscure. What if Mrs Byrne found her wanting and fired her? No, she wouldn't do that, at least not straight away. If she did, then her son would be proved right, and Mrs Byrne, she suspected, would not allow that to happen. This thought was reassuring. It meant that she probably had a few weeks' grace before her situation was reviewed, enough time, surely, to dig the dirt on Luther.

Chrissy had more than one reason to feel nervous, however. On Saturday, at Cordelia's, she'd accepted Vinnie's dinner invitation and they were due to meet in the Fox on Wednesday evening. Had she done the right thing? In the end she had gone with her gut – or perhaps another part of her body – and decided to stop running away from the things that scared her. It was just dinner, eating food with a man she liked. It didn't have to mean anything. Did she want it to mean something? No, she wasn't going to think about that.

It was crowded at King's Cross and as she pushed through the heaving mass of commuters Chrissy scoured the faces looking for Dawn's. The odds of spotting her were slim but that didn't stop her searching. What she really needed to do was to come back at the same time as she'd originally seen her – maybe Dawn had been on her way to or from work – and hope that she showed up again. But Chrissy knew this wasn't possible at the moment, not while she had the Highgate job.

She went down the escalator, keeping her eyes peeled. On the platform, she looked to her left and right, but not with any real expectation. It was simply something to do until the train came in. She didn't have long to wait and found herself in Highgate less than fifteen minutes later and with half an hour to spare. Strolling slowly through the streets, taking a longer route than she needed to, she tried to prepare herself for the day ahead.

A nasty thought entered her head as she approached the house. What if Luther Byrne had known who she was all along? What if this was an elaborate trap? Her steps faltered and she almost came to a halt. But she knew she was just being paranoid. Luther didn't even know her real name. And unless he had psychic powers, there was no way he could connect her to her mum.

Once her nerves had calmed down, she walked up the drive and rang the bell. After a short delay, Mrs Parry opened the door and stood aside to let her in.

'Good morning,' Chrissy said with a smile, thinking it would probably be smart to make friends with the housekeeper. If anyone had the gossip, it would be her. 'It's nice to see you again. How are you?'

But Mrs Parry, who looked harassed, wasn't in the mood for banal pleasantries. 'She's in the drawing room. I take it you can find your own way there?'

'Yes. Is there somewhere I can leave my coat?'

Mrs Parry opened an invisible cupboard in the wall, took the raincoat off Chrissy and hung it up. Then without another word she was gone, marching off down the corridor to whatever urgent business awaited her.

Chrissy walked at a sedate pace – she was still a little early – examining everything more closely than she had the first time. There were paintings all along the walls, portraits mainly of elegant women in ball gowns and stiff, upright men in uniform. The floor was polished wood. Once Mrs Parry's footsteps had receded, the house was very quiet, like it wasn't occupied at all.

There was neither sight nor sound of Luther. She stopped outside the drawing room, took a deep breath and knocked lightly on the door.

'Yes. Enter.'

Chrissy went inside and saw Mrs Byrne sitting by the window. Two chairs, both high backed, both pale yellow, were partly turned towards the garden. Between them was a low table. She advanced a few feet into the room and then stopped again. 'Good morning. It's Christine.'

'Well, don't just stand there,' Mrs Byrne said, flapping her hand towards the other chair. 'You're making the place look untidy.'

'Sorry.' Chrissy said. She went over to the window, sat down and asked, 'How are you?' This opening gambit hadn't worked too well on the housekeeper and it fared no better with her new boss.

'The same as I always am, my dear. Please don't ask every day or it's likely to become tedious.' Mrs Byrne sniffed the air, her nostrils flaring. 'Are you wearing perfume?'

'Yes,' Chrissy said. 'Would you rather I didn't?'

'I should think everyone would prefer that.'

Chrissy, who had saved up to buy the Dior, flinched a little at the insult, and hoped it didn't smell as bad as Mrs Byrne was implying. She'd been planning on wearing the perfume to dinner on Wednesday. What if Vinnie found it offensive, too? But she didn't have time to dwell on this. Mrs Byrne was impatiently flapping her hand again, this time towards the table.

'We'll begin with the notices.'

Chrissy stared down at the table on which lay a small heap of mail and a copy of the *Daily Telegraph*. What did she mean? 'Erm . . . the notices?'

'Births, deaths and marriages,' Mrs Byrne said tetchily, as

though she was dealing with an imbecile. 'In the paper. Look on the front; it'll tell you where.'

Chrissy picked up the newspaper and unfolded it. She checked for the right page number but then had to negotiate her way there. The *Telegraph* was big and unwieldy and kept collapsing in on her. Eventually, she found a way to control the monster, holding it at arm's length until the correct page was reached. Then she folded the paper again and laid it on her lap.

'Start with the deaths,' Mrs Byrne said, settling back in her chair as though about to listen to a good play on the radio.

Chrissy began. 'Ambrose, Margaret. Died peacefully surrounded by her family on October second, 1985. Much loved mother of Henry, Diana and Jean. Her funeral will be held at Wrexham Crematorium on ... '

'Just go through the names,' Mrs Byrne interrupted. 'I'll tell you if I want to hear more.'

So Chrissy went through the names, and was only stopped again when she came to Alice Graham, a former actress who had died at the age of seventy-eight. During the recitation, Mrs Byrne drummed her fingers against her thigh and made small clicking noises with her tongue. When it was finished, she said, 'So, she's finally dead.'

'I'm sorry. Did you know her?'

'Don't be sorry, dear. She was a dreadful woman. Couldn't keep her hands off other people's husbands. It was like a compulsion, you see, a need to have what wasn't hers.'

Chrissy heard an edge of bitterness in the tone and wondered if the late Mr Byrne had fallen victim to Alice Graham's wandering hands. She couldn't ask – it wouldn't be polite – but it piqued her curiosity.

'There are very few pleasures left when you reach my age,

Christine, but seeing one's enemies pre-decease one is right up there at the top of the list.'

Chrissy glanced at the old woman. Was she just trying to shock her? But Mrs Byrne's expression was one of gleeful self-satisfaction.

After the deaths, they moved on to the births and then the marriages. When these were completed, Chrissy was asked to go back to the front of the paper and start reading out the head-lines. When Mrs Byrne heard something of interest, she would ask for the whole article to be read out. Although a perfectly competent reader, Chrissy was constantly scanning ahead in case a difficult word came up that she might have trouble pro-nouncing. She didn't want to make a fool of herself or give Mrs Byrne any reason to criticise.

An article about Lord Scarman's 1981 report on the Toxteth and Brixton riots produced some raising of the eyebrows, as did the news that unemployment was unlikely to fall beneath the three million mark in the near future. Mrs Byrne made it clear by her interjections that she believed most working-class people were lazy and feckless, and likely to resort to protest for want of anything better to do.

Chrissy glanced round the room at all the expensive furniture and furnishings, wondering if Mrs Byrne had any idea at all how the other half lived. A week on the Mansfield would soon open her eyes. It was easy to pass judgement when you didn't have to worry about where the next meal was coming from or how you were going to feed the gas meter or whether the law were going to try and stitch you up. She almost said something but bit her tongue. It would be wise, she thought, to try and keep on the right side of the old lady, at least for now.

Once the newspaper had been exhausted, they moved on to the post. This consisted of a couple of invitations – one to the opening of a play, the other to dinner – and a letter from a cousin in Australia. The cousin's handwriting was small and spidery and Chrissy had to squint to read it. *Dear Muriel . . .* The letter was several pages long and consisted mainly of news about children, and children's children. Mrs Byrne looked bored and may have briefly nodded off.

A pre-lunch stroll in the garden was next on the agenda. Although the sky was grey, it was close and humid outside. They walked slowly along a curving path that skirted the lawn, Mrs Byrne's stick tapping against the paving stones. She stopped frequently to examine one plant or another, her fingers doing the work of her eyes, prodding and probing while she muttered about the gardener who was, it would appear, as lazy and shiftless as the people who lived on housing estates. To Chrissy the garden appeared quite lovely, but she suspected that nothing short of perfection would please her employer.

'Stanton likes to cut corners. You have to watch him like a hawk. That's the trouble with Luther: he doesn't keep on top of things. He's just like his father in that respect. Too easy-going, that's his problem. People take advantage.'

Chrissy suppressed a smile. Easy-going was not the first term that sprang to mind when she thought about Luther Byrne. 'I suppose he's busy with work and everything.'

'I'd hardly call it work, sitting around in that gallery all day. And out every other evening too. If he spent more time at home, I wouldn't have all this constant worry.'

It occurred to Chrissy that all Mrs Byrne really wanted was to see more of her son, which seemed odd, bearing in mind the ill-tempered nature of their relationship. But that was families for you; it was hard to make sense of them from the outside. They all had their own histories, their secrets and grievances.

Lunch – poached salmon, potatoes and peas – was served

by Mrs Parry in the dining room at one o'clock precisely. Mrs Byrne criticised the fish and the texture of the potatoes, but only once Mrs Parry was out of earshot. For Chrissy, who had been unsure of the arrangements and had packed a cheese sandwich just in case, the provision of a free lunch was a bonus. She was surprisingly hungry considering she'd spent most of the morning sitting down. After a few eager mouthfuls, Chrissy remembered her manners – and what she was being paid for – and attempted to make some polite conversation.

'You have a beautiful home. Have you lived here for long?'

'All my life. So, yes, for more years than I care to remember. I inherited the house from my parents and as such it was out of my husband's reach. I suppose I should be grateful for that small mercy. Jack was a profligate man. Do you know what that means?'

Chrissy didn't, but she could hazard a guess. 'A spender?' she suggested.

'Yes, a spender, a reckless spender. He liked lovely things, you see, even when he couldn't afford them. It made for certain … difficulties.'

'I suppose it would.'

'He liked to travel, too: Europe, Asia, the Far East. Often he was gone for months at a time.'

'You didn't go with him?'

'At first,' Mrs Byrne said. 'Until it became disagreeable.'

'The travelling or the company?'

Mrs Byrne speared a small chunk of salmon with her fork, raised it to her mouth, peered at it, frowned and put it down again. 'Both.'

There was a finality about the answer, a sharpness that defied further investigation, and so, after a short silence, Chrissy asked instead about Luther. 'Your son owns a gallery, then?'

'Bond Street,' Mrs Byrne said.

'That must be interesting.'

'It's a ruthless business, Christine, full of lies and greed and deception. Don't be fooled by appearances. Behind all the smart suits and the glib talk, there's only scheming ambition. Show me a dealer and I'll show you a man prepared to stab his best friend in the back.'

Chrissy wasn't sure if she was describing her son's activities or just what he had to put up with. 'Oh.'

'Oh, indeed.'

'I never realised.'

'No, people never do.' Then, out of the blue, Mrs Byrne declared, 'If you've set your sights on Luther, I'd think again. You're really not his type. You might be young and pretty but he'd never marry anyone with less money than himself.'

Chrissy, stung by the remark, was temporarily dumbstruck. She stared across the table, about to protest her innocence – it was crazy, ridiculous, she had no designs of that kind *whatsoever* on Luther – when she noticed the expression on the older woman's face. Mrs Byrne had the look of a defiant child hoping to provoke a reaction. The spiteful remark, she realised, had been designed purely to get a rise out of her.

'Well, you don't have anything to worry about on that score,' Chrissy replied calmly. 'I don't believe Mr Byrne would suit me at all.'

'I'm not worried for myself, dear, only for you. I'd hate for you to be disappointed.'

'There really isn't any danger of that.'

Mrs Byrne put down her knife and fork and pushed her plate away. Her lips pursed for a moment. Then, acting as though the exchange had not taken place at all, she said, 'I think we'll take coffee in the drawing room.'

55

After a couple of days, Chrissy had got into the routine of the Byrne household and begun to settle into the job. It was not physically demanding – sitting on her backside was hardly wearing – but the old lady kept her on her toes. It was easy to see how so many of her predecessors had fallen by the wayside: Mrs Byrne had a caustic tongue and a love of confrontation. It was only a matter of time, she suspected, before a reason would be found to fire her. This meant that she had to act quickly if she was going to get the information she needed on Luther.

Chrissy hadn't seen him once since starting work; he was gone before she arrived in the morning, and didn't return until after she'd left. Despite her best efforts, the housekeeper had proved impossible to befriend. Perhaps she had seen too many companions come and go to be bothered with trying to build any kind of relationship with them. And she didn't dare broach the subject of Luther with Mrs Byrne again. At least not directly. She would have to think of another way – but what?

All this was running through Chrissy's head as she got ready for her date with Vinnie. It was hard to know what to wear. Nothing that made her look like she was too keen, but something nice enough to show that she'd made an effort. It was a tricky balancing act. She tried on various items and eventually settled on a simple dark red shift dress. With her make-up done and her hair brushed, she was ready to go.

'Bye Nan. I'll see you later. I won't be late.'

'Have a nice time.'

Nan didn't know she was going on a date. Chrissy didn't want the interrogation – What's his name? What does he do? How did you meet him? – and so she'd just told her she was going to meet a mate in the Fox instead. It felt like she was always spouting lies these days, although she justified it by telling herself that she didn't want to cause unnecessary worry. Nan would have a major fit if she found out she was working for Luther Byrne, and a minor one if she knew she was going on a date with Vinnie Keane. Men like Vinnie weren't good news in Nan's eyes, the type who didn't even make the list when it came to marriage material. If Nan had her way, Chrissy would be speeding straight down the aisle towards Councillor Frank Yates.

In the hall she put on her raincoat, grabbed her bag and brolly, and left the flat. Vinnie had offered to pick her up but she hadn't wanted to take the chance of one of the neighbours spotting them and reporting back to Nan. Of course, there was the same risk at the Fox, but at least there she could claim that she'd just bumped into him, and that he'd only bought her a drink because they worked together.

As she walked down the high street it began to rain, and she quickly put up her brolly before the damp could make her hair go frizzy. It was barely seven-twenty but already it was dark. Cars and buses rushed by, able to gather some speed now that rush hour had passed. The streetlamps cast an orangey glow over the pavement. All the shops were closed, their metal shutters pulled down to protect against the thieves of Kellston.

Although it wasn't late and there were still people around, Chrissy stayed alert, her spare hand tight around her handbag. She had lived here long enough to know that whatever the time of day, there could be someone wanting to take what was hers. Being vigilant was second nature to her, as natural as breathing. Better safe than sorry.

The Fox was mid-week busy, not packed but with enough customers to give the place some atmosphere. She looked around for Vinnie, but couldn't spot him, so made her way towards the rear of the pub. Even though she was a few minutes early, she still expected him to be here. He was the type, she thought, never to keep a date waiting.

Chrissy was approaching the small room at the back when she noticed the couple sitting at a table in the corner, a couple it took a few seconds for her to recognise: Frank Yates and Zelda. Immediately she stepped to the side, skulking behind a pillar, not wanting them to see her. Why not? Partly it was because she was unprepared – she didn't know what to say to Zelda after all this time – but mainly it was because they appeared to be arguing. It wasn't a full-blown row but one of those restrained exchanges where they were both clearly riled and at the same time being careful not to raise their voices. She wondered if she was witnessing a lover's tiff – maybe Frank and Zelda were an item now – but couldn't see it in the body language. There was anger and disagreement, but no passion.

She peeked round the pillar, most of her attention concentrated on Zelda. Her old friend had cut her hair short and it suited her; she looked stylish and sophisticated, all shoulder pads and confidence. It was odd to think of her as a solicitor, a profession that seemed a hundred miles away from her roots on the Mansfield estate. Her clothes were smart, nicely tailored and she was wearing an expensive pair of heels.

And then something very odd happened. Frank reached into his pocket, took out his wallet and surreptitiously passed Zelda a wad of notes. It was hard to tell exactly how much it was, but the bundle was thick. Why the hell was he giving her money? She watched as Zelda quickly stashed the cash in her bag. The two of them looked furtive, guilty, as though the exchange had been a dirty one.

Chrissy jumped as she felt a tap on her shoulder, and turned to find Vinnie standing behind her. 'Oh, hi.'

'Sorry, I didn't mean to startle you. Am I late?'

'No, no, I've only just got here.'

He grinned. 'You're looking very nice.'

'Thank you,' Chrissy said, as she edged away from the pillar and back towards the main part of the pub. 'You too.' Vinnie was smartly dressed in jacket, trousers and an open-necked blue shirt. He was clean-shaven and smelled of a pleasantly subtle aftershave. She had gone easy on the perfume herself after Mrs Byrne's scathing judgement on the Dior.

'What can I get you to drink?'

'Erm . . . would you mind if we went somewhere else?'

'Somewhere else?'

She could almost see what he was thinking: first Connolly's, then the Wimpy and now the Fox. Like she was one of those women who were impossible to please. Quickly she leaned in to explain. 'There's someone here I don't want to bump into. Would you mind?'

'Of course not,' he said. 'There's plenty more pubs in London.'

Once they were out of the door, Chrissy relaxed. 'Sorry about that.'

'So who are you trying to avoid? An ex?'

'No, nothing like that. Someone I used to know years ago.'

'Someone you don't like, I take it.'

'No, I did like her. We were at school together. It's just ...' Chrissy tried to find the right words as they walked towards Vinnie's car. 'It's been a long time and ... well, it can be a bit awkward, can't it? I mean, I do want to talk to her, but not tonight. She's with someone and I think they're having a row.'

'Ah, right, yes, you never want to get in the middle of one of those.'

'Exactly.'

Vinnie suggested Islington as their next port of call. 'Do you like Italian? There's a good little restaurant there, and a decent pub just down the road.'

Chrissy said that sounded fine.

While they drove, Vinnie asked about her new job, and she gave him the same reply that she'd given her nan: that it was good, that she was enjoying it, that the old lady was nice but a touch eccentric. She asked him how his week was going and he glossed over things in the same way she had.

As they chatted, Chrissy was still thinking about what she'd seen at the Fox and wondering why Frank had been giving Zelda money. Council shenanigans? A bung? Except, if it was a bribe, surely it should have been the other way around, with Zelda providing the money from a client to secure some lucrative council contract. So perhaps it was to do with something else entirely. She wouldn't have expected Frank to be up to anything dodgy, but perhaps the whole man of the people thing was just a clever façade.

'Vinnie?' she asked. 'Do you know Frank Yates?'

'The councillor?'

'Yeah, that's the one.'

'I wouldn't say I know him, but I've seen him around. Why?'

'Do you think he's straight? I mean, is he honest? Have you heard any rumours about him?'

'No. Why? You think he's on the take?'

'What makes you say that?'

Vinnie turned his head and grinned at her. 'Because you just asked me if he was honest.'

'Well, I didn't mean . . . ' Chrissy shrugged. 'You wouldn't tell me even if you did know something, would you?'

'Course I would. But I don't. Cross my heart.' Vinnie shot her another glance. 'So what's the interest in Mr Yates?'

'Nothing, really. He's just been helping my nan with some paperwork.'

'And?'

'Why does there have to be an and?'

'There's always an and,' Vinnie said. 'Or am I just getting cynical in my old age?'

'Probably.' She looked out for a moment at the street passing by, wondering how much to tell him. Although she knew what she'd seen, she didn't know what it meant, and it didn't seem fair on Frank to go jumping to conclusions. 'I've been trying to figure him out, that's all. Some people seem too good to be true, don't they?'

'Well, no one could ever accuse me of that.'

Chrissy laughed and changed the subject.

When they reached Islington, Vinnie parked the car in a side street and they walked around the corner to the pub. It was quieter than the Fox but not empty, dimly lit with soft blues music coming through the speakers. Vinnie ordered a pint and she had a small white wine. She didn't drink much these days, didn't want to slide back into bad habits, but she needed some alcohol to help her relax. The whole Frank/Zelda business had put her on edge.

317

They chose a table away from other customers and sat down. The conversation flowed easily between them. He asked about her family and she gave him a brief history without going into detail. She asked about his and he told her both his parents were dead. He had no brothers or sisters, had never been married and had no kids.

'How come you never got hitched?' she asked.

'That's a good question.' He gave her one of his playful grins. 'You think it's too late for me now?'

'Oh, yes, I should think so. You've probably developed some dreadful habits.'

'That could be true.'

Chrissy felt easy with him, comfortable, like she'd known him for much longer than she had. Everything seemed to be going well until Vinnie leaned back and asked rather too casually, 'So what's the deal with this Luther Byrne, then?'

Chrissy, taken by surprise, took a few seconds to respond. 'Luther?'

'You were asking Terry about him, weren't you?'

'He told you that?'

'Yeah, he mentioned it. Is that a problem?'

'So much for discretion,' Chrissy said.

'Hey, I'm discreet. I've not told anyone else. And Terry only asked because I've been around longer than he has. He thought I might know something.'

'And do you?'

'Not much, but I remember the name, vaguely. I think he had a falling-out with Joe Quinn – that's the bloke who Terry took over from – but it was all years ago.'

'What kind of falling out?'

'I don't remember the details, but DCI Gaul was involved in it somehow.'

'I don't like Gaul,' Chrissy said.

'No one likes Gaul. I shouldn't think his mother's that keen, to be honest.' Vinnie sipped his pint and studied her over the rim of his glass. 'Terry said that your mum used to know Luther. What's that all about?'

'She used to work for him. I think they were friends.'

'That's why you're looking for him?'

'Yes. I thought he might be able to tell me about her.'

'Is that the only reason?'

'What do you mean?'

'It just seems a bit odd, that's all. Some random bloke who used to know your mum.'

A bad feeling – suspicion, distrust – was starting to creep over Chrissy. There was something about Vinnie, about his questions, that was setting off alarm bells in her head. 'Why are you so interested in Luther Byrne?'

'I'm not.'

'Come on, Vinnie. What's going on here?'

'Nothing,' he said, but his eyes momentarily refused to meet hers. When he did look at her again, his easy smile seemed forced. 'Forget it. It doesn't matter.'

'No, I can't forget it. Tell me.'

Vinnie sighed as though she was being unreasonable. 'All I know is that Gaul got kind of agitated on Saturday when Luther Byrne was mentioned, like it was a name he didn't want to be reminded of. Some bad shit must have gone down between them. Don't ask me what because I don't have a clue. But whatever it is, you don't want to get caught in the middle of it.'

'Why would I?'

'Look, I'm just worried about you. We both are.'

As soon as he'd said it, Chrissy could tell he wished he hadn't. 'Both?'

Vinnie's gaze slid away again. 'Well, Terry doesn't want to see you get into any trouble either.'

'What's it to him?'

'He's just looking out for you.'

But the truth was finally dawning on Chrissy. 'Bullshit. He barely knows me. That's why he asked me to go for a drink on Saturday, isn't it? So he could try and find out what I know about Gaul and Luther Byrne.'

'No. Of course not.'

Vinnie's denial didn't even come close to sounding convincing. And now Chrissy's mind was reeling back, going through the chain of events that had led her to sitting right here, right now. 'That's why you picked me up at the bus stop, isn't it? That's why we bumped into each other outside the caff. It wasn't just a coincidence. You wanted to . . .' She took a large swig of wine as anger and humiliation rose and swelled inside her. 'Jesus, was the whole Charlie Dunlap thing a set-up too? So you could come riding to my rescue, so I'd trust you, and be grateful, and confide in you?'

'It wasn't like that.'

'So what was it like?'

'For God's sake, you're getting this all out of proportion.'

But Chrissy was already on her feet. She'd heard enough. Vinnie wasn't interested in her – he never had been – not in a romantic way. It had all been a ruse, a means to an end. If she hadn't desperately needed what little wine she had left, she'd have gladly thrown it in his face. As it was, she downed the last few drops in one, slammed the glass down on the table and said, 'You can go to hell, and by the way, you can tell Terry to stuff his job, too.'

Chrissy stormed out of the pub. She'd only covered a few yards when she saw the light of a black cab and quickly raised her arm to flag it down. 'Kellston, please.' She climbed into the back and slumped into the seat.

As the cab moved off, she saw Vinnie come out and look around for her. Too late. She sat shaking, seething, her cheeks burning. What was wrong with her? Idiot! She'd been taken for a fool once before but at least then she'd had the excuse of being young and naive. At twenty-four she should know better. She should have realised that Vinnie was only playing her. As her anger grew, her hands curled into two tight fists. Well, she'd had it with men. From now on she was done with the whole damn lot of them.

56

The next morning, Chrissy was still hopping mad. She stood at the bus stop in the pouring rain, huddled under her brolly, going over the previous night's events and wondering if she had mug tattooed on her forehead. She could imagine the kind of banter that must have passed between Terry and Vinnie after she'd turned one down and then accepted the other, all the chauvinistic sexist comments that the two of them would have exchanged. And how far would Vinnie have gone to get the information he wanted? All the way, no doubt. Her lip curled in disgust. The man had the morals of a pig.

She still didn't know exactly what it was that Terry was after. Was he working for Gaul or against him? He'd said he didn't like the DCI but that could have been a ploy to put her off her guard. It was all connected to Luther Byrne, but perhaps it was connected to her mother's death, too. If Vinnie had just been straight with her, she would have told him the truth. Well, maybe. And anyway, that wasn't the point; the point was that he had wheedled his way into her affections and tried to take advantage.

Did she have the worst judgement in the world? She must have. She trusted the wrong people and continued to make the same mistakes. What she wanted was to get a grip on things, to look forward instead of back, to lead a normal life. What she probably needed was a good psychiatrist.

Just to make matters worse, every time a car went by, the tyres sluiced up the water from the gutters, sending a wave across the pavement. Although she was standing well back, her shoes were still soaked. She'd be sitting in wet feet all morning, another reason to feel utterly dejected. If she had any sense, she thought, she'd drop the whole Luther thing, leave the job and concentrate on moving on.

But she was already one job down. Having resigned from Cordelia's she was now wholly reliant on her position with Mrs Byrne. This was not a good time to be thinking about chucking that in too. It was clear that she wasn't going to be able to find out about Luther in a hurry, but that didn't mean she wouldn't ever uncover something useful. She'd just have to be smart, patient, conniving and eventually she'd get a break.

Chrissy was trying to console herself with this plan when a car pulled in beside the bus stop. Immediately she thought of Vinnie, but it wasn't his motor. She saw DS Sutherland lean across and open the door.

'You want a lift?' he called out to her.

Chrissy went over and leaned down to talk to him. 'It's okay, thanks, the bus will be here in a minute.'

'I need to talk to you.'

'What about?'

'Get in and I'll tell you.'

'I'm on my way somewhere.'

'Where are you going?'

'King's Cross,' she said, not wanting to mention Highgate.

'Hop in. I can drop you off there. We can talk on the way.'

There were only two other people at the bus stop, neither of whom she knew. She had a quick look round to make sure no one else was watching – hopefully the Dunlaps were still snoring in bed – and decided it was worth taking the risk. Being seen consorting with a cop was not advisable, but the car was unmarked and Sutherland was in plain clothes. She was curious as to what he wanted to talk about, and it was no great loss being able to get out of the rain.

Chrissy fastened her seatbelt as Sutherland pulled back out into the lane of traffic. 'Is this about Tina? Is she okay?'

'I think so. As she'll ever be. You did the right thing getting her inside on Friday. What made you take her to Frank Yates's?'

'I couldn't think of anywhere else.'

'I didn't realise you two were mates.'

'We're not, not really. I just figured it was somewhere she'd be safe, and I knew he had a phone. Is this what you wanted to talk to me about?'

'Not exactly.'

By now they'd cleared the traffic lights down by Kellston station and Chrissy was starting to relax. The further they got from the Mansfield, the less chance there was of anyone seeing them together. 'So, what is it?'

Sutherland shot her a glance. 'Don't get mad, but I overheard you talking to Frank about Luther Byrne. I wasn't eavesdropping – well, no more than a cop ever does – and I just … I suppose it's been playing on my mind. Have you found him yet?'

'Why would I even look after what you told me?'

'Because you're stubborn like your mother.'

Chrissy stared at him. 'I thought you barely knew her.'

Sutherland pulled a face. 'I suppose I may have been a little economical with the truth there.'

'You mean you lied.'

'It's complicated.'

'Go on, then. I'm listening.'

Sutherland seemed to be struggling to find the right words, his lips parting momentarily, only to close again. His fingers danced on the steering wheel. Eventually he said, 'This is just between the two of us, right?'

'Sure,' Chrissy said, growing more curious by the second.

'Okay. We were . . . your mum and me . . . we were close, you know, really close. We were seeing each other before . . .'

'What? You were going out with her? You were a couple? You're kidding!'

Sutherland gave a rueful smile. 'It's not that shocking, is it? I mean, we're talking twenty years ago. Don't judge me on how I look now; I was quite a catch back in the day.'

Despite his feeble attempt at a joke, she could see how tense he was. 'So why lie about it?'

'Like I said, it's complicated. We couldn't be open about it at the time – dating a cop was strictly off limits if you lived on the Mansfield – so we had to keep quiet. People make presumptions. She'd have been labelled a grass, and all the rest. It would have been a nightmare for her. And now . . . well, things don't change much, do they? Mud sticks. Even after all these years it wouldn't be good news for your nan, for any of you, if it became public knowledge.'

'Does Nan know?'

'She found out just before your mum died. Why do you think she dislikes me so much? She blames me for what happened.'

Chrissy frowned. 'I don't understand. Why would she blame you?'

'Because of the whole Luther Byrne business. She reckons I encouraged your mum to go after him, to help bring him down,

325

but that wasn't how it was at all. I begged Laura to stop, to leave that job, but she wouldn't. She could have turned a blind eye to what was going on or just walked away and left it to us, but she didn't. She knew we wouldn't get him without her help – he was too smart, too bloody careful.'

'So what are you saying? That she was working for you?'

'She was trying to stop him. Rascals was just a front for all sorts of bad stuff, mainly drugs and prostitution. It was the girls she was really concerned about: they were young, you see, *too* young. She wasn't the type who could just turn her back and pretend it wasn't happening. She wanted to protect them. That's the sort of person she was. She had a big heart, your mum, and a lot of courage.'

Chrissy gazed through the windscreen as she tried to assimilate all this new information. It was like meeting Laura Moss for the first time, getting to know a part of her she'd never known before. If what Sutherland said was true, she supposed she should be proud, but she felt a spurt of anger too. If her mother hadn't deliberately put herself in danger, she might still be here today.

'Do you think Luther found out what she was doing and killed her?'

'He had an alibi for the night it happened.'

'That doesn't mean anything. He could have got someone else to do it.'

Sutherland gave a nod. 'That's why I want you to stay away from him. There's no saying how he'll react if you start throwing accusations around. He's a dangerous man, Chrissy. To be honest, I don't even know if he's back in the country. After your mum died, he sold the bar and went abroad. He could be living anywhere.'

Chrissy reckoned Sutherland was either the worst cop in the

world – it didn't take two minutes to open a phone book and check the listings – or that he was deliberately trying to mislead her as to Luther's whereabouts. She suspected the latter and she understood the reason why: it was his attempt to keep her safe, to prevent her from meeting the same fate as her mother.

'He shouldn't be allowed to get away with it,' she said. 'It's wrong. He should pay for what he did.'

'There was no proof that he was involved, not directly.'

'*You* don't think it was an accident, do you?'

'The driver didn't notice anyone else on the platform, but it was dark and it was raining so . . . ' Sutherland tightly gripped the steering wheel as though even talking about it caused him pain. 'Sorry.' He cleared his throat before continuing. 'She just lurched forward, apparently, as the train was coming in. There was nothing the driver could do. Look, you don't want to hear about this. All I'm saying really is that there's nothing in the police reports or from the coroner to suggest it was anything but a tragic accident.'

'You haven't answered the question. What do *you* think?'

'I don't know, and that's the honest truth.'

Chrissy turned this over in her mind as she gazed out at the long line of cars and buses. The closer they got to King's Cross, the more clogged up the traffic was becoming. 'Nan told me Luther wasn't a villain, that he was a straightforward businessman.'

Sutherland smiled wryly. 'She's just trying to look out for you. That's what nans do, right? They take care of their own.'

'I don't like being lied to.'

'A white lie, that's all. What would telling you the truth have achieved? Put all sorts of ideas into your head, no doubt, about confronting Luther Byrne. She's already lost a daughter; she doesn't want to lose a granddaughter too.'

They were silent for a while as the car stopped and started, snarled up in a tailback. A fog of exhaust fumes belched into the morning air. There was a honking of horns, a rise in frustration as everyone went nowhere.

'We did everything we could,' Sutherland eventually said. 'It was a thorough investigation. We raided Rascal's soon after your mum's death, but it was clean as a whistle. No sign of anything illicit, not even a receipt out of place.'

'He'd have guessed you were coming.'

'Yes.'

'I still don't really understand why Nan kept quiet about it all. I'm not just talking about now, to me, but back when it happened. You know what she's like. Why didn't she kick up a stink when she found out what Luther was really like, go public, shout about it? She's not the type to let things lie. She must have known there was a chance he'd been involved in Mum's death.'

'And then what?'

Chrissy glanced at him. 'What do you mean?'

'If she'd gone down that road, then it would all have come out about her daughter passing on information to the police. Everyone on the Mansfield would have been aware of it. She couldn't have stayed there; it would have been impossible. It doesn't matter about motive – if you're a grass you're a grass, and that's the end of it. And she had you to think about, and Pete. So, after some discussion, we decided to keep a lid on a few things.'

'Like Mum's relationship with you?'

'It was for the best.'

Chrissy narrowed her eyes. 'That was convenient.'

'It wasn't like that. I know how it looks and you're right – cops aren't supposed to have relationships with their informants – but that wasn't why we all decided to keep quiet about it.'

'There was a cover-up, though.'

'You can call it that if you like. But it was for the right reasons. It's not black and white. Yes, we could have all told the truth, the whole truth and nothing but the truth, but how was that going to make anything better? Fact is, it was only going to make matters worse. We had nothing on Luther Byrne – well, nothing we could prove – so it made more sense to let certain things lie. Don't blame your nan. None of it was easy. She had some tough decisions to make.'

Chrissy was still trying to get her head round what she'd been told. What hurt her most, she thought, was having had it all concealed from her. Being kept in the dark was a sore point at the moment after what had happened with Vinnie. Nan, the one person she could normally rely on, had hidden the truth: she might have had her reasons, but that didn't make it right.

'Your mum was a special person,' Sutherland said. 'I still think about her every day.'

Aware that they were finally edging around the corner into Euston Road, and unsure as to when or if she'd ever get the chance to talk to him again, she blurted out, 'Did you love her?'

'Of course I did. I've never met anyone like her. She was a one-off.'

Chrissy would have liked to ask more – what her mum had really been like, how they'd met, if she'd ever talked about *her* – but the station was looming into view. 'You can drop me anywhere round here.'

Sutherland pulled in by a bus stop, turned and said, 'I hope I haven't upset you.'

Chrissy shook her head. 'It's just a lot to take in.'

'Your nan won't be happy if she finds out I've told you all this.'

'I won't tell her. I promise.'

'Thanks. I appreciate that. Mind how you go.'

Chrissy got out of the car, walked a few yards along the road, went down the steps into the grey underpass and joined the throng heading towards the station. It was strange, perplexing, to think of her mum and Sutherland as lovers. Had he really cared for her as much as he claimed? If she took the cynical view, she could view the whole cover-up as being mainly to his advantage, but she didn't want to judge him too harshly. There had been something persuasive, something genuine, about his declarations.

Carried along by her fellow commuters, she walked at speed, climbed the steps at the far end and emerged in front of King's Cross station. She understood now why DCI Gaul had been so aggravated when Terry had raised the subject of Luther Byrne: Luther was the one who'd got away and nobody likes to be reminded of past failures.

As she was entering the station, Chrissy experienced one of those odd feelings, like she was being watched: a sense of eyes on her, a prickling on the neck. She looked over her shoulder, searched the faces in the crowd, but came up with no likely candidate. It was only her imagination playing tricks. She was just off-kilter, agitated, churned up, after all the unexpected revelations. The only person on her heels was a ghost from the past. She glanced back again, almost expecting her mother to be there, but she saw only strangers.

57

Chrissy's state of mind was not improved by finding Luther Byrne at home when she arrived at the Highgate house. She had to pass his study on the way to the drawing room: the door was open, the radio playing, and he was rifling through a filing cabinet with his back to her. Remembering what Sutherland had told her, she felt simultaneously angry and afraid. Was this the man who, one way or another, had brought about the death of her mother? The music from the radio – a classical piece – had disguised the sound of her footsteps on the wood floor and for a few seconds she stood quite still, able to observe him without being noticed. He seemed as agitated as she was, his shoulders tight and tense, his fingers searching for something that continued to elude him. She moved swiftly on before he became aware of her presence.

Mrs Byrne was in one of her more erratic moods and the morning was a challenging one. Perhaps she too was affected by Luther's proximity. One minute she was calm and friendly, the next impatient and critical. Chrissy found it hard to concentrate, her thoughts continuously straying, and she stumbled over words in the newspaper, eliciting long, pained sighs from her employer.

'What's wrong with you today?' Mrs Byrne asked. 'Did you have a late night?'

'No,' Chrissy replied honestly. 'Just a difficult one.'

'Man trouble, I suppose.'

Chrissy didn't bother to deny it. Better that Mrs Byrne thought she was suffering from boyfriend issues, she decided, than from problems related to someone closer to home. Her chat with Sutherland had temporarily pushed Vinnie Keane out of her mind, but now he returned with a vengeance, making her scowl.

'They're more trouble than they're worth,' Mrs Byrne said. 'Take my word for it. If I had my time again, I'd stay a spinster.'

Chrissy gazed into the middle distance, thinking what an awful word spinster was and wondering if she'd end up as one. The way things were going there was every chance of it.

'What are you looking at?' Mrs Byrne asked, turning her head slightly. 'Is it the stubs?'

'The stubs?' Chrissy replied, confused.

'The painting, my dear. The horse. It's by George Stubbs.' Mrs Byrne spelled it out for her: 'S.T.U.B.B.S. Didn't they teach you anything in school?' Before Chrissy got the chance to answer, she continued, 'Do you know how he got to paint horses so well? He used to dissect them in his studio, take them apart piece by piece so he could study every bone, every muscle, every ligament. That's dedication, don't you think?'

If Chrissy hadn't been feeling queasy before, she certainly was now. She refocused her gaze to look more closely at the painting. The horse, accompanied by a gentleman, was chestnut brown, sleek and sinuous. 'It sounds messy.'

'You mustn't ever touch it,' Mrs Byrne said. 'It's alarmed.'

'Why would I touch it?'

'It's an original. It's worth a lot of money.'

Chrissy stiffened, offended by the implication. Was Mrs Byrne suggesting she might try and nick it? She opened her mouth to protest but Mrs Byrne, perhaps suspecting she had gone too far, got in before her.

'All I mean is that even if you brush against it accidentally, the alarm will go off. It can be a nuisance. I just thought I'd better warn you.'

Chrissy didn't think this was what she'd meant at all. 'I'll bear it in mind,' she said through gritted teeth.

The morning progressed in the usual way – the perusal of the newspaper, the reading of the mail, the walk in the garden – until it was time for lunch. On entering the dining room Chrissy was startled to find Luther Byrne at the table. She had presumed he'd left the house hours ago and gone to the gallery in Bond Street. This change to the normal routine made her jumpy and anxious, afraid that his reason for being there was something to do with her. He stood up as they came in, like one of those gentlemen in Victorian novels. Not that she'd read any of those but she'd seen the TV versions. Her heart started beating faster and she had to take a few deep breaths to try and calm herself.

As they all sat down, Mrs Byrne said to him, 'Did you sort it out?'

'Sort what out?'

'Whatever it is you've been fretting about all morning.'

'Oh, *that*. It was nothing. Just some VAT receipts. What delights is Mrs Parry conjuring up for lunch today?'

'I believe it's roast chicken.'

'Ah, very nice.'

'Yes, I've noticed that she always makes an extra effort when you grace us with your presence.'

'Does she?' Luther shot Chrissy a glance that could almost be described as mischievous. A smile played around his lips. 'If that's the case, I must have stern words with her.'

'For all the good it would do,' Mrs Byrne said.

He looked at Chrissy again. 'So, Miss Cope, how are you settling into our little household? I hope it's not too quiet for you.'

'Not at all. I'm finding it quite—'

'Christine was just admiring the Stubbs,' Mrs Byrne interrupted, with what might have been a hint of slyness.

Luther nodded. 'Yes, it's very fine. A copy, of course, but a decent one. Sadly, Father sold the original.'

'A copy?' Chrissy said, raising her eyebrows and looking at Mrs Byrne. 'I'd never have guessed.'

'Ah, yes, a copy,' Mrs Byrne said softly. 'I'd quite forgotten. The memory goes when you get to my age.'

Mrs Parry arrived with a tray, placed the plates of food on the table and departed again without saying a word. The three of them picked up their knives and forks and started to eat. Although Chrissy had no complaints about any of the lunches she'd been provided with, this was certainly the best, as good as Nan's Sunday roast with all the trimmings.

'Will you be going to the gallery this afternoon?' Mrs Byrne asked her son.

'No, I have some paperwork to do. Terence can manage on his own.'

Seeing as the subject had already been broached, Chrissy took the opportunity to try and wheedle some information out of Luther. 'Have you had the gallery for long?'

'Only a few years. Before that I was in New York.'

'Oh, how interesting. Did you like it there?'

'My son likes anywhere that isn't England,' Mrs Byrne said, apparently disinclined to let anyone answer for themselves. 'Before that he was in Europe: France, Italy, Greece. He's inherited his father's wanderlust. In fact, I strongly suspect he wouldn't have come back at all if it hadn't been out of a sense of duty.'

'Nonsense, Mother,' Luther said. 'I'm glad to be home. You can grow tired of hamburgers after a while.' He said to Chrissy, 'And in answer to your question: yes, I did enjoy it there. New York is a place full of possibilities.'

Chrissy tried again to delve into his past. 'So, have you always worked in the art world or . . . ?'

'More or less.' He ate a piece of chicken, chewing slowly, before he spoke again. 'I wanted to be a professional artist – it was my ambition for a long time – but I didn't have the talent. Sometimes you have to accept your inadequacies. Now I do the next best thing. I can't create great paintings and so I sell them instead.'

Mrs Byrne quickly contradicted his version of events. 'You had plenty of talent, Luther. You just didn't apply yourself. If you'd spent less time on your madcap schemes and more in the studio, you might have had some success.'

'Madcap?' Chrissy asked.

'Well, I'd hardly call them that. I've always thought it's good to try your hand at different things, see what suits. I've been involved in various—'

Again, Mrs Byrne interrupted. 'Luther never could settle, not when he was young. He was always jumping from one thing to another. He even owned a bar once. A bar,' she repeated, as if the very idea of it was preposterous.

'Where was it?' Chrissy asked, her ears pricking up. 'In London?'

'Mayfair,' Luther said.

'What happened to it?'

Luther left a long pause before answering, and Chrissy wondered if she'd asked one question to many. But eventually he replied. 'There were some ... problems. In the end I decided it wasn't for me.'

'Of course it wasn't for you,' Mrs Byrne said. 'Any fool could have told you that before you bothered to waste your money.'

'You're probably right. Still, we learn by our mistakes.' Luther glanced at Chrissy again, that small smile back in place as though they were co-conspirators in a plot to keep his mother appeased.

That was the last Chrissy heard about the bar. The conversation moved on and she didn't dare return to the subject in case Luther became suspicious. For the rest of the meal – the main course was followed by apple crumble and custard – he continued to be courteous, asking about her life and making enquiries about her grandmother's health. She didn't like this pleasant charming Luther any more than the rude, irritable one, but made the effort to be polite. A wolf in sheep's clothing was how her nan would have described him, but she wasn't fooled. She knew who he really was, had a good idea of what he'd done and was determined that he wouldn't get away with it.

58

It was only when she was on the bus, on the second leg of her journey home, that it occurred to Chrissy that Luther could have been doing as much digging as herself. A brief moment of panic made her heart race as she replayed the conversation in her head. Had she said anything she shouldn't? Had she given any hint to her true identity? She had the horrible feeling that a game of cat and mouse had taken place over lunch – and that she had been the prey.

These thoughts continued to haunt her as the bus made slow progress through the streets of London. It was scary to imagine that Luther might be on to her. Could Mrs Byrne be in on it too? The two of them had their differences, but blood was thicker than water. Chrissy was in no doubt that if it came to it the old lady would protect her own. Their relationship might be quarrelsome but families stuck together.

She continued to torment herself, searching for signs, for clues that she was about to be exposed, until her journey came to an end. She got off the bus and walked along the high street, into Mansfield Road and on to the estate. The paths were busy with people returning from work, their faces tired, their bodies moving sluggishly.

Frank Yates was in the throng and he stopped to talk to her. 'Have you ... erm ... heard anything – there's a rumour going around – about the police reopening the case on Dawn?'

Chrissy thought he looked worried, but she couldn't figure out why. 'Wouldn't that be a good thing?'

'I suppose so. It's just ... you know, everything getting stirred up again. Have you told them about King's Cross?'

'No, not yet.'

'Are you going to?'

'I haven't made up my mind. Do you think I should?'

Frank took what felt like a long time to answer. 'Only if you're a hundred per cent sure. Otherwise ... well, there's Tina to consider and ...'

'Perhaps I should ask Zelda what she thinks. Do you have her number?'

'Erm, no. I haven't seen her, not since ... not for months.'

Chrissy stared at him, vexed at being lied to. 'What's going on, Frank?'

'What do you mean?'

'I saw you with her in the Fox last night.'

Frank looked mortified. 'Did you? Oh. Christ. Sorry.' He shuffled from one foot to the other and glanced around as if searching for inspiration. 'I should have said, but I knew she hadn't been in touch with you yet and so ...'

'Oh, come off it, Frank. What's going on with you two?'

'Going on? No, there's nothing like that. We're not ... I just bumped into her. It wasn't planned or anything.'

Chrissy could see how flustered he was and it was down to more, she reckoned, than being caught out in a lie. 'Just bumped into her?'

'Yeah, I popped in for a drink and there she was. She was meeting a friend.'

Under different circumstances, Chrissy might not have mentioned what she'd seen, but her mood wasn't the best. She was sick of being lied to. 'So why were you giving her money?'

Frank's mouth dropped open. 'What?'

'It's none of my business what you two are up to, but you might want to be more careful in future. If I saw you, anyone could have. People could jump to all sorts of nasty conclusions.'

'No, it wasn't ... She's just a bit short at the moment and asked if I could help out.'

'She's a solicitor, isn't she? I thought they got pretty well paid.'

'She's only just qualified. She's not earning that much.'

'And since when did you become Mr Moneybags?'

'It wasn't that much,' he said weakly.

'Right, so you accidentally bumped into her, she asked if she could borrow some money and you just happened to have a wad of cash on you?' Chrissy didn't believe a word of what he was telling her. If it smelled wrong, it *was* wrong. 'Fine. Have it your own way. I've got to go. I'll see you around.'

'You won't tell anyone, will you? What you saw?'

'For Christ's sake, Frank, why can't you just tell me the truth? Are you in some kind of trouble?'

He shook his head, but not with much conviction.

Chrissy gave up and began walking towards the door again. Frank hesitated for a moment, but then followed her.

'I promised Zelda I wouldn't tell,' he said.

'Tell what?'

Frank kept his voice low, as though afraid of being overheard. 'We can't talk here. Come over to my place about seven. Can you do that?'

'Okay,' Chrissy said. 'I'll see you later.' She went inside, pressed the button for the lift and stared back out through the doors. Her gaze followed Frank as he hurried towards Haslow House. The hunch of his shoulders spoke of a man with a lot on his mind – and none of it, she suspected, was good.

59

Terry Street viewed DCI Gaul as one of life's necessary evils. Their relationship, which was based as much on mutual distrust as mutual advantage, had nevertheless allowed both parties to flourish over the past ten years. Neither of them liked the other, but this had never been an impediment to a profitable working relationship. Not, that is, until recently.

Terry's patience was being stretched to the limit by Gaul's constant demands. It was as though the cop thought that Terry's pockets were a bottomless pit to be mined to his heart's content. And then there were the favours, the free drinks, the girls. And now this. He stared across the table at the fat slob, trying to keep his expression neutral. He recalled all the other places they'd met up – the backstreet cafés, the pubs, the bars and hotel foyers – skulking around like guilty lovers. Terry would be glad when the ties were severed. Gaul's retirement couldn't come soon enough.

'We've been thinking of reopening the case,' Gaul said slyly.

'And why would you want to do that?'

'Loose ends. You know how it goes. No one likes unfinished business.'

No one likes a greedy, manipulative bastard, either, Terry thought. 'What sort of loose ends?'

Gaul heaved out a breath that travelled across the table. Onions and whisky. 'There's always someone who saw something, even if it was a long time ago. A little jog to the memory and . . . Well, you never know what might rise to the surface.'

'Good luck with that,' Terry said. 'As you say, it was a long time ago.'

Gaul's heavy shoulders rose and fell. He ran his tongue across his fleshy lips and smiled. When he spoke again his voice was low and wheedling. 'Come on, Terry. It's not that much to ask, is it? Not after everything I've done for you.'

'You've had plenty back.'

'I've got a lot of dirt on you, Terry.'

'Likewise,' Terry said softly.

'Yeah, but who's a jury more likely to believe? An upstanding cop who's dedicated all his life to protecting society, or a known villain? You really want to go there? You really want to take that chance?'

Terry didn't lose his cool – he rarely did – but he could feel a low-level heat simmering in his guts. He didn't care for being threatened, and especially by the likes of Gaul. Back in his more impulsive days, he wouldn't have stood for it, but experience had taught him the importance of guile. He gazed into the middle distance and pretended to ponder on the proposition. 'It's not impossible, but I'll need some time to sort it out.'

Gaul nodded, his expression one of smug satisfaction. 'Not too long, huh? Neither of us are getting any younger.'

60

While she ate her tea, Chrissy surreptitiously watched Nan while she thought about what Sutherland had told her. Why hadn't she been trusted with the truth about her mum, about Luther Byrne before? Why did she have to hear it from him? There were more questions, lots of them, but she wasn't going to ask right now. And it wasn't because she'd promised to keep quiet – a promise to a cop didn't mean a damn thing – but because she didn't feel ready yet. She needed some time to sort her head out, to get things clear.

Chrissy was only half listening to Nan talk about that day's visit to Betty Cope. Something about the old woman not being too well, but then she never was. The monologue rolled through her, in one ear and out the other, as she mused on everything that had happened since she'd got up this morning.

'You're very quiet,' Nan said.

'Am I?'

'You've barely said a word since you got in.'

'I'm just tired. It's been a long day.'

'I don't suppose that journey home helps. How was your Mrs Parry today?'

Christine had a moment of confusion, wondering why she was inquiring about the housekeeper, before remembering that Parry was the name she'd substituted for Mrs Byrne. 'Oh, yes, all right. She's fine.' Then, hoping to distract her – she didn't want too many queries about her employment – she quickly said, 'I saw Frank on the way in. He still hasn't got any news on the flat.'

Nan looked pleased, despite the lack of progress. 'He said it could take a while.'

'Will Uncle Pete really be out before Christmas?'

'He should be. If he keeps his nose clean.'

'Do you think there'll be trouble, you know, with Jacko and the others?'

'Why should there be?'

'I wouldn't be happy if I was Uncle Pete, not after what they did to him. If they'd come clean, he could have served half that sentence.'

'Well, he made his choice. Not much he can do about it now.'

Chrissy didn't see how he'd had much choice. If he'd grassed up the ones who'd really done it, told the whole story, he'd never have been able to come back to the estate. It was just like what had happened with her mum, she thought. If the other residents had found out she'd been a snitch – no matter how honourable the reason behind it – Nan's life wouldn't have been worth living.

'Did Frank have anything else to say?'

Chrissy, who'd been gazing down at her plate, glanced up. 'Huh?'

'Frank. Did he have anything else to say?'

'Like what?'

Nan gave a small despairing shake of her head. 'Haven't you youngsters ever heard of conversation?'

'No, he was in a hurry. He had someone to see.' Then, before Nan could start extolling Frank's virtues again, she added, 'I'm going over to Sheila's later. She wants to borrow an album.'

'Sheila?'

'Sheila Mackie. She used to work in Connolly's.'

'You've never mentioned her before.'

'Haven't I? I must have. Tall, long brown hair. She lives in Haslow.'

'I thought you were tired.'

'I'll only be half an hour.'

At five to seven Chrissy went to her room, chose a random album – Alison Moyet's *Alf* – shoved it in a carrier bag and returned to the living room. 'Okay, I'll see you later.'

'You be careful, walking around on your own,' Nan said. 'And put your coat on, it's raining again.'

Chrissy swung the bag by her side as she crossed the estate to Haslow. If Nan had known where she was really going, she'd have been jumping for joy, thinking love was in the air. Whereas nothing could have been further from the truth. The only thing in the air was a thin drizzle and the faint but lingering smell of rubber from the tyres of a car that had been burnt out yesterday.

Although she didn't harbour any romantic notions about Frank, she understood why Nan liked him. And he'd been good over Tina Kearns. There were plenty on the estate who wouldn't have let them in, not wanting to get involved or fearing repercussions. At least he was his own man. But was he an honest one? She thought about the money changing hands and hoped he hadn't spent the last couple of hours concocting some cock and bull story to fob her off with.

She went up in the only lift that was working and walked

along the deserted corridor to Frank's. She rang the bell and he opened the door almost immediately, as though he'd been standing on the other side waiting for her.

'That was quick,' she said.

'I saw you walking along the path. Come on in.'

Chrissy followed him through to the living room, where she was surprised to find Zelda sitting on the sofa. 'Oh, hi. I didn't realise—'

'I thought Zelda should be here too,' Frank said. 'So we can both talk to you. So we can explain.'

Zelda looked less than impressed about this arrangement, but made the effort to smile. 'How are you? It's been ages.'

It wouldn't have been so long, Chrissy thought, if her old friend had made the effort to get in touch. And everything suddenly felt awkward. But she smiled back anyway, despite the feeling she had that they both knew this reunion wouldn't be taking place if it had not been for the situation. 'I'm good, thanks. You're looking well.'

'You too.'

Zelda must have come straight from work; she was wearing a silver-grey suit and white blouse. Chrissy, who had thrown on a pair of jeans and an old jumper, wished she'd worn something less casual; she felt shabby in comparison

'Would you like a drink?' Frank asked. 'Tea, coffee?'

'No ta,' Chrissy said.

'Grab a seat, then.'

Chrissy had a choice between sitting on the sofa beside Zelda or taking the armchair. She chose the latter. Frank sat down beside Zelda, laid his palms on his thighs, took them off and put them back again. He looked nervous, slightly sweaty, like a man with something to hide. There was a silence, broken only by the ticking of the clock on the mantelpiece.

It was Zelda who took the initiative. She leaned forward and said, 'Frank told me that you saw her. At King's Cross.'

Chrissy, who hadn't been expecting this – she'd been waiting for some excuse to emerge about the cash she'd seen Frank hand over – was caught off guard. 'Dawn?'

'She doesn't call herself that any more. It's Kara now.'

Chrissy's eyes widened. She wasn't exactly surprised by the news that Dawn was still alive, but she was shocked by the fact that Zelda clearly knew a good deal more. 'How long have you known that she wasn't . . . that she wasn't dead?'

Zelda's mouth twisted a little. 'Always.'

'What?'

'You have to let us explain. We couldn't say anything back then because—'

'Hang on,' Chrissy interrupted. 'Always? You've *always* known?' She looked at Frank. 'You've *both* known? Right from the beginning? Right from when she disappeared?'

Frank winced and glanced away.

Chrissy, bewildered, returned her attention to Zelda. 'You lied to me, you lied to everyone! Why? How could you?'

'We didn't want to,' Zelda said. 'I swear. Everything just went so wrong.'

Chrissy thought of Uncle Pete climbing the steps to the Kearns flat, the flash of his red T-shirt. Her voice rose a pitch, and anger surged through her body. 'It did that all right. They all thought Marlon had killed her. That's why they . . . Jesus! And all the time you knew that she was still alive and didn't say a bloody word.'

'I know. I'm sorry . . . we're sorry.'

'Sorry?' Chrissy said with incredulity. 'How does that change anything?'

'It doesn't. It can't. We really messed up.' Zelda, like Frank, didn't seem to know what to do with her hands. They wrestled in her lap, the fingers interlocking, separating, twisting together again. 'Can I tell you what happened? Can I try and explain?'

Chrissy leapt up from the chair, unable to contain her rage and frustration. Frank and Zelda both flinched, drawing back as if she was about to launch a physical attack. But once she was on her feet, Chrissy didn't know what to do next. Feeling the need for some distance, even if it was only a few yards, she strode over to the window and, with her back turned, said tightly, 'Okay, start explaining.'

Zelda took a deep breath and began. 'Dawn just wanted to scare her mum, to make her think she'd gone missing. You know what Tina was like, always drunk, hardly ever home, barely aware of Dawn's existence. And meanwhile Marlon was ... well, doing exactly what he wanted. Preying on her. He was a pervert, Chrissy, an abuser. She was just a kid and she couldn't stop him. She couldn't do anything about it.' There was a catch in Zelda's voice. She paused for a moment before carrying on. 'Dawn reckoned the police were bound to suspect him, that they'd lock him up and then she could go home and ... She had this idea in her head that once he was out of the way, Tina would believe her about the abuse, that she'd change, get her act together, that she'd wake up and realise what a bloody terrible mother she was.'

'That didn't work out so well,' Chrissy said drily.

'No,' Zelda agreed. 'We didn't consider the fact that she was so God awful she wouldn't even notice Dawn was missing.'

Chrissy looked over her shoulder. 'So you planned the whole thing with her?'

Zelda held her gaze. 'She just wanted her mum to care. It's not that much to ask, is it?'

'So where was she?' Chrissy asked. 'Where did she hide?'

'That was down to me,' Frank said.

Chrissy moved away from the window but didn't sit down again. She folded her arms across her chest and stared at him. 'You?'

'Mum had keys to quite a few flats on the Mansfield. She was the district nurse, remember? She had to be able to get into the homes of people who weren't mobile. There was a flat just along from us – the old woman had died a week or so earlier – and Mum hadn't given the key back to the council yet. I got a copy made and gave it to Dawn. Everything was still in there, the furniture and the rest. All she had to do was lie low and keep quiet.'

Zelda nodded. 'We thought it would only be for a couple of days, but then Tina didn't raise the alarm so we had to ...'

'Move things along?' Chrissy suggested.

Zelda nodded again. 'I'm sorry about your Uncle Pete. I never meant to get him involved.'

Chrissy recalled them all visiting the Kearns flat together, going up in the lift and knocking on the door. Marlon Pound being his usual nasty self. And later, searching the Mansfield for any sign of Dawn while Uncle Pete went down to the Fox to look for Tina. Zelda had played her part to perfection, anxious and afraid, while all the time she'd known exactly where Dawn was. 'You could have told me. We were supposed to be mates.'

'We just thought the more people who knew, the more chance there was of her being found out.'

'You mean you didn't trust me.'

'It wasn't that,' Zelda said, although she didn't go on to explain what it was. 'Anyway, then they discovered that woman's body and the police were crawling all over the estate. Dawn thought they were looking for her – you know, checking out all the flats – and got scared that she was in big trouble. She waited until the morning, until it had quietened down, and then took off.'

'Took off where?'

'The West End,' Zelda said. 'She says she caught an early train from Kellston. There was some loose change in the old lady's flat, not much but enough to buy a ticket with. We didn't know any of this back then. When we found out she'd gone, we thought she'd come back again before long so we just waited, and then . . . and then all that awful stuff happened with Marlon Pound and we didn't know what to do.'

'You could have told Tina she was still alive.'

'We should have,' Frank said.

'It was my fault,' Zelda said. 'I was too scared to tell. If we hadn't helped to hide Dawn, Marlon would never have been killed.'

'It was both of us,' Frank said. 'I was worried, too. I didn't want to get in any more trouble with the law.'

Chrissy sighed, trying to make sense of it all. 'What about the cardigan?'

'That was me,' Frank said. 'I panicked. She left it in the flat and I was afraid the law would find it there, or the council, so I threw it under the stairwell.'

'I don't understand how you even got involved. You and Dawn were never friends.'

Frank shrugged. 'I felt sorry for her.'

'She made him,' Zelda said.

Frank glared at her.

'Well, aren't we supposed to be telling the *whole* truth? Isn't that why we're here?'

'None of that matters any more,' Frank said.

Chrissy unfolded her arms and finally sat down again. 'If it doesn't matter, you might as well tell me.'

But Frank stayed silent.

It was Zelda who provided the explanation. 'Dawn found out he had a crush on you. She said she'd tell everyone, spread it round the school, if he didn't help. You know what it was like; they'd have made his life a misery.'

Chrissy barked out a laugh. 'That's rubbish. Frank never even used to speak to me if he could avoid it.' Then she noticed his face, red as a beetroot, and realised it wasn't as ridiculous as she'd thought. Suddenly she could see an entirely new reason as to why he'd often been so abrupt with her back then. 'Oh.'

'It's ancient history,' Frank said quickly, looking like he wished he was a hundred miles away. 'Just a schoolboy thing. I should have told her to get lost, do her worst, but I didn't dare. She knew Mum had all those keys – she'd seen her going in and out of flats – and so ... I should have said no, but I didn't. I was a bloody fool.'

Chrissy, who was starting to share his embarrassment, decided to move swiftly on. 'Like you say, it's ancient history. We all do stupid things when we're young. But what's all this got to do with the money? I'm guessing there's a connection.'

'It was for Dawn,' Frank said. 'She got in touch with me a few weeks back. She spotted my picture in the evening paper – some council do – and rang me at work. Said she needed to see us urgently.'

'That must have been a shock. Was it the first time you'd heard from her?'

Frank nodded. 'She hadn't been in touch with Zelda, either. Anyway, the three of us met up in a pub and that's when she asked us for the cash.'

'She was struggling,' said Zelda, taking up the thread. 'She just needed a loan, a few quid to tide her over.'

'A loan!' Frank scoffed. 'Why don't you call it what it is? Blackmail. She's blackmailing us.'

Chrissy frowned. 'What? How can she be?'

'Think about it,' Frank said. 'If she goes to the press and tells them she's the missing girl from all those years ago, it'll be a damn nice headline for them. I dare say they'll be willing to pay big for the inside story. Of course, they'll want to know all the juicy details – like who helped her, what they did, why they didn't tell the law. She's got nothing to lose, but we've got everything.'

'I'll be sacked,' Zelda said. 'I know I will. Who wants to employ a solicitor who can't be trusted, who keeps quiet about something like that?'

Chrissy looked from one to the other. 'But you were both kids. You can't be blamed for what you did back then.'

'We're not kids now,' Frank said. 'We've had years to come clean and we haven't. Tina still doesn't know if her daughter's dead or alive. How's that going to look?'

Chrissy could see that it wouldn't look too good. 'How much cash have you given Dawn?'

'Two hundred,' Zelda said, 'but she wants more.'

'She's always going to want more,' Frank said. 'She's going to bleed us dry.'

'I thought you and Dawn were mates?' Chrissy said to Zelda. 'Why's she doing this to you?'

Zelda stared down at the floor. 'She says it's been hard for her, that we've both got good jobs but she's got nothing. She's ... she's different to how she used to be.'

Frank pulled a face as if to indicate she wasn't different at all, but he didn't say anything.

'What's she been doing for the past ten years?'

'She won't talk about it,' Zelda said.

'She's living in Soho,' Frank said. 'I reckon she's—'

'You don't know that,' Zelda interrupted. 'You're just presuming.'

'I know her address, though – a place in Dean Street. I

followed her after we met in the pub. There's names on all the bells, girl's names, like Roxanne, Lola, Suzy . . .'

'And Kara,' Chrissy said.

'Yeah.'

Chrissy didn't want to think too much about how Dawn had survived through the years. There weren't many ways a fourteen-year-old could make a living but prostitution was one of them. At some point, she supposed, Dawn had heard about the killing of Marlon Pound, thought she'd get the blame and decided she could never come home. 'Do you really think she'll go to the press?'

'Why not?' Frank said.

'Then there's no point in giving her any more money. If it's going to happen eventually, it might as well be before she's emptied your bank accounts.'

'She might change her mind,' Zelda said, but there wasn't much optimism in her voice.

'Perhaps you should go to the police,' Chrissy suggested. 'Get in before her. Say it's been weighing on your conscience or whatever. At least that way you don't look so bad – and you get to put your side of the story first.'

Fear flashed in Zelda's eyes. 'We can't do that!'

'Then what are you going to do?'

But neither of them seemed to have an answer to that.

'Are you . . . are you going to tell anyone?' Zelda asked.

Chrissy shook her head. 'It's not down to me. But what about Tina? She's her mum. Don't you think she deserves to know the truth?'

'She doesn't deserve anything,' Zelda retorted sharply. 'That woman can't call herself a mother. If it hadn't been for her, if she hadn't been such a complete waste of space, if she hadn't taken up with Marlon Pound, Dawn would still be here.'

To Chrissy, Zelda seemed stuck between the loyalty she felt towards an old friend and the resentment she felt towards the person Dawn had become: even now, when Dawn was putting on the screws, she couldn't quite bring herself to condemn her. 'Did she mention seeing me at King's Cross?'

'Yes, but we told her you weren't sure and that Frank had managed to persuade you to keep quiet about it in case you were wrong.'

Chrissy remembered Frank's attempt to do exactly that. She would have got mad at him, mad at them both, if they hadn't looked so scared and miserable. Feeling that there wasn't much else she could do or say, Chrissy rose to her feet. 'I'd better get back. I told Nan I wouldn't be long.' She smiled at Zelda. 'Take care of yourself. I hope you find a way to work it out.'

And then Zelda said something surprising. 'Would you like me to contact Cowan Road about your mum's accident? Frank told me you were trying to chase up the reports.'

Chrissy shot a disapproving look at Frank, annoyed that he'd shared the information. 'No, it's all right, thanks. I can manage.'

'Sorry,' Frank said. 'We were just talking and ... erm, I thought Zelda might be able to help. These things are always easier when you go through a solicitor.'

'I don't mind,' Zelda said. 'I'd like to. I mean, it was me who mentioned it in the first place. If I hadn't said anything all those years ago ...'

Chrissy suspected Zelda might be trying to make sure she kept quiet – buying her silence – and she took exception to it. She was about to refuse again, but then changed her mind. What was more important: her pride or retrieving the information she wanted? She had to get off her high horse and grab what was on offer. 'Well, if you're sure.'

Zelda looked pleased that she'd accepted. 'Do you know the date she died?'

'Not exactly. It was November, though, 1965.'

'That's okay. Leave it with me. I'll see what I can do.'

Chrissy reached down and picked up her carrier bag. 'Thanks. Frank's got my number if you need anything else.'

Frank walked her to the hall. He looked downcast, like a man who was already resigned to the very worst outcome. He opened the door, stepped aside and asked, 'What would you do if you were in my shoes?'

'Call her bluff, probably. Tell her she's had all she's getting.'

'That's a risky way to go.'

'Go to the police, then. When are you seeing her again?'

'She wants another hundred quid on Monday.'

Chrissy gave an exasperated sigh. 'For God's sake, Frank, you can't keep paying her. It's never going to end.'

'I know, I know. I just need to buy some time until I can work out what to do.'

Chrissy said her goodbyes, took the lift down to the ground floor and walked slowly along the path towards Carlton House, musing on everything she'd just learnt. It was hard not to feel bitter about events from all those years ago; if she'd known what was going on she could have stopped Uncle Pete from going round to Marlon's, found a way to convince him that nothing bad had happened to Dawn, and he wouldn't have spent the last ten years in jug. But there was nothing she could do about it now.

She sniffed the night air, breathing in the acrid smell of rubber again. Old memories coiled around her, pressing on her heart, reviving all those adolescent feelings of hope and despair and crazy dreams. Three girls sitting on a wall. Three girls with their futures still ahead of them. All it had taken was one big mistake and everything had changed for ever.

Seeing Zelda again, talking to her, had reminded her of how

close they'd once been. Had she been wrong about Zelda's motives in offering to chase up the police reports? Perhaps it had just been down to a guilty conscience. Or even an olive branch, offered as a way to make amends. She didn't know, probably wouldn't ever know for sure. Anyway, she was glad that she hadn't refused the help.

Distracted by all these thoughts, Chrissy didn't even notice the man standing near the main door until she'd almost reached it. He stepped out from the shadows and greeted her.

'Hello, Chrissy.'

She almost jumped out of her skin, her heart missing a beat, her right arm automatically rising in defence.

'It's only me,' he said.

'Christ,' she said, recognising the voice just before his face came into focus. *Vinnie*. Her arm dropped back down to her side. 'What are you trying to do, give me a bloody heart attack?'

'Sorry, I didn't mean to—'

'What are you doing here?'

Vinnie pushed his hands into his jacket pockets. 'I rang the flat and your nan said you'd gone out for an hour so I thought I'd just walk over and wait.'

'You talked to Nan?'

'I didn't tell her who I was. I just said I was calling from work, from Cordelia's.'

Chrissy was glad about that, at least; she didn't need Nan giving her the third degree about some random bloke who'd rung up out of the blue. 'Don't call the flat again.'

'I have to talk to you.'

'Whatever you've got to say, I don't want to hear it.'

'It's important. Come on, five minutes, that's all I'm asking.'

'Five minutes too many,' Chrissy said.

'Don't be like that.'

Chrissy glared at him. Vinnie, she decided, was one of those men who couldn't take no for an answer. Well, on this occasion, he was going to have to. 'Good night, Vinnie.'

As she walked through the door, he tried to follow her. 'I messed up, I get that, but there's more to it than you think. Just give me a chance, yeah? Let me explain.'

Chrissy whirled around, barring his way. 'Just go away, okay? Leave me alone.'

'I only want to—'

'I don't care what you want. This conversation is over. I don't want to see you again, and I don't want to talk to you again. *Ever.* Is that clear?' And then, before he even had the chance to reply, she crossed the foyer, ignoring the lift in case he got in with her, and hurried up the stairs.

61

Will leaned against the bar of the Fox, lit a cigarette and let his gaze float out across the room. Even when he was off duty he was still on the lookout, checking who people were talking to, supping with, sleeping with or rowing with. It was something he did instinctively now, as natural as breathing. He drank in the information and filed it away for future reference.

Tonight, he was feeling pleased with himself: the rumours he had started about a fresh investigation into the Kearns case were beginning to bear fruit. Word had spread across the Mansfield, whispers about fresh evidence and new lines of inquiry, and already there was talk among the residents of imminent arrests. There was nothing official about what he was doing – Gaul didn't share his enthusiasm for digging over old ground, worried perhaps that proof would be found of incompetence in the original investigation – but he was sticking with it, anyway. If you stirred things up enough, there was no telling what might happen.

Will beckoned over the barmaid, a curvy blonde with dark

eyes. He grinned, pushed his glass towards her and said, 'Put another in there, will you, love. And take one for yourself.'

'Ta. I'll have a voddie.'

He was openly studying her backside as she stood at the optics when Gaul appeared at his shoulder, gave a snort and said, 'You've no chance, mate.'

'Not now, I haven't,' Will said.

'Not ever.'

When the barmaid came back with his whisky, Will ordered another one for Gaul. Unlike the DCI, he always paid for his drinks. Just working with Gaul was enough to cast doubt on his integrity, to tarnish his reputation, without compounding the problem by cadging freebies everywhere he ate and drank.

'Let's sit down,' Gaul said.

Will had barely seen his boss all day. This was no great loss but it meant they had some catching up to do. They took a corner table near to the bar but not too close to any other customers, and for the next ten minutes exchanged information about the various cases they were working on.

'You made any progress with the Moss girl?' Gaul asked.

Will had good news on this front. 'Yeah, I saw her this morning. We had a chat and I put her straight. I told her there's nothing in the police reports, and that Luther Byrne is beyond dangerous. I laid it on thick so I think we can safely say that she won't be going anywhere near *him* in a hurry.'

'This morning, huh?'

'She was at the bus stop so I gave her a lift to King's Cross.'

'Did she tell you where she was going?'

'I didn't ask.'

'Maybe you should have,' Gaul said.

Will looked at him. The DCI was wearing an expression that could only be described as a disturbing combination of grim and smug. His confidence instantly took a nose dive. 'You trying to tell me something?'

'You want to know where the girl spent the day?' Gaul didn't wait for Will to answer. 'Highgate. At the home of one Mrs Muriel Byrne and her son, Luther.'

Will's jaw fell open. 'No way. She couldn't have. She said ... Shit, are you sure?'

'A hundred per cent sure. I had her tailed. Nothing official, of course. I got Freddy Reed to do it; he owed me a favour. Luckily, he didn't go alone, so when you dropped her off at the station, Freddy followed on foot.'

'They tailed us from Kellston?'

'I won't pass comment on the fact you didn't notice.'

'Yeah, well, I had other things on my mind.' Will was still trying to process what he'd been told, his guts twisting at the knowledge that Chrissy Moss had taken him for a fool. 'What the hell was she doing at the Byrne house?'

'What do you think?' Gaul said. 'She and Luther were holed up there till four o'clock. Not what I'd call a flying visit so, whatever they're planning, it's going to be big. I always knew that shit would crawl out from the woodwork one day.'

'Christ, she lied right to my face.'

Gaul gave a mocking laugh. 'You should have learnt by now: you can't trust any fucking woman.'

'So what next?'

Gaul knocked the rest of his drink back in one. 'You stay away from her, that's what. Leave this to me. I'll sort it out.'

62

It was Saturday morning and Chrissy was at a loose end, alone in the flat. She couldn't settle and kept wandering from room to room. As the flat wasn't very big, this didn't take long and she soon found herself back in the kitchen again. She sat down at the table and sighed. Although she'd had all day yesterday to think about it, her head was still full of what Frank and Zelda had revealed and the more she dwelled on what they'd told her, the more worried she became.

Strictly speaking, it was none of her business – it was *their* problem, not hers – but she still felt bad about the situation. If – when – the truth came out, they'd be in major trouble over what they'd done ten years ago. How would the men who were coming out of jail react? She wouldn't want to be in Frank or Zelda's shoes when they found out. And what about Uncle Pete? He could easily get dragged into it all again and end up right back in the slammer. Which would break Nan's heart, and hers too.

It seemed to Chrissy that both Frank and Zelda were

paralysed by indecision. Someone had to do something. She was embarrassed by the thought that Frank had ever harboured feelings for her, even if it was only a schoolboy crush. It made her feel partly responsible for what had happened. But that was ridiculous. She couldn't be held to account for other people's emotions. It had been his choice to take the key, to copy it, to hand it over – and Dawn's to use it for her own ends.

Chrissy stood up and went through to the living room. She circled the sofa while an idea slowly formed in her head. No, she should keep out of it. What if she made matters worse? But then they couldn't really get any worse. Dawn wasn't going to stop until she'd squeezed every last penny out of her victims. Before Chrissy could change her mind, she hastily scribbled a note – Nan was along the landing having a brew with her friend Jean – saying she'd gone up West to do some shopping and wouldn't be back late.

On the bus she was still reflecting on the wisdom of what she was doing. Maybe she should have talked it over first with Frank and Zelda. But she already knew what they'd say. Neither of them would agree to it; they would be too afraid of repercussions. And what if it all went wrong, if she misjudged it completely? What would happen then? She argued back and forth with herself, convinced one minute that it was right to take action, the next equally convinced that it wasn't.

By the time she arrived at Shaftesbury Avenue, she was no closer to making a final decision. Still, now she was here there was no harm in finding out where Dawn worked. She made her way to Dean Street and walked its length, looking in each of the doorways for the bank of bells Frank had described. With no success on one side, she crossed over and continued her search on the other.

It was hard not to feel self-conscious. Soho was the centre of the sex trade, the place where people came to ply their trade or satisfy their urges. What if someone mistook her for a tom? She was careful to avoid making eye contact with anyone she passed and tried to look like a woman with purpose, someone who was going somewhere, someone who wasn't touting for business. Trying to do this whilst also checking out the doorways proved to be tricky. She was afraid of walking too quickly in case she missed the bells, of walking too slowly in case it looked like she was loitering.

Eventually she came across the place she'd been searching for, a narrow building squashed between a shop selling porn and an off-licence. What now? Her finger hovered over the bell marked Kara while her head went through all the pros and cons again. Finally, she threw caution to the wind, hoped for the best and pressed the bell.

Once she'd done it, made the leap, it was disappointing to get no response. She tried again, a longer ring this time, but still nothing. Standing back, she gazed up at the windows, but there was no sign of life. She had no idea whether Dawn actually lived here or just came here to work. If it was the latter it could be hours before she showed up, maybe even as late as this evening.

Frustration began to gnaw at her. Having made the journey, she was reluctant now to turn around, admit defeat and go home. As she glanced along the street, she noticed a café and decided to wait there for half an hour. If Dawn still hadn't put in an appearance by then she'd call it a day.

Chrissy ordered a coffee and found an empty table by the window from where she had a clear view of the building. The café was busy but not crowded and no one took any notice of her. She sat and gazed out, praying that Dawn would show up before she lost her nerve. The longer she dwelled on what she intended to do, the less likely she was to do it.

With so much else on her mind, she had been able to consign Vinnie Keane to a far distant corner where he didn't impinge on her thoughts, but now he crept back into her head again. She wondered what it was that he'd wanted to say. He'd told her it was important, but that was just man-speak. Men always reckoned that what they had to say was of great significance even when it was nonsense. It was possible that Terry had sent him, peeved at being a waitress down on a busy Saturday night and hoping Vinnie could persuade her to come back to work.

She supposed she should have let him speak, but wasn't sorry that she hadn't. There was nothing worse than having to listen to someone's wheedling excuses as to why they'd done what they'd done. He was probably the sort who couldn't deal with rejection, whatever the reason, and couldn't let things lie. Well, if that was the case, she'd had a lucky escape. Except she didn't feel lucky. Vinnie was the first bloke she'd genuinely liked in a long time. Which, sadly, didn't say much for her taste or her judgement.

Half an hour passed and no one went in or out of the building. Chrissy was on the verge of giving up when she saw the young woman come round the corner. Her heart skipped a beat. Dawn. It *was* her, wasn't it? She stared hard at the face, not wanting to make a mistake. Yes, it was definitely her. She pushed back her chair, stood up and dashed out of the café.

Chrissy caught up with Dawn just as she was putting the key in the door. Her pulse was racing, partly from the sprint down the street, and partly because she was about to take a major gamble 'Dawn!'

Dawn turned, peered at her and scowled. 'Oh, it's you,' she said dismissively. 'What do *you* want?'

Chrissy had a sense of the surreal at speaking to someone who had theoretically been dead for the past ten years. 'I need to talk to you.'

'I'm busy.'

'You'll want to hear this.'

'I suppose they sent you, did they?'

'If you mean Frank and Zelda, then no, they don't know I'm here.'

'Yeah, right.'

'They don't,' Chrissy insisted. 'I swear. Look, just five minutes, that's all I'm asking. Let me buy you a coffee.'

Dawn pushed a strand of brown hair behind her ear. 'How did you find me?'

'Frank said he thought you lived somewhere in this area so I've just been walking around checking out all the bells.'

'Frank!' Dawn scoffed. 'I knew he wouldn't be able to keep his mouth shut.'

'He didn't have a choice. I said I was going to the law – I saw you at King's Cross, remember? – unless he told me what was going on.'

'You're going to get your mates in a lot of bother if you do that.'

'They're not my mates,' Chrissy said. 'I've not come because of them.'

'So why the fuck are you here?'

'Do you want that coffee or not?'

'Like I said, I'm busy.'

'Okay, suit yourself. But don't say I didn't try to warn you.'

Dawn's face grew wary. 'What's that supposed to mean?'

'You'll find out soon enough.' Chrissy took a chance, turned away and started walking back towards the café. For a moment she thought Dawn wasn't going to follow – damn it – but then she heard the rapid click of high heels on the pavement.

Dawn drew alongside, shooting her a series of fast, mistrustful glances. 'What's your fuckin' game?'

'No game,' Chrissy said. 'This is deadly serious.'

'So stop pissin' about and tell me.'

'I will – in a minute.' Chrissy didn't want to have the conversation in the street where Dawn could easily walk away from her, disappear into the building and refuse to answer the door. She wanted to be able to put forward her argument and make sure it was properly understood. Of course, there was nothing to stop Dawn from walking out of the café, but at least there was a chance she might listen to her in there. They went inside and stood by the counter. 'What would you like?' Chrissy asked.

'I'll have a brew,' Dawn said to the woman who was serving. 'And a bacon sarnie.' She looked at Chrissy. 'You're paying, right?'

'Yeah, I'm paying.'

They carried the mugs over to the same table Chrissy had been sitting at before. Dawn sat on one side and Chrissy sat on the other. Chrissy took a deep breath, knowing that the one thing she couldn't show was any sign of weakness. 'So, what are we going to do about this mess?'

'I don't see any mess,' Dawn said, spooning a couple of sugars into her tea.

'Frank says you're threatening to go to the papers.'

'I ain't threatening nothin'. Just thinking about it, that's all.'

'Well, maybe you should stop thinking about it.'

Dawn's small mouth widened into an unpleasant grin. 'You reckon? And why's that, then?'

Chrissy gazed at her, seeing some of Tina in her face. 'If you go to the papers, everyone's going to know you're alive and well and that nothing happened to you all those years ago.'

'That's kind of the point, isn't it? Shit, you ain't changed much. You always were slow on the uptake.'

Chrissy was reminded of all Dawn's other taunts when they were kids, but she wasn't going to rise to the bait. Instead, she smiled sweetly and said, 'I think you'll find you're the one who's not getting it.' She took a sip of tea, put the mug down and continued. 'You see, all the men – the ones who got sent down for Marlon Pound's murder – are coming out of jail soon: Jacko, Pat Dunlap, John Fielding and the rest. Not to mention Uncle Pete. They're not going to be happy when they discover they got sent down over something that never happened. They all thought Marlon had killed you.'

'That ain't my fault. I never made them go there. I never made them do nothin'.'

'No, well, that might be true, but they're still going to reckon you made mugs out of them. There you were, hiding in that flat, perfectly safe, while they were sure you were dead. And then suddenly you pop up all these years later, flogging your story to the press, making money out of their time in the slammer, cashing in on all that misery. God, they're going to be well pissed off.'

'So? That's their problem, not mine.'

But Chrissy heard a hint of apprehension in her voice and quickly took advantage of it. 'Do you think?'

'They can't touch me. They wouldn't dare.'

The waitress arrived with the sandwich and put the plate down in front of Dawn. Chrissy waited until the woman was out of earshot before responding. 'Seems to me that the likes of Jacko do exactly what they want. Do you really think he's going to let it go? I can't see it myself. It's a respect thing, isn't it? You're going to make him look a fool and he's not going to like it.'

Dawn was messing about with the sandwich, opening the bread and pouring brown sauce over the bacon, but Chrissy could tell she was listening, taking it all in.

'It won't take them long to find you. I mean, I did it in fifteen minutes. Of course, you could move, go live somewhere else, but you'll always be looking over your shoulder. I'm not sure if any amount of cash is worth that.' Chrissy didn't reckon Dawn had much of a conscience, but she ploughed on with the next part of her argument anyway. 'And then there's Zelda and Frank. If they hadn't kept their mouths shut, Marlon would still be alive today. Jacko's not going to let that go, either. You won't be the only one he'll have in his sights. And the thing about Jacko is that he's got a temper that he can't control; once he's got an idea in his head—'

'Okay, okay, I get it,' Dawn interrupted. 'I didn't say I *was* going to papers, did I? Just that I was thinking about it.'

'And are you still thinking about it?'

Dawn's mouth grew sulky and her eyes flashed. 'You don't scare me.'

'It's not me you need to be worried about. And I wouldn't take too long to make your mind up. Frank's got the jitters; he's on the verge of going to the law. So, if you don't want it taken out of your hands, you'd better let him know one way or the other.'

Dawn's appetite seemed to have diminished. She pushed the plate to one side and glared at Chrissy. 'I don't see how this is any of your fuckin' business.'

'It's my fuckin' business because my Uncle Pete has spent the last ten years inside.'

'I didn't make him throw Marlon off the balcony.'

Chrissy was about to protest that *he* hadn't thrown Marlon off, but knew she had to stay calm. If she let Dawn provoke her, they'd end up in a full-blown row and that wasn't going to improve the situation any. Instead, she tried a little appeasement. 'I get it, how bad it was for you back then. No one can blame you for wanting it to stop, for taking off like that. You couldn't have realised what was going to happen. But if you try to make money out of it, everything's going to blow up again. What Marlon did to you was terrible and—'

'What Marlon did?'

'Yeah, you know. Zelda told me how he used to . . .'

'Used to what?'

Chrissy didn't want to have to spell it out. She glanced away, looked back. 'What he did to you. How he . . . took advantage.'

Dawn rolled her eyes. 'Shit, you think I'd let that idiot anywhere near me?'

'But Zelda said—'

'Zelda jumped to her own conclusions. I just didn't put her straight. She always did have a vivid imagination.'

Chrissy could hardly believe what she was hearing. 'So he didn't . . . But what about the bruises? I saw them, everyone did.'

'Oh, those. Have you ever tried to take a bottle of voddie off a drunk? Mum wasn't what you'd call friendly when she'd had a few. I didn't want Zelda to know it was her. I mean, what kind of a mother beats up her own kid? It was embarrassing.'

'But everyone thought Marlon was . . .'

Dawn shrugged as if Marlon's fate was neither here nor there. 'He was all Mum was interested in. Well, that and the booze. She didn't give a toss about me.'

Chrissy was racing back in time, her memory reviving all the bits and pieces that had come together to create a distorted picture from an ill-formed jigsaw. If it hadn't been for this, for that, for the other, Marlon wouldn't be dead now and Uncle Pete wouldn't have gone to jail. Her hands tightly gripped the mug as if it could anchor her to the here and now, to stop her being pulled down into the horrors of the past.

'It wasn't my fault,' Dawn said. 'I never meant for . . . They can't blame me for it.'

Chrissy observed the face that was too thin, the grey skin

pulled tight over the cheekbones, the hollowed-out eyes. Dawn's fingernails were bitten down and she had the haunted look of the junkies that roamed the Mansfield estate. She knew that Dawn's life must be a hard one, but she couldn't afford to feel sorry for her. There was too much at stake, too many other lives that could be ruined, too. 'They can't blame you if they don't know you're still alive.'

While Dawn was considering this, Chrissy took the opportunity to ask about something she'd always wondered about. 'What did Vic Hooper say to you that day we went to Anita's flat? You know, when he called you back?'

'What does that matter?'

'I'm just curious.'

Dawn, as if unwilling to volunteer anything she didn't have to, paused for a moment but then eventually said, 'He told me to come back later if I wanted to make some easy cash. Said he'd make it worth my while.'

'But you didn't go back?'

Dawn's upper lip curled. 'What do you think I am, fuckin' stupid? But I figured it was a good a time as any to disappear, just in case he came looking for me. Frank had already given me the key to the old woman's flat. All I had to do was pick up some stuff from home, food and clothes, and lie low until Mum realised I was missing.'

A plan that had gone fatally wrong, Chrissy thought, although Dawn wouldn't need to be reminded of that. Instead she said, 'So what happens now? What are you going to do?'

Dawn gazed out of the window for a while. Then she looked at Chrissy and smirked. 'I was never going to go to the papers anyway. Why would I want that kind of aggro? Frank never could take a joke. I only wanted to borrow a few quid.'

Chrissy stood up, deciding to quit while she appeared to be

ahead. 'Good. That's settled then.' She was about to leave when she remembered something else. Reaching into her pocket she took out a slip of paper and put it down on the table. 'This is your mum's number if you want to call her. You'll have to tell her to keep quiet, though.'

Dawn stared at the slip of paper, shaking her head. 'I don't want it.'

But Chrissy left it there. 'You might, one day. Bye, Dawn.'

'You never did like me, did you?'

Chrissy hesitated, trying to think of a suitable reply. 'I was just jealous. I thought Zelda liked you more than me.'

A small smile slid across Dawn's lips. 'It's true. She did.'

Chrissy let her have her moment of triumph – she didn't have much else.

63

There was no way of knowing what would happen next, and Chrissy spent the next three days stressing over whether Dawn had only said what she had to get rid of her. By Wednesday, she was hoping that no news was good news but she still couldn't relax. Had she done the right thing? Perhaps it would be better if it was all out in the open. But not better for Frank or Zelda.

She played with her cornflakes, anxiety blunting her appetite. Although Dawn had been the one doing the blackmailing, Chrissy felt faintly guilty about the way she'd behaved. Threatening her with Jacko hadn't been a nice thing to do. Perhaps she should have tried to reason with her, instead. Fighting fire with fire was all very well but it didn't always make you feel proud of yourself.

'Are you going to eat those cornflakes?' Nan asked.

'I'm not hungry.'

Nan had a cold and her voice was hoarse. She took a tissue from the box on the table, blew her nose, got up, dropped the tissue in the bin and sat down again. 'You look worn out, love. Is that Mrs Parry working you too hard?'

'No, I'm just . . . I didn't sleep too well.'

Nan gave her one of her probing looks. 'Don't let her take advantage. I know what that sort are like; they'll have you fetching and carrying till your arms drop off.'

'Unlike Connolly's, where they used to let me sit down and put my feet up all day.'

'I'm only saying.'

'It's nothing to do with Mrs Parry.'

Nan poured herself another cup of strong tea to gird her for the hours ahead. She glanced at the clock, sneezed, sniffed and reached for another tissue.

'Why don't you take the day off, Nan? You're full of cold.'

'It's only a sniffle.'

'They can do without you for once. The customers won't want you sneezing into their pork chops.'

But Nan would never let anything as mundane as a cold keep her off work. 'I'm fine. I only take the money, don't I? I'll be right as rain by tomorrow.' Then, after another slurp of tea, she said, 'Have you heard about Dawn Kearns?'

Chrissy almost jumped out of her seat. She dropped her spoon and it clattered into the bowl. 'What?'

'Oh, sorry, love, I didn't mean to—'

'Heard what?' Chrissy asked, swallowing hard, afraid that the secret was out.

'I dare say it's nothing: you know how people talk. Only the word is the law have got some new information.'

'What sort of information?'

'Arrests, they're saying, but it's probably nonsense. Who could they possibly arrest? Marlon Pound's dead and gone so . . . Don't you go getting upset about it.'

This, however, was easier said than done. Chrissy recalled what Sutherland had mentioned in the caff, about having missed something. Had they found out Dawn was still alive? Perhaps it was Frank and Zelda they were going to arrest. And maybe she'd be pulled in too when they discovered what she'd known.

'Are you all right, love? You look white as a sheet.'

For a moment Chrissy was tempted to tell Nan everything – she felt the urge to confide, to ask for advice – but forced herself to hold her tongue. Once it was said it couldn't be taken back. 'No, I'm okay, really I am. It's just odd, isn't it, after all this time? I mean, what could the law have suddenly found out?'

'Exactly,' Nan said. 'I reckon it's just idle gossip. Tina turning up like that has set all the tongues wagging. You know what they're like on this estate.'

Chrissy raised her eyebrows. Nan, of course, was no great slouch herself when it came to gossip. 'Will you let me know if you hear anything else?' She stood up and carried her bowl over to the sink, poured out the milk and scraped the cornflakes into the bin. 'I'd better be off or I'll miss the bus.'

'It's still early,' Nan said. 'You don't need to rush.'

'There were some hold-ups yesterday on the Tube – works on the line or something. I don't want to be late again.'

The house in Highgate was as quiet as always. Chrissy felt like she could hear the dust settling as she sat in the drawing room. A thin shaft of sunlight, devoid of any warmth, slanted through the window, creating a pale patch on the carpet. Mrs Byrne was in a nostalgic frame of mind, reminiscing about old parties and the people who had come to dine: lords and ladies, artists, writers and poets. Chrissy hadn't heard of any of them but she nodded and smiled and made the effort to look impressed.

It was hard to imagine the house so full of life, of voices.

Laughter must have echoed through the rooms. Men and women, dressed to the nines, would have clinked their glasses and toasted their good fortune. As Mrs Byrne talked about these times her eyes lit up, and Chrissy wondered what it was like to have nothing much to look forward to, when so much more of your life was in the past than in the future. It made her feel sorry for the old lady, but not for long.

Chrissy thought about Nan, who was getting on too, although she still had a few years on Mrs Byrne. What would *she* look back on? There had been no fancy parties for her, no lavish meals, no gatherings of the rich and famous. Nan's life had been a hard one, a struggle to survive, the past tainted with grief. If anyone deserved pity it was her – not that she'd welcome it, not for a minute. Nan came from a world where you dusted yourself down, put on a brave face and just got on with whatever you had to do.

Some of Mrs Byrne's more familiar grievances re-emerged during their morning stroll. Nothing in the garden was quite as it should be. The leaves were already falling from the trees, not in huge quantities but enough for her to be bothered by their presence on the lawn. She seemed to think that the gardener had nothing better to do than to stand to attention with a rake waiting for the next offending leaf to flutter down.

Despite Mrs Byrne's running complaints Chrissy still enjoyed the walk. This was always her favourite time of day. She liked the smell of the earth and the wafting scents of shrubs and herbs. Having been raised surrounded by concrete, the concept of a garden was still a novelty to her, and here, enveloped by greenness, her troubles slipped away for a while. She could forget about Dawn and Frank and Zelda. She could push her mother's death into the back of her mind and relax into being Christine Cope, a girl whose only purpose was to be companionable.

Lunch passed without incident, and at half past one precisely Mrs Parry brought the coffee into the drawing room.

'I'll be off now, Mrs Byrne,' she said. 'I'll be back by four.'

'Off? Off where?'

'To see my sister in Finchley. I always go on Wednesdays.'

Mrs Byrne flinched a little as though the regularity of such excursions caused her some element of personal pain. 'Well, we shall have to try and manage without you.'

'I'm sure you'll do very nicely.'

Before anything more could be said, Mrs Parry laid down the tray and quickly retreated.

Mrs Byrne released a long sigh. 'I sometimes think that woman spends more time at her sister's than she does here.'

This was quite obviously untrue, but Chrissy didn't pass comment. Instead, she picked up the coffee pot and asked, 'Shall I pour?'

By a quarter to two Mrs Byrne had finished her coffee, sat back and nodded off. Small whispery snores escaped from her nose. From past experience Chrissy knew she would be asleep for about an hour. She usually spent this time reading a magazine or, if she was restless, quietly roaming the room gazing at the paintings, the books or out at the garden.

When she was sure she wouldn't disturb Mrs Byrne, Chrissy rose from her seat and went to the bathroom down the corridor. She had a pee, washed her hands and gazed at her reflection in the mirror. It was odd to think of being paid to do nothing, but that was precisely what was happening at the moment. And, as regards wages, Luther had been true to his word, leaving an envelope containing a hundred and fifty quid on the hall table on Friday.

Thankfully, Chrissy hadn't set eyes on him since lunch last week. She could never be comfortable in his presence, knowing what she did about him. What was it Sutherland had said? Drugs, prostitution, underage girls. Men like Luther didn't change. There had to be evidence somewhere of what he was really like.

On her way back Chrissy had to pass Luther's study. She stopped outside the door and felt temptation run through her. With Luther at work, Mrs Parry out of the way and Mrs Byrne asleep, there was nothing to prevent her from going in and having a good look round. Her hand hovered over the handle, but fear held her back. What if she was caught? What if Mrs Byrne woke up and discovered she was gone?

Chrissy crept back to the drawing room, checked that the old lady was still asleep and then returned to the study. She put her ear to the door and knocked very lightly just in case, horror of horrors, Luther was actually inside. No response. Holding her breath, she slowly turned the handle, almost hoping the room would be locked. It wasn't.

She pushed the door open and peered inside. The study was lined with books. There was a desk with a phone on it, a swivel chair, an easy chair, a lamp, a couple of filing cabinets and, on a pedestal, a bronze statue of a young man who seemed to be staring straight at her. A few paintings, more modern-looking than the ones in the drawing room, adorned the pale grey walls.

There was still time to change her mind, to withdraw, to not take that fateful step across the threshold. But when would she get an opportunity like this again? Well, maybe *next* Wednesday, if Mrs Parry always went to her sister's, although there was no saying she'd be any braver then. She strained her ears, listening for other signs of life in the house apart from Mrs Byrne, but there was nothing.

Tentatively she stepped into the room, feeling the hairs on the back of her neck stand on end. If she got caught . . . No, she couldn't afford even to think about that. With one brief glance over her shoulder, she walked over to the filing cabinets and tried to open them. All locked. It was a disappointment but no great surprise. It was where all the important stuff, the incriminating stuff, would be kept. Would he have the key with him or would it be hidden somewhere? In the desk, perhaps.

The desk was one of those wide, sturdy pieces of furniture with a bank of tiny cubby holes to the rear of the top. She poked her fingers into each of them in turn but found only loose change, dust and paperclips. Next, she turned her attention to the drawers that ran down either side. The very fact that these were unlocked suggested that nothing of significance lay inside them, but there was still a chance of finding the key.

She slid them open, one after another, but discovered only stationery, old art magazines, receipts, pens and pencils. It wasn't until she reached the bottom drawer on the right-hand side that she found something of interest: a heap of black and white photographs, some loose and others in cardboard covers. She took them out, placed them on the desk and began to quickly flick through them. The people in the photos were mainly strangers to her, elegant men and women sitting around a table in one club or another, dancing or gathered in groups with drinks in their hands. Luther was in a few of them, much younger than he was now and looking almost raffish. She moved swiftly on and was getting towards the bottom of the pile when she came across a picture that made her heart skip a beat: her mother, wearing a short white dress and white boots, standing right beside Luther Byrne.

Chrissy sucked in a breath. Her mother looked happy in the picture, smiling, her eyes full of warmth. She was leaning slightly against Luther, their elbows touching. There was an intimacy about the stance, something that spoke of trust and affection. It must have been taken, Chrissy thought, before her mother had learnt what he was really like. Or had she just been playing a part, putting on a show while she gathered information for the law?

Chrissy was still poring over the photograph, engrossed in it, when she heard the tiny hiss of breath. As she swung round her heart was already in her mouth, her pulse starting to race, the blood draining from her face. And she was right to panic. Standing in the doorway was Luther, his expression grim, his eyes flashing with rage.

'I was wondering how long it would take for you to show your true colours.'

'It . . . it isn't—'

'Oh please, spare me.'

'I was just—'

'I can see what you were *just* doing.'

'It isn't how it looks.'

Luther made a snort of derision. 'No, it never is with your sort.'

'Really, you don't understand.' Chrissy was desperately searching for an excuse, a reason – any reason – why she should be in his study. 'I know how it must seem. I-I know I shouldn't have come in here without permission, but I was trying to find some envelopes. Mrs Byrne mentioned writing a few letters this afternoon and I noticed she hadn't got any.' Why was she talking such nonsense? All he had to do was wake up his mother and ask her. But she persisted anyway, playing for time, hoping that she might be able to find a way out of this nightmare. 'I'm sorry. I didn't know where else to look.'

'There's no money in there,' Luther said, nodding towards the desk. 'Do you really think I'd be so stupid as to leave cash lying around?'

'I'm not a thief,' she said indignantly.

Luther advanced into the room, closing the door behind him. There was something ominous about that soft click. He walked to within a foot of her, folded his arms across his chest and glared. 'Only because I got here in time.'

'That's not true.'

'I knew exactly what you were from the day you came to this house. If my mother wasn't so stubborn, she'd have seen it, too.'

Chrissy's guts were churning, her chest so tight she thought it might burst. Fear was pressing in on her, squeezing out her breath, strangling her voice. 'What are you going to do?'

'What do you think?' He noticed her glance towards the door and said coldly, 'Feel free to make a run for it if you want, but you won't get very far. The front door's locked.'

Chrissy knew then that everything Sutherland had told her was true. Luther was cruel, ruthless, a man without boundaries. He was going to make her pay for what he thought he'd caught her doing. And how far would he go? She'd betrayed his trust, his mother's trust and that was unforgivable. She couldn't think straight; terror seized her, froze her. As all reason drained away, panic made her blurt out, 'People know I'm here. They'll come looking. You won't get away with it.'

Luther stared at her like she was mad. He took a step back as if to distance himself a little from her craziness. 'What?'

'You heard me,' she said. 'Whatever you're planning on doing—'

'What I'm going to do,' he interrupted, 'is call the police.'

This took Chrissy completely by surprise. 'The police?'

'I believe that's the normal procedure when you find someone trying to steal from you. And I don't suppose it's the first time you've made their acquaintance.'

As it happened, this was true, but not for the reasons Luther imagined. She was simultaneously reassured and alarmed, relieved that she didn't appear to be in any imminent danger, but troubled by the thought of having to face the law. They would take his side, she was sure of it, even if there wasn't any proof. Families like the Byrnes had influence. She would be taken down the station, interviewed, treated like dirt and, even if there wasn't any solid evidence, they would still find a way to charge her. 'All I was doing was looking at some photos.' The picture was still in her hand and she waved it at him. 'That's hardly a crime, is it?'

Luther snatched it away from her. 'It's not yours to look at.'

'She's a pretty girl. Who is she?'

'None of your business.' Luther stepped forward again, put the photo down on the desk and reached for the phone.

'Don't call the police,' Chrissy said.

'Give me one good reason why I shouldn't?'

And suddenly Chrissy had a clear choice: either she kept quiet about who she really was and waited for the law to arrive, or she came clean. She realised that this might be the only chance she ever got to confront him, to see how he reacted, to finally bring the truth out into the open. She picked up the photograph again and took a deep breath. 'Because of this,' she said, holding it up in front of him. 'Because this is my mother, Laura Moss.'

An almighty silence greeted the revelation. Confusion, disbelief, bewilderment passed across his face. Then he gave a small shake of his head. 'No.'

'It's true, I swear. I'm Chrissy Moss. Laura lived with her mum, right, my nan – Elsie – and her brother Pete. They lived on the Mansfield in Kellston. I still live there. Mum died in a train accident when I was four.' She racked her brains for more information, for more proof that she was who she said she was.

'She worked for you at Rascals. My bag's in the drawing room. There's stuff in it, letters and that, with my real name on.'

Luther had gone pale. His gaze flicked between her and the photograph as though he might find some corroboration through comparison as to whether what she was telling him was true or not.

Chrissy, afraid to stop talking in case he reached for the phone again, pressed on. 'I don't look much like her, at least I don't reckon I do. And I didn't mean to deceive you. I know what you're thinking: why not just give you a call right at the start? But I wanted to talk to you face to face. That's why I applied for the job, so I could get to meet you in person, speak to you about her, but when it came to it, I lost my nerve and it all seemed like a really bad idea. And then your mother offered me the job and . . . ' Not wanting to confess her true motivation, or to hint that she had any suspicions at all about his part in her mum's death, Chrissy quickly glossed over this part. 'I didn't know what to do. I shouldn't have taken it, but I wasn't really thinking straight.'

Luther's mouth, partly open, gradually closed, his lips compressing together in a thin, straight line. The seconds ticked by.

'Say something,' she said.

And finally he spoke. 'I need a drink.'

64

Luther took a bunch of keys from his pocket, opened the filing cabinet and brought out a bottle of brandy and two glasses. She wondered, irrelevantly, why he kept the booze in there. Perhaps Mrs Parry, or the cleaner, couldn't be trusted to keep their hands off it. She gave herself a mental shake. *Concentrate, you're not out of the woods yet.* She might have temporarily stopped him from calling the law, but that didn't mean he wouldn't.

Without asking, he poured her a drink and passed it to her. 'All right,' he said. 'So you've explained how you came to be in my house, but what about my study? What exactly are you doing in here?'

Chrissy took a gulp of the brandy. She needed it. It was the good stuff, the kind of brandy that slid down your throat like liquid silk. She knew she was on dangerous ground, quicksand, and any hopes of a permanent reprieve could easily sink without trace. 'I'm not sure, really. Looking for something that connected you to her, I suppose. It was stupid, a spur-of-the moment thing. I'm sorry.'

'What sort of something?'

'I don't know.' She glanced down at the photograph. 'Something like that, I guess. Nan won't talk about Mum; it upsets her too much. But someone told me that her death might not have been an accident and . . . I don't know whether it's true or not. I've been trying to find out more but I'm not getting very far.'

Luther's eyes darkened. 'And you thought you might find it in here?'

'I didn't know what I thought. I was just . . . just clutching at straws.'

But Luther wasn't a fool. He was quickly putting the pieces together and working it out for himself. 'You suspect I had something to do with her death.'

'No, no, of course not,' she said, acting mortified. 'Not for a minute. I didn't mean that at all. But you worked together, didn't you? You were friends. You would have known if she was in trouble or . . . or if there was anyone who wanted to harm her.' She noticed his expression, the rise of colour in his cheeks, and knew that he wasn't buying it. Rather than digging a bigger hole for herself, she rapidly changed tack. 'Okay, it crossed my mind. I heard some rumours and I listened to them. I didn't know you, did I? I had no idea what might have happened back then.'

'What sort of rumours?'

'That the two of you were close. That there were things going on at the bar – things that weren't exactly legal – and that Mum might have got involved in it, somehow. Nan said it wasn't true, that you were a straight-up businessman, but I wanted to see for myself. I needed to be sure. I feel like I owe it to her – my mum, I mean – to find out if her death really was an accident.'

Luther considered all this for a moment and then flapped a hand towards the easy chair. He sat down himself on the chair at the desk. He sipped the brandy and studied her. 'You have a somewhat unconventional approach to gathering information.'

Chrissy slumped down, nestling the glass in her lap. Had she said too much, too little? Everything felt like a gamble now. Trying to win him round, she said contritely, 'I've behaved badly. I know that. I shouldn't have taken the job. I should have been straight with you from the start.'

'I won't argue with that.'

'It all got so complicated. You didn't seem to like me very much and by the time I should have said why I was really here, who I really was, it was too late. Not that that's any excuse. I know it isn't. I couldn't blame you if you did ring the police.'

Luther crossed his legs, sat back and continued to stare at her as if still trying to decide which choice he would make. 'Who told you that your mother's death might not have been an accident?'

'A friend, a girl I knew. It was years ago. She'd heard it from her mum, and she'd heard it from someone else, and . . . I don't know where it came from originally. Nan said it wasn't true but . . . well, sometimes people just try and protect you, don't they? They think they're doing the right thing even when they're not.' Chrissy paused to drink some more brandy, conscious that if she wasn't careful her tongue might run away with her. The alcohol was blunting what was left of her fear. 'And then there was a cop – a policeman – who told me I should stay away from you, that you were bad news. He didn't come right out and say it but he kind of hinted that you could have been connected with her death.'

'Perhaps you should have listened.'

Chrissy gave him a wary glance. 'I don't trust the law.'

'And what else did this *cop* say?'

'That the club was just a cover for other stuff, bad stuff, drugs and such.'

'And was this cop called Tony Gaul?'

Chrissy shook her head. 'No, but I know him. Everyone on the Mansfield knows him.'

'The other one, then – Sutherland?'

Chrissy hesitated, not sure if should tell or not. But her hesitation was enough to confirm his suspicions.

'Will Sutherland,' he said. 'Last time I heard he was working at West End Central.'

'He came back to Kellston. He knew my mum, didn't he?'

'Yes, they both knew your mum.'

Chrissy's hand gripped the glass. She was aware in the silence that followed that Luther was constructing a story in his head, deciding perhaps what he would tell her and what he wouldn't. And she would have no way of knowing, other than by her own instinct, whether it was the truth or a web of lies. She waited impatiently, wanting to urge him on but aware that she mustn't.

'I liked your mother,' he said eventually. 'She had a lot of spirit. And whatever you may have heard she was a good friend, a loyal friend to me. As I was, I hope, to her.' His voice was soft, with a slight waver in it. A frown appeared on his forehead. He cleared his throat and continued. 'We need to go back to the sixties – sixty-five, to be exact. I'd owned Rascals for a couple of years when Joe Quinn first took an interest in it. Do you know who Quinn was?'

'Yeah, I've heard of him. Terry Street's boss, yeah, back in the day?'

'That's the one. Well, Quinn was after a foothold in the West End and decided that Rascals was just the place for laundering his ill-gotten gains. He tried to buy it off me and, when I refused, he wasn't best pleased. That's when he recruited his old friend Tony Gaul to help things along. Mayfair wasn't Gaul's patch but he had contacts in all the right places, fellow officers prepared to look the other way if the price was right.' Luther stopped and glanced at her. 'Are you sure you want to hear this?'

'Yes, of course. Why shouldn't I?'

'Knowledge isn't always power. Sometimes it can be a burden.'

But Chrissy hadn't come this far to back off now. Despite his warning, she nodded. 'Go on.'

'Well, I suppose I might have sold the bar to Quinn if he'd offered a fair price, but he wanted the place for peanuts. Naturally, I declined and that's when it got nasty. Quinn wasn't the sort of man who understood the word no, and he got Gaul to start putting pressure on me, spreading rumours about drugs being sold on the premises, arranging for the bar to be raided at regular intervals, threatening to get it closed down . . . Well, you get the picture. And when none of that worked, Gaul turned to Laura.'

'To Mum? What could she do?'

'Dig the dirt, or at least that's what he was hoping. When all else fails, there's always blackmail. He wanted her to feed him information, anything he could use against me, something that would force me to change my mind.'

Chrissy sat forward, hanging on every word. She was rapidly comparing what Sutherland had told her with what Luther was saying now. 'But why would she do that? Why would he even *think* she'd do that? I mean, you two were friends. She wouldn't betray you.'

'Everyone has their Achilles heel, their weak spot. All you have to do is find it.'

'And what was hers?'

Luther gave a wry smile. 'Pete,' he said. 'Your uncle was her weak spot. He was in trouble, on bail for robbery, but Gaul suggested that the charges could be dropped if she'd cooperate.

He was basically asking her to make a choice – Pete or me.' He refilled his glass and held up the bottle. 'Yes?'

'No,' Chrissy said. 'No, ta.' Much as she would have loved another, she couldn't afford for her head to get muddled. Fearing that she already knew what the reply would be, she asked tentatively, 'So . . . so what did she do?'

'What would *you* have done?'

Chrissy lowered her eyes, avoiding his gaze. It was a while before she looked up at him again. She still didn't have an answer.

'What is it they say?' Luther continued. 'Stuck between a rock and a hard place? Except Laura wasn't the sort of girl to be pushed around. She wanted to save Pete from going to jail, but not at my expense. So she decided to try and turn the tables, to play Gaul at his own game, to start gathering information on him, instead. It was risky, dangerous, and she knew it.'

'Why didn't you stop her?'

Luther raised a hand and dropped it back to his side again. 'And how could I do that? If there was a way of saving Pete, saving him from years behind bars, your mother was going to grab it. She figured the best way to Gaul was through Sutherland and so that's the road she took.'

Chrissy, aware that Sutherland's story and Luther's had diverged a while ago, was still no closer to knowing which one of them was telling the truth. 'What does that mean, exactly?'

'Sutherland was obsessed with her, and she used it to her advantage.'

'Did she have . . . a relationship with him?'

'Of some kind or another. I don't know all the ins and outs. Laura kept some things to herself.'

'But she wasn't in love with him?'

Luther provided another of his wry smiles. 'No, she wasn't in love. He was a means to an end, that's all.'

'I don't suppose he'd have been very happy about that if he found out. Did he find out?'

'I don't know.'

Chrissy took a moment to digest all this new information. Putting aside her mother's relationship with Sutherland for a moment – and its possible consequences – she returned to something he'd mentioned earlier. 'If everything was above board at the bar, then what kind of "dirt" could she have passed on to Gaul about you?'

'It was my personal life he was interested in.'

'Ah,' Chrissy said. Sex, she thought, sleeping with people he shouldn't have been sleeping with: underage girls, prostitutes, married women. Take your pick.

'Gaul knew something about me, but he couldn't prove it, something he knew I wouldn't want made public.'

Chrissy stared at him, uneasy at the thought that he might be about to make a confession, some awful revelation that he wouldn't ever want repeating. She shifted in the chair and gazed longingly at the bottle of brandy. 'Maybe I will have another,' she said, holding out her glass.

Luther stood up, carried the bottle over and poured her a generous measure.

'Thank you.'

He sat down again. 'You don't need to look so worried. It's not anything that matters much these days, but back then, of course, it was illegal.'

Chrissy gazed at him blankly. 'Illegal?'

'To be homosexual,' he said. 'Gay, queer, whatever you want to call it. I could have gone to prison.'

It wasn't what Chrissy had been expecting. She took a large

swig of brandy, swallowed and waited for the alcohol to have its effect. What she felt, more than anything else, was relief. Personally, she didn't give a damn whether he preferred men or women, so long as they were consenting adults. 'Why are you telling me all this?'

'Because you've been blundering around in the dark, and sooner or later you're going to bump into trouble.'

'The same kind of trouble as my mother?'

Luther didn't answer her directly. 'I suppose you have a choice to make.'

'Do I?'

'As to who you believe. I'm presuming you've been told a different story, one that doesn't put me in an entirely good light. So now you need to make up your mind as to who's telling the truth.'

Chrissy wondered how she was supposed to do that. Right now, right this minute, she was inclined to believe Luther, but then Sutherland had been convincing, too. And Luther was a clever man, smart enough to spin her a tale that would sound convincing. 'Do you think Mum's death was an accident?'

'I think it's unlikely.'

Anger rose up in Chrissy. 'Why didn't you do something about it?'

Luther answered calmly. 'What would you have liked me to do? Accuse the police of killing her, of trying to blackmail me, of corruption on the worst level? I didn't have any proof. They look after their own, Christine; it would have been their word against mine. And they'd have thrown it all straight back at me, told the world she was an informer and made your nan's life intolerable.'

'So you did nothing?'

'I went to talk to your nan, but Gaul had got there first. I

390

don't know what he said exactly – you'd have to ask her that – but it was enough to make her think twice about pointing the finger at anyone. She was scared about what might come out.'

'And then?'

'And then I sold the bar to someone else, went abroad and stayed there until it became clear that my mother needed me back home.' He sighed into the still air of the study. 'I suppose you think I'm a coward – perhaps I am – but at the time I thought it was the best thing to do.'

Best thing for who, Chrissy thought, but didn't say it out loud. And perhaps she wasn't being fair. She could see that it wouldn't have been easy going up against the law on his own. There was more she wanted to ask – questions about her mum – but she needed time to absorb what she'd already learnt. She felt tired and confused and just wanted to get away, away from this room, this house, from *him*.

Standing up, she went over to the desk and placed her glass on it. 'I think I'd better go now.'

'Yes, that's probably for the best.'

'What will you tell your mother?'

'I'll say you were taken ill, that you had to go home. I can stay with her this afternoon and keep her company.' He stood up too and drained his glass. 'In fact, why don't you take the next couple of days off – I'm sure you've got a lot to think about – and come back on Monday?'

'Come back?' Chrissy said, frowning.

'Unless you'd rather not. I'd understand if you don't wish to continue with the job. Only Mother seems to rather like you – for now, at least – so I've no objections if you haven't.'

Chrissy wasn't sure if she had objections or not. She was still too surprised by the offer. 'But I lied to you, pretended to be someone I wasn't, sneaked around behind your back and—'

'I think we should draw a line under all that. Have a think about it and let me know what you decide. Give me a call at the gallery on Friday.' He hesitated and then said, 'I take it I can rely on your discretion?'

'Discretion?'

Luther gave a half smile. 'As regards my being unlikely to marry any time in the near future.'

'Ah, right. That. Of course. She doesn't know?'

'Oh yes, she knows, on some level or another. She just refuses to acknowledge it. That her only son could be queer is a truth she finds too offensive, too wounding to accept.'

'I won't say anything.'

Chrissy retrieved her bag from the drawing room, going in and out on tiptoe so as not to wake Mrs Byrne. Luther walked her to the hall, helped her on with her coat, opened the front door and stood aside. 'If I don't see you again, take care of yourself. But you know where I am if you have more questions.' He paused, took the photograph from his pocket and offered it to her. 'Would you like to keep this?'

Chrissy smiled, took the photo and slipped it into her bag. 'Thank you.'

'Goodbye, then.'

She stepped out on to the path. 'Goodbye.'

There was one of those moments where neither of them moved, where they seemed poised in time, as still and silent as the two figures in the photo. Then Chrissy turned and walked away. She heard the click of the front door closing. It was only then that she looked back over her shoulder, wondering if she'd ever return.

65

Chrissy had a restless night, her sleep constantly interrupted by bad dreams, nightmares from the past. She woke over and over again, rising from the horrors of a graveyard, of a man falling from the sky, of her trust betrayed. Awake, she gazed into the darkness as all her old fears mingled with her current ones. They coiled around the inside of her head like snakes, slithering into every corner.

By the time morning came, she felt weak and drained and more than glad that she didn't have to go to Highgate. She got dressed and stumbled through to the kitchen, where Nan wasn't exactly at her best, either, coughing and spluttering and generally looking like death warmed up. It was clear that her cold had got much worse and Chrissy insisted that she stayed off work. 'I'll give them a call. Maybe I should call the doctor, too.'

'Oh, you don't need to bother the doctor. I'll be right as rain by tomorrow.'

'You said that yesterday and look at you now. You should be in bed, Nan, or you'll end up with bronchitis. I'll stay home with you. You shouldn't be on your own.'

'You can't go taking time off. You've only been there five minutes.'

Chrissy, of course, hadn't told her about what had happened with Luther. 'It's not a problem. They'll understand. She's got a son and a housekeeper; they'll manage between them.'

It was a sign, perhaps, of just how sick Nan was that she didn't put up more of a fight. Chrissy went to the hall, rang the butcher and told him Nan wouldn't be in before Monday. Then she loitered there for a couple of minutes to make it look like she'd made more than one call, picking up the phone and listening to the dialling tone for a while before she put it back down again.

Nan refused to go back to bed and so Chrissy put her on the sofa in the living room, got a blanket and wrapped it round her. She turned on the TV and they sat and watched breakfast television together until Nan dozed off. While Nick Owen and Anne Diamond entertained the nation, Chrissy's thoughts drifted off in other directions. Luther's face kept rising into her mind, and then Sutherland's. One of them was lying, but which one? For a while she would incline towards Luther, but then consider again and decide that Sutherland must be the guilty party – and so it went on, round and round, in a cycle she didn't seem able to break.

For lunch she opened a can of tomato soup, warmed it up on the stove and buttered some bread. They ate in the living room with trays on their knees. She gave Nan the last two aspirins – she'd have to go out later and buy some more – and surreptitiously scrutinised her for any signs of deterioration.

'Stop doing that,' Nan said.

'Doing what?'

'Sneaking all those looks at me like I'm about to drop off my perch.'

'You don't look well, Nan.'

'I'm not well, love, but I'm not at death's door.' Nan reached for a tissue and blew her nose. 'You don't have to worry about me.'

But Chrissy did worry. Nan was her rock, her anchor, even if she hadn't always been completely straight with her. Although, if the truth be told, she was just as bad, keeping quiet about everything she'd been doing. None of it was right and she resolved to come clean as soon as Nan was back to her old self. It was time to clear the air, to wipe away the secrets that lay between them.

In the afternoon, Chrissy nodded off too, the lack of sleep catching up with her. She was woken by the sound of the phone ringing. Bleary eyed, she hurried to answer it before Nan was disturbed.

'Hello?'

'Hi, it's me. It's Zelda. I just wanted to let you know that I got hold of a copy of the coroner's report today.'

Chrissy was instantly alert. 'Anything interesting?'

Zelda hesitated. 'Erm . . . '

'What is it?'

'An open verdict. That's what was given.'

'Open? What does that mean?'

'It means that there was doubt about the cause of death, that it could have been suspicious.'

Chrissy gripped the phone, pressing it closer to her ear. 'So definitely not an accident, then?'

'No, it could still have been that. It's more that there was insufficient evidence to reach a firm conclusion. They give an open verdict when the cause of death can't be proved beyond reasonable doubt. I think it was down to the train driver's testimony. He thought he might have seen someone else on the platform with your mum, but he couldn't swear to it. It was dark and everything happened quickly.'

None of this was coming as any great surprise to Chrissy, but it was backing up her own beliefs. 'I reckon he was right, that he did see someone else with her.'

'That gangster bloke?'

'No, not him. I don't know – I don't think so.'

'Who, then?'

But Chrissy didn't trust Zelda enough to share her suspicions. 'I'm not sure. I'm still working on it. Anything back from the police yet?'

'No, that's probably going to take a while, but I doubt there'll be anything more there. There were only a few other passengers at the station and they were sitting in the waiting room so they didn't see anything.'

'Okay, well, thanks for all your help. Thanks for doing that. It was good of you.'

'That's all right. We should get together sometime and have a drink.'

'Yes,' Chrissy said. 'That would be nice.'

But neither of them suggested a time or a place. Chrissy was about to end the conversation when Zelda thought of something else.

'Oh, I meant to tell you: Dawn got in touch with Frank on Saturday and said she didn't want any more money – and that she didn't mean it about going to the papers.'

'That's great news.'

'Yes, and she says she'll pay us back as soon as she can.'

Chrissy could have told her not to hold her breath – she was pretty sure Dawn would never return the cash – but knew that it would only sound spiteful. 'That's good. You must be relieved.'

'Yes. She's not so bad, is she? I think she just had money

worries and . . . Anyway, it's all over, thank God. Frank reckons that she means it, so we don't need to worry.'

They finally said their goodbyes and Chrissy hung up, hoping that Dawn wouldn't have second thoughts. She resolved never to mention their talk to either Frank or Zelda. The threats she had used were nothing to be proud of, even if they had made the problem go away. Would it stay away? She thought it would, so long as nobody else came along who recognised her.

Chrissy didn't go straight back to the living room but instead went to her bedroom and took down the copy of Rudyard Kipling's *Just So* stories from the shelf. She sat on the bed and flicked through the pages until she found the photograph Luther had given to her. She still couldn't figure out if it had been an act of kindness or a clever ploy to put her off the scent. If only pictures could talk. She stared at her mum, drinking in every detail, feeling a dull ache in her heart.

The doorbell went and she quickly slipped the photo back into the book. Nan's friend Jean was at the door, here to see Nan, and Chrissy invited her in.

Jean bustled into the hall. 'How's she doing, love?'

'Not too good, to be honest. Are you in a hurry? Only I need to do some shopping: would you be able to stay with her for half an hour or so?'

'You take your time,' Jean said. 'I'll keep an eye out until you get back.'

Chrissy popped her head round the living room door. 'Jean's here, Nan. I'm just nipping down the Spar. I'll get food for tonight and some more aspirin. Is there anything else you want?'

'Get us a small bottle of Scotch, will you, sweetheart? There's money in my purse.'

'That's okay, we can settle up later.'

Chrissy put on her coat, slung her handbag over her shoulder and left the flat. Some fresh air would do her good, she thought, as she went down in the smelly lift. Once on the ground floor, she crossed the foyer and pushed through the doors. Automatically she scanned the surrounding area for the Dunlaps – she could do without any more grief from them – but the coast was clear.

While she walked, she went over what Zelda had told her. If Nan hadn't been ill, she might have confronted her about the coroner's verdict. An accident, that's what Nan had said, nothing about it being open – although Chrissy had only been fourteen when she'd asked. Perhaps Nan just hadn't wanted to complicate matters or to put ideas into her impressionable head. But she sensed there was more to it than that.

In the Spar she bought a pack of sausages – her culinary skills weren't up to much, but she could just about manage bangers and mash – a tin of baked beans, bread, aspirin and a bottle of Scotch. Nan wasn't a big drinker but she firmly believed in the restorative powers of a hot toddy when she was under the weather.

Chrissy was about to make her way back to the estate when she suddenly remembered what day it was. Nan must have forgotten too; she always visited Betty Cope on Thursdays but she wouldn't be today. The state she was in, she wouldn't be going further than the kitchen. If Chrissy had thought on, she could have given the home a ring and let them know. Would the old lady be sitting there, patiently waiting? Nan was probably her only visitor.

She looked at her watch. It was past three already but Silverstone wasn't far away, only around the corner from the station. She could easily drop in and get the staff to pass on a message. At least that way Betty wouldn't be left in the dark, confused or worried, fearing perhaps that Nan had deserted her.

Chrissy hot-footed it to the nursing home, the shopping

swinging by her side. She had never passed through the gates before. It was a massive red-brick building, imposing but sinister, and there were bars on the windows, giving it an unpleasant, prison-like quality. She slowed as she walked up the drive, feeling reluctant to get there any faster than she had to. The place had a gloomy, oppressive quality, as though a weight of misery was contained within its walls. She stared at it, frowning, assailed by a wave of apprehension. It took an effort of will to propel herself forward, to approach the front door and ring the bell.

66

Chrissy waited in the porch, ringing twice more before a crackly voice eventually came over the intercom. 'Hello?'

'Oh, hi, I'm here about Betty Cope.'

'Come on in.'

There was a buzz and Chrissy quickly pushed open the door. She entered a wide hallway with cream-coloured walls and worn lino on the floor. Instantly, she was aware of a mingling of smells – stale air, old cooking, a whiff of urine, bleach – all of them hitting her at the same time. A middle-aged woman dressed in a green uniform, presumably the person who'd let her in, was already walking away down the corridor.

'Excuse me,' Chrissy called out.

The woman stopped, turned and waited for Chrissy to catch up. 'Yes?'

'It's about Betty Cope. My nan usually visits on Thursdays, but she's not too well and she can't make it today.'

'The lounge is just along there,' the woman said, pointing off to the right. 'Follow the signs and you can't go wrong.'

Chrissy, realising her intentions had been misunderstood, was about to explain that she didn't have the time to stay and to ask if a message could be passed on when she thought of Betty sitting there waiting. Now she was here, it wouldn't hurt to pop in for five minutes. It seemed mean not to. 'Oh, okay. Thanks.'

The lounge was large and overly warm, with a patterned carpet and groups of mismatched armchairs set around low tables. There were about twenty people in all, some of them residents, some of them visitors. She scanned the room for Betty – it was years since she'd last seen her – until her eyes came to rest on an elderly lady sitting on her own. Was that her? She thought it was, but didn't have much to go on other than a few vague childhood memories.

She hesitated, looking around for any other likely candidates – there were a couple of women sitting by the window – and dithered for a few more seconds, before deciding that her first choice had been right. Anyway, she couldn't stand there all day and there were no staff members to ask. She advanced across the room, hoping she wasn't about to embarrass herself. 'Betty?'

The old woman, whose gaze had been fixed on the carpet, raised her pale, rheumy eyes and stared at her.

Chrissy smiled. 'Hello. I'm Chrissy Moss, Elsie's granddaughter. It is Betty, isn't it?'

'Where is she? Where's Elsie?'

This seemed to confirm to Chrissy that it was actually Betty Cope she was talking to. 'I'm afraid she can't come today. She's really sorry. She's got a terrible cold and she didn't want to pass it on to you.'

'Not coming?' Disappointment was etched on her features. 'Why not?'

Chrissy sat down beside her, unsure as to whether Betty was

a bit deaf or just hadn't grasped what she'd said. Raising her voice, she repeated, 'A cold. She's got a bad cold.'

'There's no need to shout.'

'Sorry. I'm sure she'll be better by next week. How are you? It's been a long time since I last saw you.'

Betty was tiny, skin and bone, and looked as frail as a bird. Fine strands of silvery grey hair barely covered the pink of her scalp. The skin on her heavily lined face was thin and papery, almost translucent, and her bony arthritic hands danced in her lap as though she couldn't keep them still. Her voice, though, still had strength in it. 'Elsie has a lot to put up with.'

Chrissy, wondering if this was a dig at her, raised her eyebrows. 'I suppose she has.'

'It's never easy. I remember when . . . ' But Betty never finished the memory. Instead she leaned towards Chrissy and said confidentially, 'They're always watching you in here, always listening, always creeping around. They put poison in the food.'

'How awful,' Chrissy said, thinking it best to humour her.

'I want to go home but they won't let me. They have rules, you see. They never let you do anything you want.'

Chrissy took off her coat. 'It's warm, at least. They don't skimp on the heating.'

A man at a nearby table, bearded and hunched over, was beating his fist against the arm of the chair, a steady banging while he muttered to himself. The woman he was with, his daughter, perhaps, gazed into the middle distance with a blank expression on her face.

'You look different,' Betty said.

'Do I? Well, it's been a while. I was only a kid last time—'

'A bit peaky. Maybe you're coming down with something.'

'I hope not.'

'Mrs Howell caught a cold and she was dead within the week.'

'Oh dear. But I shouldn't think that happens very often.'

'You'd be surprised what happens in here.'

Chrissy glanced around the lounge and was reminded of prison again, of the visiting rooms she'd been in, of the rise and fall in conversation. The first fifteen minutes were always noisy, full of talk, a busy exchange of news, until it gradually ran out. She'd never known what to say to Uncle Pete, but Nan had made the effort to keep things going.

'How's that boyfriend of yours?'

Chrissy focused on Betty again. 'Boyfriend?'

'It was a shock for her, finding out about you and that copper.'

Chrissy started. 'What? Who do you mean?' She wondered if Nan had found out about her chat with Sutherland, maybe heard about her getting in the car with him and jumped to the wrong conclusion. But surely she'd have mentioned it, said something, asked her if it was true? She wouldn't have just kept quiet.

'You should watch your step. Coppers are all the same, backstabbers the lot of them. They'll walk all over you given the chance and not think twice about it. Reckon they own the world, don't they? Show me a copper and I'll show you a liar.'

'I don't have a boyfriend.'

Betty gave her a sceptical look. 'Your mum worries about you, love. She was only saying so the other day. Sleepless nights, that's what you're giving her.'

Chrissy stared at the old lady, wondering at first if Betty believed she was channelling spirits from the other side, before coming to the more likely conclusion that she was just getting her confused with her mother. 'I'm not Laura,' she said. 'I'm Chrissy.'

Betty ignored her. 'She didn't mean it, you know.'

'Mean what?'

'All those things she said. It was just the shock talking; we all say stuff in the heat of the moment. There's not a day goes by she doesn't regret it. You storming off like that and then ... Well, it's not an easy thing to live with, is it?'

'I don't understand.'

'I can't tell you the amount of times I've told her: "It's not your fault, Elsie," but she won't have it. It's up here, you see.' Betty pointed to her head with a trembling finger. 'And once it's there it's never going away.'

Despite the warmth of the room, Chrissy suddenly had the shivers. 'Are you talking about the accident?'

'What accident? Has there been an accident?'

'No, I didn't mean ... Not recently. Years ago. My mum's accident.'

Betty frowned. 'People should be more careful. There wouldn't be so many accidents if they just looked where they were going.'

Chrissy felt the frustration of having the truth dangled in front of her, but not quite being able to grab hold of it. 'What wasn't Elsie's fault?'

But Betty's train of thought, if she even had one, had already drifted on. She gazed down at a half-drunk cup of tea on the table and asked, 'Are there biscuits?'

'I don't know. Would you like me to find someone and ask?'

'Elsie always brings biscuits.'

'Oh, I'm sorry. I'm sure she'll bring some next week.' Chrissy tried again. 'You were saying about Elsie thinking it was her fault?'

'Why should it be her fault? You can't help catching a cold. Mrs Howell caught a cold and she was dead within the week.'

'Yes, I think you told me.' Chrissy tried to reign in her impatience. 'What about Elsie?'

'What about her?'

'What was . . . What can't she get out of her head?'

Betty leaned back her own head and closed her eyes. Chrissy waited, hoping it was just a temporary pause, but the old lady seemed to have fallen fast asleep. She touched Betty lightly on the arm but she didn't stir.

Chrissy decided that this was as good a time as any to leave. She rose quietly to her feet, picked up her carrier bag and headed back to the hall. Here she had to wait for another few minutes until someone turned up to let her out. She hurried along the road and up the high street, aware that she'd been away longer than she'd intended.

While she walked, she went over what she'd been told. But what was that, exactly? Betty wasn't what you'd call a reliable witness; things were muddled in her mind and there was no knowing what was real or what wasn't, what had happened last week or twenty years ago. What she did believe, however, was that Nan blamed herself for something. Betty had seemed plausible – well, as plausible as she could ever be – on that score. Now all Chrissy had to do was find out what it was.

67

When Chrissy got back to the flat, Jean was still there, chatting away to Nan. Jean could talk for England, and Nan wasn't far behind. The two of them had the lowdown on the whole estate, hoovering up gossip at a rate of knots and blowing it back out to anyone who'd listen. Chrissy apologised for her lateness and explained how she'd called in at Silverstone to let them know Betty wouldn't be having a visitor today.

'Oh God!' Nan exclaimed, her hand flying to her mouth. 'It's Thursday, isn't it? I forgot all about poor Betty.'

'I wouldn't worry about it,' Jean said. 'She won't remember whether you were there or not. The old dear's away with the fairies.'

Nan blew her nose and sighed. 'She has her good days. Lord, I haven't missed a visit in years.'

'You're a bloody saint, Elsie. There's not many who'd traipse round there, week in, week out. Especially when you don't get any thanks for it.'

'It's not her fault. And she was always a good friend, bless her.' Nan smiled at Chrissy. 'Ta for doing that, love. It was good of you.'

'That's okay.'

Chrissy took the shopping and went through to the kitchen, where she unpacked it and started preparations for the evening meal. She hoped Jean would go soon so she could ask Nan about what Betty had said. The two women, however, seemed to have an inexhaustible supply of information to exchange and it was another twenty minutes before Jean finally said her goodbyes.

Once Chrissy had heard the front door close, she went into the living room. 'Are you feeling any better, Nan? There's some aspirin on the kitchen table.'

'Thanks, love. I'm not so bad. Did they tell you anything at Silverstone? Did they tell you how Betty was?'

'Oh, I went in to see her.'

Nan seemed suddenly wary. 'You saw her?'

'I thought I might as well pop in and say hello as I was already there. I'm not sure if she knew who I was, though. She was all right, a bit confused.'

'Yes, she gets mixed up about things.'

Chrissy watched her closely. She didn't like putting Nan on the spot, but couldn't see any other way of getting to the bottom of everything. 'She seemed to think you blame yourself for Mum's accident. Why would she think that?'

Nan shook her head, her gaze flitting around the room and refusing to meet Chrissy's. 'I've no idea, sweetheart. She gets all sorts of strange ideas; they don't mean anything. Have you put the tea on? Don't make much for me. I'm not very hungry.'

'What happened that night, Nan? What happened the night Mum died?'

Nan didn't answer. Instead, she picked up the two mugs she

and Jean had used, and bustled through to the kitchen as if urgent matters needed her attention there.

Chrissy followed, watching as she dropped the mugs in the sink and turned on the tap. 'Nan?'

'What?' Nan asked, scrubbing the mugs with unnecessary force.

'Why won't you talk to me about it?'

'Because there's nothing to talk about.' Nan rinsed the mugs and placed them on the drainer. 'It's nonsense. Betty's memory isn't all it was. You shouldn't take any notice.'

'I know Mum was seeing that cop,' Chrissy persisted.

'A cop? What are you talking about? Did Betty say that because—'

'No, it wasn't Betty. I'd already heard it from someone else.'

'Who?'

'It doesn't matter.'

Nan turned off the tap and dried her hands on a tea towel. 'You shouldn't be listening to gossip.'

Chrissy took a glass out of the cupboard, opened the bottle of whisky, poured in a generous shot and filled it with hot water from the kettle. 'Here,' she said, passing it to her nan. 'And this isn't just gossip. It's true, isn't it? Was that why you argued? Because you found out she was seeing Will Sutherland?'

Nan looked as though she was going to protest again, but instead she sat down, took a gulp of the whisky and ran her tongue nervously over her lips. 'It's all in the past, Chrissy. Why does it matter now?'

'Because I want to know, *need* to know. And don't ask me why because I can't really explain. Not properly. It's like … God, there's just so many unanswered questions, things that don't make any sense.'

Nan drank some more whisky and took a deep breath. There

408

was a short silence. When she finally spoke again her voice was small and quavering. 'If it hadn't been for me, she'd still be alive today.'

Chrissy sat down beside her. 'Don't say that, Nan.'

'Why not? It's true. We *did* argue that night. There was talk on the estate about her and that Sutherland, but she said it was rubbish, kept on denying it till she was blue in the face. When I asked why she'd been seen with him, she told me it wasn't any of my business, that there were things I was better off not knowing about. I mean, what kind of answer is that? I told her she was a liar. Anyway, things just went from bad to worse and she ended up storming out.' Nan put her elbows on the table, stared briefly at the wall and then looked at Chrissy. 'You know what the last thing I ever said to her was? *Don't bother coming back.* What kind of thing is that for a mother to say?' Nan's voice was breaking now. 'And she didn't, did she? She never did come back.'

'You didn't mean it,' Chrissy said, taking her hand and squeezing it. 'Jesus, Nan, she knew you loved her. It was just a stupid row. And you can't blame yourself. The accident wasn't *your* fault. How could it be?'

'Because she was angry, wasn't she, not paying attention. That train platform wasn't lit well and it was raining and she must have just . . . It would never have happened if her mind hadn't been somewhere else. She was thinking about what I'd said instead of taking proper care of herself.'

'You can't know that.' Chrissy wasn't sure how much further to take it, for fear of distressing Nan even more. But then the words came out of her mouth before she could stop them. 'It might not even have been an accident. I heard what was in the coroner's report. Didn't the train driver say that he thought he saw someone else? Maybe she was pushed.'

Nan's eyes widened. 'Who'd want to do a thing like that?'

Chrissy had Sutherland at the top of the list – especially if he'd found out she'd been playing him – but Luther wasn't in the clear, either. Or Gaul. And then there were any number of lowlifes on the estate who could have suspected she was informing. 'I don't know,' she said. 'It's possible, though, isn't it?'

'No one would want to hurt your mum, not deliberately.'

'But what if—'

'Let's not talk about it any more, love. Do you mind?'

Chrissy couldn't bear to see the hurt in her eyes. 'No, of course not. Just don't ... don't keep blaming yourself, Nan. Mum would never have wanted that.'

Nan smiled weakly. 'We should get on with that tea or we'll still be sitting here tomorrow.'

No sooner had Chrissy got to her feet than the phone rang. She went through to the hall to answer it. 'Hello?'

'It's Vinnie. Please don't hang up. I really have to talk to you.'

Chrissy rolled her eyes. 'Haven't we already been through this? I thought I—'

'I'm not messing about, Chrissy. This is serious. Meet me on the green tomorrow morning. About eleven. Can you do that?'

'What's the point?'

'I can't talk about it over the phone.' Vinnie's voice sounded stern, demanding, even slightly anxious. 'Just meet me there, yeah? At the bench near the high street. Will you do that?'

Chrissy was too tired to argue. After all the emotional upheavals of the day all she wanted to do was get rid of him. 'Okay. Fine. I'll be there.'

68

Chrissy woke up on Friday morning with no intention at all of going to the green. She had better things to do – like watching over Nan, for example – than pander to Vinnie Keane's wishes. But as the morning wore on she began to worry that if she didn't show up he might come to the flat, might kick up a fuss or create a scene, and she didn't need that kind of hassle. Perhaps it would be better to just bite the bullet and get it over and done with.

At a quarter to eleven, deciding that meeting him could, on balance, be the lesser of two evils, she told Nan that she was going to Connolly's to pick up some wages that were owed to her. 'I shouldn't be long. Will you be all right on your own? If you like I can give Jean a knock on my way out, see if she can come and sit with you.'

'Oh, don't go bothering Jean. I'm much better today. You get on.'

Chrissy wasn't convinced that she was any better: she looked pale and her chest still sounded wheezy. 'Are you sure?'

'Don't start fussing again.' Nan waved a hand at her in a shooing motion. 'I'm fine. Do you want that money or not?'

Chrissy made her way off the estate, trying to prepare herself as she walked. The anger she felt towards Vinnie was still there but not as strong as it had been. With everything that had happened with Luther and Betty and Nan, she didn't have the energy to hold on to grudges. That didn't mean she'd forgiven him, though, not by a long chalk.

She saw Vinnie as she approached the green, not sitting on the bench but pacing across the grass with his hands in his jacket pockets. He had the look of a man with things on his mind and her heart sank. She wasn't in the mood for a load of half-baked excuses and hoped he wasn't going to spend an eternity expressing them.

She was only a few yards away when he turned. 'You came,' he said, with what sounded like relief.

'I can't stay long. Nan's not well.'

'Sorry to hear it.' Vinnie nodded towards the bench. 'You want to sit down?'

'No, I can't hang about. Just tell me what's so important that you have to keep harassing me.'

Vinnie's eyebrows went up. 'Well, I wouldn't call it harassment exactly. I've only—'

'Can you just get on with it, Vinnie?'

'Sure,' he said, his gaze fixed on her. 'It's about you and Luther Byrne. Whatever the two of you are plotting, Gaul's on to it and he's not happy.'

Chrissy's mouth fell open. She was shocked by the fact both Vinnie and DCI Gaul knew that she was in contact with Luther. 'What the hell are you talking about?'

'Are you saying there's nothing going on?'

'I'm saying it's none of your damn business.'

'Ordinarily, it wouldn't be, except Gaul's made it our business. He wants the problem to go away, for Terry to sort it out for him.'

As Vinnie's words sank in, Chrissy instinctively took a step back. Fear rose up in her and her heart began to race. She knew what sorting things out meant in Terry's world. Quickly she glanced around, just to reassure herself that other people were in the vicinity.

'For Christ's sake, Chrissy, what do you think I am?'

'How should I know?' Chrissy snapped back, trying to disguise her fright with a boldness she didn't feel. 'You stand there threatening me and—'

'Nobody's threatening you. The very opposite. Shit, we just want to help. You're in trouble, big trouble, although you don't seem to realise it.'

'There's nothing going on between me and Luther; we're not *plotting* anything.'

'What are you doing then?'

'I'm just working for him, that's all. Well, for his mother. She's old and . . . Anyway, that's all there is to it. There's no plotting, no conspiring, no nothing.'

'Trying telling Gaul that.'

'It's *true*,' Chrissy insisted. 'And if Terry wanted to help, why didn't he just say no to him?'

Vinnie lit a cigarette, sheltering the flame with his hand while he stared at her. 'Oh, he could have done – and then what? Gaul would have gone to someone else, someone who might not be quite as concerned with your well-being.'

'I hardly know Terry. Why should he give a damn?'

'God knows. Perhaps it's your irresistible charm.' Vinnie grinned at her. 'Or perhaps he doesn't care for being pushed around by Gaul. He's funny about things like that. Look, all Terry wants is to have a chat, maybe see if we can work together to get Gaul off your back.'

'No, thanks. I'll take my chances.'

'And what about Luther Byrne? Is he going to take his chances, too?'

'That's up to him.'

'It can only be up to him if he knows what's going on. Now I've got no idea why Gaul thinks that you and Luther are out to screw him over, but I guess he must have his reasons. And I'm also guessing that you know what they are. You don't need to tell me that; it's nothing to do with me. But Luther Byrne's looking at a pile of grief and it's probably best if he's made aware of it. Don't you reckon? Nobody likes surprises.'

Suddenly the direness of the situation hit Chrissy, along with a bucketful of guilt. By contacting Luther, by spending time at the house, she'd led Gaul to believe they were conspiring together – plotting revenge for what had happened to her mum – and now the DCI was out to get them both. Even if she tried to persuade him otherwise, it was hardly likely he'd believe her. And anyway, she couldn't approach him without revealing who'd tipped her off, and that would make trouble for Vinnie, too. For all her anger at what he'd done, she wasn't prepared to throw him to the law.

'So?' Vinnie asked.

'I'm thinking.'

'Don't take too long about it. Things are moving pretty quickly here. Gaul wants results and he wants them fast. Terry can't keep putting him off.'

'Why should I trust you, either of you?'

'Maybe you're asking the wrong question. Maybe you need to decide who you *distrust* the least.'

When he put it that way, Chrissy could see exactly what she had to do. 'Okay, I'll talk to him.'

'Let's go, then. He's waiting.'

69

Chrissy rang directory enquiries from one of the phone boxes outside the station and got the number for the Byrne Gallery. It was Luther who answered and she tried to explain about Gaul and Terry Street, although it came out rather garbled. He asked her a few sensible questions and she answered as best she could.

'You'd better come over with him, then,' Luther said. 'We may as well hear what he has to say.'

'I'm sorry. This is all my fault.'

'How do you work that out?'

'Because if I hadn't tracked you down, taken the job, Gaul would never have suspected we were up to something.'

'It's not your fault what Gaul thinks or does.'

Chrissy supposed this was true but it didn't stop her feeling responsible. The next call she made was to Nan, asking if she could cope on her own for a couple of hours. 'They're short-staffed at Connolly's. I said I'd help out if it's all right with you.' Nan said that was fine, and Chrissy hung up feeling even worse than she had after phoning Luther. So many lies. Too many.

Vinnie and Terry Street were waiting by the car at the Fox. She got in the back with Terry and they set off for Bond Street. Neither of them attempted any small talk. Chrissy, knowing there was no point in holding back, got straight to the point and gave Terry a quick summary of what had happened in the past.

'I can see how it looks to Gaul, but there's nothing going on with me and Luther.'

'What could be going on?' Terry asked.

Chrissy looked at him, puzzled. 'What do you mean?'

'I mean, why should Gaul be worried? Why are you a threat? What does he think the two of you can do after all these years?'

'I suppose he's worried that Luther will expose him for the blackmail, for putting pressure on Mum to inform, for things that might all have led eventually to her death.'

'Luther's word against his,' Terry said. 'Unless he's got solid proof. Has he?'

Chrissy gave a shrug. 'I don't know.'

'You said your mother was using Sutherland to gather evidence. She must have written stuff down. What happened to that?'

Again, Chrissy shrugged.

'Do you think your nan might have it?'

Chrissy considered this possibility but then dismissed it. She'd lived in the flat for over twenty years and couldn't think of a place Nan could have hidden anything like that without her stumbling on it at one time or another. 'No, not at home. I don't think so. And I don't think she'd have held on to it, anyway. What if the flat was searched by the law? She wouldn't want them to find it, would she?'

'Anywhere else she might have put it for safekeeping – with a mate, perhaps?'

Chrissy thought about Jean, but wasn't convinced that

Nan would entrust something quite so explosive even to a close friend. And Betty too was out of the running. 'No one springs to mind.'

'Have you asked her?'

'She doesn't know that I'm in touch with Luther. She gets upset when I talk about Mum so . . .'

Terry nodded. 'Okay. Well, maybe Luther Byrne can shine some light on it.'

All the time she and Terry were talking, Vinnie kept his eyes on the road and acted like he couldn't hear a thing. But she knew he was listening. She almost asked Terry why he was doing all this – Vinnie's explanation seemed somewhat on the thin side – but decided it was smarter not to question his motives.

They spent the rest of the journey in silence. Chrissy gazed out of the window, hoping she was doing the right thing. Could she trust Terry? Could she trust Luther, come to that? She had made a choice, accepting Luther's version of events, when she'd found out Gaul was gunning for her, but only time would tell if she'd made the right one.

Vinnie dropped them outside the gallery and drove off. He was, it appeared, to take no further part in proceedings. She went inside with Terry, where Luther was waiting. Introductions were made and the two men shook hands, subtly sizing each other up. Both of them smiled, but their expressions were probing, their eyes wary.

Luther took them upstairs to his office which was stylish and comfortable, the deep pile carpet soft enough for her to feel her feet sinking into it. The pungent aroma of white lilies – heady, almost funereal – hung in the air. He sat down behind his desk and she and Terry took the chairs opposite. Chrissy was on edge, uneasy, unsure as to how any of this was going to work out.

Luther was the first to speak, putting forward the question

417

she had shrunk from asking earlier. 'If you don't mind me enquiring, Mr Street, could you tell me exactly what your interest is in this situation?'

'What's in it for me, you mean?'

'Precisely.'

Terry, unfazed by his bluntness, leaned forward with his hands splayed on his thighs. 'Let's just say that DCI Gaul has been causing me trouble recently, being even more demanding than usual. Now I'm a reasonable man – ask anyone – but I've got my limits. I want him off my back just like you want him off yours, but in order to do that I need some ... how shall I put it? ... *leverage*.'

'Some dirt.'

'I think we can be of use to each other – with a bit of give and take.'

Luther inclined his head while he studied Terry. 'And what will you be bringing to the party, Mr Street?'

'Peace of mind,' Terry said. 'I'll make sure he leaves you both alone. For ever. That's not such a bad deal, is it? I'll be the one who makes all your problems go away.'

'And what if your intervention only makes things worse?'

'Not sure it could get any worse,' Terry said.

Luther glanced at Chrissy. 'Are you happy to go ahead?'

Happy didn't seem quite the right word to Chrissy, but she nodded anyway. 'If you are. Although I'm not sure if what we know will be enough. I mean, we don't have any solid proof, do we?'

Luther opened a drawer to his right, reached into it, pulled out a large brown envelope and placed it on the desk. 'Perhaps this will help.' With his fingertips, he pushed the envelope across to Terry.

Terry emptied out the contents: a heap of photographs, about

418

thirty, and a small navy-blue diary. He began to slowly sift through the pictures, scrutinising each one in turn. Chrissy stared at them too, but she didn't recognise any of the faces other than a much younger-looking Gaul.

'I employed a couple of somewhat unpleasant but obliging private detectives to follow Gaul around,' Luther said. 'They were the ones who provided most of the pictures. Of course, they were taken over twenty years ago but they're still relevant, I think. The DCI had a wide circle of friends. A veritable rogues' gallery. The ones taken in Spain are of particular interest – Gaul and his wife sunning themselves beside the pool at Joe Quinn's villa.'

Terry came to the pictures in question and his lips widened into a smile. 'You could have nailed him with these. Why didn't you report him, hand them over?'

'Hand them over to whom?' Luther asked. 'Gaul's superior? The head of the Met? He had friends in high places. There might have been an internal inquiry of some sort but no doubt there'd have been a closing of ranks, a cover-up, a way found for the evidence to go missing. Anyway, Christine's grandmother didn't want me to pursue it. She was afraid of repercussions.'

Chrissy nodded again. 'Gaul paid her a visit after the accident. He pretty much said that if she kept quiet about Mum's relationship with Sutherland – and presumably anything else she knew – then he'd keep the fact Mum had been an informer under wraps.' In case Terry got the wrong idea, she quickly added, 'Not that she was an informer. She wasn't. She was just using Sutherland to gather information on Gaul.'

'A risky game,' Terry said.

'The diary was your mother's,' Luther said to Chrissy. 'Your grandmother gave it to me. It's got names in it, people Gaul was taking bribes from, contacts, that kind of thing.'

Chrissy picked it up and flicked through the pages. It wasn't the first time she'd seen her mum's handwriting – Nan had Christmas and birthday cards that she'd sent – but this felt different, like she was stepping inside her world for a moment, sharing something secret and valuable. The entries were small and neat, a series of meticulous entries than ran through the summer of 1965 and stopped suddenly in early November. It was a distressing reminder of how her mother's life had come to an end so abruptly. She sighed, closed the diary and passed it over to Terry. 'Do you think it will be of any use?'

'It might. I'll take a look and then return it to you.'

'Thanks.'

Terry put everything back in the envelope, pushed back his chair and rose to his feet. 'Don't get up,' he said, leaning across to shake Luther's hand. 'I'll see myself out. And I'll stay in touch.'

'No offence,' Luther said, 'but there's really no need. Unless you run into any problems . . . '

'None taken,' Terry said. 'And I can't see any problems arising. Do you want the photos back?'

'You can keep them. I've got copies.'

'In that case, it's been a pleasure doing business with you.'

Luther smiled but didn't return the pleasantry. 'Goodbye, Mr Street.'

Terry said goodbye to them both and left. He shut the office door behind him with a soft click.

'You have some interesting friends,' Luther said, sitting back.

'I wouldn't call him a friend, exactly. I used to work for him at Cordelia's. Do you think we can trust him?' Chrissy was battling with all her doubts again. 'Do we think we've done the right thing?'

'Too late to change our minds now.'

'I don't think he'll double cross us,' Chrissy said, trying to be optimistic.

'And why's that? Because he's such an honest and upstanding member of the community?'

'Because ... I don't know ... because he wants rid of Gaul as much as we do.'

'Let's hope you're right.'

Chrissy stood up. 'I'd better be going too.'

Luther walked with her, talking as they headed downstairs. 'Have you had any more thoughts about coming back to Highgate?'

'I'm not sure it's a good idea.'

'Do you need a job?'

'Yes, of course.'

'Well, I need a companion for Mother. So why not? It makes sense, doesn't it? We can help each other out here.'

'Even after everything that's happened?'

'Especially after everything that's happened.' Luther stopped and briefly laid his hand on her arm. 'I'd like you to come back. Say you will.'

Chrissy didn't have to think about it too much. She enjoyed the job, even if Mrs Byrne wasn't always the easiest of people to get along with. And she certainly needed the money. 'All right then. I'd like that, too.'

They parted at the foot of the stairs. Chrissy looked over her shoulder as she went out through the gallery door. Luther was still standing there watching her. He raised a hand and she waved back. Just like her mother before her, she had formed an alliance with him. Hopefully this one would have a better outcome.

70

Bond Street was noisy, bustling, and Chrissy had to weave between the other pedestrians as she forged a path towards the nearest bus stop. She heard a couple of whistles from somewhere behind her, but was too preoccupied to take any notice of it. Her mum was on her mind. If Terry was successful then she wouldn't need to worry about Gaul any more, but it didn't get her any closer to finding out what had really happened that November evening in 1965. What if Gaul had been the other person on the platform? She couldn't bear the thought of him getting away with murder.

Suddenly a shout cut through the air. 'Chrissy!'

She jumped, startled and turned to see Vinnie striding towards her.

'Didn't you hear me whistle?' he said, once he'd caught up.

Chrissy stared at him. 'I'm not a dog.'

He grinned. 'I was just trying to get your attention. Do you want a lift back to Kellston?'

'Where's Terry?'

'He had to be somewhere. He took a cab.'

Chrissy would have told him to stuff his lift if she hadn't been in a hurry to get back to Nan. As it was, she didn't much fancy standing around waiting for a bus for God knows how long. 'Okay,' she said, as if she was doing him a favour. 'That would be all right, I suppose.'

She wasn't so sure that it would be all right, however, as she settled into the passenger seat and pulled across her seatbelt. While Terry had been in the car, she hadn't had to talk to Vinnie, but now they were alone, she suspected things could get awkward.

'Everything sorted?' he asked.

'Early days,' she said, unsure as to how much he knew.

Vinnie pulled away from the kerb and into the stream of West End traffic. 'Could I explain something?'

'Does it involve more apologies?'

'It doesn't have to,' he said.

'Go on then.'

Vinnie took a moment, as though he was gathering his thoughts. 'That first time I gave you a lift – you know, after the shift in Cordelia's – Terry hadn't said anything to me about Luther Byrne, not a word. It was only a few days later that he mentioned him. Gaul had got all antsy when the name came up and Terry wondered what was going on. That's why I asked you about Luther when we were in the pub. It wasn't anything underhand, anything planned. I didn't even tell Terry I was seeing you, I swear. I'll put my hands up to doing some digging but that's all there was to it. It wasn't why I asked you out.'

'Why should I believe you?'

'Because I'm basically a nice guy.'

Chrissy gave a snort. 'That's it?'

Vinnie looked at her. 'You think I need to expand on that a bit?'

'I think you should keep your eyes on the road.'

Vinnie looked ahead again. 'Okay, so I should have been straight with you when it came to Luther, not tried to go at it sideways. And I shouldn't mix business with pleasure – that never works out well. I just don't want there to be any bad feeling between us. That's not such a terrible thing, is it?'

'It depends what your motives are.'

'Decent and upright, pure as the driven snow.'

Chrissy wasn't quite ready to relinquish her resentment yet. 'And what about Charlie Dunlap having a go at me outside Connolly's? That was just a coincidence, was it?'

'Well, it's hardly out of character from what I've heard about him.'

This was true, although Chrissy wasn't going to admit it. 'You think I overreacted.'

'I didn't say that.'

'Near as damn it.'

Vinnie shot her another look. 'Hey, you've got every reason to distrust me. I get it. But I never had any bad intentions. And I know you don't want to hear another apology but I screwed up and I'm sorry.'

Chrissy was aware that he could just be stringing her a line, but she sensed he was being genuine. With so much else going on, it was possibly time to start letting go of past grievances and grudges. 'Okay.'

'Okay? Is that it?'

'What more do you want?'

Vinnie wound down the window and leaned his elbow on it. 'Nothing. That's good. I'll take okay.'

Once they'd escaped the West End, the traffic began to thin

out and soon they were making good progress towards Kellston. Now that the air had more or less been cleared, Chrissy was feeling more comfortable. 'Has Terry told you what's going on?'

'Only that Gaul seems to think you and Luther are conspiring against him.'

'And that's all?'

'Sometimes you're better off not knowing.'

Chrissy thought of Luther, of their conversation in his study at Highgate. 'You're the second person who's said that to me recently.'

'Could be there's some truth in it, then.'

'So you don't want to know?'

'It's your business, not mine.'

'You're not even the tiniest bit curious?'

Vinnie grinned again. 'If you want to tell me, you can tell me. If not, I'm fine with that too.'

'It's a long story,' Chrissy said, but she didn't elaborate. She wasn't quite ready to completely trust him.

By the time they reached Kellston, the atmosphere between them had changed. They were not best buddies, exactly, but some kind of armistice had been achieved. Vinnie drew up outside Carlton House, took a slip of paper from his pocket and offered it to her. 'It's my number,' he said. 'Call me if you ever need anything. You can leave a message if I'm not there.'

Chrissy hesitated – she couldn't imagine a time when she would ever need anything from him – but then, out of politeness, she took the number and put it in her pocket. 'Thanks for the lift.'

'I hope it all works out,' he said.

Chrissy got out of the car, shut the door and walked towards the tower. She heard the car move off but resisted the temptation to turn around.

71

Terry Street had got the cab to drop him off at Kellston station. From there he'd put in a call to Cowan Road from a phone box and made an arrangement to meet Gaul that evening. He was looking forward to it. He was looking forward to the expression on the DCI's face when he pulled out the photographs and showed him the kind of evidence that could bring a policeman's career to a scandalous end.

Terry knew how the scene would play out: there would be anger and bluster and empty threats, but in the end Gaul would accede to his demands. The bent bastard wouldn't have a choice. And it wasn't as though he was asking for much, only for balance to be restored, for the extra payments and favours to stop, and for Chrissy and Luther Byrne to be left alone. A small price, he thought, in exchange for a man's reputation.

It was a pleasant day – made even more agreeable by the knowledge of what was to come – and he decided to make the most of the sunshine and go for a walk. He was by nature a sociable bloke, not much given to introspection, but occasionally he felt the urge to be alone. He strolled around the East End streets for a while before deciding there was somewhere else he had to be.

As he passed through the gates of the cemetery, he immediately thought of Chrissy Moss. He hadn't known who she was when she'd come to work for him. How could he? Although the story had been all over the papers ten years ago – a teenage girl raped in the graveyard, a man murdered – her name hadn't been published. He had probably heard it at some point, but if he had it had slipped his mind long ago.

It was only after Gaul had reacted so badly to the name of Luther Byrne that he'd become curious about Chrissy. He'd asked around and that was when he'd found out. He had felt protective of her ever since, and there was good reason for it. Odd, even fateful, that she had found her way to Cordelia's, but life was like that sometimes.

Terry could clearly recall that afternoon from a decade ago. He had been driving through Kellston when he'd seen Eddie Barr walking through the cemetery gates with the fair-haired girl. The kid was only thirteen or fourteen, too young for a grown man, but there were rumours that Eddie liked them that way. What had made him stop? Curiosity, perhaps, or just the opportunity to gather some dirt on someone he despised.

By the time he'd parked and doubled back, the couple were already heading off the main thoroughfare and along the narrow path that led into the older part of the cemetery. He couldn't follow without being seen and so had circled round by the war graves instead. By the time he'd caught up with them again, they were on the ground and it was pretty obvious what they were up to.

Now Terry was no voyeur and had better things to do with his time than to watch other people screwing. He'd been on the point of retracing his steps – he'd seen as much as he wanted to – when he'd realised something was wrong. It wasn't Eddie on top of the girl, but some other geezer. And this was no sweet roll in the hay. The girl was limp, bloodied and broken, her cries silenced by a knife to her throat.

What he had done next Terry had no regrets about. He had made damn sure that he'd brought that piece of stone down hard enough to smash the bastard's skull open. What he did regret, however, was that he'd had to leave the kid there alone. It was unfortunate, but necessary. He'd had the law to call, and then . . . well, there had been other business to attend to. It hadn't taken a genius to work out Eddie's part in all of it.

Terry sat down on a bench and leaned back his head so he could feel the sun on his face.

Gaul had always had him in the frame for Eddie's murder, the number one suspect, but had never tried to put the finger on him. The DCI had been as happy as everyone else to see the back of the scumbag. It was only recently that he'd started threatening to re-open the case, trying to put the screws on Terry. Maybe Gaul had his suspicions about Hooper too, but he hadn't been able to put the pieces together.

Terry lowered his face, got a pack of fags out of his pocket and lit one. Someone had once told him that if you saved a life you were responsible for that person for ever. It hadn't made any sense at the time – he'd thought it should be the other way around – but now he understood. Later, when he met Gaul, he would make it clear that Chrissy Moss was off limits. He was determined that no one would ever hurt her again.

The cemetery was quiet, peaceful. He smoked his fag and listened to the breeze rustle through the trees. He had never told anyone what had happened here, and never would. The best-kept secrets were the ones you kept to yourself.

72

From the moment he woke up on Saturday morning Will Sutherland knew it was going to be a bad day. Outside it was lashing down with rain, and there was a storm cloud in his head, too. The past was closing in, spinning its web, wrapping him in its lies and deceit. He had thought it was all over, but it wasn't. Nothing had been laid to rest. Even from the grave, Laura was tormenting him.

He drank two mugs of strong black coffee for breakfast, made a hasty review of his life – still as crap as it had been yesterday – and tried to push the bad stuff out of his mind. Impossible. Although he couldn't change what had happened, he couldn't let go of it, either.

Laura had been like one of those sirens he'd read about as a kid, the creatures of mythology who lured sailors to their deaths through the sweetness of their singing. Except the analogy didn't quite stack up. He had ended up on the rocks all right, but she had been the one to die.

'Give it a rest, Sutherland,' he said out loud.

It was a downhill road once you started talking to yourself, a short journey to the loony bin. He shook his head, tried to clear his mind, but the cloud didn't lift. What he needed was a drink. Already he was looking forward to the end of his shift, when he could try and find some solace in the bottom of a whisky glass.

The day didn't improve when he went into Cowan Road. Gaul was in a rage, thwarted over something, muttering under his breath about Terry bloody Street. When Will asked what was happening with Luther Byrne, Gaul bared his teeth and glared at him.

'Why couldn't you have just stayed away from the bitch?'

Will didn't know if he was referring to Laura or her daughter, but he supposed it could apply to either of them. Laura had plotted with Luther, and now Chrissy was doing the same. The apple never falls far from the tree. Wasn't that what they said? But if they were playing the blame game, the DCI was right up there, too. Gaul was the one who'd been hand in glove with the late Joe Quinn, the two of them trying to force Luther to sell his bar. And Gaul was the one who'd pushed Will into being Laura's handler in the first place. 'Use your charm,' he'd said. 'She's more likely to talk to you than me.' Except Will was the one who'd been charmed, seduced and led straight down the garden path.

Will hadn't got a direct answer about Luther Byrne, and he didn't ask again. Gaul would tell him if and when he felt like it. The news, he imagined, would not be good. Was everything that was buried going to be dug up again? Luther had kept silent for twenty years, but perhaps all that was about to change. He felt curiously indifferent about this possibility, as though nothing really mattered any more.

The rest of the shift went much as Will had expected. He dealt with a mountain of paperwork, drank more coffee and ate an indifferent lunch before he was called out for an attempted robbery at the post office. There he arrested three suspects, interviewed them at the station and was sworn at, lied to and spat at by the scumbags. Just a normal day in the life of a Kellston cop. Gaul brooded and sulked and vented his fury on anyone who came near him.

Will went straight down to the Fox as soon as he'd clocked off. It was early evening but already the pub was starting to fill up. He grabbed a spot at the bar, sat down, bought a double whisky, downed it in one and ordered another.

'Bad day?' the barmaid asked.

'They're all bad.'

'Maybe you're in the wrong job.'

By the time Will had thought of a suitable reply to this she was already serving someone else. He leaned an elbow on the counter and surveyed the customers. There was a crowd in from the Mansfield, faces that were becoming increasingly familiar to him. He saw the Dunlap brothers across the other side of the room, drinking pints with four other louts, their heads bent together in some conspiracy or another. Frank Yates was sitting alone at a corner table, reading a paper. Groups of girls in their Saturday finery were arriving, their eyes darting here and there, checking out the talent. They posed and giggled like kids playing grown-ups. He was too old to warrant any attention. Their eyes ran over him, appraising and dismissing in one fast, demoralising glance.

There had been a time, although it was a while ago, when their gazes would have lingered. He tried to remember that younger version of Will Sutherland, to fix him in his mind: cocksure, ambitious, a man with the world at his feet. It was a world he'd wanted to change. He had joined the Force intending to make a difference, to fight all that was bad, to be the scourge of every criminal. So much for that. The moment DCI Gaul had taken him under his wing, he'd been doomed.

'You've got to play them at their own game,' Gaul had said. 'Play nice and you'll never get anywhere. They'll trample you underfoot, son. You have to fight fire with fire.'

By the time he'd realised just how bent Gaul was, it was too late. He was already infected, run through with poison. The line between right and wrong had become blurred. Idealism had been replaced by cynicism, dreams with reality. For Gaul, anything went, so long as he got what he wanted: a means to an end, he'd call it, although that end usually involved lining his own pockets.

And then Will had met Laura. He'd been the one who was supposed to be in charge, the one pulling the strings, but it hadn't worked out like that. Within weeks he'd become besotted with her. No girl had ever got under his skin the way she had. That body, that mouth, those pleading eyes. 'You won't let Pete go to jail, will you? Tell me you'll help him. Promise me.' He would have promised her the whole bloody world if she'd wanted it, and meant it.

Will was starting to feel the effects of the whisky. He'd been hoping it would calm him, blunt the sharp edges of his bitterness, but instead his resentment was growing, spreading, festering. How could you hate someone you'd loved so much? Because she'd betrayed him, torn him apart. He had thought she was the one good thing in his sordid little life, but it turned out she was as squalid and dirty as the rest of it.

An overheard call in a nightclub. That's all it had taken to rip everything up by the roots, to reveal the rot that lay at the foundations of their relationship. He had gone for a slash and she'd been standing in the corridor with her back to him, the payphone pressed to her ear, talking more loudly than she should because of the music blaring out.

'Don't worry, it's all under control ... Yes, I'm with him now ... Of course not; he doesn't suspect a thing. I think the poor sap's in love with me ... Luther, don't stress. I'm still working on it, but once we've got more dirt on Gaul you won't have anything to worry about.'

The words had sliced into him, exposing every raw nerve. It was like his flesh had been peeled away. Anger and pain surged through him. He had wanted to grab her, to smash her in the face, to break every bone in her beautiful body. It was all a lie and nothing mattered any more. But instead he had retreated, gathered himself as best he could and prepared to make her pay.

Will raised the glass to his lips, his hand shaking slightly. He looked around the Fox, but saw only that West End nightclub. He replayed the moment, watching her as she danced, her long fair hair tumbling almost to her waist. A sudden clarity as to what he had to do next had come to him. To save his pride, his life. What choice had he had? He had told her too much, been beyond indiscreet. But that was only part of it. Her betrayal had dislodged his sanity. If he didn't want to go completely mad, he would have to kill the thing he loved.

Twenty years had passed since then. Gaul had suspected, known he wasn't where he was supposed to be on the night of the accident.

'I didn't kill her,' Will had said. 'I might have wanted to, but I didn't.'

But Gaul had given him that look, the one that said he knew better, the one that said that he'd cover for him, but in return Will would always be in his debt.

73

Chrissy had intended to spend the evening watching telly with Nan, until Jean had rocked up at half past six, plonked herself on the sofa and not stopped gabbing since. First it had been her bunions, then her varicose veins and now she was on to her bowels. Chrissy was starting to reconsider Frank's offer. He had called by earlier to let them know that a flat was available in Haslow House in December and it was Uncle Pete's if he wanted it. Nan hadn't had to think twice; she'd signed the papers and showered him with gratitude, tea and cake. If she could have given him her only granddaughter, she'd probably have done that too.

As Chrissy was showing him out, Frank had said, 'You've heard about Dawn, then?'

'Yeah, Zelda told me. It's good news.'

'You don't think it's a bit odd?'

'Odd?' Chrissy had echoed, all wide-eyed innocence.

'I mean, why would she suddenly change her mind like that? One minute she's trying to screw every penny she can out of us and the next ...'

'You should be pleased.'

'Oh, I am. I think. Only I'm worried she's got something else up her sleeve. What if she's going to the papers or the law?'

Chrissy had tried to reassure him. 'I don't reckon she'll do that. She's probably just realised that she's taken you for as much as she can. And I doubt she'll want the publicity any more than you do if it all comes out.'

Frank had looked doubtful. 'I hope you're right. None of it adds up for me. Anyway, I'm meeting Zelda for a drink in the Fox at seven. Why don't you come along? I know she'd love to see you again.'

At the time Chrissy hadn't much fancied it, especially if there was going to be another post-mortem on the whys and where-fores of Dawn's sudden change of heart. 'Thanks. I'm not sure. It depends on Nan. She's still got this cold and . . . I should stay here with her really.'

'Okay. Well, the offer's open. We'll see you if we see you.'

Chrissy had been pretty sure they wouldn't see her, until now. With Jean working her way through her bodily functions, a drink at the Fox was starting to look like an attractive prospect. She got up from the chair, went over to the window, pulled aside the curtain and gazed out. It was still tipping down, and although she didn't much relish a walk in the rain, she preferred it to listening to Jean's endless list of woes.

'Nan? I said I might meet Frank and Zelda at the Fox. Will you be okay? I'll only be a couple of hours.'

Nan looked pleased at this new opportunity for blossoming romance. 'Frank, eh?' she said. 'That'll be nice. Yes, you run along. I've got Jean here to keep me company.'

Chrissy went to the bedroom, changed her tatty sweater for a more respectable one, brushed her hair and put on some lippy. Her hand hovered over the perfume bottle for a second before

435

she withdrew it. Although she was certain that Frank's crush was long over, she didn't want to turn up smelling like she'd made an extra effort. She said goodbye to Nan and Jean, put on her raincoat and left the flat.

The evening was a dismal one. Even with an umbrella, Chrissy was still getting wet. The rain was slanting down, fast and furious, seeping into her shoes and soaking her jeans. She sidestepped the puddles as she half walked, half jogged, down the high street. Perhaps this hadn't been such a great idea, after all. She'd be spending the next couple of hours with wet feet and her jeans glued to her legs.

Chrissy reached the corner, waited for the lights to change, rushed across the road and went into the Fox. Frank and Zelda were standing by the bar with their backs to her. As she crossed the pub it took her a moment to clock that Frank had his hand on Zelda's hip, and she was leaning in against him. Things had, apparently, moved on between them. She was pleased, but poor Nan was about to have all her dreams crushed. Then, as she was wondering whether she should just leave them to it – did she really want to play gooseberry? – she saw Will Sutherland push through the crowd and walk out through the door. He was drunk. Not rip-roaring, staggering, can't stand up drunk, but inebriated all the same. She could tell from the way he was walking too carefully, as though the floor was shifting a little under his feet.

Chrissy dithered, glanced towards Frank and Zelda again, and then decided to follow him. People could be indiscreet when they'd had one too many, loose-lipped, more likely to let secrets slip. She caught up with him outside the station. As she approached, she couldn't work out what he was doing. Just staring into the interior by the looks of it. Trying to make up his mind, perhaps, whether to catch a train or not. The rain was still pouring down and he was getting drenched, water running off his hair and down his face.

'Hello,' she said, drawing alongside him.

Sutherland turned and stared at her for a moment, as though grasping for a name. Then a thin smile crawled onto his lips. 'Chrissy Moss,' he said. 'Fancy seeing you here.'

'What are you doing?' she asked, following his gaze into the small station concourse.

'Thinking.'

'You lied to me about Luther Byrne,' she said, deciding to be blunt. There was no point going around the houses with someone who was drunk. Subtlety wasn't in their repertoire.

'It was as good a tale as any.'

'And what does that mean?'

'Everyone has their own story. You repeat it often enough, you eventually come to believe it.' Sutherland kept his eyes on her. 'And when it comes to telling lies, you're hardly in a position to talk.'

'It's hard to be honest when you're not sure you can trust someone.'

'I looked out for you,' he said. 'All those years. If it hadn't been for me, you would have ended up in the slammer. I looked out for you because you're Laura's daughter.'

Chrissy thought back to those bad times, back to the days she had been out of control. 'I know, and I'm grateful.'

'You've got a funny way of showing it.'

'I've never tried to do you any harm. All I've ever wanted was the truth about what happened to Mum.'

'The truth,' he murmured. 'We could all do with some of that.' Then, without another word, he moved away from her and walked off into the station.

Chrissy stood there, not sure what to do next. The rain

drummed against the canopy of her umbrella. What she ought to do was go back to the Fox and join Frank and Zelda, but she knew she wasn't going to. At least not right now. Instead she set off in pursuit of Sutherland. If she pushed him hard enough, if she didn't stop, then maybe he would give her what she wanted.

Inside the station there were two platforms, one to the left where the trains went out to Liverpool Street, and one to the right where the trains came in. She chose the latter and hurried down the steps. The platform was only partly covered and Sutherland was sitting on a bench at the far end, indifferent or oblivious to the rain.

She hesitated again, knowing this was where her mum's life had ended. Usually she tried to avoid the place, especially at night; for her it had an eerie, haunted quality. She shivered, even though it wasn't cold. Goosebumps were breaking out on her arms. A couple of passengers were huddled in the shelter, but otherwise the place was deserted. There were lights but there were dark shadows, too, especially near the old brick wall that ran adjacent to the platform. She took a deep breath, walked up to the bench and sat down beside him.

Sutherland looked at her. 'You should go home.'

'I need some answers.'

He didn't reply.

'This is where my mum died, wasn't it?'

Again nothing.

'I don't believe it was an accident.'

Sutherland wiped the rain from his neck and gazed at the tracks. 'I used to come here a lot after it happened. Just come and sit here and think about her. She wasn't like you imagine she was. You've got an idea in your head that she was kind and sweet and loving but she wasn't any of those things.'

Chrissy heard an edge to his voice, something hard but also self-pitying. 'You said she was special, that you loved her.'

'I've said plenty of things.'

'You didn't love her at all.'

Sutherland's head swung round and he glared at her. 'What the fuck do you know about it?'

Chrissy flinched, recoiling from him. It was as if he had suddenly tipped over the line, the way drunks often do, shifting from maudlin to angry at the flick of a switch. 'Nothing,' she said, trying to appease. 'Nothing at all.'

Sutherland jumped to his feet and strode over to the edge of the platform. He stood there for a while, hands in his pockets, his shoulders tight and hunched. Then he turned and came back to her. 'Go home,' he said again. 'You shouldn't be here. Leave me alone.'

Not liking him looming over her, Chrissy stood up, too. She knew that leaving would be the sensible option. She could sense the rage growing in him, knew that he was becoming increasingly erratic. But with that could come carelessness or confession. If she goaded and prodded, she might eventually get the answers she wanted. 'I don't understand. What did she ever do to you?'

'Your mother was a liar,' he hissed into her face. 'A liar and a slut.'

'She wasn't. Don't say that.'

'Why not? She thought she could take me for a sucker, a fool, and that I'd be too stupid to realise. She underestimated me. She made a big mistake.'

Chrissy said softly, 'But weren't you using *her* too, trying to get information on Luther Byrne?'

'That wasn't the same.'

'Why wasn't it?'

'You're as stupid as your fuckin' mother. She thought she could walk all over me but she was wrong.'

'So what did you do about it?'

He gave a low laugh and the roughness in his voice slipped into something sly. 'You see that wall over there? It wouldn't be difficult to climb over if you wanted to get away in a hurry. Over the wall and into the alley and gone.'

Chrissy felt her stomach clench. 'Is that what you did?'

'What do you think?' Sutherland's mouth slid into a rictus grin. 'She betrayed me. I'd have given her anything, everything, but it wasn't enough.'

'You killed her, didn't you? Go on, why don't you say it?'

Sutherland's eyes, hard and cold, bored into her. She heard a faint click on the tracks, a sign that a train was approaching. He must have heard it too. Suddenly he reached out and grabbed her arms, causing the brolly to tumble to the ground. She struggled, trying to free herself, but his grip only tightened. They were barely a step or two away from the edge of the platform, close enough for him to give her one hard shove and . . .

'Let go of me. Please, don't do this.'

He leaned in close and she could smell the whisky on his breath. His eyes had narrowed into two savage slits. 'The bitch deserved to die. She got what was coming to her.'

Chrissy could have cried out, shouted for help, but by the time anyone got to her it would already be too late. Had he stood here in this very spot with his hands grasping her mother's arms, waiting, waiting for the perfect moment? The train was drawing nearer – she could see the lights now – and panic coursed through her. She tried to wrench herself free, but she wasn't strong enough. '*Please.* You're hurting me.'

'You shouldn't have done it,' he said. 'Why did you do it?'

She heard the anguish in his voice and knew that he had

slipped into the distant past. History repeating itself. The girl he was holding on to now wasn't her; it was Laura Moss, the love of his life, the girl he was fated to destroy. His face was twisted and there were tears running down his cheeks.

The train was fifty metres away, slowing as it prepared to pull into the station. One last chance before she ended up on the tracks. 'Stop it! Look at me! Look, it's Chrissy!'

But she couldn't reach him. It was too late. He was lost to another time, to an act of vengeance he was doomed to repeat. She saw his body stiffen, saw him ready himself for the push that would hurl her into oblivion. Death travelled towards her. *Please, God.* She closed her eyes, terrified, knowing what was coming, knowing she couldn't prevent it and trying to gird herself against the impact.

But as the train glided into the station, instead of pushing her away, he abruptly pulled her to him, wrapping her in his arms and holding her tight. They stayed like that until the train had moved off again, a man and a woman caught in an embrace. To any passenger staring through the window they would have looked like lovers unable or unwilling to part. Her head was against his chest and she could feel the rapid beating of his heart. Confusion came first, then relief. Euphoria swept over her. She was still alive. She'd survived. She'd come through it.

Eventually Chrissy felt his grip relax. He let go of her and stepped back, swaying a little on his feet. Knowing how close she'd come to death she didn't have to think twice. Without even stopping to pick up the brolly, she fled along the platform, running as fast as she could, up the steps, across the concourse and out of the station, not looking back until she'd reached the corner of the high street.

74

Chrissy was still in a state of shock, dazed, driven purely by adrenalin, as she stumbled up the high street towards the Mansfield. She looked over her shoulder again and again, petrified by the thought he might change his mind and come after her. What if he had his car? What if he tried to run her over? Every set of headlights made her flinch. If she'd had any sense, she'd have chosen a right turn out of the station instead of a left, taken refuge in the Fox and sought help from Frank and Zelda. But it was too late for that now. She couldn't risk going back.

The rain was pelting down, soaking her from head to foot. Her breath came in short fast pants. She forged on, desperate to be home. Sutherland had come within a hair's breadth of killing her. The thought of it made her want to heave. The smell of him still lingered in her nostrils: sweat and cigarettes and whisky. Her heart thumped against her ribs. The man was more than drunk; he was crazy, deranged, capable of anything. At the very last moment he had drawn back from murder, given her a reprieve, but the knowledge of what might have been sent a tremor through her body.

Chrissy didn't slow down even as she passed through the gates to the estate. She wouldn't feel safe again until she was inside the flat. Hurtling along the path, she burst through the doors to Carlton House and staggered into a lift. She punched the floor number with the flat of her hand and prayed for the lift to be working. It was. As she travelled up, she tried to get herself together, to calm down, to bring some coherence to her thoughts.

She could hear the TV as she unlocked the door. She tried to close the door quietly – there was so much she had to tell but she wasn't going to blurt it out in front of Jean – only Nan's hearing was as sharp as a pin.

'Is that you, Chrissy?'

'Yeah, it's me.'

'What are you doing back so soon?'

Chrissy fumbled for an answer. The truth, that Sutherland had almost thrown her under a train, would have to wait for a while. A slight feeling of hysteria was rising in her. 'I need to get changed, Nan. I'm soaked.' Before any more awkward questions came her way, she walked along the hall to her bedroom, peeling off her raincoat as she went.

Nan, sensing that something was wrong, wasn't far behind. She stood in the doorway and said, 'Look at the state of you. Has something happened? Are you all right, love?'

Chrissy glanced in the mirror, seeing what Nan saw: a drowned rat with a face so pale it was like all the blood had been leeched from it. 'I'm all right. I'll tell you later.'

'Tell me now.'

'I can't, not while . . .' Chrissy inclined her head in the general direction of the living room. 'Later, yeah?'

'Did that Zelda say something to upset you?'

'No, of course not. Why would she?'

Nan's lips puckered. 'That one seems to make a habit of stirring things up.'

'No.'

'Was it Frank, then? Did he—'

'No, not Frank, not Zelda. It's nothing to do with either of them.'

Nan clearly wanted to ask more, but could tell Chrissy wasn't going to go there until they were alone. 'Well, get those wet things off before you catch pneumonia.'

While Chrissy was getting changed, she heard Jean being ushered unceremoniously out of the flat and wondered what Nan had said to get rid of her. She tried to prepare herself, to get the words right in her head before she spoke them. The revelation was so huge, so forbidding, she didn't know where to start. But she had to find a way.

After putting on a warm sweater, she ran a comb through her bedraggled hair, took two deep breaths and went through to the living room. Nan, aware that this was something serious, was nervously pacing with her arms folded across her chest. Chrissy thought how small she looked, how weary. Nan stopped pacing and stared at her.

'What is it, love? What's going on?'

'Let's sit down.' Chrissy's legs still felt as shaky as the rest of her. She lowered herself onto the sofa and waited for Nan to join her. Suddenly her mouth was dry, her throat like sandpaper. She had to force herself to speak. 'I saw DS Sutherland tonight.'

'What? At the Fox?'

'Yes, no. I mean, I got talking to him at Kellston station. The thing is, Nan, he was drunk and I asked him about Mum.'

Chrissy swallowed hard and forced herself to carry on. 'He told me what happened to her. He said it wasn't an accident.'

'Oh, Chrissy, not this again. Your mum wasn't pushed. She just—'

'No, you have to listen. He *told* me. He virtually told me that he killed her.'

Nan flinched as if she'd been hit. 'He couldn't have! Why on earth would he say a thing like that?'

'Because it's true. And he'd had a skinful. Perhaps he has a guilty conscience. Who knows? It doesn't really matter why. He went down onto the platform and I followed him and he showed me where . . . And he was saying all these awful things about Mum. Then he went all weird, like he thought I was her. I was terrified. He grabbed hold of me. A train was coming and I thought he was going to kill me, too.'

Nan took her hand and squeezed it tightly. 'That must have been terrible. He had no right to scare you like that.'

'He confessed, Nan. He said she was a liar and a slut. He said she deserved to die.'

'That was just the drink talking. He didn't mean it.'

Chrissy gazed at her, bewildered. 'Of course he meant it. You didn't see him, the look in his eyes, the way he was acting. He did it, I'm telling you. Why are you defending him?'

'I'm not. He's the last person I'd defend. And I'm not saying that he didn't *want* to kill her. The truth is he had a thing about your mum. He thought he was in love with her, but she didn't love him back.'

'People don't go around confessing to murders they haven't committed.'

'Sometimes they do.'

Frustration and confusion were growing in Chrissy. Why wouldn't Nan believe her? Perhaps it was because she simply

445

couldn't accept that her daughter had been murdered. 'He did it, I'm sure, and I'm going to report him to the law. He killed Mum. I heard it from his own lips and I won't let him get away with it.'

'And what do you think that's going to achieve? You reckon Gaul's going to arrest his own sergeant? That's hardly likely.'

'Not Cowan Road, then. Somewhere else. Scotland Yard.'

'You can't start accusing people of murder.'

'He *confessed*, Nan. Well, near as damn it.'

'And you think he's going to repeat that when he's sobered up? Mark my words, he'll think better of it. And then where are you going to be?'

But Chrissy didn't care about the repercussions. 'I can't keep quiet. Why should I?' She glanced towards the photo of her mum on the mantelpiece. 'For her sake. Doesn't she deserve some justice?'

'You'll only make things worse.'

Chrissy let go of Nan's hand and rose to her feet. 'They can't get any worse. I'm going to make that call. I'm going to do it right now.'

'You can't. It was an accident, love. You have to accept it.'

Chrissy was striding towards the door, her eyes grim with determination. 'Why do you keep saying that? *You* don't know. You weren't there.'

'No, but your Uncle Pete was.'

The revelation hit Chrissy with the force of a jackhammer. She swung round, her mouth dropping open. 'Uncle Pete?' she croaked.

Nan wouldn't meet her gaze. She leaned forward, covering her face with her hands. 'He didn't mean it. He never meant to hurt her.'

It was a few seconds before Chrissy could even move again.

The world had shifted, was still shifting, under her feet. 'No, that's not true. It can't be.'

A terrible silence filled the room.

'Nan?'

But all Nan did was shake her head.

'Nan, talk to me. What are you saying?' Chrissy's heart was thrashing in her chest. She had thought things couldn't get any more shocking, but a new nightmare, cruel and monstrous, had crept out of the darkness and into the light.

Eventually Nan dropped her hands and looked up at her. 'I never wanted you to know, love. I couldn't tell you. How could I tell you something like that?' She was trembling and tearful, her voice barely a whisper. 'He never meant to do it. He went after her, didn't he? That night we had the row – your mum and me – Pete was here, too. He was really mad, raging, and he followed her to the station. I tried to stop him but . . .'

Chrissy wanted to put her hands over her ears, to deafen herself, to block out the horror of what she was hearing. She was struggling to take it all in. Her own uncle had killed her mum? No. It was too immense, too shocking to accept. 'Are you sure, Nan? Did he tell you that he'd done it?'

'He wouldn't ever admit it. He couldn't. Said he'd changed his mind and gone to the Fox instead. But I saw the state he was in when he went after her – and when he came back. He couldn't face it, what he'd done, couldn't even talk about it.'

But now Chrissy was starting to question Nan's beliefs. As the initial shock subsided, she was replaying the scene with Sutherland again, remembering all the things he'd said and done to her. None of it had been the behaviour of an innocent man. And suddenly she knew with absolute certainty that her grandmother was wrong. All these years Nan had been convinced it was her own son who'd killed her daughter but she'd been mistaken. 'God, Nan, don't you see? He was telling the truth! Uncle Pete was telling the truth!'

It was then that the noise came, odd and guttural. Nan lurched forward and then slumped back on the sofa, her head lolling, her hand raised to her chest. Chrissy rushed over and knelt by her side. 'Nan! Nan!' Her grandmother's lips moved but no sound came out. She stared at her, feeling helpless, paralysed by panic.

The knowledge of what she had to do eventually permeated her brain. She dashed through to the hall and called an ambulance, so frantic she could barely explain what had happened. When she got back to the living room Nan's face had turned grey and her breathing was shallow, like the life was ebbing out of her. Chrissy gently grasped the thin shoulders, willing her to stay alive. She held her in her arms and wept. For the second time that night she prayed. 'Please God, don't let her die.'

75

It was the waiting that was intolerable. Chrissy had been at the hospital for half an hour and all she knew was that Nan had suffered a heart attack. Try not to worry, the nurse had said, but that was like asking fire not to burn. In her head she kept going over everything that had happened, revisiting every minute of the night from her encounter with Sutherland to Nan's dreadful collapse. She felt guilty, responsible, as if she had forced Nan into making an admission that had almost killed her. Might still kill her. If she hadn't threatened to make that phone call to the law, they wouldn't be here now.

Chrissy couldn't sit still. She paced up and down the corridor, desperate for news, terrified that it might be bad. A kind of clarity was descending on her thoughts. She couldn't blame Nan for not sharing her suspicions, for keeping it all to herself for the past twenty years. Her grandmother had lived not just with the horror of losing her daughter, but also with what she thought her son had done.

There was a vending machine near the end of the corridor

and, as she was rooting in her pocket for change, she came across the slip of paper with Vinnie's number on it. She remembered what he'd said. *Call me if you ever need anything.* Well, she did need something – a friend, someone to be with her, to help her get through the waiting, someone who wouldn't try to make her explain everything. But still she hesitated. She wasn't good at asking for favours.

Chrissy bought a coffee and carried the plastic cup to the pay phone near the entrance. Before she could have second thoughts, she quickly dialled the number. It went to the answering machine and she hung up. Of course he wasn't home. It was Saturday night; he'd be at Cordelia's. She called directory enquiries and got them to put her straight through. As the phone was picked up, she could hear the sounds of the bar in the background: the babble of voices, the music, the chink of glasses. 'Hang on,' a man said – she didn't recognise the voice – after she'd told him who she was and asked to speak to Vinnie. 'I'll see if I can find him.'

It was a few minutes before Vinnie came on the line. 'Hey, Chrissy, what's up?'

'Nan's collapsed. She's had a heart attack. We're at Kellston hospital.' The words came tumbling out before she'd even said hello to him. She paused, swallowed, tried to recover some composure. 'God, sorry. I don't even know why I'm calling you.'

'It's fine. I'll be there as soon as I can.'

Chrissy took her coffee and went back to sit in the corridor. She drank without tasting, sipping the hot, insipid liquid just for something to do. Gradually the pieces of what had happened all those years ago were starting to slot into place. When the law had turned up at the flat – Gaul and Sutherland – Nan must have been petrified, scared to death that they suspected Uncle Pete, prepared to agree to anything if it would make them go

450

away. It was only later, when Luther had come to see her, that she'd found out what her daughter had really been up to. Which must have broken her heart for a second time.

Chrissy stood up, paced for a while, sat down again. She looked at her watch. Time seemed to have slowed down, to have almost stopped. The minutes stretched out, each long second as unbearable as the last. Nan couldn't die. She couldn't. How could she survive without her? Nan had always been there, strong as iron, carrying everyone's burdens as well as her own. The world would stop turning without her.

Chrissy stared at the floor, at the walls and back at the floor again. On the next occasion she looked up it was to see Vinnie striding towards her. She was glad to see him, tried to smile, but her lips weren't being cooperative. His mere presence, however, was enough to bring her comfort, although she couldn't have explained exactly why.

He sat down beside her and sighed. 'These are bloody awful places, aren't they? You heard anything yet?'

Chrissy shook her head. 'Thanks for coming.'

'You want me to try and find someone?'

'They said they'd tell me as soon as . . . ' Suddenly everything was too much for her. Tears rose to her eyes and she turned her stricken face towards him. 'This is all my fault. I made her tell me. She didn't want to but I forced her. I pushed and pushed until . . . '

Vinnie laid a hand on her arm. 'Hey, you can't blame yourself for this.'

'I *can*. It was a secret, something awful, something she'd kept hidden for years, and I made her tell me and now . . . '

'Maybe you need to look at it in a different way. Maybe it was the keeping quiet that caused the heart attack. That kind of thing can be a strain.'

451

Chrissy wanted to believe him, but she couldn't.

'You'll get through this,' he said. 'You're stronger than you think.'

Chrissy didn't believe this, either.

A few more minutes ticked by. Vinnie sighed. 'I'm sorry it took me so long to get here. There was a snarl-up at Kellston station, a load of cop cars and an ambulance blocking the street.'

This news jerked Chrissy out of her introspection. 'What?'

'Yeah, apparently some poor sod jumped in front of a train.'

Chrissy felt her body stiffen, her blood turn to ice. She stared at him, eyes wide, her pulse starting to race. 'Was it ... was it Will Sutherland?'

'Sutherland?' Vinnie frowned, half laughed. 'Why the hell would it be him?'

'It was,' she gasped. 'I know it was.'

'God, what's going on, Chrissy?'

And so she told him, a stumbling, fragmented account of everything that had happened. And while she was talking, a swell of emotion was rising and crashing through her. *Sutherland was dead.* It was a kind of justice, she supposed – an eye for an eye – but she had not wanted it to end like this. Behind bars, yes, but not splattered on a railway track. Was it guilt that had made him do it, despair or the knowledge that his life was over anyway? She'd never know for sure.

'Jesus,' Vinnie said when she'd finished.

At that very moment the doctor came to talk to her. Her grandmother, he announced, was stable and was going to be okay. Relief made her knees go weak. If Vinnie hadn't held on to her elbow, propping her up, she would have ended up on the floor. She was allowed to go in and see her but only for a few minutes.

'I'll wait here,' Vinnie said.

Chrissy was shocked at how tiny Nan looked, adrift on a sea of white. There were tubes and drips attached to her, all the paraphernalia that came with keeping someone alive. She sat down, took her hand and tried to hold in the tears. 'It'll be all right, Nan. I promise.' And she knew that it was true. The past could never be wiped out, but they'd face it together. They'd find a way to get through it all. They were family.

Nan was too weak to speak but she gently squeezed Chrissy's fingers.

It was hard to leave, but eventually Chrissy had to. She bent and kissed her on the forehead. 'I'll be back tomorrow. I love you, Nan. You get some sleep.'

Vinnie was waiting for her in the corridor. 'Come on. Let's get you home.'

As they walked out of the doors into the cool, damp air she asked, 'Do you believe in God, Vinnie?'

'When it suits me.'

'I've been praying all night for Nan to pull through.'

'Yeah, I put in a word myself.'

Chrissy gazed up at his craggy face, at all six foot five of him, and smiled. Perhaps even God was disinclined to get into an argument with Vinnie Keane.

Don't miss the brand new pulse-racing novel
from Roberta Kray . . .

DOUBLE CROSSED

Coming November 2021.

Available now to pre-order